HOMO SAPIENS

IT IS UNIVERSALLY CONCEDED THAT STANISLAW PRZYBYSZEWKI IS PO-LAND'S GREATEST LIVING WRITER

HOMO SAPIENS IS HIS MOST FAMOUS BOOK

HOMO SAPIENS

A NOVEL IN THREE PARTS

BY

STANISLAW PRZYBYSZEWSKI

TRANSLATED FROM
THE POLISH BY
THOMAS SELTZER

AMS PRESS
NEW YORK

Reprinted from the edition of 1915, New York
First AMS EDITION published 1970
Manufactured in the United States of America

International Standard Book Number: 0-404-05147-2
Library of Congress Number: 72-127895

AMS PRESS INC.
NEW YORK, N.Y. 10003

CONTENTS

PART ONE

PART TWO

PART THREE

PART ONE
OVERBOARD

HOMO SAPIENS

CHAPTER I

FALK jumped up in a rage. Who was that knocking at the door? He wanted to be left alone, having made up his mind to settle down to work at last.

Thank the Lord, it was not a friend. It was the postman.

He was about to toss the letter aside. There was no hurry.— But what was this? From Mikita!

Now he was in a quiver. Mikita, the dear fellow!

He tore open the envelope.

" Be at home in the afternoon. I am returning from Paris."

The lengthiest composition from Mikita's pen since that famous German essay of his written several years before.

Falk burst out laughing. A marvellous production, that German essay. Strange that they hadn't expelled him from college for it. A miracle.

It was a series of reflections, daringly heretical for a student of those days, couched in the form of New Year's greetings and resolutions.

And old Fränkel, how he had stormed! Delicious! Mikita had certainly taken a risk.

Falk recalled having urged him to write down his reflections, the basic idea of which was a capital German pun: —" *Was einem Schiller erlaubt ist, sollte einem Schüler nicht erlaubt sein?* "

And then, the next day.— They had been up the whole night writing the essay, in the morning had sent off their explanation to Fränkel and lain down to sleep. How they had escaped without punishment, remained a puzzle.

Imagine sending in an excuse like this: "Of course, it is out of the question for us to attend classes after working a whole night on an essay."

Apocryphal!

"Now I must get to work," Falk said to himself.

He sat down. But all desire for work had gone from him. He tried to force himself, made a strenuous attempt to collect his thoughts, chewed the tip of his penholder, wrote a few sentences — the veriest banalities. No, impossible!

The inability to work when he wanted to work invariably threw Falk into a state of despondency that had to be drowned in alcohol. To-day he remained in excellent spirits.

He flung himself back in his easy-chair. The dingy attic they had shared during their last days at college arose to his mind — three windows that were never opened because the panes threatened to drop out at the slightest touch, the walls all covered with mould, and the icy temperature.

One morning they both awoke early, and gazed around the room in surprise.

"The air is fresh," said Mikita.

"Yes."

"What do you think is the matter?"

Later the cause of the amazing phenomenon became clear. It was so cold outdoors that the birds dropped dead in their flight.

Falk rose from his chair. Those were the happiest memories of his life.

And that tall, uncouth individual who supplied them with

books — what was his name? — An interesting character. What was — what was his name? Oh, yes, Longinus. It came back to Falk how he and Mikita had once broken into his hovel, which he always kept locked, and made away with a book that he had refused to lend them.

It was on a Sunday. The room was cold again. Falk woke up to an uncommon spectacle — Mikita with nothing but his shirt on, the key of the attic door in his hand, and Longinus trembling, beside himself with rage.

" Open the door," cried Longinus, with dramatic pathos.

" Put the book down and I'll open it."

Longinus paced up and down the room, taking long, heroic strides.

" Open the door! "

" Put the book down."

" You are an intelligent, educated man. You will not permit an infringement of my rights, will you? " Longinus said, addressing Falk. He was fond of flowery phrases.

" I am extremely sorry, but what can I do? Mikita has the key."

" Hereafter I shall not regard you as an educated man." It was the gravest insult Longinus ever offered any one.

How they had laughed. It was on a Sunday. They really should have been at church but, true to their atheistic principles, they abhorred church-going. Yet it was not safe to stay away, with their fanatical teacher of religion spying for absentees.

Ha, ha, ha!

Falk remembered sitting in church once opposite his " goddess." In an effort to look interesting and attractive he posed in an extremely uncomfortable position throughout the whole interminable mass like Byron, in the picture, sitting on Shelley's grave.

The incident had its sequel.

Falk set to work again, but his mind still refused to enter harness. His thoughts kept dancing and turning round those glorious memories. Unconsciously chewing the tip of his penholder, he kept saying over and over to himself: " Great times! Great times! "

And when Ibsen rose in their firmament! When " Brand " turned their heads! When their slogan became: " All or nothing! " Ah — glorious!

Then they began to scour the slums and gather the children of the proletariat about them. The picture of the attic came to his mind again. Five o'clock in the morning. The knock of wooden slippers as of some one dragging artillery up the stairs. The door opens and one by one they file in, a boy, a girl, then two boys and two girls, and more boys and girls. The room fills up with them. They group themselves round the oak table near the stove.

" Get up, Mikita, I am awfully tired."

" I can't," angrily growls Mikita. " I've been cramming Latin the whole night."

Suddenly they both jump, looking daggers at each other, unable to make their jaws meet from the cold.

Then Falk goes to work at the stove, blowing and swearing because the wood won't burn, while Mikita lights the alcohol lamp and puts a large pot of milk on it.

Gradually the expression on their faces thaws.

The children attack the bread and milk like hungry wolves. Mikita stands by, radiant with joy.

" Now, children, get out! "

Then they exchange friendly looks.

A warm feeling of tenderness smote Falk. All this had long lain stowed away in the background of his consciousness. Yet how much of humanity and beauty it held.

Falk pursued his reminiscences.

Next came the sense of shame they always had felt at catching each other in a throb of emotion — no, they called it æsthetics, and it ended in an argument.

"The Niebelungenlied is nothing but empty twaddle." Mikita well knew Falk's weak points. Falk, of course, could not assent to such an opinion of the Niebelungenlied, and expressed his disagreement with heat, all the while slicing the bread. Mikita was shrewd. He made a habit of starting an argument during the operation of bread-cutting when Falk would keep slicing absent-mindedly, and the slices would disappear down Mikita's mouth.

Suddenly:—"Look here, we are two minutes late for class already." They snatched up their books and ran off, he first, Mikita limping behind.—"Wonder whether his leg is cured now?"—Not till then would it occur to Falk that he was hungry and that Mikita had eaten up all the bread. A shrewd chap, Mikita.

Then Falk grew thoughtful.

"Brand" applied to love. "All or nothing."

Again he sank into thought, this time of the present.

"Janina! I've ruined her life. Her future is gone.

"H'm. But why can't she tear herself away from me? How I've plagued her with things Brand says and the way he makes straight for his goal. Yes, there is no doubt of it, I've hypnotised her. How else explain her conduct, her running away from home and going with me? Oh, bother it! I've never really loved her. I've merely wanted to see the unfolding of a girl's love. Not a bad idea for a boy of eighteen reading Büchner and that *triste cochon,* Bourget."

He must visit her. No, he had better not. If only she would forget him. He rose and began to pace to and fro.

Why, it was contemptible to keep drawing her to him,

and then assuming a rationalistic pose, telling her that love is something to be suppressed, the primitive sentiment of primitive people, a disease, a rash on the spiritual life of the new man.

Oh, yes, in this he was inimitable. If only she could be made to take it more cheerfully.

Then he remembered how she had once responded to his cynical argumentations.

"I wish you'd fall in love some day, really fall in love." How naïve she was. No, no. The old wolf of Könisberg knew. He had penetrated the secret of love. Love, he said, is a pathological manifestation, a disease. Yes, Kant was a connoisseur in the matter of love.

Falk lighted a cigarette and stretched himself on the sofa.

"Wonder what Mikita is painting now? That man possesses strength of character, supernatural strength of character. To make his way in the world against such odds, never losing sight for a moment of the object he set himself. Had he wanted to paint as others paint, he could have accumulated a fortune already."

Those terrible years of deprivation at the university.

"Have you got five pennies, Mikita?"

Mikita hadn't a single penny. Since early in the morning he had been rummaging incessantly among his things looking for five pennies that he thought he had lost.

"So we are going to fast?"

"Seems so," Mikita said without turning from his work. Then after a pause, "You know money's below par now."

"Yes, I know."

"Well, then," and Mikita continued to paint.

They suffered pangs of hunger. Falk shuddered. He had grown so weak from lack of food that it was surprising he did not go completely insane. Once he fell in the street from faintness and was almost run over.

Finally they sank so low as to have but one pair of trousers between them. When Falk went to the university Mikita painted in his under-garments.

At this point Falk burst out laughing. His mother had sent the manager over with money in the nick of time. She had sold a piece of woodland. All three of them, Falk, Mikita and the manager, had gone to a café and stayed from morning till late at night. The manager returned home crawling on all fours. Every minute Mikita would pull his leg. Finally the manager turned upon him furiously and kicked him on the nose. Oh, Lord! And how the manager, when he began to feel sick, knocked a hole through the window with his head, because he was too weak to open it.

Those long weeks of hunger and poverty. He thought with tenderness of his mother, who always came to the rescue at the critical moment.

"Yes, yes, mother — mother.

"Mikita must have gone hungry in Paris many, many times."

Ha — ha! And they are the men who propose to carve out new paths in life.

A sad smile flickered over Falk's face.

Yes. In despite of everything. Rather perish of hunger than yield an inch.

What was it, after all? What was it that sustained him in the face of all failure, insult and hate?

He lay down on the sofa again.

It was the great, wonderful art, the art of new worlds, worlds transcending phenomena, transcending knowledge, transcending tangible forms, worlds so ingraspably fine that all distances vanish and melt, worlds comprehended in one look, one movement, one flash of a second.

He drew a deep breath.

And new symbols, new words, new colours, new sounds.

All this has already been.

No, no, my dear sir, not all! There never yet was a sorrow that excluded all other sorrows, there never yet was a joy that passed into sorrow, there never yet was that whole series of new perceptions which combine and concentrate all sensations. Yes, yes, there never yet were those thousands of impressions which only two or three, or at most a dozen, people now living are capable of experiencing. All this has not yet been, or else the crowd, too, would understand it, the crowd that needs centuries for chewing and digesting the smallest grain of thought.

After all it is perhaps better that not every newspaper hack understands, else the great artist would have to be ashamed of himself.

He looked at the puff of smoke issuing in thin streaks from his cigarette and coiling upwards in fantastic spirals. Once he had seen a similar picture, a Chinese print of a mountain torrent.

Suddenly he heard Mikita's voice.

Yes, he remembered. Never thereafter did he feel the same way, a mystical sensation baffling all description. He was sick then, he could not open his eyes, his face was swollen.

Mikita nursed him, and a good nurse he made. Day and night he watched at his bedside. And when Falk could not sleep he read aloud — Heine's *Florentinische Nächte.*

And Falk listened to the soft, monotonous song, yes, song, or perhaps prayer, which gradually dying away ascended to ·heaven, like the last waves of a lake lulled by the stillness of night — a prayer ever clearer, ever softer. He fell asleep.

CHAPTER II

"MIKITA, old boy!"
    "Yes, it's me."
They embraced warmly.

Falk ran about the room all excitement, picking things up and setting them down somewhere else, creating a mess.

"Tell me, tell me what will you have. Beer? Whiskey? No, wait, I have first-rate Tokay; mother sent it to me; it's old stuff left by my father; he laid it down years ago. He was a specialist, you know, in that sort of thing."

"Won't you settle down for once? Do sit down. Let a fellow look at you."

Falk composed himself at last. They exchanged happy looks and clinked glasses.

"Excellent stuff. Why, you're not looking well. You must have done a lot of writing. You know — the devil — that last book of yours got me so excited; it was so different, so out of the ordinary. I bought the book, began to read it on the street and stopped. It gripped me so I had to finish it on the street. Eric, you're an artist."

Falk blushed.

"I am glad, very glad. Your demands of me were always so high. Do you really like it?"

"I should say so." Mikita described a large circle in the air. Falk laughed.

"You've acquired a new gesture."

"You see, one can't always say things in words. All those impalpable fine shades that keep eluding you — nothing but a gesture can express them."

"Yes, you are right."

"Here, for example, is a wide line, do you catch me? A broad sweep, a warm undercurrent, so to speak; but it's only a few that understand it. In Paris I went to one of the great ones, the chief of the naturalists, or whatever you call them. He gathers in the coin, I tell you. Of course, the public is now beginning to buy that stuff, the *cinquième element* discovered by Napoleon in Poland, *la boue* and a few potato stalks. Before, they used to buy the gingerbread pictures of the famous draper and upholsterer of His Holiness the Pope. Raphael's his name, isn't it? Well, now the time has come for the fellows who paint potatoes and dirt.

"I asked this chief of the tribe why they were painting that which nature made a thousand times more beautiful, and the significance of which was after all not so profound. 'What?' he said, 'you call it nonsense, do you? You ask for its underlying thought, its significance? Why it's nature itself. Do you understand?'

"Yes, I understood.

"'Nature is both its content and its significance.'

"But even so, why just potatoes?

"The potato artist got excited.

"'Because potatoes are nature; everything else is nonsense. Imagination! Imagination! Fiddlesticks! Imagination is merely an aid to be used in none but cases of extreme necessity.'"

Both laughed heartily.

Mikita grew thoughtful.

"But they'll soon see. My head is fairly bursting with ideas. If I had a thousand hands, I'd draw you a thousand lines and then you'd understand me. I can't express it in words, a man sometimes forgets his vocabulary. I went to see a sculptor. You'll see his work. I have sketches of it in my room. I got down on my knee before that man. 'It's grand, it's grand,' I said. 'What?' he asked. I explained what I meant. 'Ah, do you think so?' And he drew a powerful line in space. *He* understood. But, dear me, the way I'm running on. I must stop. How are things with you? Not brilliant, eh?"

"No, not brilliant. I have had to put up with a lot of discomfort lately. Those many exquisitely tenuous feelings which as yet are beyond the power of words to express, those thousands of words which are born in the soul like a flash and vanish as quickly, evading one's grasp —"

"Yes, that's so," Mikita interrupted him. "That sculptor, that genius I told you about, do you know what he said? He put it magnificently. 'Look,' he says, 'here are five fingers. You can see them, touch them; but you can't see, you can't touch what's between the fingers, and yet that's the most important.' "

"Yes, there's no doubt of it, that's the most important. But let's drop art."

"You seem to be completely exhausted?"

"I can't say that, but there are times when I feel sick and tired of everything. Not to be able to draw directly from the treasures of life, to be compelled to live in conformity with circumstances, however they may chance to shape themselves — and why — why, after all? The very thought that I am almost incapable of feeling pain or joy directly is intolerable, enough to kill me. Everything in me turns into literature, into the artistic."

"You ought to fall in love."

"What? So you advise that, too, Mikita?"

"Yes, yes, Love! Love is not literature. Love cannot be felt indirectly. A moment of happiness descends upon

you and you are ready to jump to the sky without thinking
that in so doing you may fall and break your leg. And when
you suffer, you suffer frightful tortures that get you into
their direct grip. But there's no use; you can't describe it,
it can't be fitted into categories, it can't be covered by a definition."

A smile passed over Mikita's face.

" I have an announcement to make to you. I am engaged."

" You? Engaged? "

" Yes, and infinitely happy."

Falk could not conceal his astonishment.

" Well, here's to your sweetheart! "

They finished the bottle.

" Listen, Mikita, we are going to spend the whole day
together, aren't we? "

" Of course."

" You know, I've discovered a new café."

" No, partner. We'll go to my lady."

" Is she here? "

" Yes, the wedding is to be in four weeks, as soon as
I scrape enough money together from the Munich exhibition to make a decent affair of it. It will be a triumph,
the like of which never before happened in any artist's studio."

" I was so glad that we'd be all by ourselves to-day, and
just to-day," Falk pleaded. " Have you forgotten those
wonderful *heures de confidence* when we had our long unending arguments? "

But Mikita was not to be dissuaded. Ysa was so curious
to see Falk. She had made him promise on oath that he
would bring that strange beast called Falk *in natura*.

" I can't break my promise," he insisted. " We must go."

Falk assented. On the way Mikita kept talking incessantly of his happiness, gesticulating animatedly.

"It's amazing the way it makes a new man out of you, just as though you were reborn. Everything turns upside down. You seem to see depths that no mortal eye has visioned before. A thousand worlds pass before your eyes. And then all those strange, unseen sensations, so fleeting, so evasive, that your brain can't hold them more than an infinitesimal fraction of a second. And yet you are constantly under their influence, the whole day long. And how wonderful nature seems then! Listen! at first, before I had gained her consent, I lay at her door like a dog. In the cold, in a biting frost I slept the whole night at the door of her room until finally I won her. But how I suffered. Did you ever see the cry of heaven? No? Well, let me tell you I did. I saw heaven crying. It seemed as if the whole sky opened its thousands of mouths and hurled down molten colours into space. The whole sky, an endless expanse of stripes ranging in colour from dark-red to black. Congealed blood — no, a pool reflecting a purple sunset, and then dirty gold. Ugly, disgusting, but superb. My God, how superb! Then transport of joy. I grew, mounted up, up, to the sky, so that I could have lighted a cigarette with the sun."

Falk smiled. "Mikita," he thought, "whose head hardly reaches my shoulders. A remarkable man."

"A funny picture, isn't it, me reaching up to the sky? You know, when I was in Paris the Frenchmen used to stare at me because I walked with a friend who made me look like a giant beside him."

Both smiled. Mikita gave Falk's hand a warm pressure.

"Look here, Eric, I really don't know whom I love more.

You see, love for a woman is altogether different. It involves certain demands, and very peremptory demands, doesn't it? Love has a certain inherent purpose, whereas friendship, my boy, friendship is something intangible; it's the between the fingers. That's why, when you have lived with a woman constantly for three months —"

Falk interjected:

"You can't imagine how homesick I was for you. Here among these scribblers there isn't a single one, you understand, not one. So we must take advantage of the opportunity now and make good use of our time."

"Yes, we'll stay together."

They paused at the entrance.

"Listen, Eric, she is consumed with curiosity to meet you. Try to be interesting, or you'll make me appear ridiculous. You can be if you want to, devil that you are."

They entered.

It seemed to Falk that a large, smooth mirror-like surface was spreading out before him. Then he felt as if he were recalling something he had once in his life already heard and seen.

"Eric Falk," Mikita introduced him.

She looked at him with embarrassment, then held out her hand.

"So that's you?"

Falk grew animated.

"Yes, it's I. Nothing unusual, as you see. From Mikita's description you must have expected some strange sort of animal."

She smiled. Falk saw the smile shining through a mystic cloud of smoke.

"I was envious of you. Mikita never stopped talking

about you. It was really for your sake that we came to Berlin."

Strange. That cloud of smoke in her eyes, like a heavy curtain of mist dimming a brilliant light.

They sat down. Falk glanced at her; she at him. A smile flickered over their faces. They were peculiarly embarrassed.

"Mikita said you are always drinking brandy. I bought a bottle, but he has taken half already. Shall I pour a glass for you?"

"For heaven's sake, that's enough."

"I beg your pardon. I didn't know. You're from Russia. Isn't it the custom there to drink brandy from large glasses?"

"She has an idea," Mikita explained, "that in Russia bears regularly visit people's houses and lick out the pots and pans."

They laughed. The conversation passed from one subject to another. Mikita kept up a continuous chatter, always gesticulating.

"You see, Eric, we are both madly in love."

Falk noticed an embarrassed smile dart over her face as if she were slightly ashamed.

"You mustn't bore Mr. Falk with such uninteresting matters."

A faint frown darkened Mikita's brow. She stealthily stroked his hand. His face brightened again.

"She has him well in hand," Falk thought.

A dark-red glow suffused the room, as if the light of the lamp passed through several layers of different coloured glass. Or perhaps it was not the play of the light. No, it was something hidden in the corners of her mouth. No, it was in the thin lines round her mouth. Again it disappeared, creeping behind her soft, delicate features. It defied comprehension.

"You are quiet, Eric. Do you want anything? What can I do for you?"

"My God, how beautiful you are!" Falk spoke meditatively, with a sincerity coming apparently from such depths that even Mikita yielded to the deception.

"You see, Ysa, how candid and outspoken he is."

"A strange man. What a face!" Ysa felt the need of looking at him all the time.

"What have you done with yourself the whole winter?"

Falk controlled himself.

"Misbehaved with Iltis."

"Who is he?"

"Iltis is the nickname of a certain great man here."

Ysa laughed.

"An odd nickname."

"I like Iltis, and he enjoys the company of young people. Sometimes when their revelries go too far, he quietly steals away."

"What is he?"

"A sculptor. But that makes no difference. It is as a man that we are interested in him. And as a man he has the fixed idea that everybody can be induced to shoot himself by hypnotism. Hypnotism is his hobby. Once we happened to be spending a whole night drinking. The esteemed public, which regards us as priests of art —"

"Priests of art! Grand! Temple of the muses. Clio — ha, ha, ha!" Mikita was in ecstasies.

"As I was saying, the public has no idea how often a thing of that sort happens to the priests of art. Once after passing a night without sleep in that way, the priests began to feel a desire for fresh air. The small priests scattered on the street. Only the high hierophant —"

"Hierophant! Iltis an hierophant!" Mikita shook with laughter.

"The hierophant remained with me. Suddenly he stopped. A man was leaning against a wall, looking at the sky.

"'A man!' said Iltis with an indescribable tremour in his voice.

"The man did not stir. Iltis's eyes seemed to dart sparks of fire.

"'Look, he is hypnotised,' he whispered mysteriously.

"'Man!' he shouted in a mighty voice, like a cracked trumpet, which would have crumbled the walls of Jericho. 'Here are five dollars. Buy yourself a revolver and commit suicide.'

"The man held out his hand.

"'A perfect case of hypnosis,' Iltis whispered and with a grandiose air put the five dollars into the stranger's hand.

"The man almost jumped for joy. 'Now I needn't commit suicide. Hurrah for life!'

"'Base coward!' Iltis roared after him."

Mikita and Ysa laughed heartily.

Falk listened. There was in that laugh a sound, something — what did that laugh remind him of?

"You know, if I were minister of public education, I'd give that coward a well-paying position as professor of psychology."

"Are all of you Russians so delightfully sarcastic?" She glanced at him with large, sincere eyes.

"I am not a Russian. I was born near the Russian frontier. But, thanks to my association with Slavs and my Catholic upbringing, I have traits of character that the Germans do not possess. It's this interesting combination that people find so attractive."

Falk went on to speak of his country with tenderness and warmth, and the tone of mockery playing like an accompaniment to everything he said dropped to a subdued note.

" A wonderful people. Ninety-eight illiterates to every hundred of population. That's because at school the Poles must learn in a language foreign to them. The Germans, in their eagerness to make good German citizens of the Polish children, sacrifice everything to the German language. They hammer the pure German tongue with pure German energy into the children, and the result is correspondingly brilliant."

There was something attractive in his voice. Even when speaking of the merest trifles he was eloquent.

Mikita said in a loud voice:

" Do you remember, Falk, we had a teacher in the high school very much like Iltiṣ? "

Falk listened absent-mindedly. When Mikita spoke he looked at Ysa. Each time their eyes met they smiled. It was a feeling he had never experienced before. Something was straining in him, so it seemed, and concentrating his forces; warmth and energy mounted to his brain.

A desire was actually making itself felt in him to be interesting and witty. Yes, really, he felt something strangely like a desire to draw the woman's attention to himself, to interest her.

Who was this woman?

She glanced at him again; she was not listening to Mikita. The same peculiar light around her eyes, as if all the lines were converging behind that little cloud of smoke. He had a feeling always of wanting to take something off of her face and lips.

Mikita broke off abruptly in the middle of his story. He looked stealthily at Ysa. Her eyes were turned upon Falk. "Curiosity?" he thought. "Yes? And maybe not?"

Falk noticed Mikita's uneasiness and burst out laughing.

"Yes, it is quite amazing. Old Fränkel is the very double of Iltis. Do you remember that Sunday, Mikita? We were still in bed asleep. I was dreaming about Grieser, the chemist, who seemed to us an intellectual giant those days. He fooled us both. Suddenly I was roused. Somebody was knocking at the door.

" 'Open the door!'

"Half asleep I was still thinking of Grieser, but that wasn't Grieser's voice.

"Who is there?"

" 'Fränkel.'

"I still kept thinking of Grieser.

" 'But you are not Grieser.'

" 'It's Fränkel. Open the door.'

" 'No fooling. You aren't Grieser.'

"I realised it wasn't Grieser's voice, yet I rose in a semi-drowsy condition, opened the door, and still didn't recognise him.

" 'So you aren't Grieser?'

"Suddenly I was wide awake and jumped back in fright. It actually was Fränkel. Good God! Strauss' 'Life of Jesus' was lying on our table."

Mikita melted with a sense of warmth at these memories.

Falk felt he ought to go, but could not. It was physically impossible for him to tear himself away from Ysa.

"Listen, Mikita, what do you say to our going to the Green Nightingale? It will interest Ysa."

Mikita wavered, but Ysa immediately consented.

"Yes, yes, I am eager to see that famous café."

They put on their coats and hats. Falk went out first.
Ysa lingered behind to put out the lamp.

"Well, isn't he a trump?" asked Mikita.

"Yes, he's splendid. But I couldn't love him." And she
kissed him passionately.

They hailed a cab and entered it.

It was a bright night in March.

They passed the Tiergarten without having spoken a word.
It was very close in the carriage. Falk sat opposite Ysa.

Never before in his life had he experienced such a feeling.
The light in her eyes seemed to be pouring, steadily pouring,
into his, his body to be drinking in her body, her warmth.
Something emanated from her that entered into him and
blended all his feelings into one, into desire, hunger, thirst.
His breathing grew hot and irregular.

What was it? Maybe he had drunk too much. No, he
knew he had not.

Suddenly their hands touched.

Falk forgot Mikita's presence. For a moment he lost
control of himself. He raised her hand to his mouth and
covered it with passionate kisses.

She did not withdraw it.

CHAPTER III

Y SA'S appearance at the Green Nightingale produced an
impression. Falk observed Iltis's eyes screw up and a
grimace distort his face, his unclean imagination, apparently, setting to work at once. In this he was without a
peer.

Iltis rose instantly to shake hands with Mikita.

"So Iltis and Mikita are friends from of old," Falk noted,
greeting Iltis with a careless nod and seating himself beside
Ysa a little off from the others.

Again he saw the glow in her eyes piercing the curtain
of mist. His consciousness seemed to be ebbing away, and
it took a supreme effort to control himself.

Strange, his voice had turned hoarse, and he had to cough
to clear his throat.

"Let me introduce you to the company." He had to
clear his throat again.

"That stout man there with the small feet — a pity you
can't see his feet, they are worth looking at — yes, that
one glancing at you stealthily, inquiringly, as if scenting a
hidden social problem in you — he's an anarchist. He writes
marvellous poetry: 'We are the infantry' . . . No —
'We are the red hussars of humanity, the red hussars!'
The fiery imagination of the Prussian!"

Falk laughed hoarsely.

"Yes, an anarchist and an individualist. As for that,
they all are, all the men here round the table, they are all
individualists, all guided by the same flat, tasteless, coarse
German egoism."

There was the sound of a glass broken on the floor. Everybody turned round

Falk smiled.

"The young man who broke the glass is also a celebrity, a philosopher. He believes in the existence of a central will in the universe. According to his theory, human beings are only the emanations of that will. Its energy is stored up in the finger tips, and to break it up and distribute it he must throw glasses on the floor."

The curly haired young man glanced round with a look of triumph. Disappointed in the faint response, he called for another glass.

"Never mind, child, never mind," Iltis said to soothe him.

"We must join them at the table," said Mikita, coming up to Falk and Ysa. "They'll think we want to keep aloof."

Ysa was now introduced to the whole circle. She sat beside Falk again. On his other side was a man they called the Suckling, whose over-amiability annoyed Falk. Falk knew he loathed him.

"Have you read the new volume of poems?" The Suckling mentioned the title of a book of verse then making the rounds.

"Yes, glanced through it."

Falk felt that Ysa was listening to him, and a tremor, like an electric shock, went through him.

"Well, what's your opinion? Striking, don't you think so?"

"Not at all. On the contrary, stupid." Falk tried hard to remain calm. "Exceedingly stupid. Why will people persist in writing verses that have no content, no meaning? Just to sing about spring? There's plenty of stuff like that already, too much of it. A writer should be ashamed even to mention the word 'spring.' It's been so overdone."

Mikita looked at Falk in astonishment.

"All this spilling of ink about moods and feelings is flat, stale and meaningless. Any country yokel has them, any girl has them when a season of more brisk and rapid changes dissipates her winter drowsiness. If these moods at least lifted a tiny corner of the curtain concealing the secrets and problems of the human soul, if they dropped at least a crumb of that unseen mystery of the soul which is on the other side of the empty knowledge we so far possess. But the spokesmen of the human race, even the greatest of them, don't feel these sensations. Why? Because they stand shuddering before the peasant, thrilled with the passion of spring."

Falk grew confused and began to stammer. He felt as if he were standing on a platform haranguing an audience of thousands. He was losing control of himself and running off into nonsense, as always when so excited. The Suckling tried to interrupt, but Falk insistently went on with his argument.

"You see, those feelings have a meaning for young people, because they constitute, so to speak, the underlying motive of sexual selection."

"But my dear Falk," the Suckling profited by the pause in which Falk tried to collect his thoughts, "you ignore technique. Technique is derived from the Greek word *technikos,* meaning skilful." He stressed each word. "That is the only standard by which an artistic production may be judged, and the artistry of these poems is perfect, the rhythm is rich and free —"

Falk broke in:

"Nonsense!"

" Here's to your health," cried Iltis, stepping up to Falk. Something wrong was going on inside of Falk. Iltis had never seen him so heated.

" No, my dear fellow," Falk continued. " It is not form or rhythm by which a work of art should be judged. When men first began to create artistic forms, had to create them, in fact, in obedience to an impulse flowing from a thousand causes, then form and metre had a meaning; then only did rhythm as such possess significance, because it symbolised the circulation of the blood. When rhythm first made its appearance it was a discovery, the creation of a genius. Now it is nothing but a manifestation of atavism, an empty, fossilised classical formula. Besides, nothing else was necessary than the commonly acquired sense of form. Mind you, I do not mean to deny the significance of rhythm as a means of rounding out the artistic effect. But poetry should contain something more than that."

Iltis again clinked glasses with Falk. Falk began to be bored.

" Oh no, not the old worn-out themes, spring, love and woman. Away with all that ridiculous lyricism! "

Falk spoke with increasing vehemence. Ysa did not hear the words, she only saw the man with his thin delicate face and deep eyes aflame with passion.

" What I want? What I want? I want life and its terrible depths, its bottomless abyss. To me art is the profoundest instinct of life, the sacred road to the future life, to eternity. That is why I crave great big thoughts, pregnant with meaning and content, thoughts that will lay the foundation for a new sexual selection, create a new world and a new understanding of the world. For me art does not end in rhythm, in music. Art is the will that out of nonexistence conjures up new worlds, new people.— No, no, my dear fellow, what we need is an art big with ideas. Otherwise what's the use of art at all? It's superfluous, meaningless."

Falk suddenly recovered himself. What was he talking about? Was he trying to lay out a program for the world? He glanced at Ysa to see what impression his harangue had produced upon her. " I've made a fool of myself," he thought, " acting like a schoolboy."

" The art that you extolled," he said, " can have meaning for none but animals."

" Birds, for example, as you know, attract the female by rhythm and song; which our poets are unable to do. They can't produce an impression even on boys and girls."

A sardonic smile spread over Iltis's face, and his eyes twinkled.

Falk rose and went over to him. He was dissatisfied with himself, but felt Ysa's eyes upon him. He returned her look, piercing her through to her very heart. That was lyrical to excess. He grew heated again; which irritated the Suckling.

" I am really interested to know what you call art."

" Have you seen Rops? Well, that's art. What more can one say about life? "

" Yes, naturally."

" Naturally for those who judge superficially, naturally for those who regard everything as natural. Yes, natural for Strauss, for Vogt, for Büchner, and — and. But do you mean to say that that depth, that vertigo-producing abysmal gulf, the great war of the sexes, the eternal hatred between them — do you mean to say that that is natural? Isn't it rather a profound mystery? One and the same agency creating and destroying life, stimulating and urging us on to action, and yet in itself seemingly so irresponsible and insignificant? "

Falk floundered, groped for words, could not find them, and became still more excited.

"What we need is a brain free of existing notions, a self-comprehending brain, independent of the knowledge of things as hitherto understood, a brain that has untied the sacred knot of all understanding, for which a line is a sound, a great event a movement, in which thousands of human beings are welded into, and comprehended as, one, which passes in direct, unbroken transition from sound to word, from word to colour, and for which the present limitations do not exist."

He recovered himself, and smiled.

"No, no, don't come to me with your absurd logic, your conceptions, your atavistic, inadequate, inefficient means of sexual selection. I don't want to hear of them."

Ysa still kept looking at him, not hearing what he said, only seeing his thick hair dropping on his forehead and his deep, wide-open eyes. She was surprised to find him so handsome, so diabolically handsome.

"Mr. Falk seems to have gone to school with the theosophists," drawled the anarchist, looking up.

Falk smiled.

"No, sir, not at all. Listen. You are a famous poet. You are known wherever the German language is spoken —"

Some one burst out laughing, apparently with design. The anarchist turned round in a rage, his face reddening.

"No joking, please," he said to Falk.

Falk's expression became grave.

"I was in earnest, but unfortunate, evidently, in conveying my meaning. To be sure, I personally do not consider you a great poet. I was only echoing the opinion I hear all round me, but —"

The anarchist was furious. He saw Ysa's gaze resting upon him with frank amusement.

"My dear sir, you are going too far."

"Not at all. You see an evil intent in my remarks which I assure you was not in my mind. You have created something for me, too, a sort of picture — I may call it the sublimity of contrast. I understand your 'red hussars of humanity.'"

The man who had laughed before laughed again, and so loud that it made Falk uncomfortable.

"Now to the conclusion. Isn't it a fact that your creative moments are unusual moments for you, mystical, I may almost say, theosophical, because whatever is unusual you dismiss as theosophical. You've heard of fakirs who hypnotise themselves to sleep and then lie buried for months dead-alive. I once saw a fakir in Marseilles in a state of torpor like that. When cut, his body would not bleed. When you create you fall into a similar trance, the only difference being that you cannot induce the condition artificially. In one flash all your vital powers concentrate at a single point. You see nothing, you hear nothing, you work unconsciously, without thinking, without reasoning. You do everything as in a trance. Now tell me, isn't that mystical? Can you explain it by logic? Can you explain why just you are a famous poet and not some one else?"

An embarrassed silence fell upon the company. Every one felt that Falk had gone too far.

The anarchist rose and walked out.

Iltis had not comprehended a word. His brain was too big to bother with metaphysical trifling of that sort. Still he understood that Falk had beaten his opponent, and touched glasses with him.

"Give me your hand."

The young man who had thrown the glass on the floor rose, holding one hand to his side. With a gesture of pathos he offered the other to Falk. Falk took it with a smile.

Ysa was silent. She felt so happy. It was a long, long time since she had experienced such happiness. Falk was a wonderful man. He was positively the most beautiful event in her life, though only accidental. Suddenly she felt uneasy.

"You are so quiet," Mikita said, coming towards her.

"I am happy." She pressed his hand lightly.

"Are you tired?"

"Not in the least."

"I suppose we had better go, though?"

A mysterious power kept her chained there. Though she would have liked to stay, she yielded to the mute entreaty in his eyes.

"Yes, let's go." Her voice, almost repellant, seemed to come from some one else.

She rose.

"What, going already? Stay a bit longer," Falk pleaded, ready to detain her by force.

Mikita was insistent. He had to take Ysa home.

"Don't forget, Mikita."

"Oh, yes." Mikita had almost forgotten Iltis's invitation to spend the following evening at his studio. He would surely come, but didn't know if Ysa would care to.

"I'll be very glad to," said Ysa eagerly.

"And you, Falk? Of course you will?" asked Iltis, slapping him on his shoulder good-naturedly.

"Without fail."

Ysa turned round to Falk and gave him her hand again.

"Will you come to see me soon?" The mist curtaining

her eyes seemed to lift, the light behind to blaze up and burst on her eyelids like a hot wave.

"Your house is my country."

Mikita was disturbed. He squeezed Falk's hand and left the restaurant with Ysa.

"He's impatient," said Iltis with a roguish wink of his eyes.

The irritation surging in Falk almost vented itself in words that would hardly have been to Iltis's taste.

He resumed his seat and looked round the room. Everybody and everything in it bored him. He felt wofully alone and dissatisfied with himself. How ridiculous and puerile that twaddle of his had been! He had meant to produce an impression on Ysa, and had merely poured out empty words and phrases. Disgusting! When he might have expressed himself with far better effect. But he had trembled so, had been confused, had completely lost his presence of mind.

He was furious.

The way that fool, The Suckling, sipped his beer was so nauseating. Sickening! Everything connected with the famous "Nightingale" irritated him. Yes, everything.

Then why stay longer?

He felt a craving for fresh air, the need to go, no matter where, far, far, through all the streets of the city! He must come to an understanding with himself, make a certain something clear to his soul. A problem confronted him that he must solve, something — something new and strange.

He paid his bill and left.

CHAPTER IV

BUT in the street he fell a prey to a sense of extreme uneasiness. In the hope that physical fatigue would bring relief he walked quickly, and finally broke into a run as though something were whipping him on. But the black discomfort grew. It seethed and boiled and overflowed through every pore, every nerve. What was it?

"Can it be that the danger has returned?" he reflected.

He came to a standstill. An almost animal instinct gripped him, as if not his own soul, but another soul that had passed into him, was scenting danger.

He felt a vague indefinite animal attraction drawing him. "Run! Run!" a voice within him cried.

His mind reverted to an incident of his boyhood, when he was fourteen years old. He was sitting in a room on the third floor with two windows giving on the yard. There was a steady noise of coopers at work putting hoops on barrels. He was obliged to memorise a long passage from Ovid. If he failed, he would be punished. And he sat and studied and studied until large bitter tears rolled down his cheeks. His brain was peculiarly dull. In learning each new verse he forgot all the preceding ones.

And in the meadow behind the fortress wall his schoolmates were playing. Jans, of whom he was so fond, must be there, too. The day was fading. He dropped on his knees; a mad fear seized him; he prayed to the Holy Ghost for light. But he could remember nothing, absolutely nothing.

His eyes grew dim from sheer terror. He must learn it,

he must. And he beat his head with his fists, repeated each word a thousand times. No use!

There was no escape. Then unexpectedly an idea occurred to him, a saving thought. He must run, far, far away — to his mother.

And he ran through the night, ran, lost his breath, fell. Each little sound glued him to the spot, each spark flooded his eyes as with a sea of light. Then he jumped up again and ran, ran without respite until finally he dropped in the forest utterly exhausted and unconscious.

Now he heard the same powerful, peremptory voice: "Run! Run!"

He stopped and a smile darted over his face.

The beast has awakened: But hasn't a man endowed with reason any other means of defence than cowardly escape? Why must he run? Why must he?

A desire kindled in him, spreading like a mist over his brain and crowding out all other thoughts. He felt her hand on his lips, felt the warmth of her body making his blood hot, felt the sound of her voice streaming over his nerves like a gentle wave.

He pulled himself up with violence.

"No," he cried aloud.

Mikita! How Mikita loved her. How anxiously he had kept watching her and Falk! Was he not certain of her love?

Then suddenly:

She? Can she conceivably love Mikita? Why no, absurd. Is there another woman like her? No, no. Then how could she fail to be annoyed by Mikita's manners and gesture? — Hm, Mikita's anxiety had really made him seem rather ridiculous, and —

No! No! Falk was ashamed of himself. Mikita was

lovable. On close acquaintance every one must get to love him. She loved him, no doubt of it. She must love him.

But perhaps she loved merely his art?

Did she, or did it just seem so? But how about that look of annoyance on her face when Mikita had spoken of their happiness? And hadn't she tried to soften the hard impression by stroking Mikita's hand?

To find himself thinking of Mikita in that way infuriated Falk. The sight of him in love was unpleasant. He felt a secret hope that his conjectures would prove true.

Disgusting! Why disgusting? Ha, ha, ha! As if it were his fault that his soul harboured stupid, beastly instincts.

He was now on Unter den Linden. He was surprised. Never had he seen such magnificent trees. The great boughs radiated from the trunks like the knotty spokes of a wheel, branching and intertwining fantastically. The tops reared a gigantic network of arteries to the sky, that sacred, mysterious storehouse of light and blessings.

How beautiful! The March wind blew its warm breath upon him.

He must forget her. Yes, forget her. Again all his thoughts and plans were drowned in that familiar cry: "Run! Run."

No, why should he run? What should he run for?

But his agitation increased. He struggled with that ever-growing pain which almost brought his heart to a standstill.

Who was the woman? What was she to him? Never before had he experienced such a feeling. No, never. He thought and thought — no, never.

Was it love?

He was terrified. How could it be that in one hour

a woman should have so completely overwhelmed his soul, and focussed all his thoughts and feelings upon herself?

No, he did not want to, he must not think of it any more.

"Thou shalt not covet thy neighbour's wife."

No, that had not even entered his mind. She was Mikita's all in all, his sole happiness. God, how Mikita had fairly burst with excitement when speaking of his love! It was so good that Mikita had found happiness at last! How it would unfold his artistic powers to be able to work for Ysa and because of her!

Falk felt her thin, hot hand on his lips. She had not resisted him. He saw her cloudy smile, the brilliant glow about her eyes. And with infinite bliss he felt a tremulous warmth in his body. His eyes burned. There was a choking in his throat and a sadness in his heart.

He wanted to be near a human being upon whom he could pour out a world of tenderness.

"Janina!"

The thought darted down on him like a lightning flash. She was so good to him, she loved him so, and he loved her too, more than he cared to admit to himself. Her love suddenly seemed exceedingly beautiful. She gave the whole of herself to him, without thinking, without calculating, without doubting. She belonged to him, to him alone.

Strange, he was near her house. What had brought him there? Yes, one more block.

The night concièrge opened the door. He ran upstairs and knocked at her door.

"Eric, you?" She was all atremble.

"Hush, it's I. I had a longing for you." He entered her room.

She fell on his neck in a transport of passion.   With what ecstasy he now felt this passion!

"Yes, I began to long for you." And he kissed her and fondled her and spoke to her so that she was almost beside herself with the greatness of her happiness.

He pressed her harder and harder to him, all the while listening to his own conscience, which cried: "Mikita! Mikita!"

"Yes, now I have forgotten, forgotten everything — for Mikita's sake."

And aloud he said:

"Yes, Janina, now I will stay with you, always, always."

CHAPTER V

HE must never see Ysa again. That was the only definite thought he was able to formulate during the
whole sleepless night. Never, never again.

Fear clutched him, a pathologic fear. How would it end?
How crush the terrible desire in him? In the space of a
single hour the woman had thrust roots deep into him, spreading and enmeshing his soul. He felt cut up into two parts.
No sooner would one part direct his will on the clear path
of sobriety than the other would intoxicate his brain upsetting his resolutions, drowning the voice of duty and conscience. Anguish and desire ate in deeper and deeper so
that he stood helpless, writhing with pain, nowhere able to
find peace.

Now what had actually happened?

"Ho, you psychologists! Explain what is taking place in
my soul. You have such a mass of psychological laws and
principles. Won't you please explain?"

He started with the shock of a new thought. What had
been the matter with Mikita? Had he had a premonition
of what was coming? But nothing had happened. Why
had he been so gloomy? He must love Ysa to distraction.
His lips had trembled with grief.

Yes, Mikita could scent misfortune thousands of miles
away. He could see the grass grow. The tone with which
he had asked Falk to escort Ysa to Iltis!

"I'm awfully busy," he had said, "and Ysa's so eager
to go."

Why had he not taken her himself? "Perhaps I'll come

later," he had added. Couldn't he have put off his work till the next day?

Falk rose. No, he would not take Ysa to Iltis. He did not wish to see her any more. He might still muster the strength to forget her. If he never saw her again she would remain a beautiful memory in his life, which in time he might even utilise as a literary theme.

In literature! Falk broke into an ironical smile. Remain at home and devote oneself to literature. Ha, ha!

He conceived sudden disgust for the literary profession. That stupid, senseless scribbling! Why was he not aristocrat enough not to prostitute his deepest, tenderest, most delicate, most intimate emotions and experiences? Why cast them to the crowd? Revolting.

Now he had made up his mind. Settled. He would remain at home.

Pleased with himself for having reached this conclusion he sat down and attempted to read. As his eyes travelled over the printed page, his mind remained a blank, while his gaze went ceilingward. A character in one of Gogol's novels occurred to him, a servant who took delight in the mere mechanical process of reading though without understanding a word. Falk tried to concentrate and read again.

What fascination in her movements! Not movements, in fact, but eloquent speech, the supreme expression of his own hightest ideal of beauty. And her hands, her hands!

He shivered.

"If I only could forget it all!" He must write a postal to Mikita, telling him he would be unable to escort Ysa to Iltis.

"I must take it to the postoffice myself, and see that it goes by the tube," he thought. "I wish I had a messenger-boy and shouldn't have to mail it myself."

He went out into the street. To her! to her! It was as if some physical impulse urged him on. To see her once more, to breathe the air she breathed, to drink in once more the charm she spread around her.

But no, a thousand times no! He could conquer himself, of course he could.

Yes, conquer himself like one of his friends who had set his heart on seeing Rome. He got within a mile of it, then turned back, saying a man should be able to conquer his desires. True, on reaching home, he went insane.

So that was the result of self-conquest? Then what was the use of it? He recalled Heine's words — how did Heine put it? Something like this: " It would be good if I could conquer myself, but better still if I don't."

The cynicism of Heine's remark troubled Falk. It was like sullying Ysa to think of it. But how? What had she to do with it? He walked on and thought of the mysterious association of ideas that spring up in our brains apparently without any connection. But only apparently, for the cunning, unseen power knows well what it combines and associates.

It was with a certain satisfaction that he dwelt on the unriddling of this problem. It kept away the subject from which he recoiled in terror — Mikita. Yet the thought of Mikita pursued him relentlessly.

It would come, and his heart would contract, and his temples beat with the distressing surge of blood to his brain.

What right had Mikita to another human being? How could he claim exclusive possession of her, a sort of monopoly?

Then he felt ashamed, but simultaneously another sensation came over him — yes, a sensation of hate — no, of repulsion.

For Mikita's sake he must not go to her.

What, for Mikita's sake?

He broke into an ironical laugh. The idea of thinking himself irresistible, invincible. Was he, Eric Falk, by a certain balance of traits evolved through the ages destined to cuckold every man? Must needs every man's sweetheart fall distractedly in love with him and absolutely succumb? Ridiculous, ridiculous!

"Falk, you're making an ass of yourself."

If at least he would say to himself:

"Don't go, you'll fall in love, and you cannot count on her jilting him because she is —"

He broke off, convinced beyond peradventure that she was nearer to him than to Mikita, and equally convinced that Mikita must also feel that Ysa —

No, no.

But there was one thing he could do without offending his conscience. He could be near her, across the street, in the restaurant. He would go there and get drunk. Then it would be impossible for him to visit her. Yes, he would get drunk. He must, and he would.

He stopped in front of Ysa's house. Too late now. He could not inform Mikita in time.

What was he to do?

"My God! Of course I must go in."

He mounted the steps, his heart pounding.

He rang, and was terrified by the sound of the bell which seemed to ring an alarm through the whole house.

"Run! Run!" it cried in his soul.

The door opened. Ysa stood in the hall. He saw a light of joy sparkle in her eyes and make radiant her face.

She pressed his hand warmly, very warmly.

Did she imply anything by it?

"You know Mikita won't come till later," she said.

"I know. He was at my rooms to-day."

"So you'll take me? You don't mind?"

"I'll do anything for you." The words escaped before he could stop them.

A moment of embarrassment followed. He must be on his guard, must keep himself in hand, not lose his self-control.

They sat down, looked at each other, and smiled. She, too, was uneasy, Falk felt.

He mastered himself and began to speak on indifferent topics.

"How did you like it yesterday?"

"It was a most interesting evening."

"Iltis is an unusual character, don't you think so?"
She smiled.

"No, I mean it seriously." Ysa looked at him unconvinced.

"Iltis is positively a genius of a dilettante sort. He knows everything, has read everything, and gone through the whole gamut of experiences. His brain works with unerring logic, but reaches such extraordinary conclusions that the net result is nil. For instance, a short while ago he began to work on the problem of children — to what stage of development they belong. He racked his brain for months and months, and ended by establishing an analogy between children and women. Women are children whose development has ceased, and children are their dolls. Children and women have round forms and delicate bones. Children and women cannot reason logically, cannot submit to the laws of logic. In carrying the comparison further he stumbled up against a difficulty. Children are pure and innocent, women are faithless, vain, the very servants of Satan. So the sum total of his

profound researches was nothing but a superficial comparison."

Falk continued with growing animation.

"Once, going home with him early in the morning —
after a night at the café I always take him home — he stopped
and looked at a flock of swans swimming from under the
bridge.

"'Eric, do you see?' he said with excitement in his voice.

"'Yes, I see.'

"'What do you see?'

"'Swans.'

"'Aren't they?'

"'Yes.'

"Iltis turned around nervously.

"Just then a huckstress from Jéricho Street chanced to
pass by."

Falk broke into a nervous laugh.

"That remarkable huckstress from Jericho Street — do
you know the great Liliencron?"

"No." Ysa gave Falk a surprised look.

"Liliencron wrote a poem —'The Crucifix'— no, 'Rabbi
Jeshua.' In the crowd —"

"But how about Iltis?" asked Ysa.

"I'll come back to him presently.— Well, in the crowd
on the way to Calvary are lawyers, officers, pickpockets, and
of course psychologists and representatives of the naturalistic
school of literature and finally a huckstress from Jericho
Street.

"'But there were no huckstresses at that time,' one of his
friends observed.

"Liliencron turned on him in anger. Why, the huckstress
was the outstanding figure in the poem. She was the prin-

cipal character. It was in order to create the type that he wrote the poem."

Ysa laughed a pleasant, comradely laugh, which acted on Falk like a tonic. That was the way he always wanted to see her. Then they could really be friends and nothing but friends.

" So, when the huckstress came up, Iltis snatched a handful of rolls from her basket and threw them on the water. That made him exceedingly happy.

" ' You see? ' he said.

" ' I see.'

" ' What do you see? '

" ' Swans.'

" ' Hm, funny. Yes, of course. But what you don't see and I do with my mental eye is that children and swans are in the same stage of development. Children don't eat crusts and neither do swans.' "

Ysa gave a constrained laugh.

Falk was disconcerted. Absurd in him! How could he suppose such drivel would amuse her?

" Does Iltis mean what he says seriously? "

Falk began to justify himself.

There had not been a word of truth in the story. He had made it up as he went along in a mistaken attempt to amuse her, but had succeeded only in boring her, the last thing on earth he would want to do.

Ysa's face darkened.

" Are you angry with me? "

" No."

The day drew to a close and the gloom thickened. There was an uncomfortable pause in the conversation. A tangled web of ideas began to weave itself in Falk's brain, a thousand sensations and thoughts meeting, crossing and upsetting one another.

" Has Mikita visited you to-day? " he asked, to break the silence, surprised himself that he should have put just that question.

" Yes, he's been here."

" He's behaved oddly to-day. What's the matter with him? "

" He's a bit nervous. The exhibition of his paintings in Munich is giving him a lot of trouble."

" You know, he isn't a bit changed. We used to love each other ever so much, yet sometimes we quarrelled. His moods used to change a hundred times a minute."

Ysa cast about for another subject of conversation. Falk saw it in the nervous twitching of her fingers.

" I'll be your first man, of course? "

" Of course." Ysa fixed him with her gaze.

Why did she look at him so? A faint, scarcely perceptible smile hovered about his lips. It produced an unpleasant impression upon Ysa, who thought:

" What does he mean by that smile? "

" Yes," she said aloud. " You will have the pleasure three weeks from now."

" I am glad." Falk smiled good-naturedly.

Another pause of silence.

" I'll show you something that will interest you," she said, rising.

Falk carefully examined the Japanese vase.

" Excellent. The Japanese are wonderful artists. They catch things like snap-shot photography. Don't you think so? They can see phenomena utterly hidden to our perceptions, phenomena coming and going in the thousandth part of a second. Do you understand? "

" Well? "

" I mean they possess the power to hold in their consciousness impressions that we cannot retain more than the fraction of a second; or, to put it in the elegant official slang of our physiological psychologists, the interval of time is too brief to enable the impression to enter our consciousness."

He held the vase in his hand and looked at Ysa.

" It happens to me sometimes, too, but only very rarely. To-day, for example, when I saw you in the hall I caught the flash of joy that darted over your face and instantly vanished."

" Yes? Did you notice it? " she said in an ironical tone.

" Yes, it was like the momentary flash of a diamond, yet I caught it. Isn't it so? Weren't you glad I came? And it made me feel infinitely happy to notice it."

His voice was so sincere and cordial that she blushed.

" We must go now," she said.

" No, let's wait a while longer. It's too early. Besides, I feel so happy here. Am I too frank? I have never felt like this before, never."

Darkness brings people strangely close together.

" It is all so queer, queer that Mikita is my friend and that you are engaged to him. I have the peculiar feeling that I have known you for thousands of years."

Ysa rose and lit the lamp.

Light parts people, and she wanted to set a distance between them.

" I'm sorry Mikita won't come till later."

" Yes, it's a pity. He was so excited."

This started Falk to reasoning about Mikita again. Absurd that Mikita should have the monopoly of a human being! But there was nothing to be done; it could not be helped. Falk looked at his watch. " It's time now. Let's go."

CHAPTER VI

WHAT had given him that idea?

In the centre of the picture he would paint a woman with a mysterious, treacherous, maniac smile on her lips, and all about her a thousand outstretched, clamourous hands — thin, nervous artists' hands, fat, fleshy, be-ringed bankers' hands, all sorts of hands, an orgy of greedy voluptuous hands. While the woman looked at them with her mysterious, maniac smile.

Mikita was in a fever. He must set to painting at once, quick, quick, or it would disappear, and then would come brooding, anguish, the venomous sting of a thousand serpents.

"Falk's no blackguard! No, Mikita, Falk's no blackguard," a persuasive voice within him cried. But then he saw the two glancing at each other, and exchanging embarrassed smiles, his heart all the while palpitating in alarm.

And to-night at Iltis's! They would dance there, of course. He had not thought of it before. Dancing, dancing. Ysa loved dancing. Dancing was her sole passion.

He had seen her dancing once. It had made his head swim! Those unrestrained bacchanalian movements, that frenzy of voluptuousness!

"That's what you ought to paint, my dear naturalist friend — the soul opening and a satanic monster crawling from its depths. Paint that abomination.

Confound it!

Why could he never believe that she loved him, ought to love him? Yes, *him, him!* After all, he represented a certain value, if only as an artist.

A damnable situation, the deuce take it!

Some Liebermann or other paints three stupid sheep in a potato field, or potatoes on the field, or a field and women gathering potatoes, and he gets money for it and gold medals. I painted humanity, and something more, something lying beyond humanity, and what did I get? Nothing! Go, Mikita, you are an ass! Didn't you see how the crowd split its sides laughing in Hamburg, Paris, and Berlin too? Isn't that fame? And the jokes in the *Fliegende Blätter?* Didn't I furnish them with an admirable theme for jokes?

I had to pay taxes. Good God, not to have a piece of bread to eat and to pay taxes. Not bad. They were going to confiscate all my property for my arrears to the government. What sort of a thing is the government? What have I got to do with the government?

"Are these your paintings?"

"Yes, of course they are mine. They represent a value of forty thousand marks. Why are you laughing?"

"I beg your pardon, I can't help it. Who will buy them? You won't get a penny for them. I am sorry, but there is nothing here I can confiscate."

"Well, Ysa, dear, am I not a great painter?"

He began to paint, still laughing.

But there was grief in his soul, and it bored down deep, so that he actually jumped with pain.

Remarkable. What is Falk, after all? What has he done? As for me — I haven't fallen from the table like little Eyolf. My spinal column is perfectly sound. My brain creates thoughts.

"Did you write this composition, Mikita?"

"Yes, teacher, of course."

"Nobody helped you with it?"

" Who could have helped me? "

" Somebody's influence is quite clear."

" Well said, teacher, but the composition is my own."

" Now don't be stubborn, Mikita; confess Falk put the silk trimming on your felt slippers. Where is Falk? "

But on such occasions Falk never appeared at school. He sent in an excuse that he was ill, and stayed at home writing poetry.

Mikita shook himself as if recovering consciousness, and beat his head. " Why, it's ugly to think that way about Falk. Mr. Liebermann, paint me the black soul that throws handfuls of dirt into a man's brain. Paint me that, and I will present you with all my works. I'll send them to you postpaid."

And Ysa is dancing now — with Falk. He can dance. Oh, how he can dance.

Hatred swept over him again

Falk, my dear Falk, where is the woman that can resist you?

Ysa is dancing.

Have you ever believed in anything, Ysa? Do you know what faith is?

Of course she did not know.

Do you know what you are, Ysa?

No, she did not know.

Don't you know yourself, Ysa?

No.

And he in whose soul faith had nestled and warmed itself for centuries, for ages! Yes, it was because faith was in him and of him that he craved to possess a woman and possess her wholly; it was because of this that be believed in love transcending time.

He jumped up.

No, he would not go to Iltis's. Now he would put his self-control to the test. What, go there and see her hanging on Falk's shoulders, pressing to him, merging into one with him? Ha, ha!

Mikita pulled off his blouse. He was hot.

Stand there and look on! Othello with his dagger under his mantle!

And Iltis screwing up his eyes and saying to the Suckling:

"Ysa's danced herself into his vitals."

No, no, he must come to his senses, he must. What reason had he to doubt Ysa? None whatever.

Then what did he want, the devil take it!

His feelings grew stronger. The pain became intolerable. He would go. He would go. He must show Ysa that he had become sensible at last and had ceased to doubt her. Yes, he would go and enjoy himself and dance.

But you can't dance, Mikita. You hop like a clown in a provincial circus. And besides, you are short, shorter than Ysa. A well-matched couple!

Mikita had to sit down. It was as if his legs were being cut from under him.

Oh, how it hurts, hang it!

"Mikita, come here a moment."

"What is it, teacher?"

"Mikita, it's an outrage to fill a composition with such nonsense. At least if it were your own, but it's Falk's, there's no mistaking his touch."

How was it he hadn't slapped that old fool in the face?

Suddenly he rose.

Have I gone insane? What do I want of Falk or Ysa?

He was frightened. Why, these were actual symptoms of disease. Nor was it the first time. They had kept recurring. He remembered having gone to Brittany once so as to buckle down to work.

Ridiculous Mikita. Ha, ha! A lot of work he had done. He hadn't been able to hold out more than a few hours. The very next day in a fit of jealousy he had boarded a train and dashed off to Paris, appearing before Ysa almost bereft of his senses.

"What, back already?" He had looked very foolish to her, and was ready to sink through the floor for shame.

"You see, Mikita," he began to speak to himself, "you are an ass, a positive ass. Love is a thing to be snatched up. If one hesitates, sends out feelers, and keeps turning and turning forever like a cat around a pot of hot fat, then it's no good. One must go for it proudly and boldly, take it by force. Then it comes to one. Conquer! Don't ask for a gift, for charity. No, Mikita, you can't get it by begging for it in Christ's name."

Yes, now they are dancing.

He began to sing the refrain of a street song.

"Venant des noces belles
Au jardin des amours —
Que les beaux jours sont courts!"

Grand! There was an illustration to it by Steinlen in *Gil Blas,* a ludicrous clown and a girl slapping him in the face.

Grand, grand!

"Venant des noces belles,
J'étais bien fatigué.
Je vis deux colombelles,
Une pastoure, ô gué!"

But there was no reason at all, no reason at all. Oh, Mikitia, how fine if you were not obliged to doubt. Wouldn't it be glorious, Mikita?

Yesterday, in the cab —

He rose and began to pace the room agitatedly.

She had always showed solicitude, asked what was the matter with him, stroked his hand and laid her head on his breast.

Yesterday she had said nothing, not a word. "Good-night, Mikita." That was all.

"Good-bye, Ysa, good-bye."

He began to sing in a loud falsetto.

> "Venant des noces belles
> Au jardin des amours —"

CHAPTER VII

"NO, no, my child, take it from me, all scientists are fools."

Iltis sat surrounded by a group of young men, spreading out his wisdom before them. His forty-six years sat upon him easily. He seemed as young as any man in the gathering.

Falk, who could not forget his cynical remark of the day before, kept watching the whole evening for an opportunity to hit back.

"Yes," Iltis continued, "all of them. At least I don't know one who isn't. Here is an example characteristic of professors as a class. I was travelling with a privat-dozent in geology. He was trying to take some measurements, but the magnetic needle would not stand still.

"'Ah,' said the brilliant professor, 'I know what's the trouble, I have a magnet in my pocket.'

"'Then why don't you throw it away?'

"He threw it away, but the needle still refused to subside.

"'Have you a penknife in your pocket?'

"Yes, the geologist had a penknife in his pocket. The penknife was disposed of too. Still the needle kept dancing a jig. 'You must have some iron ore sticking to your shoes,' I ventured to suggest. 'You'll have to throw your shoes away, too, I am afraid.' Oh, no, the erudite privat-dozent wouldn't hear of it. That's the way your scientific measurements are made, and on the results so obtained, they construct goodness knows what theories."

" Are you quite sure the iron ore was the cause? "

Iltis looked up at Falk in surprise.

" Of course," he said.

" Well, you see the question of causes is a very knotty one; it isn't by any means so clear as you think. It is rare indeed that any assigned cause has not subsequently been disproved. Take, for example, your favourite theme. Can you show me the cause of why woman is on a lower plane of development than man? "

" Any text-book on physiology will tell you."

" Respiration? Absurd. Children of both sexes up to ten years of age breathe with the aid of the stomach, just as all women do who don't wear corsets, Chinese women, for example, and the women of Yuma. In fact, women's mode of breathing in general has been artificially developed. It is an artificial product, as can be seen among the women of the Indian tribe, the Chickasaws."

" Idle tales of ethnologists, my dear Falk. They prove nothing, or else they prove the very opposite of what you are driving at."

" Oh, no, they are the reports of absolutely disinterested observers. But your other proof is all wrong, too, your argument that woman represents a lower stage of development because in stature and constitution she approaches the child. This, if anything, rather proves her superiority. The child type reveals the basic features of the human species in the purest form, whereas the adult male type is, morphologically, a transition stage between the primitive type and the higher types."

" That's metaphysics, friend Eric. Altogether, you are too much of a metaphysician, too much in the stars."

" Maybe. But isn't it a fact that all your conclusions are due to your confusion of morphological factors, to your not knowing what constitutes the higher and what the lower from a morphological point of view?"

Iltis looked at Falk puzzled.

"I don't understand you," he said.

Falk's eyes haunted Ysa. "What's the use of talking, anyway? I haven't come here to lecture on morphology. I want to dance."

"*Soyons amis, Cinna!*" cried Iltis. "Here's to your health!"

Some one began to play a waltz.

Falk went over to Ysa. She was standing at the further end of the large studio, smiling **at** him with that smile of hers which defied analysis. The very dusk in which she stood seemed to smile mysteriously.

"Do you dance?"

A gleam of light shot across her face.

"Then may I?" asked Falk, beginning to quiver.

The blood mounted to his head as he pressed her shapely body to his.

He plunged into an eddy, which carried him round and round. They were growing together, he felt, and she was part of his soul. He was whirling with himself and about himself, not seeing her, she being in him. He felt the rhythm, the lines, and the delicacy of her movements, felt them as the ebb and flow of his own soul, which came and went, first strong then faint.

And then suddenly he had a sensation of something exquisitely smooth, like a soft glassy surface. She was touching her face to his.

A flame of joy burst from his heart. He pressed her violently.

She belonged to him.

He forgot everything. The figures of the dancers melted

into one blood-red ribbon, which circled around him like a Saturn's ring. He felt only himself and this woman, who belonged to him. He did not hear the music; the music was in him, the whole world played and stormed in him, and he was carrying her through the whole world, and was great and proud because he could so carry her.

Who was Ysa, who was Mikita?

There was none but he, Falk. He alone existed. She whom he pressed to his bosom was part of him.

Exhausted they dropped on the sofa.

There was talk and bustle all about. Broken fragments of speech that he did not understand reached his ears. He still saw the blood-red Saturn's ring circling around him.

At last his senses returned. The red mist dispersed, and he saw long narrow streaks of tobacco smoke.

She sat half reclining on the sofa breathing hard. Her eyes were wide open. He touched her hand lightly. They were alone on the sofa, no one could see thm.

She answered his touch with a passionate, nervous grip.

And their hands closed on each other with a still stronger pressure. She moved toward him, nearer, nearer, almost bending over him. Their heads touched.

She made no resistance. He felt how she gave herself to him, permeated him, pierced through to his heart, and laid herself on the hot couch of his blood.

Suddenly she tore herself away.

"Mr. Falk, permit me to introduce to you the first German patron of art — a patron of German nationalism," Schermer continued with a wicked smile, "by blood, flesh and bones — Mr. Buchenzweig."

Buchenzweig made a low bow.

"I don't know on what grounds I deserve Mr. Schermer's flattering introduction, but I do take great interest in litera-

ture and art." He sat down, remaining silent for a moment.
He was a comical figure — a beefy, turgid face and whitish
eyes.

"I have read your book with grea-eat interest. It's fascinating."

"Thank you; I'm glad."

"Mr. Buchenzweig is exceedingly interested in art."
Schermer tried hard not to show he was drunk.

"And do you know why?" said Buchenzweig in a melancholy tone, dropping his lower lip. "Do you know why? I
have had many disappointments in my life, many disillusion-
ments, and I am seeking consolation in art."

The Suckling joined the group.

"Well, Falk, have you discovered another new genius?"

"How about yourself? Haven't you discovered yourself
yet?"

Ysa listened distractedly. How could it have caught her
so suddenly? How could she have done what she did, give
herself like that to Falk? To permit a stranger of only a
day's acquaintance to come so close? Dreadful! She realised that Falk was nearer to her than she cared to admit, and
it shamed and worried her.

"Do you know, Mr. Buchenzweig," screeched Schermer,
"you are a man actually interested in art and literature.
You are forever talking about art and the like. Then why
don't you do something for German art? Do something.
Lend the poor German writers money, me, for example.
Lend me two hundred marks, please do."

Buchenzweig thrust out his lower lip and stuck his index
finger in his trousers pocket. Though he pretended not to
see Ysa, he kept casting stealthy sidewise glances at her.

"What a disagreeable man!" Ysa thought. "And why
isn't Mikita here yet? It's so late."

" Have you got two hundred marks? " Schermer sneered.
" How many pennies make up your millionaire fortune? "

" It doesn't seem to insult him," thought Ysa, with sudden
disgust for all these people.

" Why isn't he coming? What does he want of me? "
A great weariness settled down on her. That everlasting
jealousy.— But she was all he had. He had nobody, nothing
in the world beside her. " It seems he isn't coming. He is
in his studio now, pacing the room like a wild beast in a
cage, tormenting himself into insanity."

She listened. Falk, irritation in his voice, was saying:

" Leave me alone with your eternal prattle about literature. Surely you have something more important to do than
squabble about whether the first place in German literature
belongs to Hauptmann or Sudermann."

" Well, well," the Suckling rejoined with heat, " the idea
of comparing the two. Why, there is a world of difference
between them."

" Quite right, I never doubted it. I am a worshipper of
Hauptmann myself. I like his lyrical works best. Have
you read his prologue for the opening of the German theatre?
A gem, the crowning jewel in contemporary lyric poetry.
Ha, ha, ha! Listen.

> " ' Und so wie es uns, den Alten
> Doch gelang in diesem Hause,
> Wollen wir die Fahne halten
> Ob der Strasse Marktgebrause! '

" Have you forgotten that wonderful phrase? Let me
see, how does it begin? That one about ninety onions and
the gleam of the magic fire, and — well, it's all the same, ha,
ha, ha! a gem, a gem! "

The Suckling gave Schermer a contemptuous look, and
said, raising his voice:

" I don't know, Mr. Falk, whether that's your real opinion or whether you're joking, but consider, a man who could write ' The Weavers ' "—

" ' The Weavers ' is all played out," broke in Schermer. " The newspapers have got us so accustomed to starving workmen, strikes and all the various manifestations of social unrest, that such subjects have lost their power to move us."

The Suckling vouchsafed the opinion that it was unpleasant to be in the society of a drunken man, and received a reply in kind; upon which the group broke up, leaving Ysa and Falk to themselves.

He looked at her, feeling that a vast distance had laid itself between them. She was a stranger now. A pang smote him.

" She's sitting on needles," he thought, " awaiting Mikita."

" No, Mr. Falk," she said, turning to him, " Mikita won't come to-night."

" Stay a while longer, he may come any minute."

" No, no, he won't come. I'm going home. I'm so tired. The company tires me. I don't want to stay here any longer."

" May I see you home? "

" As you please."

Falk bit his lips. He noticed her perturbation, and said:

" Maybe you don't care to have me go with you? "

" Oh, no, please do. But let's leave this place. I want to be at home."

CHAPTER VIII

"SHALL I call a cab?" asked Falk on the street.
"Oh, no, let's walk."

"How strange in Mikita," she thought.

He had promised to come without fail. Then why hadn't he? It worried her. She hardly dared to speak to any one, always conscious of his searching, suspicious look upon her. That incident in Frankfort, for instance. Maddening. Couldn't he understand that one would naturally be pleased to meet a countryman in a foreign city? And how he had taken it!—gone into the next room and written a letter to conceal his anger.

They were near the Tiergarten. In the warm March air her nerves gradually recovered.

He would certainly be angry with her for not having waited for him a few hours longer at Iltis's.

"Have you any idea why Mikita didn't come, Mr. Falk?"

"He's got the blues again, I suppose." But the next instant, ashamed of himself, he added: "Probably fretting over his work. When he's in that state, he can't bear to see anybody, especially such bores as to-night."

They were silent. A wonderful stillness hung in the air, a stillness, however, impregnated with the ferment of March, which stole into her soul. How good that Falk was with her!

"May I offer you my arm?"

She was almost grateful to him. She thought of the evening, of the dancing, and no longer felt ashamed or ill at ease. On the contrary, a soft sensation of warmth suffused her body.

"Why are you so quiet?" Her voice betrayed emotion.

"I didn't want to intrude. I was afraid my conversation might bore you."

"No, no, you're wrong. It was the company that bored me so. Now I'm glad we're alone together." She repeated the last sentence with the emphasis of sincerity.

"You see," Falk smiled, "I have good cause to be silent and meditate deeply upon myself." She was listening intently. "You see, the situation is unusual, it is strange. You mustn't misunderstand me. I'm talking to you about it simply as of a riddle, a mystery, a miracle, like resurrection from the dead."

Falk coughed. There was a slight tremor in his voice.

"I remember when still at high school being struck by an idea of Plato's. He holds that our earthly life is but a reflection of another life lived by us in some past time as an idea. All we see is merely a recollection, a reminiscence of what we have seen before entering this existence. The idea then appealed to me simply for its poetical beauty. Now I am constantly reminded of it because I see it realised in myself. I'm telling you this quite objectively, as when I spoke of the insensibility of fakirs last night. You mustn't take it in a bad way. I know I'm nothing to you but a stranger."

"You are not a stranger to me."

"No, really not? Ah, that makes me happy, I can't tell you how happy. Of all the people in the world you are the only one to whom I should not like to be a stranger, the only person in the world. You see, no one knows me. That's why none of them understands me, why they all hate me and are distrustful and suspicious. But to you I should like to open my whole soul."

He wavered. Had he not gone too far?

She made no reply, which meant that he was permitted to continue.

"Yes, what was it I was going to say? — Yesterday — strange it should have happened only yesterday — when I saw you yesterday, I knew I had known you long before. I must have seen you somewhere. Of course, I had never seen you before, but still I've known you for æons. That's why I'm saying all this to you. I've got to say it to you.— Yes, and then.— As a rule I'm able to hold myself in check, but yesterday in the cab I could not resist. I had to kiss your hand, and I am profoundly thankful that you didn't withdraw it.

"It's a puzzle to me. Between me and everybody else there is always a big barrier. I see people, as it were, only from a distance. My soul is as shy as a maiden's which permits no one to come close. But you I feel in myself, I feel every movement of yours streaming through my nerves, and then I see all the other people circling round me like a ring of fire."

Ysa listened as though mesmerised. She knew she ought not permit him to say such things. She felt Mikita's eyes upon her, penetrating to the bottom of her soul. But those passionate, fiery words! Never had any man spoken to her like that.

Falk was urged on by an impulse that drove him farther and farther. It was immaterial to him now what he said. He no longer tried to check himself, yielding completely to the need he felt to speak on. Something seemed to have opened in his heart and released a smouldering fire that instantly burst into a blaze, a conflagration.

"I don't want anything of you, I know I have no right to want anything. You love Mikita —"

"Yes," she answered perfunctorily.

"Yes, yes, yes, I know it. I also know that what I'm saying is stupid, frightfully stupid, insipid. But I must speak. This is the most important event in my life. I have never loved nor known what love is. I held love to be an absurdity, a disease that mankind ought to fight off and try to overcome. Now, suddenly it has come to me — in one minute, the moment my eyes fell on you standing in the waves of red light and you said in that enigmatic, I may say, cloud-covered voice: 'So that's you?'

"I felt I knew your voice, and I knew it was just the way you ought to speak. I expected it. And I knew that the woman I could love had to look precisely as you look, just like you. The riddle of my soul was solved, everything I had not known before became clear. I was able to peer into the abyss, to see the deepest depths."

"Mr. Falk, please don't, don't talk to me like that. It pains me, grieves me beyond measure, that you should suffer on my account. I can't give you anything — anything at all."

"I know it, Ysa, I know it well. And I don't ask anything, I only want to say —"

"You know I love Mikita."

"If you loved a thousand Mikitas, I should have had to tell you. I simply had to, there was no avoiding it."

He suddenly fell silent. What was it, he thought, that he really wanted? He laughed out loud.

"Why are you laughing?"

"Nothing, nothing, Ysa, I'm taking myself in hand," he said, serious now and despondent. He raised her hand to his lips, and a feverish heat passed into him from the long, narrow hand that he kissed.

"Don't be angry with me. I've lost control of myself. You should understand me. I've never loved in my life.

And now this new, unseen sensation has descended upon me with such violence that I'm stunned. Forget all I said."

A melancholy smile passed over his face.

"I shall never again speak to you about it. I shall always love you because it is impossible for me not to love you, because you are my soul, my holy of holies, because you are that in me by virtue of which I am I and not some one else."

Again he kissed her hand.

"Let us remain friends. Yes? You will have the gratification of knowing that you are the best, the greatest, the most important event in my life, my —"

His voice broke, and he kissed her hand. She remained silent, pressing his hand tightly. Falk grew calm.

"You are not angry with me?"

"No."

"And you will be my friend?"

"Yes."

The rest of the way they walked in silence.

Opposite Ysa's house was a restaurant which was still open.

"Now that we are friends, Ysa, may I ask you to take a glass of wine with me to clinch our friendship?"

Ysa wavered.

"It will be the greatest pleasure to me. I'd like to speak to you as a comrade."

They entered.

Falk ordered a Burgundy.

They were alone. The room in which they sat was divided from the large hall by a portière.

"Thank you, I have never had a friend."

Mikita's name was on Ysa's lips, but she shrank instinctively from pronouncing it.

The waiter put the wine on the table.

" Do you smoke? "

" Yes."

Ysa leaned back on the sofa, lighted a cigarette and puffed out a ring of smoke.

" Here's to our friendship." He gave her a friendly glance.

" I'm so happy. Ysa, you're so good to me, and we'll make no demands on each other, will we? "

Again he noticed the hot gleam about her eyes. " Not that, not that," he said to himself, afraid to encounter it. Drinking off the glass of wine hastily, he filled another, and said:

" Yes, yes, the human soul is a curious enigma."

Another pause of silence.

" Have you read Nietzsche? " he asked suddenly, raising his head.

" Yes."

" Do you remember this passage in Zarathustra: 'The night is deep, deeper than the day could ever have conceived'? "

She nodded yes.

" Hm, isn't it true? " he asked, smiling at her. " The soul too is deep, deeper than ever appears to our stupid consciousness."

They exchanged glances, their looks flowing into each other.

Falk gazed into his glass again.

" I'm really a specialist in psychology, a specialist, you understand? That means that I have measured the velocity with which external impressions are received, and have measured the time required for the impressions, aided by the feelings, to reach the consciousness; but in the province of

love I have never made researches and have been totally ignorant." Then suddenly: "Well, here's to your health!"
He drank off his glass.

"All those measurements have led to nothing. This one night has taught me more than the whole four or five years wasted in studying the so-called science of psychology. I dreamed —" he raised his head —" but I'm boring you."

"Oh, no, far from it."

They both smiled.

"Well, as I was saying, last night I dreamed I was sailing with you on the ocean. A dense fog enveloped the ship, heavy as lead, close, stifling. I was sitting in the saloon with you, talking — no, not talking. Something in my soul was talking in a voice without sound, a sort of disembodied voice. But you understood me.

"Then we rose. We both knew very well what was going to happen — something terrible — and it did happen. There was a fearful crash as of some sun breaking away from its orbit, an infernal din as of a mass of icebergs tumbling down upon the earth. It was a collision with another steamer. We were the only ones who felt no fear. We saw none but each other and understood each other.

"I held your hand tight in mine, but of a sudden you disappeared.

"I found myself in a boat. The sea tossed us up to the sky, then plunged us deep down into a bottomless abyss.

"I was indifferent to my fate, yet my head felt ready to fly apart from terror of what had happened to you. Then I saw the ship sinking rapidly. The only part still visible above the water was the tall mast, and on it, at the very top, were you. I leapt into the sea, caught you, and you hung on my arm limp and unconscious. The weight was awful, I couldn't keep up any longer; one minute more and we'd both have gone down.

"The mist and the clouds rolled together into one gigantic figure, and then spread all over the heavens, cold, terrifying, indifferent."

Falk smiled a strange, troubled smile.

"The sea and the sky, you and I, the whole world, were one. It was Destiny."

Ysa became uncomfortable again under his strange look. He broke off abruptly.

"An odd dream, wasn't it?" he asked, smiling.

She made no answer, in an effort to appear indifferent. Falk's burning eyes rested on hers a full minute. Then he looked into his glass again.

"This is the first time that fate, imperious necessity, has entered into my life." His voice had a measured, monotonous cadence, with a suggestion of easy carelessness. But he held her spellbound as though wielding a hypnotic power. She was perforce compelled to listen to him.

"I never knew what necessity was. Now I know. You see, I went through life unconcerned, with no premonition of evil; I had perfect mastery over myself, was able always to consult my reason. There was no feeling I could not control. Suddenly you come, strange emblem of my soul, you, the idea that I had already conceived in another existence, you who contain the whole mystery of my art.

"So, you see, I was firm, strong and cold, when along you came, and my whole life centred upon this one event. You have taken possession of me. I can think of nothing else. You are the contents of my brain."

"Don't, Falk, don't speak like that. The idea that I am the cause of your suffering is dreadful."

"No, Ysa, you are mistaken. I am happy. You've made

a new man of me, you've given me countless wealth. Why, I don't want anything of you, I know you love Mikita."

Ysa felt her disquiet growing. Mikita had been completely forgotten. No, she must not sit there longer, or listen to another word of Falk's. She rose.

" I'm going."

" Stay, stay a while longer."

Something forced her back into her seat. But Mikita came to her mind, and her restlessness grew.

" No, no," she said with a gesture of haste, " I must go, I can't sit here any longer, I can't, I'm so tired."

Falk tried to suppress a nervous laugh.

CHAPTER IX

THEY stopped before her door. Falk fumbled for the keyhole. At last.

She entered the vestibule. He followed. They stopped again.

Why was he lingering? What did he want?

"Good-night, Falk."

He held her hand in a hard grip, his voice trembled.

"I believe our leave-taking should be more cordial."

The door was half open. Broad bands of light streaming from the street lamps fell upon her face. Her look of surprise embarrassed him.

"Good-night," she said.

He heard the key in the lock, and stood still listening to her light, quick step up the stairway. Then he faced about and walked away.

Suddenly he gave a loud whoop. What did that mean? Was he giving vent to his energy in a senseless explosion of sound? Admirable. What a donkey he had been. Annoying! How stupid that stuff about a cordial leave-taking! What an absurd jackanapes she must think him! He, the great, scornful ridiculer of all things and all people suddenly in love like a freshman. To add to his misery there rose in his mind an incident in his boyhood, with all its sting revived by his present situation.

It had happened when he was only thirteen years old and was making his first attempt at falling in love. He held himself to be infinitely great. The profound, intellectual conversations he carried on with the lady of his heart —

Schiller and Lenau — yellow gloves bought for the occasion.

One night his teacher caught him in a tête-à-tête. The next day — great!

The bell rang. There was a ten-minute recess. All the boys rushed to the door.

"Falk, you will please stay in." He knew what was before him.

"Come here."

He walked to the platform as though going to the gallows.

"Bring your chair."

He obeyed.

"Lie down."

He lay down.

The thick rush cane whizzed in the air, trembled, bent, descended and whizzed faster, faster, ever more painful.

My, how it hurt! Why are you laughing, sir? It's a tragedy. Rarely in my life have I suffered as I suffered then. If you laugh at it, you simply show up your stupidity. Don't you understand life itself? The ridiculous next to the tragic, gold in dross, the most sacred mingling with the most commonplace.

Hegel, the old Prussian philosopher, was one of the wisest of men. What, you don't know Hegel? Well, his whole philosophy focussed in one question, "Why does nature use such unæsthetic means to attain her loftiest aims?" The sex organs, for instance, serve for both procreation and the elimination of the waste products of metabolism.

Odd, isn't it? So odd as to be absurd, nay, revolting. But so it is with the most sacred things. It's a way they have.

Falk worked himself into a rage.

The thing must be thought out, must be settled once for all. Love, love! First a bewilderment, a being overcome with a sense of perplexity; then embarrassed looks and flaming eyes; next a quivering of the hands as though one were telegraphing across thousands of miles; next a raising and lowering of the voice, now hoarse, now shrill, as when reading the odes of Horace. Then a whole series of unconscious motions, an aimless catching hold of objects and swinging them in the air, a weakness in the knees, coughing, spitting. Isn't it laughable, side-splittingly laughable?

And opposite me sits Ysa encouraging me with her sweet smile, revealing the knowledge of good and evil, and with her enigmatic look.

But we know all these theatrical tricks. Didn't I prove myself to-day to be a perfect adept in the art of attitudinising.

I am what they call a highly differentiated individual. I have, combined in me, everything — design, ambition, sincerity, knowledge and ignorance, falsehood and truth. A thousand heavens, a thousand worlds are in me; yet, notwithstanding, I am ridiculous.

And there is no help for it, absolutely none. The "iron law," the most constant of all the laws, is this, that a man in order to attain his ridiculous aim must make himself a thousand times ridiculous in the eyes of the woman he loves.

He broke off the thread of his reflections.

"So there is still shame in my being. Yes, yes, I feel as shy as an infatuated schoolboy, who's afraid he'll fall off his horse in the presence of his adored one."

But why? Ysa was a complete stranger. He knew nothing of her. He had not penetrated the fraction of an inch into the mystery of her smile, into the mystery of herself, so infinitely sweet, so infinitely near him.

And with that strange woman of whom he knew nothing he had fallen in love. At once, in a second.

Ho, you thousands of learned psychologists, come hither! Come hither, you who know it all, you anatomists of the soul, analysts "pure and simple"! Come hither and explain!

This is the fact. It took one second for me to fall in love with a woman, the first time I ever loved.

"Because the sex emotion has awakened in you," you say. You are wrong, it was never asleep.

"Because you worked yourself into it." No, I worked myself into nothing. My brain had nothing to do with it. I had no time for reflection. You ought to be ashamed of yourselves, founders of the science of the physiology of love; you ought to know, you fantastic physiologists, that sex love is not the result of reflection; one does not go to work and deliberately think it out. The sex emotion is a blind, stupid beast — stupid and ridiculous.

Lastly, I don't care, it's absolutely immaterial to me. The man who is to be twenty-five years old next June has ceased to ask for the causes of things. The question "Why?" does not exist for him. He accepts things as facts. So.

He looked around. What park was this? He did not know. "Not a bad place," he thought, and seated himself on a bench. His head was a little heavy, he must have drunk too much. Resting brought him no relief. The whole night a thought boiled and seethed within him, giving him no peace. Though he tried to stifle it, it kept rising to the surface and finally poured over.

"Mikita!"

Falk rose, paced to and fro, and sat down again.

You see, Mikita, you mustn't be angry with me. What can I do? It's not my fault. Why did you take me to her? I wanted to drink wine and talk with you, I didn't want to go to her. One shouldn't take a friend to one's sweetheart. That's a fundamental in the code of love. Never, never should a man take his friend to his sweetheart. Even if she be as grand a creature as your Ysa.

Don't, Mikita, don't be so frightfully miserable. I love you dearly and it drives me mad; I'm suffering the torments of hell.

He examined his own feelings.

Really, I'm not to blame. Judge for yourself. I enter the room. A magic red wave of light. It envelops a woman whom I know even better than you, although I had never seen her before.

Was it the fault perhaps of that red light? You are an artist to the fingertips, you should know how a red light affects a soul.

There is a certain Du Bois-Raymond, also a psychologist in a way, who says the colour red is composed of waves that make five-hundred billion vibrations in a second. These vibrations cause vibrations in the nerves, as a result of which I tremble, quiver.

Now do you understand why I have fallen in love? Because I tremble.

It is as clear as the sun. I tremble, ergo I love.

Falk rose and walked aimlessly on. The streets were empty, and silent, except for the hoarse, insistent voice of a woman saying every now and then:

" Come, sweetheart."

No, he had not the least desire to go. What did he care for cocottes? He was not a Berlin author seeking experiences and petticoat states of mind to write a novel about. No, he hated all women, all, especially her who had artfully stolen into his soul and stirred up a sea of hellish tumult.

No, Mikita, you must not be angry with me. No, no. You can't imagine how I suffer. Something has been clutching at my throat all day. I haven't eaten, I've just been drinking.

Do you know what I dreamed? I dreamed I was falling from a high mountain. I was sitting on an iceberg, rushing along at terrific speed. What could I do? How could I try to save myself? The vast mountain of ice dashed on, furious, irresistible, and I was borne along with it.

See for yourself, can I help it? Can I change the arrangement of the atoms in my nerves? Can I rearrange, recorrelate them? Can I check the movements of my brain? Can I? And you, can *you*?

The iceberg is carrying me, jolting me, tossing me from one side to another, and I roll about, slip down. Finally I shall be thrown into the sea.

"Such is the 'iron' law!"

Falk almost shouted it.

Yes, I'm drunk, but in such circumstances it is hard to control oneself.

No, Mikita, no, you're infinitely dear to me. I'm not guilty, not in the least guilty toward you.

He was suddenly overcome with rage.

But didn't you try to excite her, my dearest Falk? Didn't you endeavour to arouse her curiosity in a thousand different ways?

Remarkable, this sudden sense of guilt. Yes, I'm taking my conscience, charged with sin, laying it out before the Almighty who created me, not an irrational four-footed animal, but a two-footed human being endowed with a soul and reason, with the power to distinguish between good and evil, and the power, by virtue of what is called his free will, the quintessence of it all, to govern his conduct.

Yes, my dear Mikita, *mea maxima culpa!* I have sinned before you.

How tired he was. Noticing a café he entered.

The room was full of noises — shouting, swearing, quarrelling, haggling. He looked round. "I wonder if there's a Berlin litterateur here gathering material for a book?" he thought. "A colleague — ha, ha, ha!"

Resting his elbows on the table he gazed at the large white blotch of the electric lamp. There was a twinkling in his eyes, a hot haze quivered about the lamp. It circled faster and faster, ever hotter and more impetuous.

He felt Ysa in his embrace, her face close to his, her movements streaming through his nerves. Ah, bliss! He saw that light like a red Saturn's ring.

It was a great problem. He straightened himself up.

The problem of his love. Ysa had been born out of him, or he out of her. She was the complement, the perfection of his life. Her movements were so utterly the movements of his soul that they stirred him to ecstasy, the sound of her voice awakened a something that held the mystery of his existence.

Stupid brain, whence do you know this with such confidence?

He laughed an ironical laugh.

He went into a revery. He saw Ysa and himself in strange circumstances. They were sitting opposite each other, exchanging cold glances as though indifferent strangers. Rays of light, a sort of Roentgen rays, passed through her eyes, and he saw himself and herself through and through, as though something had emerged from deep down in them, as though the two hidden I's had approached and were scrutinising each other eagerly.

But no. They were sitting at the table, indifferent, talking about commonplaces. Those other I's, however, were infinitely near, locked in intimate embrace, fused into one.

That other I, Mikita, whom I do not know, who has suddenly appeared without cause, without reason, knew her before you and I met, these thousands of years.

You see, Mikita, my stupid mind can perceive the greatest things ever; it can affirm an accomplished fact.

Yes, friend Mikita, it is an accomplished fact — I love her.

But why did I try to win her interest, impress her, make myself attractive in her eyes? For heaven's sake, Mikita, be reasonable. The Great Agent wound up the spring so that the wheels perforce were obliged to turn in this, not in any other, direction.

How can you fail to understand?

" Why didn't Mikita come? " he heard Ysa's question.

Ah, Ysa, you don't know Mikita at all, not at all. Mikita's instinct has hands that reach out thousands of miles, hands that can grasp the ungraspable. Mikita sees how sound turns into colour. He has painted harmonies, which, could you hear them, would drive you to distraction. But the gross eye, it seems, can bear everything. Mikita sees the grass grow, sees the heavens cry. Yes, Mikita sees all that; Mikita is a genius.

" And I, what have I done? " Falk groaned inwardly.

Nonsense, Falk. Are you really drunk?

Oh, no, I'm a psychologist, and am dissecting Mikita's soul.

Mikita pretends to see nothing. He lets the poison penetrate deep until his whole soul corrodes. What does he get by it? Nothing. Useless impediments are dumped in the sea, and the vessel sails on freely. Mikita is not the first; he will not be the last.

The noise in the café became too much for Falk.

"Quiet!" ·he cried, jumping up; then sat down again. That confounded buzzing of the flies kept him from thinking.

The next idea carried him off in a wave of excitement. He must see Mikita, instantly, without fail. He must see what he was doing now.

"Who's there? I'm busy."—"It's I, Eric Falk." Mikita opens the door, and looks at Falk sidewise, his eyes, of course, glaring ferociously.

"What do you want?"

"What do I want? I want to explain that it isn't I who love, but my other I, which I do not know, but which has come and gripped me suddenly. I want to explain how it all happened. I was sitting with her at table, indifferent, cold; but while I was talking about commonplaces, that other I, acting independently, drew her to me and worked on her until she yielded. No, no, not she. She laughed at me, made fun of me because my stupid conscious I craved for a warmer leave-taking. You see, she is a stranger to me, a perfect stranger. But those other I's in both of us know each other well, love each other infinitely and inseparably."

I thank Thee, Almighty Creator, that Thou hast fashioned me a two-legged creature endowed with reason having the power to distinguish between good and evil, and not to desire Ysa, seeing that Mikita was so fortunate as to meet her first.

And there, there sits a young animal next to one hundred and fifty pounds of carrion — ha, ha! — a stupid little tradesman. There he is without reason, without the power to distinguish between good and evil.— You understand, you silly puppy? Do you know what you are in comparison to me? You are without reason, without a will, don't you know?

He broke out into a roar of laughter.

For this unbecoming conduct — he gloated over the phrase " unbecoming conduct "— he had to leave the café.

And it was high time.

In that atmosphere, fouled with the greasy odours of meat and perspiration, it was impossible for a creature of the genus *Homo sapiens* to hold out any longer.

Outside day was breaking. The deep blue of the sky spread over the dark roofs in ineffable stillness and grandeur.

The grandeur of the Berlin sky! — He laughed sardonically. But such is the stupid way of nature; she reveals her wonders equally to oceans and mud puddles.

CHAPTER X

"WHY didn't you come to Iltis's studio last night?"
Ysa asked hesitatingly.

"Why should I? I was positive you'd enjoy yourself without me."

"It was ugly of you. You know how I enjoy being with you."

"Really?" he looked at her sceptically.

"Don't you know it?" She felt miserable, but observed a tremor in his pale, tired face. She knew that tremor well.

"Aren't you ashamed of yourself? You're horrid." She took his hand and began to stroke it.

He pulled his hand away softly and paced the studio.

"What's the matter?"

"With me? Nothing, nothing."

She looked at his twitching face. There was a fire burning in him that threatened every minute to burst into an explosion.

"Do come here."

He paused before her.

"What do you want?"

"Sit down beside me, here."

He sat down. She took his hand.

"Now what *is* the matter, Mikita?"

"Nothing."

"You see, Mikita, you're not frank. You don't want to say it, but I know you're jealous of Falk."

Mikita made as if to interrupt her.

"No, no, I know you. You are jealous, and it's fearfully stupid of you. Falk is an interesting man, next to you perhaps the most interesting man I've met. But I couldn't ever love him, no, never. When you didn't turn up last night I knew you were staying home and working yourself into a frenzy of jealousy. The whole night long I kept wondering what I had done to make you jealous. I haven't given you any cause to be jealous, have I?"

Mikita's face turned red with shame.

"You mustn't be jealous. It's torture to me. Besides, it's awfully tiresome. If you keep on, soon I won't dare to say a word to anybody for fear you'll be hurt. It's intolerable. I simply can't stand it. You haven't the slightest cause to act this way. You are killing our love."

Mikita, utterly crushed, kissed her hand.

"That eternal distrust of yours is fearfully insulting. You used to be so proud of my independence; now you want to crush it and cow me. You'll soon be wanting to isolate me from the rest of the world."

Mikita was in despair.

"No, no, Ysa, I'm not jealous. But you can't imagine what your love means to me. I can't live without you. I've grown into you with all the roots of my being. You "— he made a wide, droll gesture with his hand —" you don't understand, you haven't my crazy temperament, the — the — in a word, you can't feel how it tortures me, how it flashes like lightning in front of my eyes and makes me blind to everything else."

She held his hand in hers and kept stroking it.

"No, you can't tell what you are to me. I'm not jealous. I only feel an insane terror that I may lose you. I can't satisfy myself as to why you love me, I — I —"

"Look here," he said, suddenly rising and straightening up. "Just look at this funny little Mikita. Why, you're taller than I am."

" Stop, I love you. You are a great artist, the greatest of all."

" There you are, you see. You love only the artist in me; the man you don't even know. As a man I'm nothing to you, nothing at all."

" But the man and artist in you are one. What would you be without your art? "

" Yes, yes, you're right. It's as you say, Ysa, I've gone clean mad. But don't be angry with me, for God's sake, don't. I'll be rational now. It's not my fault. What can I do? You know I live only by you. If I were to lose you I'd have nothing left, absolutely nothing."

Tears rolled down his cheeks. She embraced him.

" But, my dear, stupid Mikita, I do love you."

" Really? Do you really love me? You — you? "

With trembling hands he stroked her face, caressed and pressed her to him passionately.

" You'll never give me up? "

" No, no."

" You love me? "

" Yes."

" Say it again, once more, a thousand times, my precious, my only. I can't — I can't tell you how I suffered yesterday. I thought I was losing my mind. I wanted to run to you but couldn't, I didn't know what to do with myself, I couldn't sit, I couldn't stand. Ysa, you'll never forsake me, will you? Don't, don't! If you do I am lost; if you do, then — then —"

His feeble, exhausted body shook.

" You see, I'm going to paint. You have no conception yet of what I can do. You'll see. I'll paint you, only you, always you. I will make the whole world bow to you — I can paint everything — thoughts, music, words. . . . And *you,* yes, *you.* You'll be proud of me, believe me, you'll be proud of me."

He dropped on his knees, his voice sank to a vague murmur of confused, broken words, and he clasped her knees.

"You're mine — you're — m — m —"

His excitement irritated and made her uncomfortable. If she could only quiet him.

"Yes, yes. You are my great Mikita. And I'm yours, yours. . . . But you mustn't be so mean."

"No, no, I know you love me. I know you're mine — Forgive me. It shall never happen again. Do you forgive me?"

"Yes, yes."

He closed her in his arms in a grip so hard that she had to gasp for breath. A vague fear stole over her. She felt it rising higher and higher, and shivered. Above everything else, she would have liked to leave him now.—

She tore herself out of his grasp, but he seemed not to notice it. A wild passion, long suppressed, broke through to the surface.

"I am so happy, so infinitely happy. I owe everything to you. You have given me all, all —" he mumbled. A blind, raging, beastly desire took possession of him.

"Without you I am nothing, nothing. I felt it yesterday. Yesterday I knew that without you I'm lost, utterly gone." He pressed her still harder.

"You — you —" he gasped.

She felt his sultry breath burning her neck. Her soul shrivelled up like a dry leaf. Her fear grew worse. It took away her strength, bewildered her. Oh, God! What was she to do? The image of Falk arose before her. Indignation and rebellion, savage, desperate, took fire in her.

"Be mine," he entreated. "Prove to me that you love

me." His eyes were the unseeing eyes of a madman.

Oh, God! God! She roused herself. She wanted to push him away, to run away, never, never to see him again — not to yield to that abomination. But that instant her strength failed. Overcome by a sickening weariness, she was unable to offer resistance. She had to. . . .

" I love you — I'm dying for the longing of you —" he lisped like a child.

Her feeling of revulsion grew, mounted to her throat, choked her. A cold shiver of disgust ran through her body, but she was powerless. She heard nothing but Falk's voice, saw his eyes — no, she hadn't the strength. She closed her eyes, and in despair, awful, hideous despair, yielded to the revolting outbreak of passion.

.   .   .   .

"You have given me happiness."

His happiness contorted Mikita's thin, nervous face with an imbecile grimace.

All she felt was revulsion, loathing, hatred. Yet on her lips a smile played, all unconscious to herself, a smile revealing the knowledge of good and evil.

She struggled with herself. Shame blurred her eyesight. It was only by a mighty effort that she checked the word she felt like flinging into his face for his outrage upon her. And the thought of Falk bored still deeper into her soul. A terrific pain drove like a wedge through her head, splitting it apart.

" Oh, Ysa, now I'm happy, infinitely happy."

She controlled herself and smiled. Yet all the time she felt that revulsion, loathing, hatred — of his words, his hands, his hot breath.

But Mikita thought solely of his happiness. The woman

belonged to him. His head was ablaze with joy and the consciousness of power.

She wished to stop thinking, but the thought of Falk clung, made her suffer intensely, stung her, burned her heart with shame and hate. She had to gasp for breath. If only Falk would not come! O God! If only he would not come!

"Is Falk coming to-day?"

He gazed at her in surprise.

"Who? Falk?"

She recovered herself.

"I should very much like him to see your paintings. He hasn't seen them yet, and he is the only one who's capable of understanding them."

Mikita heaved a sigh of relief.

"I'll write him this minute, Ysa, and ask him to come at once."

She jumped up.

"No, no, not to-day!"

"Why not?"

"To-day I want to be alone with you."

He kissed her hand feelingly, raising his eyes to her with a look of thanks.

What abject, canine devotion!

It grew dusk.

What right had he to make such a savage assault upon her — such a — no, no, she must not think, she must not think. Yet she could not rid herself of the sense of having been besmirched. He *had* besmirched her.

She felt his hand on her shoulder.

She shivered with fright. His touch was repugnant to her.

"Light the lamp."

Mikita rose and lighted the lamp.

Then he sat down and pierced her with his gaze.

She could no longer hold herself in check. It rushed upon her — Falk, Mikita, and disgust — that terrible disgust.

In him also sudden fear awoke; for a moment a panic paralysed his brain. She saw a quiver dart over his face. His eyes opened wide.

"What's the matter?" he asked in a hoarse voice.

"Nothing, nothing." She tried unsuccessfully to force a smile.

At that moment the bell rang.

Mikita started, unaware whence the sound came.

"Do you hear? The door-bell. Don't answer, please don't," she begged in terror.

But he had already run out of the room. Her strength failed. It's he, it's Falk. She knew it. Oh, my God! It's he.

"Ah, great, first rate! We were just going to write a letter asking you to come." Mikita was beside himself. "Well, Ysa, here's Falk at last." He made a desperate effort to regain self-control. "I'm so glad, awfully glad, old fellow. We'll have a great time together this evening. What'll you have — whiskey, beer? Eh?

"You want to see my pictures, the stupid pictures. You think they're worth looking at? Go out into the street, into life, yes, then you'll see pictures. What's this daubing and painting for? God! What is it all for? Didn't you tell me yesterday that all the screaming and smearing of the poets and artists can't attract even a goose? Yes, go out into the street — no, go into a café at night. There you'll see pictures, striking pictures! The pictures I saw yesterday no human being can paint. Listen to what I saw. I was

in a resturant a long while. At a table opposite was a man
with two women, one of them his mistress. With the other
he kept exchanging telegraphic messages under the table
while eating sausages. Then suddenly there was a moment —
ha, ha! a wonderful moment!" Mikita gave a hoarse laugh.
He spoke indistinctly. "A rare moment! The official mistress"— every instant his nervous, unpleasant laugh interrupted his story —"suddenly picked up the dish of sausages
and threw them in her inconstant lover's face. It was a sight
worth a hundred of my pictures. The gravy dripped from
his forehead and face, you know the sort of dark chocolate-
coloured liquid they put into all the dishes here in Berlin.
The sausages flew in all directions. The fellow was a sight."
Mikita shook with laughter. "It was a picture, I tell you.
You should have seen it."

Falk could not understand what was happening to Mikita.
He glanced at Ysa, but she was lying back on the sofa, her
eyes upturned.

Evidently there had been a stormy scene of jealousy between them.

"And do you know what the man did?" Mikita nervously twisted the buttons on Falk's coat. "Nothing, absolutely nothing. He calmly wiped the gravy off his face;
that's all. And the woman of the telegraphic messages almost died laughing. Her erotic cravings were gone, washed
clean away.

"Do you know why?" Mikita cried.

"Because the man had been made ridiculous. When a
man appears in a ridiculous light to a woman, all's lost for
that man."

This remark awakened an unpleasant feeling in Falk.
He recalled last night's leave-taking from Ysa.

"Have you an idea of what it means to appear ridiculous

in a woman's eyes? Of course, of course, not always,"
Mikita stammered. " No, not always. There are women
in whose eyes a man can never become ridiculous — they are
the women who love! love!" He calmed himself. "You
see the women who love are oblivious of themselves and everything. They have no eyes for the ridiculous in a man, they
don't think about it, they don't notice it." He had worked
himself into excitement again.

"Well, Ysa, what do you say, isn't it so? You are a
woman. You know."

Ysa tried to change the subject of conversation. How
ugly, how revolting he was! She burst out laughing.

" Yes, I should think you were right. The story's amus-
ing. What was the sequel?"

Mikita searched her with his eyes.

" Oh, yes. As I said, the stewed, roasted and derided
gentleman sat perfectly still, although every one else in the
room was almost rolling over with laughter. His exquisite
high collar had been metamorphosed into a rag, and you
could have hung his starched shirt-front on a match. The
cause of it all, I mean the woman in whose eyes one may
not make oneself ridiculous, turned pale now, I noticed, and
trembled. Her expression was like a dog's about to snap.
Goya saw people that way, the great, inimitable Goya, the
only psychologist in the world. He alone saw the beast in
man; for all human beings are beasts, either dogs or don-
keys.

" But the other girl had temperament, had love in her
heart, infinite love; she loved him, yes, she loved. . . .

" What, it doesn't interest you? The sentiment of jealousy that leads to crime doesn't interest you? One throws
sausages, another throws vitriol; but the sentiment is always
the same, a strong, all-powerful emotion — love, life itself,

that's what it is, in one manifesting itself one way, in another, another way. My mother had a servant girl who read novels day and night. Don't you think humanity lost another great Rodziewicz in her? Isn't it so?"

Falk was ill at ease. What was happening to Mikita?

"Now, old man, is there any use in looking at pictures?

"Yes, that's the way of love. Well, then, the man calmly and triumphantly left the restaurant, the women with him. But out in the street there was a sensation. It needed to be seen to be appreciated. The official mistress was suddenly bowled over in the gutter by a terrific slap in the face. But she crawled back on her knees and implored his pardon. He kicked her, yet she ran after him crying and begging."

Mikita grew more vehement.

"Do you know what I did? I went up to him, bowed very low, and said, 'Permit me to express my great esteem and admiration.' Yes, you see —" Mikita's excitement became alarming.

"For heaven's sake, what's the matter with you? Are you ill?"

"I? Ill? Absurd! Why, don't you think the man acted right? A woman must be subjugated, with the fist, the whip; love must be wrested by force, must be conquered." He stuttered and fell silent.

There was an awkward pause. Falk's eyes haunted Mikita and Ysa. Yet all in all the scene gave him satisfaction.

Ysa suddenly sat up and said:

"An excellent opportunity for you to quote Nietzsche, 'When you go to a woman don't forget to take a whip along.' Else what you say may sound like plagiarism, you know."

There was unwonted aggressiveness in her voice. Falk

looked at her in surprise. Could it mean a rupture? With Mikita? The hatred in her eyes!

Mikita leaped from his chair and broke into a laugh.

"Yes, Nietzsche put it magnificently, wonderfully.— But what's the matter with you? You look so solemn.— Or have I turned altogether silly?"

Suddenly his manner softened.

"Don't be angry with me for being so excited. I'm beginning to believe I really have delirium tremens. I boozed the whole night with that creature, which isn't good for me, to say the least. My uncle died of delirium tremens, the genuine article, the best that ever shattered the human brain. It was as towering as a tall palm tree, under which, as our knights of the intellect tell us, no man can go with impunity."

He paced about the room and straightened the pictures here and there.

"God! what pictures! A self-complacent man ought really rest content with these and never again handle a brush and smear paint.

"So you want to see my paintings? If you do, you'd better come to-morrow in the daytime. It needs a lot of light, a million square miles of light in each eye, to see what no man has yet seen — not one — I neither — but which I must see some day, yes, I must!"

Falk had never before beheld Mikita in such a state. It was abnormal.

"But what is the matter with you, tell me, won't you? Why are you playing this game with me?"

"What's the matter with me? What's the matter with me? I am happy, happier than I've ever been in my life."

"But you needn't shout it from the roof tops."

"I've got to shout, confound it! because I notice a quiver

round your lips sometimes, a sort of tinge of irony, as if you didn't believe in my happiness. Say, Ysa, aren't we happy?"

Ysa's endurance was at an end. He was going to drag their relationship through the mire now. It was too much.

She rose, put on her hat and coat, and walked out of the studio without saying a word.

Mikita, stunned, stared at her vacantly; then turned to Falk.

"You go, too! Leave me! I am terribly excited. I must be by myself. Go, go!" he cried at the top of his voice.

Falk shrugged his shoulders almost contemptuously, and left. Below he found Ysa waiting for him.

Left by himself Mikita locked the door, stopped in the middle of the room, and then suddenly knocked his head against the wall.

The pain sobered him.

No, he had really gone out of his mind.

He flung himself on the sofa. His head ached fearfully. It grew dark before his eyes, and his head began to turn.

What a disgrace! To outrage an unprotected girl, forcing her against her will. That's what he had done. She had given herself to him because she couldn't help it, she had had to submit, had to, because — because —"

He cried aloud:

"Abominable!"

He was on the rack of torture. Every muscle of his quivered. His soul boiled over with ever-mounting rage. He felt he was falling into pieces, that every joint was dropping apart. A panic seized him.

"Something bad is happening to me, something bad," he kept repeating.

He clutched at his breast with both hands.

"I have outraged an unprotected woman, a woman who felt disgust of me. Why did she yield? Because I asked her? Because — because — Oh, God! She gave herself to me out of kindness, Heaven knows why."

Suddenly a wild thought blazed up like a lightning-flash. "And now she will give herself to Falk because he will ask her for it, she will give herself because she'll be sorry for him, because she won't want to see him suffer, because — because —"

He broke into insane laughter, flung himself on the sofa, and at length burst into a fit of convulsive weeping.

He heard his own sobbing and again an unreasoning panic possessed him. He jumped up. He must go and find her, so that Falk should not take her away from him.

In a flash he put on his hat, opened the door, bounded down the stairs and ran through the streets to her very house; then up the steps, trembling, pale, foaming at the mouth.

"Miss Ysa?"

"Not at home, sir."

He stood in front of the house. Everything in him crumbled away.

He tried to walk, but his legs would not carry him. He could not make a step.

He remained standing a while; still he was unable to collect his thoughts. A sign on the opposite side of the street caught his eyes: —"Café and Restaurant."

Aha! A café. He would go there and sit down and rest. It would be quiet there — tranquil. He would sit down on a sofa, drink a cup of coffee — read the newspapers —

CHAPTER XI

YSA and Falk were sitting in the same restaurant as on the night before, this time in a room by themselves.

Ysa had never felt so at ease when alone with a man. She lay stretched out on the sofa, smoking a cigarette, indolently and mechanically blowing rings of smoke into the air.

Mikita, she had completely forgotten; and if he came to her mind, it was in the shape of a wicked, dirty gnome, a dwarfish monstrosity.

How ugly he could be! Those horrid insinuations in his stupid story of the sausages.

Falk kept his eyes fixed upon her.

He noticed with surprise that at times a hot red ring quivered on her face, and each time this happened she would rise nervously and empty her glass.

How he loved her! How he thirsted to put his arms about that graceful figure, stroke her soft bright hair, cover and hide her head on his bosom. Why had he not the courage to do it?

Why?

He felt, he knew she loved him. Then why?

Was it pity for Mikita? But did he, Falk, not suffer as much as Mikita? Perhaps even more?

The unpleasant scene at Mikita's that he had been obliged to witness recurred to him in every detail. Strange! he almost felt glad of it. What kind of a devil dwelt in him to take joy in so heart-rending a tragedy! He remembered how he had once forced a girl's sweetheart into intoxication and then felt devilish glee in the girl's despair at seeing him so scandalously drunk. From that time on, he was certain, she had begun to detest her lover. What a demon he harboured in himself!

A nervous, sickly smile trembled round his lips.

Ysa glanced at him. How handsome he was! She could sit for hours looking at him, at his large, sparkling eyes turned upon her with a feverish glow. And when he walked about the room, those supple, danger-threatening movements of a graceful panther!

Again she felt the red ring of shame flash on her face and black hatred stir in her heart.

Mikita was simply a rude boor.

She drank off her glass greedily.

They said not a word. Falk had already spoken much; now he longed to bury himself in her soul and enjoy the moment, to breathe it in with every nerve of his body.

She had listened and intoxicated herself with the even sound of his voice. Something in that voice paralysed her will, hypnotised her. She remembered when she had heard " Tristan and Isolde." She had felt then as she was feeling now — sitting in a box forgetful of where she was — ah, that sweet somnolent state! That somnolent, yet voluptuous music — She heard the wonderful strains of grief streaming into her soul —

She threw herself back on the sofa and closed her eyes.

It was so good to be here — with him — alone with him. Falk arose, made a few turns round the room, then sat down beside her. He took her hand, looked into her eyes. It was as though a magic phosphorescence poured all about them. He saw the light, a hot, quivering, alluring, inviting light, the same as when he had first met her.

The peace of a blissful sorrow descended upon their souls.

"Now I shall continue."

"But don't forget."

"What?"

"The terms."

"I've already forgotten them."

"You mustn't forget."

"No, no." He kissed her hand.

How she drew him, fairly pulled him to her with those eyes of hers. Could she be doing it consciously?

"Whence did you come here?"

"Is it not more important to know where I am going?" She smiled.

"Yes, yes. You put me to shame. You're right.— And your hands are so beautiful, I have never seen hands like yours."

She looked at him.

He suddenly lost control of himself, dropped on his knees, and began to kiss her soft, narrow, long hand passionately, pressing it to his lips.

She slowly withdrew it.

"Don't. It hurts."

She spoke in a low, broken, choking voice.

Falk sat down again. He wiped his forehead, took a drink, trembled with excitement, and was silent.

The silence lasted a long time.

Then he began to speak again, calmly, with a sad smile.

"Two or three days have passed since I met you. I don't understand it. As a matter of fact, there is nothing to understand. It is an incontestable, accomplished fact. Be kind and let me tell you everything. It will relieve me. I must speak about it. Perhaps you don't understand it, but this is the first time in my life that I have loved." He drank greedily, scarcely knowing that he drank.

"Yes, you don't understand. But it's terrible to fall in love at my age. It entirely upsets one's soul and tangles up one's brain. You have become my fate, my ruin."

His excitement waxed.

"I know, yes, I know I oughtn't to say it to you"—he warded off the thought of Mikita—"and I don't know why I am speaking. This terrible mystery! I am a different man from what I was three days ago. I don't understand what has happened to me—I am carrying you in myself, I have carried you in myself all my life as a great sorrow and martyrdom, and—I've told you so now for the hundredth time, but—" he broke off—"I am in such terrible anguish. I am so tormented, overwhelmed with a senseless fear—no, no, I am not insane, I am well aware of what I am saying and doing. I also know I shall be able to restrain myself. Yes, I'll go away, carrying you off in me. I shall remain with this eternal sorrow in me—let my soul break and perish—"

He dropped to his knees again. It grew dark before his eyes. He felt two hearts beating one against the other.

"Only love me—say, say that you love me."

He embraced her and felt her body yielding, coming nearer, nearer, bending over him.

"Mine, mine—"

She strained herself with difficulty out of his embrace, not knowing why she resisted. Suddenly she became conscious of a terrible hatred of Mikita, who had sullied her, trampled on her.

Falk glanced at her.

Her eyes opened wide and filled with tears. She turned away, clutching the sofa arm nervously.

He controlled himself.

"Yes, you are are right," he said in a tired voice. "Yes,

it wasn't nice of me. Forgive me. You are too worn out to love."

She looked at him with soft, melancholy reproach.

"And then," he said, growing excited again, "what unutterable bliss to sit near you like this without desire, no outburst of passion.— Yes, let's be friends — shall we?"

Falk strove to appear cheerful, but could not conceal his fatigue and distress. And why should he conceal it? Why? He turned spiteful and stubborn, and could scarcely refrain from picking up the table and hurling it down again, though he had never before desired to vent his feelings in violence.

Again he rose, walked about the table, and sat down next to Ysa on the other side.

"No, it would be absurd in me to play a comedy with you. I don't want to. But I must tell you how I feel, I must. You might have, Ysa — let me call you Ysa. I have nobody in the world. For me merely to call you Ysa constitutes unutterable joy. Thanks to the little word Ysa, I can look on you as mine. It would make me happy to shout Ysa with all my strength — Ysa! Ysa!"

A whirlwind of passion swept down on him. He no longer saw anything. He hid his head on her lap, and she caught it in her hands and kissed him, timidly, then ardently, again and again, with growing passion. He was all a-tremble, fiery streams of bliss flowed through his body.

Her passionate broken words, spoken in a low voice, poured into his soul as if from a distance, from beyond seas and mountains.

"I took him, I thought I could get to love him. He loved me so much — if you only knew how I am tortured. You I have loved from long ago, from ever since he began to tell me about you. I persuaded him to come here. The first time I saw you I shivered and lost my senses — but I can't,

I can't! I don't want to pass from hand to hand, from one to another. Let me go, let me go!"

Falk no longer heard anything. He put his arms around her, drank in her lips, caught her head, pressed it to his face passionately, madly.

At last she tore herself away and began to cry.

"Let me go. Don't torture me. I — I can't."

He rose, infinitely distressed. Then he took her hand, and they looked long into each other's eyes.

"And so we must part?"

"Yes."

"Forever?"

She was silent. Tears rolled down her cheeks.

"Forever?"

Falk trembled fearfully. He waited to hear his death sentence.

"Forever."

CHAPTER XII

FALK stood in the street so completely lost in thought that it was a long while before he became conscious of his whereabouts.

Yes, it was the first time in his life that he experienced such terrible, crushing grief. It utterly weakened him.

" Forever," he said to himself.

" Forever." But he could not comprehend what that unintelligible " forever " signified.

He stopped at a corner.

" Shall I go home? What am I to do at home? "

On the other side of the street he noticed an electric light in a café. He crossed over to it, not knowing why.

Glancing about the room for an empty table, he started back in fright. There in a corner sat Mikita, his appearance terrible.

Could it be blood?

Yes, blood.

Falk went up to him.

" For heaven's sake, what have you done to yourself? " There was blood on Mikita's temples, and congealed blood plastering his hair.

Mikita gave him a glassy stare. A large bottle of absinthe stood on the table in front of him.

" Oh, it's you. Good evening, good evening. Very glad, indeed."

" What have you done to yourself? "

It was so repulsive.

" Well, my dear Falk, how are the love operations proceeding? I am speaking of the chief thing in love. You look as if you had come here straight from the seat of bliss. It was dead easy, wasn't it? Ysa *is* a dancer, a godless dancer — Ha, ha, ha!"

Mikita laughed a revoltingly cynical laugh. Falk controlled his disgust.

"But what have you done to yourself?" he asked scrutinising Mikita's face.

"What have I done? Ha, ha, ha! I broke my head on the wall. What of it? A few drops of blood. That's all. But it makes everybody look at me, and that gives me an excellent opportunity to observe and jot down sketches." He pointed to the marble table-top covered with drawings. "No, no. It won't do me the least bit of harm. But tell me, Falk, how far have you advanced in your love?"

Falk gave him a look of contempt. But then he noticed his glassy, roving eyes. They frightened him.

"You're an idiot," he cried.

Mikita's artificial mood vanished. He sank into thought, his face took on a dull expression, his eyes came to a standstill, and he mechanically nodded his head.

"I know, I know."

Falk was struck. He sat down next to him.

"Listen, Mikita, you're an idiot. But what do you want of Ysa, of me? Tell me, point-blank."

Mikita flashed a spiteful look at him.

"Maybe you expect to fool me, too. Haven't you spent the whole night with her?"

Falk turned indignant.

"It's your own fault if I've been with her. First you turn people out of doors, then you expect them to go quietly home. You tortured her the whole evening, plagued her with base, stupid insinuations, and then you insist that she should go home and to bed as if nothing had happened."

Not bad at all, this moral outburst. Falk was ashamed of himself. What pitiful cowardice and mendacity!

"Where have you been with her? Where?"

"Where? As her lover is subject to paroxysms of insanity, I had to quiet her. In order to explain this to the woman you insulted, we had to go somewhere. It isn't pleasant to gather a crowd round you in the street."

Mikita glanced at him incredulously.

"Well, you fool, go there and ask the proprietor. Then you'll know where we've been. As for me, I beg to be excused. I have no desire to play the rôle of mediator in your pre-marital squabbles. I don't propose to dilate to Ysa any more upon the high merits, both moral and spiritual, of her future husband, and justify him."

"So that's what you did?"

"I haven't the least cause to conceal anything from you."

"It's vile, vile," Falk repeated to him. "But why? Is it vile in me to reassure him? Ha, ha! Let them be happy. I shall never see her again."

Darkness gathered before Mikita's eyes. He seized Falk's hand and pressed it with such force that Falk almost cried out with pain.

"You — Falk —" he stuttered. "I — thank you." His voice broke.

Falk would have preferred a slap in the face. Yet after all he was making Mikita happy. At the same time he felt a dull dislike of him. Mikita seemed so insignificant. How could one go about with such a bloody face? Repulsive!

"For goodness' sake, wipe that blood off your face."

That embarrassed Mikita. He gazed helplessly at Falk, abashed, then went away to wash his face.

Falk's conscience smote him.

Disgusting! He seemed to be acting the rôle of benefactor of that poor, deceived Mikita, a protector and guardian, restoring happiness to the duped dwarf. Bah, how contemptible!

But what nonsense! Why sacrifice his own happiness for
Mikita's? Perhaps because there was still lurking in him
a remnant of stupid conscience, of the atavistic conception of
self-restraint, of private property, of the right of priority.
He might have come to Ysa ahead of Mikita, and then Mikita might have done just what Falk had wished to do, but
now no longer wished to do.— Hm, yes, now all's over and
lost — now — now —

Mikita returned with the blood washed away.

"Now you look human again."

Falk felt the need of being kind and considerate toward
Mikita — as before, like a brother.

And he made the attempt.

But Mikita was hot and cold with shame. He could
scarcely look at Falk. He was disgusted with himself.

"Let's go, Eric."

They walked side by side in silence. Mikita was boiling
inwardly, and finally broke out.

"You don't understand, Eric. You can't possibly understand. What do you know about her? Tell me, tell me,
what do you know? Nothing at all. I have been living
close to her now three or four months, and I know nothing
of her. I am throwing myself over a precipice. No, I am
not falling over a precipice. I have been caught up in a
whirlpool and sucked down, and now I am at the bottom.

"Listen, listen, Eric." He clutched his hand convulsively. "You don't know what torture it is, how madden-
ingly, excruciatingly painful it is, this distrust — this — you
understand? Sometimes it catches me in the street and

gives me a hundred stabs. I lose consciousness. I — I —"

"If he knew how I am suffering," thought Falk. "He talks to *me* about it. Ha, ha, ha!"

The whole thing struck him as the height of folly. Really, how absurd in them — like two rams affected with *avertin* turning round about the same woman. He suppressed the growing sense of enmity toward this man walking by his side, who shared the same passion, the same suffering.

"You don't know your betrothed?"

Your betrothed. How it hurt! But he must never meet her again. For the first time he understood what this "never" meant. Never again. He turned cold and shivered.

"No, I don't know her. I don't know anything about her." Mikita's voice shook. "But in point of fact —"

Falk heard a suppressed sob, but felt no pity. His voice was harsh as he said: "Listen, Mikita, I feel you're jealous of me. But you haven't the slightest cause to be. Yes, yes, I know your reason is trying to fight it down. But what comes from unseen depths cannot be subdued by ratiocination. That's why your Ysa shall never see me again.— No, no, don't interrupt. Let me finish. It isn't self-sacrifice, not at all. I love your Ysa very much, but you are mistaken if you think it's more than just a deep feeling on my part as well as hers."

Falk blushed.

"No, no, I know your disposition. But it will be best if we don't see each other for a while. Good-bye."

Mikita could not bring out a word.

"Yes, yes, good-bye."

Mikita wanted to say something, but Falk had already jumped into a cab.

"Where to?" asked the cabby.

Falk mechanically named the street that Janina lived on.
He recovered himself.

What? Where? Where had he told him to drive to?
How could that idea have been born in his mind? Why, he
hadn't thought of Janina, not once the whole day. What
did he want to go to Janina for? But after all it made no
difference where he went, and no difference whether he knew
the reason or not.

The thing that preoccupied and distressed him above all
was an unintelligible mystery. Why should he have fallen
in love with that woman? Why? Why should he suffer so
terribly? For that woman?

Ha, ha, ha! All over the world there are proud, strong
men, men of iron, you may say, who despise women.

Falk shook with laughter.

They despise women, these strong, wise males. And
they don't suffer on account of women. They are so proud,
so invincible. Yes, even Iltis, the old and ridiculous, de-
spises women.

Falk, without knowing it, laughed nervously.

" I have never suffered on account of a woman," he heard
Iltis saying.

Because your organism is very tough, a peasant's organism, my dear Iltis. Your sensibilities have not yet reached
the stage of dependence upon the brain. You are like a
hydromedusa which suddenly parts with its feelers stocked
with sexual organs and sends them off to seek the female,
and then does not bother about them any more. You are a
very happy creature, my dear Iltis. But I don't envy you
your happiness. I never envy the ox his enjoyment of grass,
not even when I am starving.

It is my own fault that I am suffering, dear Iltis. I am
suffering because my mind is trying to sound its depths, to

create links to unite me with the universe, with the whole of nature. I am suffering because I cannot merge with nature, cannot fuse with what is my complement, woman; because — but really it makes no difference what I can or cannot do. It is all nothing but a delusion of my super-sapient brain. There is only one salient fact: I am suffering, and I have never suffered before.

Falk stretched himself out in the cab.

He must never see her again. Why? Because Mikita had the atavistic right of priority, and perhaps also because he was the older. And to seniority belongs priority.— Because Mikita might suffer.

Falk broke into a sardonic laugh.

Yes, he must sacrifice himself to save another from suffering. Hadn't Christ allowed himself to be crucified in order to open up the heavens to others? So he also, Eric Falk, was taking on his shoulders the sufferings of another. He, too, was a benefactor and redeemer.

Mikita was bending under the load of his good deeds, scarcely able to stand erect, so crushing was their weight. Repulsive! Falk spat out; a breach of good manners he had never been guilty of before.

Yes, he was going away so as not to make Mikita unhappy. For no other reason.

Of course I'm really going because she asked me to, but why not give some one the opportunity to regard me as his benefactor? Why not?

I might have told Mikita it's because I fear danger ahead that I'm going, but that wouldn't have sounded so well. And besides what does it matter?

Or I might have said, " Mikita, you are an ass, and sometimes you are egregiously unæsthetic. Of course, æsthetics itself is the silliest thing in the world; still one should have the refinement not to crack one's head against the wall."

O Almighty God! I am thankful to you for not having made me like that publican.

What coarse ideas men will sometimes have.

But what was I going to say? — You see, Mikita, a man should dissemble a bit. I have nothing against your suffering. Why shouldn't you suffer? I'm suffering also. But you ought to assume a different attitude. Let's say you have detected that your sweetheart is rejecting you for your friend. Then your conduct to that friend should become exceedingly affable, yet a little cold and distant withal. You should pretend absolute indifference. Occasionally your face should suggest suffering, but only rarely, only when circumstances call for it, when it is timely. As to when it is timely, that is purely a matter of instinct and tact.

In brief, one must be indifferent, cold and distant. Had you acted that way, I should have been ashamed from the bottom of my heart, felt I was a pitiful sinner, and cut a ridiculous figure in my own eyes. Quite likely these negative sensations would have cooled me off and sobered me.

As it is, I appear in the rôle of benefactor, and it is you who are ashamed, because it is ridiculous for one's jealousy to be exposed to the public gaze and one's face to be smeared with blood.

Yes, I am your benefactor to whom you mumble your thanks. I am your benefactor.

Why?

Because you stand on a lower plane than I, because you have a slave mind, because I — because I'm a scoundrel, a plain scoundrel.

And she loves me.

On that account I am a scoundrel?

Ha-ha! Mikita, your logic is poor. Can't you see Ysa

doesn't love you any more? Confound it, are you blind?

What did Mikita want of a woman who belonged to another heart and soul?

The cab rolled from asphalt to cobblestone paving. It wasn't pleasant. But the cobblestone wouldn't last long.

But why, why does she want to marry Mikita? Why?

As he asked himself this, a conjecture flashed into his mind that made him rebound like a rubber ball.

" Or is she his mistress? "

It went through him like a stab in the breast and doubled him over with the pain of it. A thousand needles pricked at his heart.

" Hurry up, driver, hurry, the deuce take it! "

But what business is it of mine? What has it to do with me, me! I shall never see her again. It's even better so, far better so. This petty grief will pass away, and I'll forget.

Where had that idiot brought him?

Aha!

Falk jumped out of the cab. He now had to wait for the janitor.

Why had he come to Janina? He had a clear vision of what would be before him. First, of course, crying because he was so exhausted and sombre; and then — No, he wouldn't go up. He saw Ysa, her graceful figure, felt her kisses, her slender hand. No, he wouldn't visit Janina. He'd go home, home, and light the lamp. He fumbled nervously in his pockets. Thank God, he had matches.— Then he'd lie down in bed — no, no, maybe he'd fall asleep on the sofa — yes, he'd take a little morphine — only he'd have a headache the next morning — and he'd never see her again.

At home he found a long letter from his mother, giving a detailed account of the sale of her estate, a step she had been compelled to take because after his father's death the manager had begun to steal and everything was going wrong. She was going to live in the city. The letter also contained a long account of a certain Mr. Kauer, who had been very helpful to her, and his daughter, whom she described as a veritable angel of goodness and beauty.

The name " Marit " sounded strange; he had heard it only once before, in Norway.

And finally, which was the main thing — Falk breathed a sigh of relief — his mother explained at length that he must come home without fail in order to be present at the settlement of their affairs; the executors of the estate wished him to be present.

Splendid. Everything was turning out first rate. Settled then — he'd go home to his mother.

He sat down and wrote her a reply saying he was coming at once, and went out and dropped the letter in the box.

CHAPTER XIII

FALK had half an hour to wait at the railroad station. His cranky watch was always too fast. The morphine had weakened him. He was feverish, his head was heavy, his heart beat violently, and now and then a stabbing pain in his breast made him bend over.

He looked around. Two railroad officials were sitting in the lunchroom playing cards with the waiter. Falk wanted beer, but could not make up his mind to disturb the waiter. He glanced at the large glass door and read several times, "Waiting Room." So there was nothing for him to do but wait. He looked into the lunchroom again. Strange that he hadn't noticed a fourth man there before. The man had a black moustache and a deeply lined face. Now and then he watched the game, then stopped in front of the mirror and looked at his reflection with an expression of contentment.

Yes, you are handsome. I wonder whether you have a mistress. No doubt you have. Men like you always appeal to women. If Mikita were — well, yes —

Too bad, but he must interrupt the waiter. He rang the bell.

"Excuse me, but I should very much like something to drink."

The waiter took this as a reprimand, and was profuse in excuses. Falk replied with studied affability.

He felt so comfortable in the waiting-room, but it was time to go now. He found an empty compartment. How lucky! Another person's presence would have driven him wild. He was incapable of thinking out a thought to the end.

He looked at his watch. Still five minutes. He pressed his forehead against the window-pane, and his attention was attracted by the light of the gas-lamp on the platform. The flame, shaped like a triangle with its base turned upward, quivered at the breath of the spring breeze. The base was forked and burst upward in two sharp tongues. Such must have been the fiery tongues that descended upon the heads of the apostles.

He roused himself from his absorption. How clearly he saw it. A pity he didn't have his note-book along. To jot down notes, he felt, would open his soul.

The train moved. What! He must go away from her! From her? No, impossible! A cold perspiration broke out on his forehead.

From her?

Something urged him to jump out of the train and run to her, fall at her feet, put his arms about her knees and tell her he could not live without her, she must belong to him, that — that — He gasped for breath. He clutched his head, and began to sob.

He heard the train rolling on irresistibly, irrevocably. Nothing, nothing could hold it back.

Ah, if another train were to come and collide with his, and the engines were to crash into each other, and the coaches pile up to the sky!

How foul the air was in that cage, just as in a coffee-house. He threw the window open violently. In an instant an unpleasant damp cold filled the compartment.

He quieted himself again and closed the window.

One thing was clear. He could not, he must not go away. His head would split. It is true. How had he put it to Ysa? His soul would break into small pieces, like the divinity about whom Grabbe wrote: "I am broken into pieces, but each piece is a god, a redeemer, a new Messiah, sacrificing himself in order to save others."

"I do not want to sacrifice myself. I want to be happy," he cried.

Then he recovered himself. What was passing in him? Why this folly? Could it be that Kant was right? Is love really but a disease, a fever for the elimination of disease germs, a process of recovery? How madly the train was rushing!

He stretched himself the length of the seat. The train jolted fearfully. Something seemed to drop under him. He was stumbling over the cross-ties of the roadbed, walking courageously, to show the village lads that he, a noble, the son of the proprietor, was braver than they. They were cowards. Now he was going to show them. And he walked on a lake that had frozen over only the day before. The ice cracked and gave under him. He walked as on a velvety turf, and suddenly —

Falk jumped up, then lay down again. Once more he felt as if he were falling, and reached out his hand mechanically to hold on to something.

No, he could not run away from her. She must be his. He'd make her, he'd make her be his. She loved him, but like all women she was afraid. She wanted him, he knew it well, but she was afraid.

Oh, God, God, if only the train would stop!

He paced the disgusting little cage. There was a violent thumping in his temples, and a great uneasiness obscured his thoughts. Every moment he became aware of troubling ideas and sensations that crawled out heaven knew whence.

"What does Mikita want of her? She belongs to me, me. Does he want to outrage her soul?"

Ah! — the train was slowing up! He rejoiced. At last,

at last! But it passed the station without stopping, then sped on again.

He wanted to cry out. But what good would it do? He must wait patiently. A dull despair settled down on him. He was not a child. He must wait. He must learn to control himself.

Seating himself at the window he tried to observe the landscape. But the night was so profoundly dark, so profoundly dark, profounder than the day can conceive.

The depth in his soul was abysmal. He closed his eyes.

He saw a meadow clearing in his father's forest. Two elks were fighting. They struck at each other with their large horns, separated, and made another terrific lunge. Their horns interlocked. In great leaps they tried to disentangle themselves, turning round and round. There was a crunching of horns. One elk succeeded in freeing himself and ran his horns into the other's breast. He drove them in deeper and deeper, tore ferociously at his flesh and entrails. The blood spurted.

" Terrible, terrible! " cried Falk.

And near the fighting animals a female elk was pasturing unmindful of the savage struggle of the passion-mad males.

Falk tried to turn his thoughts in another direction. But he saw flaming rings, which expanded slowly into gigantic red glowing circles, ever widening, until his eyes could scarcely grasp their hugeness. And in the centre of the rings stood the victor trembling and gory, yet proud and mighty. On his horns hung the entrails of his rival. Then Falk saw the victor elk spin round and round, faster and faster. A fiery vortex picked him up and carried him off. Falk saw him fall, as though a planet had dropped out of its course. Whither, whither?

A vortex, a vortex — Where had he heard that story of the vortex, beckoning and luring people on into it?

Again darkness gathered before his eyes. He saw Mikita, and throwing himself upon him, grabbed him, dragged him through the corridor. They dropped down in a great dive. The railing broke. Panting with rage they knotted into a ball and fell down, down, down on to the stones of the black abyss.

Falk glanced about, his mind a complete blank. Presently he heard some one entering the compartment and was happy to see it was the conductor. " How soon's the next stop? "

" Two minutes."

Falk completely recovered himself. He was all eagerness. He looked at his watch. He had been on the train only three hours. So he would be back in three hours — and then to Ysa — to Ysa.

The train stopped. Falk walked out.

" When's the next train back? "

" To-morrow, nine o'clock."

His knees trembled. He lost all sense of his surroundings. " Hotel Stern! " " Hotel de l'Europe! " " Hotel du Nord! " the cabbies were crying on all sides. He gave one of them his bag and allowed himself to be driven off.

Waking up the next day, at about noon, he looked round the room.

" Hm, not a bad room for a hotel."

His limbs ached, yet he had the sensation of recovering from an illness. To be sure, he was extremely nervous; but it was a nervousness that to him meant good health. Some day the doctors would understand it.

He sat up in bed and rang. When the boy came, he

asked him the name of the hotel, and called for coffee — Strange! So he had actually not gone insane.

He felt a sort of triumphant tranquillity.

" I'll remain here," he thought, " because I feel so well here."

He called for some note-paper and wrote a letter to his mother explaining why he could not come, how to deal with the executors, and saying he'd probably spend the summer abroad.

He read the letter over. Wasn't there something else he ought to tell her? His eyes fell on Marit's name. So he asked her to convey his cordial greetings to the angel of beauty and goodness, Marit. Having finished the letter, he drank his coffee, and went to bed again, but did not fall asleep at once. In his dreams he saw the angel of beauty and goodness, Marit.

CHAPTER XIV

THERE was animated talking and laughing at the Green Nightingale.

Iltis, with a serious expression on his face, as befitted the great man, was explaining to Mikita why woman is on a lower level of development than man.

He sat with his back turned deliberately on the young author beside him, there having been an unpleasant scene between the two the night before; in consequence of which the young author made bold to observe that Iltis's hatred of women was not purely theoretical.

Whenever a lady appeared in their society, Iltis began to talk his impossible stuff about women. "You see," he said to Mikita, "you are still young, and so is Falk. You don't understand. But wait until you have debauched ten years in marital life with a woman"—the last phrase he said in a whisper, in deference to Ysa's presence— "then you'll see. My good friend Falk cites examples of women from Yuma and the Chickasaw Indians and all that kind of learned nonsense. The fact remains, woman is an inferior being."

The Suckling tried to interrupt; Iltis cut him off with an emphatic gesture.

"No, no, a fact remains a fact," he said with appropriate haughtiness. "Besides, you must not attribute too much importance to proofs."

Mikita was not listening. He was harried with pain and shame, which sent the blood rushing furiously to his head.

Why drag on further? All was lost. Couldn't he see she was disgusted with the relation between them? Wasn't it positive hate? How he had implored her, how he had crawled on his knees asking forgiveness. But she — hm, hm — that icy cold smile. Hadn't her eyes plainly said, "Why beg? Why place me in this unpleasant position? What have you and I in common any more?"

He sighed heavily.

"You seem to be down in the mouth," said Iltis, with a wink.

"Excuse me, I can't agree with you." The Suckling paused and pondered, trying to find the best way to formulate his thoughts.

That made Iltis angry. "You mustn't be petty, you mustn't be petty of all things. Or else we'll let ourselves in for the foolish absurdities they call science. Perhaps you'd like me to tell you my experiences with scientists."

"Why isn't Falk coming?" thought Mikita. "It's no use. Ha, ha, ha! It's to give me an opportunity to win her back. Here's to you, my dear Eric. Too late, too late."

But why do I plague her so? What do I expect of her any more? Love? Love cannot be forced. Ridiculous, ridiculous. Anyway, how can one love a man who is just ridiculous?

He looked at Ysa, who, as always, was sitting a bit off from the rest. She did not return his look. She was in a highly excited state, red blotches burned on her cheeks, her eyes wandered uneasily.

The door opened, and the light-haired theosophist entered.

Ysa glanced at the door and, unable to control herself, started. Though she smiled to the light-haired young man her face betrayed vivid disappointment.

Yes, disappointment. He wasn't blind, the devil take it. It was so unmistakably a look of disappointment. And those nervous, tremulous, impatient movements. Whom is she waiting for? Whom? Stupid Mikita, don't you know? Don't you know why she can't stay alone with you for even half an hour? Don't you know why she has been dragging you here for three days?

Mikita laughed bitterly.

" She's waiting for Falk, ha, ha! — Falk! " He repeated the name, and the repetition gave him immense satisfaction. Falk was his friend, even more than a friend, a brother. Evidently he was making that sacrifice for him. Yes, undoubtedly so.

" Heigh, hello, ho! " he shouted. " Here's to your health, Iltis."

All glanced at him in surprise. They had never before heard Mikita bellow in that fashion.

" The devil take you with your philosophy — woman, man, male, female! — it's all nonsense, nonsense. Let's be merry and enjoy ourselves."

Ysa glanced at Mikita wearily.

Why was he so noisy? What was the matter with him again? Whom was he jealous of now?

How repulsive the man had become to her! How could she ever have loved him? She couldn't stand it any longer. She must put an end to it, this very day, on returning home with him, yes, this very day.

But how tell him? Her heart jumped and throbbed.

How say it to him? Calmly and plainly. Could he not help her in this unpleasant situation? He knew now that she loved Falk. Or hadn't he grasped it yet? But she had so clearly shown him her indifference. He was importunate. The thought terrified her, and she did not dare to dwell on it. Yet it was so clear to her now — he disgusted her. She was surprised not to find herself pained by the discovery.

An importunate fellow. Why, it positively gladdened her to be able to repeat the phrase without grieving.

The door opened again. This time it was surely Falk. She was all a-quiver.

A stranger entered. How terrible to have to wait and wait, sitting with those disagreeable men.

She felt Mikita's eyes turned upon her and avoided them.

" God, how litttle I care for him now ! "

What was happening to Falk these five terrible days? Should she go to him? But where did he live? Should she ask Mikita? No, she couldn't.

She fell to calculating.

How manage to see him? Why have been so foolish as to adjure him by all that was sacred never to call on her again? When she had known that she loved him with all her heart, that Mikita was a stranger to her, and the whole world, absolutely the whole world, brought her nothing but misery?

She was in despair. Why was Mikita talking so loud? Her gaze involuntarily settled on the empty bottles at his place.

" Do you know what love is? " Mikita lost his self-possession. " Do you know what the pangs of passion are? Do you? Have you ever loved a woman at all? "

Iltis waved his hand contemptuously.

" Yes — yes," Mikita stuttered. " Woman gave birth to man, and that's all you expect of her. Woman is a breeding animal, but man loves. Woman never loves, never. It's enough for her to breed."

" What! You don't mean to say women love, do you? "

" But women even commit suicide on account of love," the Suckling interjected. "You can read it in the papers almost every day."

" Suicide? There's your man for that. Ask him. It's

his specialty." Mikita pointed to Iltis. "A woman commits suicide when she's pregnant and has been abandoned by her lover."

Mikita thumped his fist on the table. Ysa looked at him with infinite disgust. Drunk again! How could she ever have loved such a man? No, she never had loved him. It had been a mere illusion.

A silence fell. Ysa's presence embarrassed everybody. Mikita was too free in her presence. Now he stopped talking. For the first time his eyes caught her contemptuous look. He saw it clearly and dropped his head.

It was perfectly clear. Her look fairly drilled itself into his being. He felt her eyes within himself. How they looked at him! How would it be to paint them? Throw some blotches on the canvas. How would they look three steps away? No, not a good view. How would it be from the corner of his studio? Wouldn't do either. From the other side? Now in the looking-glass? Yes, that would do. Otherwise it couldn't be explained — it was contempt, colossal, cold contempt — and disgust, repugnance.

Ysa could bear it no longer. She felt feverishly uneasy. Her heart was thumping louder and louder. At all costs she must see Falk.

He must come some time. He used to visit the café every day. Then why hadn't he come once in these five days?

The company grew animated again.

"Oh, leave me alone with your literature — eternal palaver about poets, royalties, publishers — makes me sick." Iltis yawned. "What do you want of Falk? He's a good fellow."

Ysa listened, and saw Mikita suddenly straightening himself.

"I admit Falk has talent," said the Suckling, "but it's

just unfolding. He's still got to mature. He hasn't arrived yet. The direction his development will take is still problematic. He's still searching and groping."

"What, Falk groping?" Mikita laughed noisily. "You're great, I must say. Don't you know Falk's the only man that can do anything? Falk has introduced something new into literature, he has made discoveries. Falk can do what you would like to do, but can't. Falk — Falk —"

At that moment Buchenzweig, guessing that the conversation was tiring Ysa, came up to her and tried to be entertaining. She glanced at his fat, smooth face, the face of a lackey or a barber. What did the man want of her?

"I had the honour of seeing you a few evenings ago with Mr. Falk. A remarkable young man, very unusual. Of all the people present that evening, he interested me the most. I came here to-night just to meet him."

"Listen, Ysa," Mikita called across the table. "Did you know Falk had left Berlin?" He stabbed her with his gaze.

Ysa shivered. As she looked at Mikita's livid face, her breast contracted with pain and her eyes opened wide. Then, mechanically, she turned to Buchenzweig. She put out her hand for her glass, but it was empty. Buchenzweig ran obligingly to call the waiter. She saw nothing through the mist curtaining her eyes. Suddenly somebody's voice reached her ears. It was Buchenzweig's. She glanced at him, smiling helplessly. The wine was brought, and she drank it off.

"I know Halbe very well. An unusually fine man, and a great force in our day when there are so few big men."

Ysa glanced at Buchenzweig. Suddenly, for no reason that she could tell, he disgusted her.

"Excuse me, Mr. Buchenzweig, I'm sorry to have to leave your company, but it's time for me to be going home."

She went to Mikita.

" I'm going home."

"Yes, really? You're bored?"

She put on her wraps without replying.

Before driving off in the cab, Mikita called to Iltis, who had courteously helped Ysa in: "Wait for me, I'm coming back right away. We'll have a jolly night together."

Ysa frowned.

Both kept silent. She was all broken up and could not think. Every moment she fell into a state of despair, which alternated with a drowsy exhaustion.

" Ysa, to-morrow is the opening day of my exhibition in Munich."

"Yes."

The cab halted.

" Now, off, quick, back to the Nightingale," he shouted to the driver. The driver whipped up his horse, and the cab rolled off rapidly over the asphalting, while Mikita writhed in terrible paroxysms of weeping.

By the time he reached the Nightingale he was calm. The men gave him a noisy welcome.

"Yes, Ysa's presence seems to put constraint on every-body," he thought.

"Listen," he said, seating himself beside Iltis. "If I get drunk to-night, put me on the train to-morrow morning at half-past seven. Now remember."

" All right, all right. I've taken that train a hundred times."

CHAPTER XV

FALK sat in his room at the hotel thinking hard.

Why had he come there? The same result could have been achieved by torturing himself in Berlin. It was six days now that he had been at that hotel, wasn't it?

He counted. Yes, the sixth day. He couldn't stand it any longer. Absolutely couldn't. It was an indisputable fact, he was obliged to admit it, he could no longer endure the agony. It would be his complete undoing. Every day something tore itself loose from him, which the day before had still been firmly attached. Every day his disgust with life grew.

To perish for a woman? He, an artist? He — ha, ha, ha!

At any rate, it was better to perish for a woman than from an insane stroke of apoplexy, or typhoid fever, or diphtheria.

Ah, you stupid Iltis, how small you are! It would at least be for myself, for that which constitutes the depth of my soul that I should be perishing — because *she* is I, I whom you have never yet seen, whom I myself have just found. You, if you prefer, may die of delirium tremens, or persecutional mania. I'd rather die for myself.

But why die? I want to be happy. I want to live.

He lost the train of his thoughts. Of late his mind had taken to wandering.

Hm, never before had his conduct escaped the control of his brain. Even in the first days after the meeting of Ysa, he had still been master of himself. At any rate, he had been deliberate in the means by which he had influenced her,

Good Lord, that ridiculous story of the swans! So stupid, tiresome, puerile!

Then he was caught up in an eddy. His brain began to whirl, faster and faster. He fell and was engulfed in a bottomless maelstrom of desire.

Those dances, those dances!

His eyes were caught by a spider's web in a corner of the room. For a long time he concentrated his look on it until his lids dropped of themselves. He was tired, fearfully tired. He felt an aching pain in all his bones. Two, three, no, four hours he ran about the streets hoping to neutralise his pain by exhaustion, and so be able to fall asleep without the nauseating dose of morphine. Now he must look at some shining object. And he gazed long at the brass door knob. Tears rolled down his cheeks, soft pangs of grief.

It was a marvellously beautiful day, a clear, sunny noon. He saw the majestic tower of the Church of the Saviour in Copenhagen. Mikita was standing next to him waving his handkerchief.

"Good-bye, good-bye!" He heard the voice without seeing any one. Presently he caught sight of a boy standing beside him crying. The poor fellow. He had to go to Stettin, it seemed, to look for work.

"I wonder how many miles an hour the steamer can make."

"Look." Mikita pointed to an English steamer. Two sailors were wrestling. They flew at each other like cocks, tangled up into a knot, rolled on the ground, untwisted, twined into a knot again, jumped up, fell back on the ground; then jumped up once more and went at each other with greater fury. All that was distinguishable in the mass was the flashing of their hands. Finally they rolled down the stairway leading to the saloon, disappeared and reappeared.

Again the ball of living flesh bounded madly on the deck.

Falk awoke, opened his eyes, and closed them again.

" Look, Eric, you see this fascinating night in the water, that gleam, that scintillation? Good God, if it could be painted ! "

" Ah, you dear boy."

They were sitting and drinking. The night was pitch dark. They pressed close together.

Suddenly it was as though a madness seized them. They began to fight. Falk picked Mikita up and was about to throw him overboard, but Mikita proved to be very skilful, broke from his grasp and caught his legs. Falk beat him desperately on the head, Mikita paid no attention, and carried him, yes, literally carried him, to the side of the vessel. In an instant he would be overboard. Suddenly he felt something hard under his feet. He flung his whole weight on Mikita, trampled him, threw him back, and caught him by the waist. One violent swing, and Mikita went darting through the darkness of the night into the sea.

Falk awoke.

He was standing in the middle of the room with clenched fists.

Presently he recovered. A savage hate came over him, an unreasoning thirst for fight.

Overboard, overboard !

He clenched his teeth, trembling from head to foot; then began to pace the room wildly. Who wanted to take his happiness away from him? For whose sake must he go to destruction?

Gradually he regained his composure. Now it was perfectly clear; he saw it.

One or the other of them must go down. He was at the parting of the ways. Either he was to be happy and

Mikita undone, or Mikita was to be happy and he undone. But to live without her — he could not. She did not love Mikita, so what did Mikita want of her? What, after all, was Mikita to him? They had gone to school together, had studied together, suffered hunger together — and what else — well, what else — what else?

He sat with drooping head.

The longing for Ysa was upon him, racking, sickening, stronger than ever.

Yes, at the parting of the ways — he or I.

The vortex was dragging them both down. One of them would be drawn into happiness, but only one.

And that one was he, Falk.

He tore off his clothes, and dressed himself again; looked for his money, turned his pockets inside out; he could not find it, and losing patience, ran about the room, perspiration breaking out on his forehead.

He must go to her, he must. The agony was greater than he could bear. He removed the bed coverings and the mattress and at last found his purse tucked away.

If only it was not too late, if only not too late. He looked at his watch and rang. The boy responded at once.

"When does the next train leave for Berlin?"

"In less than an hour."

"Let me have my bill, quick, quick. Hurry, for God's sake."

When Falk reached Berlin it was late at night.

In a flash he knew what to do. He must go to Mikita and tell him point-blank not to deceive himself into thinking Ysa loved him. If she hadn't told him so yet, it was simply because she wanted to gain time and break it to him gently. She pitied him.

Yes, he must speak quite frankly.

Oh, how wretchedly disagreeable!

But why? Wasn't Mikita a perfect stranger to him? And yet, as he neared his studio, the weight in his heart grew heavier.

No, he could not tell Mikita. He kept thinking of what Mikita had once been to him, when he loved him.

Before Mikita's door he stopped irresolutely.

Yes, he must, he must. But — God! Yes. It wouldn't do, he would have to leave Berlin again. He recalled the torments of the six days past.

" Frightful, frightful," he whispered.

Then he walked up the steps.

" Is Mr. Mikita at home? "

" No, he's gone to Munich."

Falk stood on the steps, incapable of grasping immediately the fulness of the good fortune.

"What luck!" he said to himself and repeated it. Yet, notwithstanding, he felt downcast.

And now to Ysa, to Ysa!

He tried to imagine how she would receive him, pictured a thousand little things he had observed in her, thought only of her, with desperate concentration, in order to stupify himself, to silence a something in him that wanted to speak, that resisted and ran away with his immense happiness.

Now he knew — he must not go to Ysa, he must wait till Mikita returned, must tell him everything, so as to be free of the charge of cowardice and of stealing his sweetheart behind his back. Yes, he must wait.

But that was impossible, physically impossible. Everything in him was strained to the utmost. One thousandth fraction of an inch more and the string would snap.

Then what had been the use of returning? As long as

his endurance had held out, he had remained away, had fought energetically, very energetically, but now —

He started forward decisively.

Enough of struggling. He was doing what he must do, although a hundred, a thousand feelings in him opposed it. Good Lord! He was not disputing that each one of those feelings constituted a certain fraction of necessity. But in the end the final, the powerful, irresistible necessity conquers always.

He reflected on the minutest details of this thought, but soon fell a prey again to terrible disquiet. Deep down in his being there was a dull alarm, a sort of troubled, shaming pang. But all combined into one feeling, an infinitely melancholy sense of inevitable ruin and despair.

He passed by a clock and was frightened. In half an hour the door would be locked and he'd be shut out from seeing her that day still.

He must finally make up his mind. He must, he must. Each nerve, each muscle was stretched taut. He walked faster.

"I mustn't think any more. I must go to her, happen what may."

Still he continued to think, still he strove and struggled with himself. But now he knew his course was inevitable. Finally he subdued his thoughts and walked up the steps quickly.

When about to ring he was paralysed by alarm, touching the button several times, but not daring to press it. He leaned against the wall to resist the sensation of a prodigious weight pulling him down. After a moment he descended a few steps, counted them, and was suddenly aroused by the scraping of a key in the lock. Then he recollected the neces-

sity, the final necessity that always conquers.   He mounted
the steps, and this time rang.

The maid opened the door.

" Is Miss Ysa in? "

" Miss Ysa is not receiving.   She gave orders not to let
anybody in."

" But please tell her I *must* speak to her."   He almost
shouted.

At that moment the door opened.   Ysa stood in the hallway.   Falk crossed over to her without saying a word, and
they walked into the room together.

They took each other's hands.   They trembled as in a
fever.   Then Ysa threw her arms about his neck and burst
out crying.

CHAPTER XVI

MIKITA went about Munich as in a dream. He did everything his friends advised him to do, went everywhere he was told to go, but felt that something bad, very bad, was happening to him.

Now he must go away. He would so gladly have remained in Munich, but there was nothing more for him to do there, and to do something was a necessity.

He slowly made his way to the station. Yes, he must return to Berlin. He ought really take leave of his friends, but they would insist on accompanying him to the station, and thrust their services on him, and stand on the platform joking until the train came. No, that wasn't pleasant, he had to remain alone.

Strange, how concentrated his thoughts now were. Before, they had vanished as they came, so that he really could not formulate his desires. But now everything arranged itself so clearly and orderly. His voice, too, had dropped lower. The one symptom left was that strange trembling which lasted whole hours at a time, and the loss of consciousness at moments. Oh, terrible!

He feared it would repeat itself.

He stopped before a shop window in which revolvers were displayed. He remembered newspaper descriptions of many peculiar events. Something unpleasant might happen to him too. It was not beyond the range of possibility. He might be set upon. Why shouldn't the same thing happen to him as happened to thousands of others? He laughed to himself.

There was a large variety of arms in the window. " People love to invent things," Mikita thought.

" To be or not to be," flashed through his mind.

" To be or not to be? " All he lacked were the proper mantle and skull. Confound it! I must study the correct pose in front of a looking-glass. Little Mikita — magnificent! He'd look just like the short singer Silva in the mantle of the giant Victory.

He entered the shop, and his eye was caught by a large calendar hanging on the wall.

" April first," he read the big lettering, " April fool. There'll be many surprises of all kinds to-day."

He asked to be shown a revolver. Extreme fatigue obliged him to sit down.

Was it so necessary to return to Berlin that very day? Could he not wait until he had recovered his nerves?

Suddenly his thoughts became animated.

Absence plays a significant rôle in love. Falk, too, had gone away, and she had longed for him. She needed to have somebody with her all the time. If he were to return to her now . . . why could not the same thing happen to him as happened to thousands of others? Hadn't he read in numerous novels of separation rekindling a love that has been extinguished?

Good God! Writers are no fools, are they? How beautifully and circumstantially they describe it!

He paid for the revolver and walked out.

One hope stirred another. He mended his pace, straightened himself. A new strength seemed to have been born in him. He was all tense with it. Why shouldn't he be able to stand the long trip? he thought.

His brain was on fire.

He remembered Ysa, remembered how happy they had

been, how she had loved him, how ecstatically. After all, he was a great painter, before whom she had to bow. But she had seen more than the big artist in him. Yes, yes, she had liked to press herself against him, and pet and stroke him. She — she — Oh, God! How he loved her! He was not himself any longer. Each thread of his organism was tied to hers, inextricably tied to hers.

But, of course, he had worn her out by perpetually plaguing her with his jealousy — his — his —

Yes, but she had been so kind, she had forgiven him everything.

To Berlin — she would rise from her chair, put her hand out to him, throw herself on his neck. "Thank God, you have come. I have been longing for you so. I was so homesick for you."

"Yes, that's what she'll do," he cried. He was profoundly convinced of it.

"But has she written me once in answer to my letters?" He clapped his hand to his head.

Ah, foolish Mikita, what do you know of women? What do you know of their cunning? Of course, how could he harry himself so? Why, it was clear — she had a perfect right to punish him severely. And he persuaded himself with growing conviction that he did not understand anything about these matters, it was only feminine cunning, feminine wisdom — no — how had Falk put it? Inborn wisdom of sexual selection. Falk could always find the appropriate expression for everything.

As he approached Berlin, his disquiet grew. The former pain began to smart again, and during the last two hours of the ride he was a helpless prey to dismal anguish. It was almost animal suffering. Impossible, unheard of, for a man to suffer so!

He paced the compartment, flung himself on the seat, jumped up again, then fell into a nervous tremor. It seemed to him he was losing his mind from the pain and excitement.

. . . .

Ysa met him with a cold embarrassed smile. She was putting her wardrobe in order.

He understood the clear, the fatal truth. He must go away at once. But he was so tired he had to sit down.

Ysa turned round.

"Ysa!" he suddenly cried in a hoarse voice, without looking at her; then broke off. On the table a pair of silk stockings were lying. Through his mind flashed a kind of hidden sex association. He picked the stockings up and tore them to pieces.

Ysa gave him a look of contempt. At last she would gather together enough will power.

"What do you want of me? I don't love you any more."

This was only by way of experiment. Would she be able to say it to him?

"I don't love you. You are a perfect stranger to me now." She was on the point of adding something about Falk, but could not.

Again she noticed that dog-like, slavish submissiveness. He disgusted her.

She said something else, but he did not hear.

He left.

Once he had read that at such times a man understands nothing. But he understood everything, clearly, definitely. As a matter of fact, she had not needed to tell him.

Why were the streets so empty? Oh, yes, it was Sunday. The people were out of town, Sunday evening of the first of April. He looked at his watch. Six o'clock.—" To

be or not to be?"—Oh, yes, when I stand in front of the
mirror in Hamlet's cloak, with the skull in my hands, then I
must remember the soliloquy.

He had not imagined that a man could think so clearly,
calmly, and soundly before his death.

"Garborg is right. Once a man realises that death is
inevitable, he becomes perfectly calm.

"Yes, yes, the writers — they are those who always —"

He walked very slowly, then came to a standstill.

That foolish youngster had been irritating him for a long
while. Mikita kept looking at him. He was evidently going to a girl and wanted to show off the nattiness of his feet
in his new narrow shoes. That was why he had to stop each
instant pretending to be looking in the shop windows.

There, he was stopping again! Mikita conceived a great
dislike of the foolish youth. He went up to him and said
sternly, "You must have awful corns, young man."

The stranger gave him an astonished look and turned red
with anger. Mikita was disconcerted.

"You're impudent," the boy cried.

Mikita fell back, a little alarmed at what he had done.

"Excuse me. You know — wheels," touching his forehead, and he moved away quickly.

God, how unkind people are! They are plaguing me to
death.

Tears ran down his cheeks. Well, Mikita, many mis-
fortunes have descended upon you. But you mustn't grum-
ble. Calm yourself, the devil take it.

He went off into a rage again.

"Oh, you fool, you sentimental actor, what are you whim-
pering about? As if you were standing before the embodi-
ment of the fair sex and she were pitying you. Ha, ha!
Fair sex!"

He entered his studio and locked the door. He glanced at the canvas on the easel. Hideous daub! How could he have failed to see how hideous it was? He must fix it at once. He took up a brush, but his hand shook. He fell into a rage, snatched up the picture and tore it to shreds.

Then he threw himself on the sofa, but immediately jumped up as if driven by a thousand devils within.

"Ysa," he cried. "Ysa!" and began to laugh so that he gasped for breath.

He rolled on the floor, beat his head on it, snatched up a chair, and shivered it to bits. A mad spirit of destructiveness took possession of him.

When he came to himself, it was already night.

He felt utterly fatigued. The frenzy of madness was in his brain.

One more thing only, the last. God, what was it? What was it he had to do now?

He felt some heavy object in his pocket. Oh, yes. He walked about the room looking for something, and kept repeating, "Yes, yes."

Yes, that was the very thing. The revolver in his pocket seemed to grow heavier. He must sit down, mustn't he? Yes, that was the best way. He must sit down, sit down.

What a terrible stillness! It oppressed him fearfully.

He took out the revolver, but a long time slipped by before he loaded it. His hands refused to obey him. He got angry at himself. Of course, he must sit down first. That was the most important thing.

He sat down.

In the heart? Of course. Great idea. They always shoot one inch higher, and then they are taken to the hospital. Ha, ha!

Suddenly, unaware of it himself, he became immersed in deep thought, oblivious of his surroundings.

Then he heard singing outside the door. That stirred him up. He pressed the revolver firmly.

Quick, quick!

His excitement grew. One minute more and he would not be able to do it.

He thrust the barrel deep into his mouth and pulled the trigger.

CHAPTER XVII

THAT same night Falk and Ysa were sitting in a railroad coach on their way to Paris.

" Do you love me? " she asked, looking at him blissfully.

Falk did not answer. He pressed her hand, and looked into her eyes with infinite tenderness.

" You are mine, mine," she said. And they sat a long while pressed close together.

She felt terribly tired. Falk laid out some rugs for her to lie on, wrapped her up warmly, and continued to look at her with the same hot, sincere tenderness.

" Mine, mine," he said.

" Kiss me." And she closed her eyes.

He kissed her gently as if afraid to touch her.

" And now sleep, sleep."

" Yes."

He sat down on the seat opposite. Now she was his, none but his. Now he was happy. Of Mikita he had scarcely a thought. It was astonishing how little he pitied him. Only once. Yes, a man who doesn't carry the force to live within himself must die. If he hasn't the elements within himself necessary for life, it is nobody's fault, it cannot be helped.

Could *he* also have gone into annihilation? No, his suffering was of an entirely different nature. His own paroxysms were attacks of fever, the labour that gives birth to a strong will. Yes, he suddenly comprehended. But what was the name for it? The new will, the will born out of the instincts, the will — hm! How express it? The will of the instincts unrestrained by the limitations of knowledge or atavistic sentiments, the will in which the instincts and the mind combine in a united whole.

He still had to suffer because he was a man of the Transition. He was still shaken by fever because he had to conquer his brain. But he would cease to suffer as soon as he eliminated all those stupid ethical survivals, all those remnants of atavism.

He laughed in his soul. Good God, that idiotic ratiocinating and subtilising. All that senseless stuff about a new will and the like. The truth of the matter was, he was generously making himself out a superman, because, yes, because his desire knew no bounds, because Ysa had given herself to him out of love, and because he himself was a criminal. The truth of the matter was, he wanted to lull himself to sleep, to lie to himself.

"A crime!" something in his soul cried.

He glanced at Ysa. She belonged to him, because she had to belong to him, and — and they were hurrying toward happiness.

He looked through the window. Trees, fields, and houses shot by.

"All this will be yours as soon as the new will ascends the throne in you, the new will, the will of the instincts hallowed by the brain."

He thought of Napoleon. No, that wasn't it. That was the will of an apoplectic fanatic. Strange, he was all the time looking for examples of the same lack of restraint, the same egoism and criminality. Evidently a result of the illness he had been through. Now at last he had achieved happiness.

And he grew in the consciousness of his great happiness, which conquered by dint of his will. Everything else remained behind like a memory, a theme for a great stirring drama.

He looked a long time at Ysa as she slept. She was a

woman he did not know. But he did not have to know her. Why should he? He possessed her, having taken her away from another. He was the elk — no, that was too beastly, too beastly — The recollection of the entrails hanging on the horns was not pleasant.

He fought with all his might against the mass of disagreeable thoughts that crowded into his mind. It was as though a hornets' nest had been stirred up.

Then he calmed himself. Everything had to happen as it had. Only it was strange that the antiquated conceptions of freedom of the will, crime, blame, kept recurring to his memory. And perhaps —

But now, now, whither was fate carrying him? To happiness? To unending happiness? Full of new unseen joys?

Oh, how proud he felt, how happy, strong and how— unhappy!

And the train went dashing on. The houses, trees, and cities flashed past the window; and high in the sky shone a lone star misted over with violet.

PART TWO

BY THE WAY

CHAPTER I

M ARIT KAUER was sitting on the verandah happy,
excited, painfully expectant.

At last, at last! After having completely lost hope she
was to see him again. No less than ten times had he written to his mother that he was coming soon — the next day,
the day after. Then some pressing piece of work would
delay the trip home until the next month; and a month
would pass, then another, and another. But now at last
he had come, he was really here.

Her youngest brother had brought the great news. Coming home from school he had first made much of a hundred
trifling incidents of the class-room, then, by the way, dropped
the startling information that Eric Falk had waited for him
at the school door, asked to be remembered to the family,
and said he would call that very afternoon.

For an instant Marit had been stunned, it was so unbe-
lievable.

How those procrastinations had bruised her! She had
gone about like a lost soul, even sacrificed her modesty and
written a warm begging letter asking him to come for at
least a day. To be sure it was at his mother's request, as
the elderly lady was near-sighted and writing was agony to
her. But he must have had sufficient imagination to realise
how much of yearning, what a world of desire were stowed
away in each word.

Perhaps he did not want to realise. Heavens! Could
what the people were saying about him be true? No —
base falsehoods, vile slanders! They said Falk was married,

even had a son — a secret civil marriage relation — and with a Frenchwoman!

No, he was noble, frank, sincere; surely he would have written to her about it. He had told her so often that he loved her. Could he — could he possibly have deceived her? Had he not time and again declared that she, and no one else, could make him happy? No, slander, lies! He was so noble, so refined.

Her heart throbbed, her breath came and went heavily. Tears filled her eyes. A rare sense of sweetness rose in her breast. Another quarter of an hour, and she would see him; she would look into his mysterious eyes, listen to his wonderful voice. How she loved him, how unendingly!

God had heard her. She had sung three *Te Deums* that He should speed his return. Like a wounded animal she had crawled to the feet of the Saviour and prayed and wept and confessed. Could the Heavenly Father refuse her prayer? What had she done to incur His great wrath? And she fasted Fridays and Saturdays to atone for sins of which she was not even conscious. Yet the most upright of men sin no less than seven times a day, and perhaps her love for Falk was a sin.

But no, Falk had come. Therefore God must have heard her.

She rose. It was close on the verandah, the air hung oppressive in the garden. She walked out on the road leading to the town nearby, whence he would come.

A shiver went through her, her blood rushed to her heart, she shook like an aspen leaf. There he was! She saw him.

That was he, surely he. She leaned against the hedge. Then something pushed her forward. What joy it would be to throw herself on his breast.

No, no, no. Just show him how glad she was — not conceal her pleasure. He should see how glad she was.

But that wouldn't do either, it wouldn't do to reveal her joy; no, she must not, she could not. She must run away. It would not be proper to meet him there on the road. Her temples were on fire, she felt the hot glow in her eyes. She would not be able to bring forth a single word.

Back in her room, she threw herself on the bed, buried her head in the pillow, and sobbed aloud.

Old man Kauer greeted Falk with effusion.

"You still among the living? A pleasant surprise indeed. So you've at last remembered your native country. I'm glad. We've been expecting you a long while."

Falk's manner was unusually cordial. He had always remembered the place of his birth, but had been overwhelmed with work, occupied down to the very moment of his departure, his last task being the proof-reading of his new novel; a beastly job, the worst he knew of. But he was ever so happy to be back and with his mother. It was so good to feel the love all round him. One's home country was a precious thing.

"I had to come; it was a necessity. I was fearfully run down and nervous, almost an imbecile. But here, with mother, I shall quickly recover. Mother is as great an invention as printing."

"I'm very glad, very glad to see you here again," Kauer repeated. "I want to have some talks with you. Here in this damned God-forsaken place one's cut off from everything, totally ignorant and out of touch with what's going on in the world. I shall depend upon you to put me *au courant* with affairs. You must tell me everything in detail."

A bottle of wine was placed on the table.

"You know good wine, I suppose, Mr. Falk. You can't get wine like this in Paris, I don't care what they say. It's a pleasure — an unaccustomed pleasure, I'm sorry to say — to drink it with an intelligent man like you."

They were soon engrossed in a discussion of asparagus culture.

"You must try the new method, Mr. Kauer. Each asparagus root is given a little more than three feet of ground and dug all round —"

The door opened for Marit. She was pale, her face looked as though it had just been washed.

Falk jumped up and caught her hands. He had not expected to see her so soon. Ah, what a world of time had passed since they had last met!

"We had given up all hope of ever seeing you again," she said turning aside, looking for something in the window embrasure.

Falk went back to asparagus, though he was unable to hide his agitation.

Kauer listened attentively, interrupting occasionally to reiterate how glad he was that Falk had come home. Then the old man told of his own affairs. Misfortune, he said, had descended upon him of late like a hailstorm. There was last year's bad crop, then his wife had taken ill and was obliged to remain at a watering place where she had now been for six months. Marit had to keep house, and father and daughter paid for their sins by sharing the burden. So would Falk please forgive him if he left for a few moments as it was just sowing time?

Falk was alone with Marit. She stared out of the window. Falk paced to and fro, then stepped up to her. She was all in a tremble, the colour of her face ran alternately red and deadly white.

"Well, what have you done with yourself all this time?" asked Falk, with a kindly smile.

"Oh, nothing." She raised her eyes to him curiously. "It's really surprising that you've come at last. What made you?"

"When a man's done up as I am, his nerves practically all gone, he feels the need of taking a rest at his mother's. Say what you will, I shall always remain a child running back to its mother whenever it's in trouble."

There was silence. Falk walked the room ruminating.

"I love my mother dearly, but I couldn't come before. Unusual circumstances prevented me."

"Yes, I've heard something of those unusual circumstances," Marit returned ironically.

Falk glanced at her in astonishment, though his answer showed he had not been caught unawares.

"What can I do if people talk? I can't prevent them from spreading mad rumours about me. Besides, it makes no difference to me what they say. I don't give a hang."

Another pause of silence. Falk poured out a second glass of wine and drank it off at one gulp.

Marit scrutinised him sternly. His face was pale, his eyes sunken and glowing with a strange feverish light.

"He must have suffered a lot," she thought, and her heart softened.

"Excuse me. I didn't mean to mention it. I haven't the right to. It doesn't interest me in the least."

"H'm, yes," said Falk, troubled. "It's strange, I've been travelling two days and nights in succession without closing an eye, yet when I arrived I couldn't think of taking a rest. I had to go right off to see you."

The first day of flowery spring had drawn to a close. Falk and Marit stood at the window looking at the stream

and the hills beyond covered with woods. A mist rose from
the lake faintly veiling the hills and drifting in among the
trees. The lake seemed to be leaving its banks and over-
flowing the world. Gradually the hills and woods disappeared behind a vast glistening sheet of mist that closed in
the horizon.

Kauer had in the meanwhile returned, but only to an-
nounce that he would have to absent himself for another
short interval. Falk made to go, but Marit would not hear
of it — he must stay and have dinner with them.

They were left alone again. Falk drank incessantly, only
now and then, as if reluctantly, throwing out some insignificant remark.

" Don't be angry with me for drinking so much. I'm
in such a state that I'm obliged to drink. My vitality is
low, but I haven't got delirium tremens yet; still far from it.
In fact, I should like to get it.

" I want to tell you something — don't think I've turned
sentimental. Oh, no. I simply want to state a fact — a
worm is gnawing at my heart. I'm not happy.— But that's
all nonsense. Don't let it affect you too much."

" Falk," said Marit, going up to him, " don't play with
me. Be frank. When you were here a year ago — you
remember, the first time I met you? — you told me you
loved me. You even wrote me so. I have kept all your
letters. They are my dearest possession. You know what
my feelings toward you are. I love you with all my heart.
Do please tell me everything. I should like to stifle this
feeling in me, but it's useless to try. I can't. You told me
you can't promise anything, that our love has no future.
I did not want, nor ask for, oaths or assurances. I wanted
nothing of you. I loved you, and still love you, because I
cannot help it."

Marit grew confused. There was so much to tell him, but her thoughts rambled away out of her control.

"That isn't what I wanted to say. I just want you to be frank with me; tell me everything, the whole truth. I've suffered so, I've been through such agony."

Falk looked at her in surprise.

"But what do you want me to tell you?"

"You know what's on my mind. There's so much being gossiped about you, it can't be unfounded. Is it true, is it true about the Frenchwoman and the child? No, it's impossible!"

"What?"

"The child."

"The child?" Falk took long strides up and down the room.

A painful silence fell. The voices of workmen in the distance were audible. Suddenly Falk stood before her.

"Well, I'll tell you the whole terrible truth. I'm going to be quite candid, as candid as I can, though you turn me out of doors for it. I have a child. I had a son before I met you. A child is a wonderful thing. It's like a ramrod driven down your spine. It gives you backbone and strength. I was crawling in the mire, I was worse than the worst.— Hear me out calmly. I was a male like all other males, with a right to beget children."

He became excited.

"If you can't rid yourself of your silly prudery, then why did you ask me to be open with you?"

Marit's eyes filled with tears.

"I beg your pardon, but I'm really nervous." The tears rolled down her cheeks.

"My dear precious Marit, be good, listen to me like a

sister, please,— like a sister. Listen, even though you don't understand half of what I say."

"You can't possibly mean to play hide-and-seek with me, can you? I won't permit it. I love and respect you too much for that."

"Very well. You know now I have a son. I love him more than anything else in the world. But his mother — h'm, his mother I cannot bear. I've been unhappy. When she came across my path, she was so good to me, we lived together for a time; and — well, it happened. . . ."

"Good God! Is it possible?"

"H'm, everything is possible in this world."

Falk spoke in a weary voice, pacing to and fro; then stopped and took her hand.

"Marit, now I'm going to speak to you frankly, tell you everything. You mustn't love me, Marit. It's true, I begged you to love me, but I thought then I could make you happy, a little bit. I believed it. I wanted you to become my wife. You'd have loved my son. But that woman has clung to me like a burr. I've tried a thousand times to separate from her. I couldn't. It seems to me I never shall, I'll never have the strength to."

Falk was fearfully excited.

"No, no," he went on as Marit was about to interrupt, "let me tell you all. I thought I could make you happy. That was the only reason I dared to ask for your love. You mustn't think I'm a rascal. But now I no longer ask you to love me. I know it can't be. I'm not able to give you the tiniest crumb of happiness. I beg only one thing of you — be my sister, my friend, my only —"

Marit remained sitting as if petrified.

Falk dropped on his knees at her feet and took her hand.

"Be kind, be good to me. You can't be my love, so

be my friend. No, you can't be my friend either, no.— I'm going now, at once! Answer me. Shall I go? Shall I? All right, good-bye, I'm going, I'm going."

Marit jumped up in a panic of despair.

"Stay, stay! Do what you please, but I must see you. I'm ill when I don't see you. O God, God! How horrible it all is!"

Falk flung himself at her.

"No, for God's sake, don't!" She pushed him away and ran out of the room.

Falk sat at the table, emptied the whole bottle, and gazed into space. The darkness was soothing. Suddenly he recoiled. Strange that a light could frighten one so. Marit was entering with the lamp.

"The truth is, my nerves are shattered," Falk said to himself.

Marit, looking worn out, smiled as she put the lamp on the table.

"Father'll be here in a moment. You must stay and have dinner with us."

"Yes, I'll stay, I'll stay. I'm a gentleman. If I were to make off, your father might suspect me."

CHAPTER II

THE next day he came again.

He was uncommonly agreeable, with an outward air of cheerfulness, though it cost him a supreme effort to conceal his nervousness.

"Nothing has passed between us, Marit, has it? You have forgotten everything,— yes? I don't remember a word."

Marit held her eyes fixed on the ground.

"It's a dangerous symptom. Sometimes I lose consciousness completely — no, only my memory, and not when I'm drunk either. I know I drank a lot yesterday, but I didn't give the impression of being drunk? Or perhaps I did? Then it was only because I made myself look drunk so as to be able to tell you all I wanted to tell you with impunity. I often do it." Falk spoke loud and laughed excessively.

Marit looked at him amazed.

"Something very pleasant seems to have happened to you?"

"Just had pleasant news from Paris. My books have been translated into French and were well received. It's gratifying. It makes me feel good. I don't care much for the French, but after all Paris is the centre of present-day culture. And then — yes, I'll tell you — a most peculiar story."

Marit stared in amazement at him. He was behaving so queerly to-day.

"You know your father sent me home in a carriage yesterday evening. Of course you remember. Well, we were driving along briskly when all of a sudden the horses stopped short and refused to budge. They reared and plunged and neighed like animals in a story under a spell. The coachman whipped them, which only made matters worse. Finally we both got out and tugged at the bridles. Still the horses refused to budge from the spot, in fact, became still more unmanageable. At last the coachman came to the conclusion that their minds had been definitely made up and there was no use trying to urge them.

"What do you suppose it was? The night was so dark you could have slapped a man and he wouldn't have known who did it. I screwed up my courage and felt about with my hands and feet. Suddenly — my heart stood still — I stumbled over a coffin and fell across a body."

Marit jumped.

"Horrible! Impossible!"

"It's the truth. I screamed, but the next instant felt ashamed of my cowardice. I hardly had time to recover from my first fright when another struck me. The body began to whine. I can't recall ever having heard anything so blood-curdling.— Why, you're pale, Marit. Don't be frightened. It was funny. It wasn't a dead man, it was a peasant dead drunk. His wife had died and he had gone to town to buy a coffin. On his way back, sodden and sleepy, he had removed the coffin from the wagon, let the horses go their own way, and disposed himself comfortably in the coffin for a good night's sleep."

Marit laughed heartily.

"I'm glad to have made you laugh so. You ought to laugh, laugh the whole day long. Let's laugh like little children. I'll always be like to-day, a merry boy on the street. Maybe you think I'm not a good boy. I'm jolly though. Very well, then. I'll be this way the rest of the day."

Falk laughed, then abruptly turned serious. Ah, what a sweet child she was!

"Marit, my joy, I should like to be lying at your feet on a Persian rug.

"Well, well, you mustn't wrinkle your forehead. I'll never speak like that again." Falk's eyes moistened. Marit looked at him with ineffable love.

"Why have you turned so sad all of a sudden? I can't stand it, I get ill when I see you so sad."

"What makes you say I'm sad? I'm very, very happy."

A silence fell.

"Would you like to take a walk? Let's go on a stroll round the lake."

"I'd love to."

It was a wondrously beautiful day, the verdure still youthfully tender, the trees in their garb of fresh young leaves, and the hills on the opposite shore spreading out to full view luxurious green carpets of young grass.

They walked in silence, their feet sinking into the moist sand. Now and then Falk would pick up a flat stone and send it skipping over the surface of the lake. His face was serious, like the face of a man whose heart is weighted with a great grief. He walked straight on, only stopping from time to time to skip the stones.

Marit glanced at him sadly.

"Why do you torture me? Why don't you say something? I can't stand this silence."

"Yes, yes." Falk seemed to be rousing himself from a long sleep. "Wait a moment, wait a moment. I'll tell you wonderful things."

He laughed merrily.

"Shall I tell you something about Paris? I've met celebrities there. You know what celebrities are? Well, if you do I needn't explain. A singular species, these celebrities. I've met many of their kind, though at this moment I have a particular one in mind. He was inimitable. He hated women because he loved them so. Excuse the expression I'm going to use, but it describes him exactly — he was an excited stallion.

"No, no, don't take offence, please don't. You shan't hear words like that from me again. I won't tell you about it. I know you're a devout Catholic and are not likely to have come across such expressions in the writings of the Holy Fathers. Well, then, the celebrity — don't be scared, I won't say anything bad — said to himself, 'Why should I view the moon through a telescope when I can obtain the same result by observing it through a microscope?' He was a bundle of paradoxes, this great man, as you see. He wanted to do everything differently from other people.—

"But Heavens alive! How beautiful you are! I love you, oh, so much. You remember I loved you last spring already?—

"So the celebrity turned the tube of the microscope so that the objective was on top, put in a few drops of mercury, which seems to magnify some, and began to view the moon. Of course, seen that way the moon was a strange, misty-looking object. But that was a mere trifle. That blotch over there was Europe — what else could it be? The rectangle was Australia, just as certainly —

"Your laugh is charming! It gives your eyes a fascinating depth.—

"Well, this is the conclusion our celebrity deduced from the remarkable phenomenon: the moon has neither mountains, nor craters, nor volcanoes. The moon is simply a glass disk reflecting our earth."

Marit laughed like a child.

" How you ridicule the great men. Don't you feel the least respect for them? "

" Not the least. I've seen them in full dress and in negligée. Whatever their costume they are just as ridiculous. They take themselves so seriously, assume airs in public that remind one of Gothic architecture, set themselves up on pedestals. Oh, it's so funny."

Falk became reminiscent.

" Only once I saw a genuinely great man, for whom I felt profound respect."

" Tell me about him, do please. He must be interesting indeed to impress you, to impress Mr. Falk."

" It really is remarkable. But then he was a genuinely great man. I met him in Christiania. Once I spent a whole summer in Norway, you know. He was short and spare and homely. A quiet man with large wonderful eyes. They did not have that official sapience, or that official fire, which glow in the eyes of the ordinary great man. There was something in them that reminded me of the broken wings of a great, kingly eagle. He played the violin exquisitely. Once, after drinking a lot, we went to an acquaintance's house. He played there almost in the dark. He was a shy, modest, sensitive, profound soul. I had never in my life heard such music. It bared one's very being. It was as though a dove's heart just torn out of its breast were palpitating there. The anguish in those notes cut open one's breast and clutched at one's throat. Marit, Marit, it was you I saw before me. You were the dove's heart, you were the sound that cried for happiness and died away in agony.— Oh, do let me speak, let me say it at least once."

" No, no, I forbid you absolutely. It will lead to the same scene as yesterday. You are so nervous. Be sensible."

Falk said nothing. Marit swallowed her tears. For many minutes they walked in silence.

"You asked me yesterday to be your friend. As a friend I have certain rights."

"Of course."

"Are you really married?"

"No, but I have a child whom I love dearly. I mean to go back, take him to southern Italy, and live with him and for him. My mind's made up. Nothing will change it. I love that child, I can't imagine loving anything or anybody so much."

That wrought upon Marit, but she kept silent.

"The child's really a wonder." Falk entered into a description, speaking with unusual tenderness, yet all the while watching the effect of his words upon her. Her face plainly indicated that she was suffering.

"Of course you can't know what it means. I was very ill in Paris — nicotine poisoning. I'd have been in Abraham's bosom by now if it hadn't been for the nursing I got."

"Who nursed you?"

"A girl, a wonderfully bright girl, who plays the piano beautifully."

"The mother of the child?"

"Oh, no, I don't see the mother any more."

Marit looked at him in astonishment.

"But only last evening you told me you can't get rid of her, that she clings to you like a burr."

"Is that so? Did I say that?" Falk asked, colouring.

"Yes, that's what you said. You also said it was the only thing that stood between us and our happiness."

Falk reflected.

"I must have been drunk. I couldn't have said it if I hadn't been."

He affected astonishment and Marit had to repeat word for word his utterances of the night before.

"I surely must have been drunk. Never pay any attention to what I say when I'm in that state. I fib scandalously."

Marit scanned his face dubiously.

"Believe me, I say the most impossible things then. No, no — the mother of my child has gone from my world completely. I think she's an artist's model living with some artist."

Somehow this gave Marit satisfaction.

"Yes, I left her quickly enough. The girl who nursed me during my sickness is quite different. Her family name is — Perier. She watched over me two whole weeks, day and night. She put up with my most exasperating whims — was an angel of patience, and played the piano so beautifully. Day and night she was at my side."

"Do you mean to say she lived with you?"

Falk pretended great amazement.

"What's so strange in that? In *Europe* —" he stressed the word —" in Europe the greatest freedom prevails in the relations between men and women. There are none of those stupid prejudices, none of those antediluvian conventions which cling to people here. Here, even though a girl is formally and publicly engaged, her mother and aunts feel obliged to trail her at every step. No, in Europe there are no precepts or rules in love. Each human being is a law unto himself.

"God, how stifling it is here — suffocating! There's a law for everything, nothing but rules, restrictions, barriers. People are bound hand and foot. This you may do; this you may not do. Or, in your jargon, this is proper and this is not proper; or, better still, 'not correct.' Ha, ha — not correct!

"Why did you break away so brusquely last night? Or isn't it *correct* to kiss a sister or friend?"

"No, I couldn't do such a thing. I'd despise myself. I couldn't look you straight in the face again. And you, would you have the least respect for me?"

Falk burst out laughing.

"Respect? Respect? What's that? Does such a funny word really exist? It's not in my vocabulary, nor have I a conception of the idea it's meant to convey. I know free women, to whom their will and theirs alone is the only law; and I know slave women without a will of their own, who do nothing but what the world tells them to do. I know strong women who despise the crowd and have beauty enough in their souls to go where their instinct leads; and I know women, like sheep, who can be bought and sold as need be on the marital market."

"So you esteem highly the woman who bore you your child and then left you and went to another man?"

"Esteem is not the word. It implies moral standards, which I do not recognise. She went where love bid her go, and she acted beautifully."

"No, it's ugly."

"As you please."

Marit grew excited.

"And that Miss — what's her name?"

"Miss Perier."

"According to that you must look upon her too as the ideal woman."

"Of course. She's the most intelligent woman I've ever met."

Marit quivered.

" Then why don't you love her? "

" It's the fault of sex, or, rather, of that in us with which we love, which does not depend upon the brain. I might consider a woman the most excellent person in the world, yet not fall in love with her."

" So that's the kind of woman you bow to? " Marit almost cried. " Yet I know, I'm positive, Miss Perier is a bad woman."

Falk shrugged his shoulders contemptuously.

" Well, yes, from the point of view of the Church and established morality."

He suddenly grew cold, made it clear that he did not care to continue the conversation.

Marit suffered. One question especially harassed her — Why had he concocted that piece of fiction about the child and its mother?

" So the mother ran away from her child? Be truthful. I was so miserable all last night."

" Why do you insist on knowing? "

" I must know, I must."

Falk glanced at her in astonishment.

" I've told you once already."

Now he spoke sincerely, convincingly. Marit believed him, was grateful, and looked at him with mute entreaty in her eyes, the entreaty of a child ready to ask for pardon, but still wavering.

Falk did not return her look, but kept his eyes fixed stubbornly on the ground. Thus they approached the garden gate.

" You're going to have dinner with us, aren't you? Father told me to be sure to make you stay."

Falk, not to be shaken, declined politely, yet coldly, took grave leave of her, and walked off down the road.

Marit followed him with her eyes. Surely he would look back at least once. But he walked straight on and disappeared round a bend.

" My God, my God! " she groaned. " What have I done to him? "

In her room she lit the lamp in front of the Virgin Mary and prayed fervently.

CHAPTER III

FALK, instead of going back to town, turned off from the road and walked along the shore of the lake.

The woods on the opposite side were enveloped in deep twilight. The smooth mirror of the lake reflected the sheen of the darkening sky.

He stopped.

How could he have forgotten what he had said the night before? The whole story had now resolved itself into a silly, pitiful comedy.

But Marit — she believed him blindly, unsuspectingly, with implicit trust in his every word. Gradually he regained composure, sat down at the water's edge, and gazed into the distance mechanically.

His thoughts jigged in his brain, a chaos, with an image or a broken impression flashing out only from time to time.

Then he rose and walked on, slowly, almost painfully. He wanted to remember something, forced himself to think — think something out to the end.

It grew dark. Little lights went up in the neighbouring villages. Now and then the rumble of a peasant's wagon was heard, then everything went still, and Falk listened to the chatter of the grasshoppers and the croaking of the frogs.

What did he really want? He was not a professional Don Juan. He never tried to attract women merely in order to possess them.

His thoughts refused to disentangle themselves. Gradually there emerged before him the image of a woman with the infinite grace of the races that are now becoming extinct. Long narrow hands seemed to be stretching out to him, wondrously good kind eyes to be looking into his very soul.

It was his wife — ha, ha! Miss Perier!

He smiled sardonically, then instantly turned grave again.

He loved her, oh, how passionately!

Something stung him.

Ha, ha, ha! Before his eyes arose the man who had possessed her before him.

He sprang up in a rage, smarting as with the pain of a sword thrust.

God, God! Only not to think of it! No, never think of it again. Was he never to be rid of that terrible torture, those senseless memories? Was it her fault that she had not met him before giving herself up to that first man? Her instinct had deceived her — she had made a mistake — she had not loved him . . .

No, no, no! She was so beautiful — she had a veritably masculine mind. She understood him as no one else did.

He saw her as she had appeared the first time he had met her. Ha, ha! Mikita's fiancée — a sea of red light, an indeterminate luminosity about her eyes — that movement of her hand, and the subdued voice, " So that's you? "

Yes, it's I, dearest, and I fell in love with you at once.

Yes, he loved her truly, was longing for her, wanted to sit in his large easy-chair at home, hold her on his knees and feel her arms about his neck.

But why in the world couldn't he forget Marit?

In the greatest transports of love, he would suddenly behold his wife's face changing, changing into a delicate little face — the face of Marit, Marit . . .

His strength left him. He looked at that face like a madman, and his thoughts stubbornly reverted to the two weeks he had spent with Marit when a year ago his mother had summoned him home on very important business.

Again he felt the anguished longing for the love that could be nothing but torment, the awful torment of desiring a woman never to be possessed.

Oh, how happy he had been with his wife before he had met Marit. Happy? H'm, h'm! He saw Mikita again, her betrothed. He trembled. But granted he was happy, loved her, loved . . . And now there arose between them Marit, who separated them, and whom he must continually suppress in his heart in order to remain close to his wife.

But why had he come here now? What did he want of Marit? Why was he deceiving her? Why playing this comedy?

If only he could understand it himself.

There must be some purpose in it; and that hidden purpose must be somewhere within the limits of logical reasoning.

Or was it only sexual attraction lying in wait for a new victim?

No, impossible. It would be despicable to sully that pure dovelike soul. Never would he do it. In two weeks he would return to his wife. If he were to go back having possessed Marit, his conscience would gnaw at him, pursue him remorselessly.

Oh, that accursed conscience!

To be in Paris forever thinking about her — always to be saying to himself, " Now she's lying face downward with arms outstretched in the shape of the cross, writhing with pain, praying to God for mercy." Not for a minute would he have peace. It would be hellish to live a life with that one thought, that one image, that eternal fear and torture.

He walked on slowly. It had grown quite dark, and over the meadows rose a mist hot with the glow of a golden moon. He stopped, looked at the sea of light, and tried in vain to recall a certain something.

Not a single definite thought emerged, only this one damnable question: What did he really want?

Then he had a picture of Marit. How beautiful she had been sitting on the stone with the red reflection of the brim of her summer hat on her face. How supple, how graceful!

Conscience! Ha, ha, ha! Conscience! Good heavens! How ridiculously silly is your superman! Herr Professor Nietzsche left out of account tradition and culture which created conscience in the course of hundreds of centuries. Ha, ha! Of course, dull reason aided by logic may eliminate conscience, yet up to that time it had proved impossible. Oh, how ridiculous is your superman sans conscience!

His thoughts returned to Marit. The problem interested him, this problem of dual love.

It was clear as the sun. He loved both, without a doubt. Why delude himself? When he wrote passionate, oh, very passionate love letters to his wife, he was not lying. He really loved her. Nor, when a few hours before he had assured Marit of his love, had he lied either. God saw it.

He laughed aloud, but instantly fell a prey to a tormenting pain, a biting rancour.

He had a right to love Marit. Why not? Who could prohibit him? Should the stupid mob-made laws of morality prove stronger than his feelings?

Why not deceive her if he desired her? Why not possess her if they loved each other?

She loved him. Then what was to hinder the realisation of their desire? Morality? Merciful heavens, *what* was morality? He knew no other force than the force of his feelings — the feeling now in his heart. There were no laws to bind his will.

He walked along the path through the cemetery.

The leaves of the silver poplars rustled mysteriously. The marble slabs rose in sharp relief against the dark background of the night. A strange sensation stung him. That solemn rustling of the leaves reminded him somehow of the rattle of skeletons.

How absurd in him to be impressed by those foolish superstitions of the people about death.

His nerves were overstrained, he was utterly fatigued, his thoughts became more and more confused, he could not think a thing out logically, to the end — Oh, the devil take it!

What was all that logic for? Something was being born in his soul that united his thinking centres with motive forces lying beyond the limits of his knowledge, possessing a logic of their own that laughed at conscious ratiocination.

Passing by the monastery garden, he stopped to look up at the high white walls.

Yes, a year before she had come out of the monastery, where she had been educated — ha, ha! — educated! They had broken her, bound her hand and foot with the fetters of moral and religious rules, and now these were stifling her. She could not take a single free step.

Why couldn't she say to him: " Here, I love you. Take me."

Ha, ha! Again that absurd reasoning!

But he would be stronger. He would root out of her soul the weeds of prejudice and religion. He would subjugate her, make her his slave — or, rather, the opposite — set her free, and himself also. For was he not himself a slave, the slave of his wife, of his conscience, of all the prejudices that now crept out of him like earthworms after a spring rain?

He would see who was stronger, himself or religion. A savage energy seemed to cleave his brain.

He walked briskly, constantly hastening his pace.

He reached home all in a sweat, and found his mother waiting up for him.

"Oh, mother dear, why haven't you gone to bed?"

"I was so afraid you'd forget to put out the lamp. So many accidents happen that way."

"But, mother, you can't come to Paris every night to see that I put out the lamp."

"Unfortunately I can't. You're right, of course. But a mother will always remain a mother."

"Yes, yes, a mother. It's a sacred thing to have a mother." Falk kissed both her hands. "Is there any brandy in the house?"

"Yes, but I hate to give it to you. You drink a great deal, and your nerves are unsteady anyway."

Falk laughed. "The best medicine for me, mother. Besides, I'm feverish, and alcohol takes the strength out of fever."

His mother brought in a bottle of brandy. Falk pondered. Finally he made up his mind.

"I must tell you something, mother. I have kept it a secret from you a long while. But it bothers me not to have you know. Only promise me you will listen calmly."

"Quite calmly, my child."

"Well, then, mother dear, I am married."

Mrs. Falk looked at him for some time as if dazed. Alarm gathered in her large, deep, kind eyes.

"Don't, dear, don't joke like that with me."

"It's the truth, mother. I fell in love and married. She's of a good family. She loved me, too. So we went to the mayor and got married."

" What, not in church? "

" Of course not. What's the use of a church for getting married in? You know my views on religion. I never kept them a secret. Then, too, my wife is a Lutheran."

" Lord Jesus! A Lutheran! " Tears glistened in Mrs. Falk's eyes.

Falk caught her hands, kissed them, and spoke of his happiness so much and so ardently that the old lady finally composed herself.

" But why didn't you tell me before? "

" Why should I have? Marriage hasn't the slightest religious significance to me. It is simply a contract made in order to secure the wife economically and guard her against annoyance from the police."

" Do you really live with her, with your so-called wife? "

" So-called? " exclaimed Falk resentfully. " Of course I do. Mother, you should get into the habit of respecting civil institutions as much as Church institutions. I want to ask you," he added, " to be sure not to say anything to anybody about it — to absolutely no one. I don't want people mixing up in my private affairs. I'll never forgive you if you do."

" I will gladly refrain, both for your sake and mine. What would people say? I couldn't show myself in the street.— A Lutheran! "

" Yes, yes, the people, those people! And now do go to bed. I'll be very careful about the lamp. Good night, mother."

" Good night, my child."

Falk fell again to pondering. He sat down. His brain now worked with unusual lucidity.

What was impelling him toward Marit with such irresistible force? Could it be only sexual attraction? But there were thousands of incomparably more beautiful women whom he could get without the least difficulty. Then what did he want of Marit, that child still deaf to the voice of sex?

A child deaf to the voice of sex — the only correct description of her.

Or was it true love, such as he felt for his wife, such as he had first learned from his wife?

No, impossible.

He rose and began to pace the room. He must at last come to a clear understanding with himself about it. He tried to think with strict logical precision.

Good God, how often he had already thought all those thoughts! Each time with brand-new arguments, with greater psychological subtleties.

Now, then, in the first place —

He laughed merrily, remembering a high school mate of his who always started to answer a question with " In the first place " and rarely got any farther.

What nonsense!

Well, then, his first acquaintance with Marit . . . that strange hallucination of the fragrance of roses and something else, something uncommon, mystical.

An old, long-dormant memory flashed up in his mind. He saw a large room with a coffin in the middle and round the coffin candles, tall wax candles. The room was filled with white roses exhaling an odour that drugged the senses.

Then the long funeral procession moving slowly to the church on the hill; a wonderful summer evening; every one carrying torches or candles A gust of wind blew out the candle of some one walking near him. This focussed his attention. Then they put the coffin on the catapult. Nearby stood eight priests in their churchly vestments.

From all round the odour of white roses was borne in waves to his nostrils.

Marit had said something, walked away, come again. But he could not rid himself of that hallucination.

Finally he made the strange discovery — Marit had white roses in her hair.

Falk ruminated.

Is it possible that the white roses are the cause of my so desiring to possess her? What connection is there between my desire and that reminiscence?

The other unseen self which was in him understood much better. From the very beginning there had been a certain sexual impression brought to the surface by the fragrance of roses in Marit's hair.

And in what way, or better — what connection was there between the smell of roses and his sexual attraction? Between an impression received in his early boyhood and his adult impulses?

I don't know, I don't know, my esteemed public.

Well, and what else?

Another, still stranger circumstance.

Their hands had met accidentally — perhaps not accidentally. He had felt a sensation as of a naked child's body pressing to his.

Now he recollected whence that feeling had come. When twelve years old he had gone out bathing with a girl. In his country the boys and girls bathed together naked. You needn't smile your cynical smile, my highly moral public. There's nothing improper in that. It is the lovely purity and innocence of those who know not yet the forbidden fruits of bourgeois society.

The girl, caught by an undertow, had been drawn into a deep place. Falk had made toward her quickly, succeeded in grabbing her by her hair, pressed her to him, and carried her out of the water.

It was then that the male in him had first awakened.

Falk thought with peculiar tenderness of the girl of the same age as himself and now the mother of two children.

Strange, inexplicable — after seeing Marit to recall those long-forgotten impressions of still longer ago.

Oh, yes! He recalled another thing — when he had stood at the parting of the ways and love and friendship were waging a terrific struggle in him.

The man who had been engaged to his present wife had been his friend. Falk had not wanted to deceive him. He had been in anguish, had writhed with pain, had run away so as not to see her again. — Just then it was that he had received a letter from his mother for the first time mentioning the angel of goodness and beauty, Marit.

Marit, Marit! That odd name had wrought upon him powerfully, preoccupied his mind whole days, stamped itself upon his soul. It sounded like music in his ears, like a mysterious presentiment of something beyond the ordinary.

Marit, Marit! The name characterised her perfectly. — A Norwegian shore dissolved in the spring — gold on her small head, as if the marvellous Norwegian spring sun were playing upon it.

He did not understand . . . in fact, what was there to understand? Could his love for Marit have been born of those few trifling impressions?

No, impossible. The cause of it must be rooted deeper. There must be something in Marit not amenable to definition, something reaching to the very depths of his being.

Suddenly he understood. It must be so — Marit and his mother country were one and the same thing.

There was something broad and expansive in her, a melancholy pensiveness; certain sharp, well-defined lines reminding him of a plain he loved. That absurd mother country which any fool might sketch in a few strokes.

Why were his very deepest sentiments cast in those simple forms? Why did he love her so — her head with the bright luxuriant hair? What was passing in him? Was it really love?

No, truly, no. He loved only his wife, his beautiful wife, the soul of his soul, the heart of his heart. . . .

So it was merely sexual attraction?

Also absurd. That stupid desire could find satisfaction in a thousand other women.

H'm!

But Falk was highly cultured, refined, not to be satisfied with the first article to hand. His preferences were retiring, discriminating.

Well, and what else?

What else? Besides, I have a thirst for Marit. I want to possess her and will possess her, because such is my will.

Falk began to be feverish, seized suddenly with an eager, savage longing for Marit.

She was now lying in bed, her hands folded in a cross on the sheet, holding perhaps the bronze crucifix he had once noticed that she owned.

"To conquer a saint . . . that was something out of the ordinary," he thought.

But saint or no saint, he would do what he desired, what he was compelled to do.

That terrible yearning, that desire was eating his soul away, consuming his peace like gangrene, racking his nerves. It would not let him work.

He must, he had a perfect right to do it.

Am I not right, gentlemen? No, there is no right or wrong. That is a conception governing the conduct of Tom, Dick, and Harry. But if we must perforce speak of whether I am right or wrong — and speak of it I must in order to appease the atavistic prejudices called conscience — then I resort to the following arguments.

I am a man capable of taking and using life far more strenuously, broadly, many-sidedly than a girl whose sole function in life is to give birth to children and rear domestic fowl.

This speech, gentlemen, I address to the philosophers.

To the doctors I say I am a man who is simply perishing with desire and longing for a girl. And to the lawyers I say, " I am in the position, therefore, of a man who has to act as I do in self-defence."

Hence, I am perfectly within my rights.

Then comes some Mr. X and says, " You're an immoral man."

" Why ? " I ask most amiably.

" Because you have seduced an innocent girl."

" And nothing else ? " I ask surprised. " Then listen. I haven't seduced her. She gave herself to me of her own accord."

You know that passage in the Napoleonic Code forbidding the hunting out of the fathers of illegitimate children. Don't you know the capital anecdote? Then you're not an educated man. Napoleon was no less great as a lawgiver than Moses.

Now listen. The most sacred aim of nature is to create life, for which the sexual co-operation of two individuals of different sexes is necessary. I wanted to attain that aim, so I fulfilled the most sacred duty imposed on me by nature.

Then comes Mr. Y.

" Go to all the devils! " I shout. " I am I, and that's sufficient."

Falk grew more and more excited. He was in a rage. His thoughts whirled chaotically.

Dawn was breaking. The world melted in majestic twilight. The birds began to chirp.

Falk drank a glass of brandy and lit a cigarette. Gradually he calmed himself.

Marit, dear sweet child. Ah, those eyes looking at me, now with unutterable love, now with anxiety and fear.

He felt her hands on his temples, he heard her gentle voice whispering with a passionate tremor, " Eric, my Eric, mine only. . . ." He felt her on his knees, her hands round his neck, her whole body pressing to his.

Falk drank and became more and more sentimental.

Suddenly he jumped up. I know you, you cunning lust. You want to conceal your bloodthirsty passion under a cloak of sentimentalism. No, no. Thank you for your hypocrisy. When I do anything, it is with the full knowledge of what I am doing. I love only my wife, and if I want to possess Marit, I by no means deceive my wife. On the contrary, I should belong to her more than ever.

The sky lit up the room as with a dull purplish red blaze. The light of the lamp dimmed.

Falk looked at himself in the mirror. His lean face in that half light was Mephistophelian. His eyes burned feverishly.

He sat down on the sofa feeling a great fatigue.

It was ridiculous that he should suddenly have become utterly indifferent to the girl — astonishing. He was not in the least drawn to her.

But to-morrow it would return. To-morrow he would burn with desire again.

Yet it was plain insanity to live longer in such an atmosphere, to continue to meet her and dispute with her. No, he must put an end to it once for all.

Falk jumped up. To-morrow or the day after he would return to his wife — to Paris.

He already saw himself in the train.

Cologne! Good Lord, ten hours still! He was all aquiver with impatience. The train was dragging on an eternity. He would have liked to jump out of the carriage and run, run, faster than all the expresses in the world — three hours more — two hours — he held his watch and followed the hands — half an hour — his breath caught. It grew dark before his eyes, his heart throbbed. There — now the train was pulling into the station. His eyes darted into the crowd like two swallows. Now he caught sight of her — there in the yellow cloak. He recognised her at once. She was looking for him eagerly, running down the platform alongside the train. Now they met, took each other's hands — then he caught her in a close embrace.

He awoke from his revery. He must wire her at once — " Coming in a few days."

Then he felt nervous. He would not have the strength, he felt, for so long a journey. He sat down, his hands dangling.

Paris seemed somewhere far off, at the other end of the world.

Strange, he could not recall his wife's face. The girl's face . . . Good God, by what name had he referred to his wife?

He paced the room, unable to recollect.

Why, he had heard the name, had read it in the parliamentary records.

At last. He sighed with relief. Miss Perier — Perier — Perier —

He grew excited again, felt immensely dissatisfied with himself.

Oh, that stupid idiotic comedy. Once you lie, you should at least not be caught lying. He had given himself away and Marit would be more careful.

But perhaps not. Certainly not. She would rather let her head be chopped off than believe Falk had lied. No, never in her life. Of course, she believed that he had been drunk.

The room turned light. Now he must lie down. His head was on fire, his hands hot. Ah, for something cold on his head. Her hands . . .

Whose hands?

He burst into a sardonic laugh.

Marit's hands, of course, Marit's hands.

The birds chirped noisily in the garden. He opened the window. A cold stream of fresh air struck his head and refreshed and sobered him. Wisps of mist were dissolving and fading away. The meadow, green and distant, was opening to view. In the orchard adjoining the meadow, the trees all in blossom, emerged one by one, a waving floral sea that benumbed the senses, and on the meadow lay whole oases of yellow daisies.

CHAPTER IV

FALK jumped up. He had fallen asleep on the sofa. In the daylight softened by the leafy trees in the garden an expression of profound melancholy lay on his wasted face.

His mother was bending over him, about to slip a cushion under his head.

" What awful dreams I had! "

" You'll wear yourself out, my child, spending whole nights up like this."

" Not at all, mother dear, I slept very well. I don't require long, steady sleep. There are people who can sleep even while walking. I knew a letter-carrier who could, and he lived to be ninety years old.

" Mother, another thing I have to tell you is, I'm going away in a day or two. I've got to return to Paris."

His mother felt aggrieved.

" Then why did you come at all? Why take that long journey for just a few days here? Your wife can get along very well by herself for a few weeks, can't she? God knows whether I shall ever see you again," she added sorrowfully.

" I should love to stay, but I can't possibly."

There was a knock at the door. Marit entered, greatly embarrassed. She kissed Mrs. Falk, and Falk shook hands with her coldly.

" Don't be angry with me, Mrs. Falk, for making such an early call. Father had important business here in town — and — and —"

Mrs. Falk excused herself for the room still being in disorder. That idler of hers had just got up, she said, adding:

"Just think, my child, Eric is preparing to leave us already. You must make him stay."

Marit quivered inwardly.

"What, going already?"

"Yes, I must. I must get back to work. I can't work here."

Marit remained seated as if petrified, looking at him with frightened eyes.

"Besides, there's no sense in my remaining longer. Life here is so close, so stifling. One keeps going round and round as in a charmed circle — don't be angry, mother. I'm accustomed to the broad, unrestricted life of a large city. Here I feel as if I were bound."

Marit sat thinking, then rose abruptly.

"I've got to go. You'll come to say good-bye, of course, before you leave, won't you?"

Mrs. Falk pressed her to remain for breakfast, laying a white cloth on the table and giving orders for the meal to be served.

Falk sat opposite Marit, gazing in absorption at his plate and only from time to time taking her in with a concentrated glance.

"Queer how much you resemble a girl I met in Norway, and still queerer that you have the same name." Falk spoke drily as if mentioning an ordinary incident. "She was a very lovely girl, with a crown of abundant golden hair, which made her look as if the first rays of the northern sun were casting a halo round her head.— But you don't look well. And why are you so sad? It's odd you never can be gay. Evidently your religion forbids it. Cheerfulness seems to be a sin.— Don't make such a serious face, mother — just a little remark thrown out."

Silence again.

Then Mrs. Falk spoke at length of her husband. Tears came to her eyes.

Marit rose.

"Now I'm going. I can't wait for father any longer."

Falk also rose. "May I accompany you? I take long walks at this time of the day anyway."

"If you like."

For an interval they walked in silence. Falk, with his hat drawn down over his eyes and his hands thrust carelessly in his pockets, was to all appearances lost in thought. Every now and then Marit would glance furtively at him, but he pretended not to notice.

"Do you really mean to leave?"

Falk looked at her with a cold wearied expression as if failing to understand her question.

"Oh — go away? Yes, absolutely. What have I got to do here? You don't suppose it's a pleasure to be near you and to be suffering agonies. Yes, I'm leaving, perhaps to-morrow. However, I'll do whatever occurs to me."

Marit's eyes filled with tears.

"Don't go. Else everything you said about your love is a lie. A man who loves doesn't act that way."

"Then tell me what you expect. I want to kiss you — you know how happy that would make me — and you won't let me. I want to speak to you about what is more important to me than anything else, and you won't listen. Then what do you expect — what?"

Marit cried.

"Didn't you say I mustn't love you, that you can't give me anything in return?"

"But I explained why I spoke that way. And suppose it actually were so, can't you conceive the infinite bliss of one moment?"

Marit looked at him in surprise.

"What am I to do? What do you want?"

"What I want?" he rejoined. "I? What I want? Do I know?"

"To ruin me and make me unhappy and then go away—"

"To ruin you—make you unhappy—h'm! Happiness —a paltry English invention. What a low, despicable thing is that satiated, complacent, contented happiness of your Mr. Smith and Mr. Brown! The highest, the only real happiness concentrates in a single moment. For that moment it is worth sacrificing one's very life. Would you your lifelong wallow in the filth of bourgeois happiness? What I want of you? Two—three hours of happiness, then on again—far away. Happiness is retiring. If too long enjoyed, it turns stale and muddy."

"Don't torture me. I can't stand it. You want to ruin me."

"Not at all. But don't let's speak of it. It's stupid to keep turning round and round the same idea all the time. I won't say any more. I'll be nice and jolly, only don't cry, don't cry."

Falk was very sorry for her.

"Don't cry. I'll be nice and jolly, only don't cry. Shall I tell you something interesting?"

"Yes." She was always glad to listen to him.

There was brief silence.

"I had a wonderful dream last night. You know when my father was still living we had an estate at the Russian frontier. The Russian sentry post was stationed right behind our barn. Once a peasant stole some corn from the field. My father was a hard, impulsive man. He used to beat me mercilessly, which, of course, made me not a whit better. I hated him as only a child can hate.

"He instituted a search for the thief and his booty. The whole village was summoned. The thief appeared before my father.

"'Did you steal the corn?'

"'Yes,' he answered audaciously.

"'What would you rather have, six months or thirty lashes?'

"Without saying a word, the thief lay down on the ground, and the flogging commenced.

"'Hit hard, or you'll get it yourself,' my father cried to the coachman.

"And the leather thong whistled through the air down on the peasant's back.

"'Now you do it,' my father ordered the half-witted herdsman. His broad face went still broader in a great grin.

"A terrific blow — but why are you so upset?

"Well, then, a terrific blow descended on the man's back. He jumped up, his teeth set, then lay down again. Another terrific blow.

"The peasants standing round laughed. The herdsman flogged with all his might. He was a powerful man.

"Another blow — two, three, four, five —

"I was beside myself. In my hiding-place I dug up the earth with my nails and stuffed it into my ears so as not to hear anything. I was going crazy. Children are compassionate to the point of stupidity.

"Finally the horror ended. The peasant got up, but fell to the ground again. He could not remain upright on his feet, and those human swine standing about laughed.

"But he had tremendous will power. At last he rose by himself and left.

" Father was satisfied.   He went to the breakfast table, and ate with great appetite, I remember.   I wanted to throw myself on him like a wild-cat and scratch and tear him to pieces.   Of course I didn't.

" That night our estate was in a blaze, set on fire from all four sides.   I jumped up out of bed in glee.   Never since has anything given me such satisfaction.   Father was punished.   The gates of the stables had been opened wide and the cattle driven out.

" At that point my mother came into the room and my dream ended."

The story moved Marit.

" Did it really happen, or was it only a dream? "

" That makes no difference.   The important thing is the velocity with which the sleeping consciousness works. It evoked all those memories at the very moment that mother opened the door.   Which is nothing unusual.   Hippolyte Taine mentions the case of a man who during a faint lasting no more than two seconds lived through fifty years of his life."

No, Marit could not understand.

" It isn't important that you should.   *Rassurez-vous*. I don't understand it myself.   The first memories were supplemented by succeeding impressions, and all combined into one dream."

The explanation did not satisfy Marit.   Falk must try and make it clearer to her.

" It won't make you any wiser, Marit.   The soul is different, altogether different from what crude people imagine, that's what you must learn to know.   Listen some more.   The peasant in my dream, for example, wriggling and jumping under the knout, in all probability came from impressions received in another field. You know, I suppose, that I studied the natural sciences and vivisected frogs and rabbits. I was obliged to, but always chloroformed them beforehand. Once, however, I pinned an unchloroformed frog to the board and opened its ventral and thoracic cavities. Its contractions were so violent that its body jerked up to the very heads of the pins. Then I cut out its heart . . .

" You can't listen? Well, then, let's speak of something else.

" I'm cruel? Not a bit. It would be foolish to compare pain in human beings to pain in animals, or my feelings to the feelings of those coarse peasants who laughed while looking on at the cruelty perpetrated against one of their own class."

For some time they walked on in silence, and entered a grove at the lake's edge.

The air was sultry, the midday sun blazed down on the woods and water, the lake lay spread out indolently at rest. Upon the whole plain hung oppressive quiet.

" Shall we rest a little? Dont be afraid. I shan't be importunate or rash. Oh, no. I'll keep at a respectful distance."

He flung himself down on the moss, and she sat on a stone two or three feet away and played mechanically with her sunshade.

Suddenly he raised himself on his elbow.

" Tell me, why do you go to church? Haven't you enough pride not to go where all the rabble goes, to a place reeking with the foul odour of sweat and horrid undigested food? "

Marit recalled how she had once fainted in church on

account of the nauseating air, how they had carried her into the vestry and unbuttoned her dress — indeed it was ugly. But she said nothing.

"Don't you see it lowers one to mingle with the rabble?"

"No, I don't see and don't want to see. My religion is my only refuge."

"Yes?" Falk drawled. "Very well, then, very well."

He looked extremely tired, and again stretched himself out on the moss and half closed his eyes. There in the deep shadow of the trees his face bore an expression of one who has gone through profound suffering.

Marit scanned him. A terrible man! She could not rid herself of the thought of the church reeking with the odour of sweat and garlicky breaths. And then that mechanical, tedious service, that never-ending mass, those monotonous soporific vespers — she did not dare to think on — God, God, what else was he going to do to her?

The expression of suffering on Falk's face deepened. He was pale, deep furrows showed round his mouth. Now she felt like throwing herself on his neck and gently stroking those furrows away.

Oh, what joy it would be to see him happy! What rapture to give him but a little happiness! Tears glistened in her eyes.

"Falk!" She wanted to say something, but could not.

Falk jumped up, greatly amazed. She looked at the ground in embarrassment, struggling with her tears, which now rolled down her cheeks.

Falk moved toward her. She wanted to rise.

"Don't be afraid of me, for God's sake! I'm not asking anything of you. And if I should, it would only be on condition that you give it to me of your own accord, willingly.

No, no, I didn't even think of touching you. You can rest perfectly easy."

He fixed his eyes on the lake and the glowing woods on the opposite shore.

Marit wanted to begin a conversation again.

" Why were you so angry last night? "

" I angry? " Falk yawned. " Angry? Not at all. I was only a bit excited. I love you and should like you to live the same life I do and think the thoughts I think; whereas you love and honour all I hold to be stupid and trivial. I can't tell you what I should so very much like to tell you. I am a free man. I cannot look on calmly and see a woman I love living in debasing enslavement to laws and formulas created for the sole purpose of crushing and suppressing the bloodthirsty impulses of the vulgar rabble.

" Thanks to that I am losing you," he continued, beginning to grow heated. " Your image is dimmed in my heart and brain. You dole out charity. I can say *a priori* that you do it because it is so prescribed in your churchly code, or, rather, because your churchly code bids you be charitable so that you may enter the kingdom of heaven. And if you visit the sick, it is with the idea of being liberally rewarded in the life to come. You expect a reward for everything. For each good deed you are promised compound interest. Therefore you are no better than a usurer. Shame on you! For the mere reading of prayers you demand remission of sins at some time or other. Ha, ha, ha! " he laughed contemptuously.

Marit turned pale.

" Do something not because the Church promises you a reward, but because your heart bids you do it. Do it without pay, without compound interest. Break all the precepts. Scorn that shameful traffic in virtues, that mean usury. Be yourself, nothing but yourself, the beautiful, lovely Marit . . . ha, ha, ha! You say you love me. But a stupid formula about impure desires — so the Church calls the most beautiful and profound of instincts — yes, a stupid formula is enough to suppress your strongest and noblest impulses, to silence the voice of your heart, to quench the fire that consumes you. Then you read another ten acathisti so that the Virgin Mary may rescue your soul from the clutches of the devil. Is that love? Is that love? Love which a formula, a law, the fear of your absurd hell can silence? Ha, ha, ha!"

Falk laughed still more contemptuously. Marit's whole body quivered.

"Well, answer me, is that love? Tell me, what do you call love?"

Marit was silent.

"Well, answer me. Do answer me. I don't want to plague you. I love you. I'm going mad from longing for you. And I know you love me. I know —"

He pressed himself to her and put his arm about her waist.

"Don't, for God's sake, don't. What are you doing? Eric, Eric, don't torture me."

"Oh, I beg your pardon, a thousand pardons. The devil! I've begun to forget myself so often. But that's unimportant. It won't happen again. . . . Shall we go? What do you say? It seems to me it's time for dinner."

Falk yawned purposely.

Marit walked at his side heart-stricken and desolate.

"Good-bye." Falk held out his hand. They had reached the garden gate.

Marit trembled.

"You won't go away, you won't go away!" her heart cried. Oh, if only he would not go away!

She grasped his hand impetuously.

"You won't go, will you? Do what you please, but don't go away. Don't go away."

Her lips trembled visibly. Her whole body shook.

"Don't go away, don't go away. I'll die here."

She burst into tears.

Falk looked at her sternly.

"I really don't know. That depends on circumstances. At any rate, I'll see you before I go."

He took leave coldly and walked away.

CHAPTER V

IT was night. A storm was raging. The rain beat
against the window panes in intermittent torrents.

Marit sat half dressed on her bed, too faint to take off the
rest of her clothes. Why should she? That night, she
knew, would be the same as the nights that had gone before.
She would lie down, the bed would dance with her in it,
she would sit up, bolster up the pillows, lean against the
wall, and remain like that staring into the darkness. Then
she would rise and press her forehead to the window pane
to cool it. And so the whole night long.

"Well, now all's over," she kept repeating in growing
anguish.

Before the wonder-working image of the Mother of God
glowed the ominous red of the lamp, lighting up a fraction
of the room. Suddenly the wick dropped, the oil took fire,
and the room filled with the nauseating smell of lamp smoke.

"The church reeking with the foul odour of sweat
and horrid undigested food." Falk's denunciation flashed
through her mind. The fire in the oil went out. Dreadful
night!

With her mind utterly blank she stared into the voiceless emptiness of the dark, stormy night.

Great heavens, what did he want of her? What was
he asking of her? The blood poured hot into her face.

She had a premonition of it, without understanding.
Suddenly she felt his quivering, thirsting lips upon hers. A
flaming serpent of passion coiled about her body. She
thought of nothing definitely, only thrilled all over with
great desire. She pressed her hands together between her

knees and sat that way cowering, shrunken, all ablaze, hearkening to the unseen tremor that set her vibrating with bliss and terror.

What was it? It recurred so frequently, and she feared it so. Ah, with what wild joy she would throw herself on his neck, with all-devouring passion, and kiss him, kiss him. . . . Again the blood poured hot over her, her head reeled. Everything flowed together into a raging whirlpool.

It was sin.

Sin, sin!

She jumped up, shivering as in a fever, and began to look for matches. She could not find them and threw herself on her knees before the image.

She wanted to concentrate her mind for prayer. In vain.

Again she jumped up in terror; she heard clearly the mocking words, " Stupid formulas."

No, that was something in herself mocking: Falk, Falk.

" You do everything for pay, to be rewarded in heaven with interest."

" Oh, God, God! " she sobbed.

Something, it seemed to her, kept her from praying; and with still greater ardour she threw herself on her knees searching for words. She was ready to tear the words of a prayer out of her heart along with a bloody piece of it, but could not find a single one. The Mother of God had abandoned her.

" Sin, sin! " sounded, hummed, howled like a storm in her troubled brain.

Why was God punishing her so? Why, why?

All that Falk had said took life in her brain again. Blank despair removed her last vestige of strength.

" And he said I didn't love him, that laws and formulas

are stronger than my love. No, no, a thousand times no! To-morrow, to-morrow he'll see how I love him. I'll fling myself on his neck. I want to love him and I will love him. Let God hurl me to the very bottom of hell, yet I will love him."

She jumped up and leaned against the window trying to think. In the garden the storm raged and broke off twigs and branches.

Again she felt his arms winding about her neck. And she did not resist, yielding to the awful caress, drinking in the poison of bliss, hanging impotently in his embrace.

No, no, no!

At last she found the matches and lit the lamp. The wavering light fell on the Byzantine image of the Mother of God. Marit was frightened. She stood motionless and looked with mounting terror. To her heated imagination the face of the Virgin was distorted with a caustic smile, then with anguish, and finally congealed into an austere, menacing expression.

Marit wanted to throw herself on the ground. Something kept her. She stood as though held fast. Terror constricted her heart. Her breath caught.

There, the mouth of Our Lady of Mercy lit up with a kind, benign smile.

Something rustled under the bed. Marit started in fright, not daring to breathe.

Oh, it was only the crackling of the torn wall paper.

She wanted to run. The whole house was full of apparitions. With a shiver she listened to the tense stillness.

Quiet.

Heavens, how terrible it all was! To run, oh, to run — to him, to him.

No, no.

"Pray, pray!" something in her cried.

No, she could not pray — not any more. Her hands folded for prayer dropped of themselves. The thought of the odours in the church picked her up from her knees.

Oh, how miserable she was! And it was he had brought her to this — oh, no, not he. He, too, was unhappy and miserable.

So what was to be done, what was to be done? Everybody had abandoned her. She threw herself on the bed and buried her face in the pillow. She sobbed and choked.

Then she grew calm.

He was so kind. She would beg him so, so hard, not to ask anything of her, only to remain and speak to her as he alone could speak.

"But he's going away, to-morrow he's going away."

She ran to and fro in the room.

"Perhaps he's gone already?"

She fell to the floor shaken again by a storm of sobs.

"No, no, impossible. He's so kind. He won't leave me."

"Eric, Eric," she groaned. "I'm yours, I'll do everything, only stay here, stay here."

She listened to her own groaning.

But her uneasiness kept rising, frothed up and overflowed. No longer had she the strength to bear the fearful anguish. God, those awful monstrous shadows, those fiendish shapes on the walls, that stern inexorable face of the Mother of God.

Run, run!

She dressed with feverish haste and ran out in the park. The cold wind refreshed her as she walked along the poplar avenue, and quiet and calm settled in her heart. She ceased to think.

The rain soaked through to her very skin. Getting cold she returned to her room, undressed, and lay down in bed, utterly worn out.

She was already asleep when suddenly she saw Falk's face looking at her sarcastically and laughing a Mephistophelian laugh. His eyes pierced to the very bottom of her soul. She looked at him in terror, ready to sink through the ground. An intolerable weight lay on her heart. Gathering together the remnant of her strength she jumped up. The face disappeared, leaving behind only the sound of mocking laughter in the stillness of the night.

Panting for breath she sat down on the edge of the bed, listening to a something in her that endeavoured to talk, to give warning.

And she rose higher, ever higher. Now, now she would learn the awful secret, she would look into the most hidden depths of Falk's soul.

She had never yet seen him like that. Her brain began to clear. In fearful alarm she heeded her own agitation.— Suddenly, suddenly — was he lying?

He? No, no. He was not lying. But what was it?

She was overcome by a deadly fatigue, lay down, and looked into the dark, voiceless emptiness.

It grew quiet in the garden. The wind ceased to whistle and howl. And on the kindly face of the Holy Virgin shone a sweet, quiet smile.

Everything tangled up in her brain. Before her eyes spread the broad open meadow. Falk was approaching from a distance, and she was running to meet him all out of breath. Now he was so good, so unendingly good . . .

CHAPTER VI

IT was a wonderful morning. The sun rising over the fields and meadows made diamonds of the dew drops. The torn shreds of mist floated upward to join the fleecy clouds in the deep blue of the sky.

Marit was on her way to matins. She was extremely pale, but in her sad, tired, child's face was the stamp of a sacred peace.

She walked slowly, counting her beads and praying to the Holy Ghost.

As she approached the monastery, the bell began to ring. The priest was conducting services in the corner chapel. Marit went down on her knees before the main altar and began to pray fervently. The young priest, who sat alongside the confessional, cast curious glances at her while mechanically fingering his rosary.

Marit rose and went over to the confessional.

Her confession drew itself out to great length.

Suddenly she got up and hurried nervously across the church to a seat under the choir. There she covered her face with both hands and burst into tears.

The unscrupulous man! To ask her such things! She couldn't even think of them. Her brain was confused. No, impossible. Could a servant of God put such questions? Her face glowed.

The coarse peasant! He must be a peasant surely. Hadn't Eric told her they were all peasants?

But all people are sinners. The priest might also commit an error. Evidently his wasn't a distinguished intellect.

Yet in the depths of her heart Marit suffered with a sense of shame and insult. She cried, felt debased.

Neither God nor the Holy Virgin nor the priest, no one, no one wanted to help her. They had all abandoned her. Almighty God! Merciful heavens! What a misfortune!

The vile creature rang the bell three times.

No, to-day she would not take part in the services — she did not want to, she could not.

She looked about in embarrassment.

This church, this church steeped in the foul odour of sweat. Falk was right. The smell was unendurable.

Marit left the church.

Should she go to Mrs. Falk? No, impossible. How clearly Marit saw the old lady's searching eyes turned now upon Falk, now upon herself.

Eric would probably come to see her to-day. Now she would listen to him eagerly. He didn't exaggerate a bit. The priests, they were indeed peasants, who went to the seminaries because it gave them an easier way of earning a living — ha, ha, ha! She laughed Falk's caustic laugh. She recalled what he had told her of priests a year before.

He had a kinswoman with seven children and a mother to support, her husband, a bricklayer, having lost his life by falling off a scaffolding. It had happened while Eric was still at high school.

"And so," Marit distinctly heard Falk's voice, "I went to their poverty-stricken room, not because I wanted to look at the dead man. That's unpleasant. His wife was to go to the priest and tell him about her plight, so that he would bury her husband free of charge. The priest — what do you think the priest said to her?"

At that time Marit had refused to believe him; now she was convinced he had told the truth. Eric would not lie.

Behind the monastery flowed a narrow stream spanned by a half-ruined bridge. Marit stopped on the bridge to look down at the current's languid flow.

So what had the priest said?

Again she distinctly heard Falk's ironic voice, " If you pay me three dollars, I'll bury him. If not, you can bury him without a priest. It'll cost much less."

A shiver of disgust went through her. She recalled the confessional.

Mechanically she walked on.

Ah, if only she were to meet him now. He often took walks alone.

Her heart beat tumultuously.

Now he could tell her everything, absolutely everything, and she would listen and agree.

She waited — in vain. She waited the whole day. Falk did not come.

A hundred times she walked round the garden, sharply scanning the road from town — still he was not to be seen. From time to time a cloud of dust arose, drew nearer — a buggy from one of the small surrounding estates.

" He'll come to-morrow," she thought, slowly undressing in the dark. She had refrained from lighting the lamp for fear of seeing the image of the chaste Virgin. She did not want to, she could not look at it . . .

Seized with uneasiness she stopped in front of her bed. Pray?

Once more she asked herself, " Pray? "

" The stupid desire for childish happiness beyond the grave," some one's voice laughed in her soul.

Would the all-powerful and almighty God strike her down for it on the spot?

She waited in tense fear.

No, nothing happened.

The clock struck into the profound stillness.

She felt a great lassitude and wanted to sleep. Her brain refused to work. Only once the terrible question sounded in her mind, "Will he come to-morrow, or will he not?"

"Has he gone already?"

No, no. She was convinced, she knew he had not gone, not now, when she belonged to him wholly, only to him. He could not have gone.

Strange that she should be so convinced of it.

The next day she again waited for him in vain. She waited the whole endless, infinitely terrible day.

Could she stand the torture longer? No, it was too much.

Involuntarily she looked at herself in the glass. Her face had grown thin, her eyes were reddened from the sleepless nights with blue rings round them; a hectic red burned on her cheeks.

She felt sorry for herself. How could he torture her so? Why did he wreak his vengeance upon her? What for? What for? She seemed like a child to her own self, punished unjustly.

She attempted to think but was unable to collect her thoughts.

What was the matter with her? She heard with perfect clearness Falk's words and broken phrases. She had fallen into a large, strong net — or, no, not a net, an iron cage out of which she was too weak to break away.

My God, my God! What was happening to her?

She was defending herself with all her might, struggling, fighting. But the mad, poisonous thoughts of Falk had her in their clutches.

Everything sacred seemed to be bared to nakedness. Ugh! Ugly nakedness . . .

And yesterday in church — from under his mask of servant of God the peasant had stared out with coarse curiosity.

Now what was happening to her? Oh, almighty heaven! She did not want to look, yet each moment her eyes involuntarily turned in that direction . . .

What was happening? The expression of holiness and unearthly goodness had vanished from the Byzantine Madonna's face. A scoffing smile met Marit's gaze.

What a ridiculous picture!

She sat for a long time perfectly still. Yes, the whole world had abandoned her — and he, too.

When she entered the dining-room it was already evening.

"Listen, Marit," her father greeted her. "I must go to mother. She's worse. There's no danger, but I don't feel easy. I'm going to-morrow." Kauer buttered his bread busily as he spoke.

Mother, mother! Marit had forgotten her, forgotten everything, was indifferent to everything. A fearful, silent, evil hand, she felt, was upon her, a cloud ready to burst in torrents.

"The landrat has invited us for dinner to-morrow evening," Kauer added after a pause.

That set Marit trembling with joy. Falk would be there surely. At last, at last, she would see him. He was very friendly with the landrat.

"Father dear, we must accept."

Kauer had meant to leave the next morning, but Marit begged him to stay over. Kauer loved his daughter above all else in the world, could not deny her a thing.

"Well, in that case I'll take the night train. But then you'll have to come back home by yourself."

"Not the first time, father. I'm quite grown up."

Kauer sat silent evidently thinking about something.

"Strange," he said, "strange that Falk doesn't show up here any more. I've got a weak spot in my heart for him. He's a remarkable young man. The whole town is furious at him, yet in ecstasies over him, too. He does wild things sometimes. Yesterday his mother bought a pig in market and was obliged to drive it home herself as she happened not to have anybody to do it for her. So what do you think our Falk does? Takes the rope, sticks a monocle in his eye, and with the solemnest air in the world drives the pig all through town. Everybody turned out to look at the unusual spectacle."

Marit laughed heartily.

"Ha, ha, ha!" Kauer chimed in. "A swineherd with a monocle stuck in his eye! Only he drinks inordinately. Yesterday he asked the head master of the gymnasium to allow him to slap him in the face. The head master was dumbfounded.

"'I'd love to give you a slap,' said Falk sort of dreamily, 'but I'm too lazy.'"

"What did he want to do that for?" Marit asked.

"I don't know. Just think, Marit, the head master of the gymnasium! Falk's an eccentric. It's amazing that one has to love the rascal in spite of one's self. It's a pity he drinks so much."

"Does he really drink very much?" Marit asked.

"That's what they say."

Marit remembered Falk telling her that he drank only when he felt miserable.

It both grieved and delighted her.

And to-morrow, to-morrow she would at last see him and tell him everything, everything.

CHAPTER VII

MARIT'S face lit up when she caught sight of Falk among the landrat's guests.

Yet he seemed in no haste to greet her, standing aside engrossed in conversation with the young physician of the town.

He had seen her, however. She had caught his searching look.

Quite a while later he stepped up and greeted her with cool formality.

"Where have you been hiding so long?" Kauer pressed Falk's hand cordially. "I have been eager to speak to you before going away."

"Going away?"

"Yes, I'm off to-night to visit my wife. She's worse. I commend Marit to your care."

The young physician broke into the conversation, insisting on an account of the latest developments in neurology. Falk, he had heard, had made a careful study of the subject.

"That was long ago. I've forgotten all I ever knew. Now I'm occupied with literature, and write books. But perhaps I can give you a little information."

"So there is no direct contact? In that case, how is the nervous current transmitted from one nerve to the other? It means a positive revolution in the science."

Marit sat nearby listening attentively while giving the prosecutor's wife absent-minded answers to her interrogations.

The strange-sounding, erudite words penetrated to her soul — Golgi — Ramon — Cajal. Falk knew everything.

How pitiful and insignificant the little doctor seemed listening like an attentive schoolboy, eager to know everything and knowing nothing.

Her heart filled with glad pride.

He, he, Falk, loved her! How handsome he was! She trembled suddenly.

They were summoned to dinner.

Conversation, at first scattered, soon became general and turned upon the social wrongs of the day.

Marit sat opposite Falk striving in vain to catch his look. He seemed to see nothing.

Why did he refuse to look at her? She longed for him so. Never before, it seemed to her, had she felt such a longing.

They spoke of the activity of the plunderbund in Posen.

"A phenomenon I cannot comprehend," said Falk decidedly. "It's not a question of which side my sympathy is on. I simply can't understand it. See how absurdly the Prussians contradict themselves. They maintain they are one of the most powerful nations of Europe. Ha, ha, you remember Bismarck's *Wir Preussen fürchten nur Gott, sonst niemand?* And here is Bismarck himself, the great and powerful, afraid of none but God, thrown into a panic by a handful of Poles. A few million Poles reduced to beggary against fifty million Germans! And your powerful Prussians literally quaking with fear. They are defending Germanism. Ha, ha, ha! I'm beginning to feel respect for that handful of people so menacing to Germany the proud and mighty. Gentlemen, it's no joke. If two or three millions can crowd out fifty million Germans — *à la bonheur*. Here's to your health!

"But the Prussian state for all its strength acts like a plain idiot. Giants always are idiots, you know. Here you have a huge state forbidding the teaching of the Polish language and pestering the Poles in every way it can think of — a striking historic example of a government trying to convert a part of its subjects into imbeciles. I know from personal observation that the Polish children forget their mother tongue and speak a hideous dialect hardly suggestive of human speech.

"But I'll discount this particular inanity. There's a still greater one that the government is guilty of — in the economic field. For what can be more destructive to society than economic stupidity?

"The colonisation commission buys up the land of the Poles, parcels it out, and settles poor German colonists on it. What can your poor settler do? His German stolidity does not replace the immense working capacity for which the Polish peasant is famous, and so he either becomes Polish-ised, as happened to the colonists that Frederick the Great settled in Netze, or he completely degenerates, as have the large majority of the present colonists in Posen.

"I admire the Polish peasant's contempt and dislike for the German colonist. He won't sell him a pound of butter even for its weight in gold."

"My dear man," the landrat interrupted, "it is neither fear nor stupidity, but simply a precautionary measure. The Poles are an explosive element in the body politic, and there are many such elements in Germany — Papists, Bavarians, Socialists, Danes."

"Very well. But if that's the case, then why boast of fearing nothing but God? Why lie about it? Why not openly admit that Prussia is a weak state, or, better still, not a state at all? Admit that Prussia is poor and insignificant, because a handful of Poles can thrust your pitiful *Grosse Nation* from the saddle, and in union with the Wends on the Spree and the Silesian Lusatians can capture Berlin and crush that wretched nation of half-breeds composed of Jews, the dregs of the Slav races, and militarists. Therefore the Poles must be destroyed. Your sour patriotism in face of this fear of the Slavs looks very much like the ludicrous somersaults of a clown through a paper ring."

Falk spoke with heat.

"Very well, granted Germany is not a separate nationality, nor even wants to be one; yet it is important that she achieve economic power; and therefore, it may be said, the means by which she obtains economic power make no difference, since her concern is not Germany, but money. At the same time you must also frankly say: 'We are a nation of half-breeds. Three wars have thrown us together in a heap without rhyme or reason. We are not a nation. We are tradesmen, farmers. Everything in the way of our economic development we will trample under foot ruthlessly.' — But, gentlemen, to speak of danger to the country is a disgrace; to speak of the patriotic necessity for the complete destruction of the Poles is cowardice; to say *Wir fürchten nur Gott* is a decoy for none but fat saloon-keepers.

"In a word, either we must set aside hypocrisy and confess we are scoundrels violating the rights of nations and caring not a hang about them, because we are a nation of tradesmen, usurers, insatiable, greedy, grasping — all right — or else we are a nation so weak that a handful of foreigners can crowd us out, and therefore we must once for all give up the claim to being the *Grosse Nation* and drop *Vom Fels zur Meer* and *Wir fürchten nur Gott* and all the other high-sounding phrases.

"And don't drag in your Goethe and Schiller either. Ha, ha, ha! Not bad — a nation of ideologists, a nation of thinkers, with all her forces and energies concentrated against a handful of Poles, loyal Poles, Prussian subjects of the Polish nationality."

Falk laughed a quiet, caustic laugh.

"The inferences you draw are absolutely false," the physician joined in. "Absolutely false. The Prussians don't fear the Poles at all. It so happens that they have to deal with a highly volatile, restless element. Each minute fresh disorders are to be expected. The Socialists are only waiting for that. So, of course, the government feels endangered."

"What are you talking about? Maybe you'll say the Poles have an arsenal somewhere? Ha, ha, ha! In England, perhaps? Or maybe you think Krupp will send a few hundred cannon to Posen on the order of the Poles? He would, to be sure, but the Poles don't enjoy government credit. Ha, ha! Five cannon would be enough to disperse the Polish army, whose only weapons would be pitchforks, scythes, and the crude shot guns of Lefaucheux.

"It's nothing but the paltry hypocritical policy of the tradesman who fears that some one else may succeed in snatching up a crumb of the fat Prussian loaf. It's a monstrous policy. Look at Galicia. There the official language in all the Polish schools is Polish; the Poles have their two universities conducted by gentlemen pleasing to God and the Pope, agreeably to the doctrine that education is the most devoted servant of the Church.

"And what a splendid show when the professors parade to church in their gorgeous robes. The Poles have the right there to wear their national garb. Nowhere can you see more sumptuous apparel and handsomer figures than in the Lemberg Diet.

"In return, the Austrian Poles are the most loyal subjects in the Empire. They are mild, patient, gentle as lambs.

Have you ever heard of the Poles committing disorders in Austria? On the contrary, when there is any cutting off of a hydra's head to be done, the Poles are the first to do it. They are, as your Schiller says, *frisch und munter zur hand.*"

"You seem not to admit even Schiller's greatness," the editor of the local newspaper observed.

"On the contrary, on the contrary. It was from him that Bismarck got all his bombastic phrases."

The landrat, who had been thinking seriously, said:

"You have never paid any attention to Czech politics, have you? The same relations exist between the Austrians and Czechs as here between the Germans and Poles."

"Oh, no. The Czech question is primarily economic, at least so it seems to me. Bohemia is the largest province in Austria. Czech industry having reached a high degree of development is naturally looking for the largest possible outlet, and is trying to crowd the Germans out of the world market."

Kauer, who was already in his cups, burst out laughing.

"That is to say, the Prussians are imitating the Czechs in their Polish policy?"

"By no means. Prussia's economic policy is even stupider than her policy of fear. For example, German industry wants to conquer Poland. The colonisation commission comes along and buys up the estates. The Polish nobility is scattered all over the world, and so the best consumer is lost. The estates are parcelled out and settled with poor colonists. The Polish peasant is not a consumer because he himself produces all he needs. So what good has been done to German industry?

"As to Polish industry, it is not worth talking about. It is going into decline because the Germans can produce and sell cheaper. But there isn't the least advantage in this to German industry. So what's the use of it all? No, it's sheer insanity, or else amazing blindness. You are angry, gentlemen. But what is it, if not blindness — the deliberate destruction of a large part of one's country?"

Falk grew more vehement. For a second his gaze travelled to Marit's fever-flushed face. She seemed to be drinking in his every word.

"Yes, this Prussian policy" — Falk crumbed his bread, rolled it into tiny balls, and arranged them mechanically in a circle — "this ridiculous Prussian policy with regard to the Poles is absolutely unintelligible to me either from the political or economic point of view. Yet, as a bit of unwise speculation, I might understand it; but one thing positively beyond my comprehension is the Pope's attitude on the question."

Again his look travelled to Marit.

"Don't be angry, Father Superior. I think you and I will agree on this. I haven't the least desire to start a religious dispute. I shan't touch a single question on which the Pope is held infallible. I am only referring to his politics. And the Pope has never yet been pronounced infallible in politics, has he?

"I once saw Pope Leo XIII in Rome. He was the most beautiful old man I've ever seen — the noblest, wisest face — and his long, white, aristocratic hands. His poems, I think, are very good, written in excellent classical Latin.

"It seems that the Pope would naturally be the refuge of the down-trodden; and the Poles, being the most oppressed people in Europe, would be nearest to his heart. What do we see in actual fact? I can imagine the astonishment of the Poles when after Bismarck had driven about twenty thousand of them out of Prussia he received the order of Jesus, the highest order the Pope can bestow.

"Ah, Father Superior, don't be angry. I am keeping strictly to politics."

The priest was greatly wrought up. The company exchanged anxious glances.— How audacious of Falk to talk that way to the old father. Their looks travelled from Falk to the priest.

The face of the old cleric paled.

"Young man, you are too young to settle the most weighty questions of Church and politics, with your mind infected by foreign heresies."

Falk did not flinch.

"Quite true, Father Superior. It is really a matter of indifference to me what the Pope or the Prussian government does. I am simply making the statement that in relation to the Poles both the Papal and the Prussian governments act, to say the least —" He broke off.

"Ha, ha!" jeered the priest. "The things left unsaid are more insulting still."

"Therefore we'd better drop the discussion. I see you cannot listen to my opinions, calmly; and I've become disaccustomed to disputes abroad. Sometimes people understand each other, sometimes not. I don't want to force my notions on anybody."

All were silent except the editor, who was curious to find out what Falk thought of the Socialists. The editor was suspected of harbouring Socialist sympathies without daring to profess them, and Falk, he felt sure, would speak up.

"Quite true, Mr. Falk, you are a real revolutionist. Fine! Living under a monarchy you cannot, of course, be satisfied. What is your opinion of the monarchical form of government?"

The editor was glad that an authority like Falk would

support and defend the idea for which he, the poor provincial editor, was condemned.

"What my opinion is? H'm! Are you laying a trap for me? Well, once I was in Helsingborg with a friend of mine, a rabid anarchist. We were on a boat, from which we had a view of the marvellous castle mentioned in ' Hamlet.' Can you guess what my friend the rabid anarchist said? Fancy! That such a wonderful piece of architecture was possible only under a monarchical régime. You are surprised? Well, look at the art of the Renaissance. Find Mæcenases now for Titian, Michael Angelo, Tintoretto, Giorgione. Look at the Bourbon period when the great collections at Paris, Burgos, and Toledo were made. And consider the scandalous, barbarous economy of the Commune, which came near destroying the collections of Notre Dame and the Louvre.

"You want more proofs, eh? No? That's enough?

"Indeed, I abhor democracy. It commonises, levels down, reduces people to a lower plane, turns them into a horrid undifferentiated mass, with thought for nothing but money and a moralising theatre. No, I don't want democracy. Democracy means the inauguration of the reign of Cleon, of tailors, of Savonarola who ordered the burning of the priceless art treasures; it means the rule of gross shopkeepers who hate everything great and beautiful. Oh, no, we must not let loose the plebeian instincts which will turn against all that is beautiful and noble."

Falk quivered. The company's sympathies went over to him. He cleared his throat and continued:

"Nevertheless I sympathise deeply with the revolutionary ideal. I am not active myself because life interests me little. I view evolution as an astronomer views the movements of the stars through a telescope.

"If I sympathise with all these offshoots of democracy, it is only because the economic equality for which they strive so vigorously is totally different from intellectual and cultural equality. In the future state, I am profoundly convinced, an oligarchy of the intellect will arise and gradually acquire possession of the reins of government. Then will begin a new economic development a million times better than the one bequeathed to us by barbarism.

"Now the government is in the hands of an impoverished and beggared aristocracy, with the danger ahead of its giving way to the vile rule of low upstarts and money-bags with their sordid, grasping hands. I should not like to live to see it."

The editor looked like a drowned poodle.

"One more question: What do you think of the present government?"

"H'm, the present government — that's Emperor William. I admire him. I like him. Not long ago he promoted an officer of the fire department to the rank of colonel. Why? Because the officer had skilfully kept the Berlin mob away from the palace during a parade. And he conferred the promotion without any of your Prussian bureaucratic red tape. That's the beauty about him — his independence. He's a great soul. H'm, h'm. Yes, long live the German Kaiser Wilhelm the Second!"

Embarrassed glances were exchanged, but all rose and clinked glasses.

The editor with his secret sympathy for the Social Democrats, though he looked sheepish, also rose, conscious that the landrat was eyeing him.

They left the table.

Falk felt hot yearning eyes upon him. Looking around he saw Marit radiant, happy.

She dropped her eyes.

Falk walked up to her.

In the general exit from the dining-room they found themselves thrown close together.

Contact with her sent a warm flood pulsating through his body.

" Eric, you are a great man."

Marit was flushed.

Falk fairly bathed her in his warm glance. What had happened to Marit?

Kauer approached.

" You're the very devil. You spoke like a man. No one would have dared to speak as you did, though sometimes one should like to say a few things. Look out, though, don't spoil my girl. You mustn't talk to her like that."

Falk was about to protest.

" I'm only joking. I have the greatest confidence in you. What's in your mind is on your tongue. That's enough for me. I shall be back in a week. Now I must take French leave. Stay until I come back."

Kauer left.

Ah, how well he had spoken! Marit looked at Falk in ecstasy.

" I spoke well? Stupid stuff, Marit. Everything I said could have been met by a thousand objections. But these gentlemen who extract their wisdom from the local papers — ha, ha, ha! — of course it satisfies and impresses them. Well, well. Did you like what I said about the Pope, too? "

Marit answered hastily.

" Oh, very, very much. I've been thinking so much about all those things, and I have to admit you're right even in what hurt me so only a few days ago."

Falk, unprepared for this, glanced at her in astonishment. A most surprising metamorphosis! How quickly it had been effected.

"Why haven't you been to see us? I waited for you two whole days. And I suffered so. I tell you frankly, I suffered terribly."

"My dear good Marit, you know very well why I didn't come. I simply did not want to interfere with your peace. Then you know I'm awfully nervous. I mustn't expose myself to the wear and tear of being with you, else — a cord drawn too tight will snap. Ha, ha!" Falk smiled agreeably.

They fell silent. The editor approached. He could not forget the toast to the Kaiser and was eager to push Falk to the wall.

"What is your attitude toward anarchist assassinations? You are a connoisseur of the human soul, a psychologist. How do you explain them?"

"You're a mighty curious man. You surely don't expect me to expound my political creed here to-night? However, it's possible to take a bird's eye view of the thing, so to speak.

"Now, then, I can perfectly well understand the anarchist propaganda of the deed — as a fierce protest against what we are accustomed to call justice.

"We prosperous people, able to get at least one meal a day and do a luxurious form of work — we hold it to be just that our brethren in Christ should rise at four o'clock in the morning and go forth to a twelve-hour day of hard work in order to produce necessaries for our consumption. Some people, you can easily imagine, refuse to reconcile themselves to such a state of things and filled with naïve indignation are trying to destroy it.

" Take a man who sees this fearful social cruelty enacted every day; in times of strikes sees the workingmen dropping like flies before the guns, sees capital starving them out like Indian coolies; then can't you understand that a man possessed of a strong warm heart would be filled with the desire for vengeance, with a fierce blind thirst for vengeance, with the fury of an enraged bull charging the first man he meets — in this case the first of the well-fed privileged class?

" We don't understand such hearts, because our own hearts are small, poor, mean. But the heart that throbs in response to poverty and need is stirred to indignation over the injustices of life."

A group had gathered about Falk. Marit was listening rapturously.

A smile flitted over the editor's face.

" So you justify anarchistic attempts? "

Falk narrowed his eyes.

" I justify them? That would be the height of folly in me, having, as it chances, a well-to-do mother and so belonging to the class that can live without performing labour. I can *understand* anarchistic attempts, is what I said, not that I justified them."

Falk looked round languidly. For a moment his gaze rested on Marit, to whom he smiled kindly. Then he caught sight of the head master of the high school.

" Yes, I understand crime, murder, whatever you call it, committed in a rage, in a moment of excitement. There's the head master, for instance. I was so angry at him yesterday that I told him I'd like to slap him, but it wasn't worth the while."

All eyes turned on the head master.

" I'm sorry I said it in a moment of wrath . . .

" Why did I? Because, gentlemen, if a teacher is shocked

by an author's works, he should not say so to his pupils . . .

"Oh, yes," he went on, addressing the editor, "you want to know what I deduce from all this. Ha, ha! Very well, the deduction. You see, I understand the propaganda of the deed because I understand the conditions out of which the idea of political murder springs.

He laughed pleasantly.

Falk never fumbled, but always managed to wriggle out of a situation like an eel.

Marit remained close by with her eyes fixed upon him radiant, happy. And several times he turned toward her as if to question, "That's right, isn't it, Marit?"

He alone had the big beautiful heart that he had spoken of, a heart bold, filled with indignation. He was ready to proclaim what he felt and thought before the whole world.

Rapture swelled her breast. There was such unutterable bliss in that feeling of unending devotion. She quivered. Her face burned.

Falk disappeared somewhere for a while.

Suddenly he caught her hand.

"Come, Marit, come," he whispered in her ear.

Marit drew close to him.

"Come, come!"

At the landrat's, guests could depart without taking formal leave.

CHAPTER VIII

OUTSIDE, Falk was not quite so easy.
"I sent the coachman on ahead. It's such a wonderful night, I'd like to walk and speak to you a little. Will you walk, yes?" His voice shook slightly.

Marit made no answer. A vague sensation caught her breath. They passed out of the town, both of them thoughtful and silent.

There came the moment when one reads in the soul of a beloved creature as in his own.

"Will you take my arm? The road is rough, you may stumble."

She took his arm silently. He pressed her hand, and felt how she trembled. He knew he ought to speak now, yet was afraid to trust his voice.

His agitation grew.

"No, not yet," he thought. "It isn't time. Only peasants go at it so precipitately."

The moonlight flooded the meadow. In the distance they could see high rows of peat stacks.

Falk controlled himself, feeling he must wait still; it was better to sip happiness slowly. The sensation would be the stronger for it.

He stopped and looked at the meadow and peat stacks; then they walked on again without looking at each other, as if moved by something akin to shame.

Falk stopped again.

"Queer, every time I look at peat I think of my father's peat digger. He was a hard drinker and got a mild form of delirium tremens, then developed a curious mania."

Falk instinctively diverted her attention in order the more surely to catch her off her guard later.

"He fancied that will-o'-the-wisps were the souls of dead masons. Just at that time the Pope had issued an encyclical proclaiming that the masons were possessed by the devil.

"He took his old rifle and wandered whole nights through the peat pits, jumped across the widest ditches with the marvellous precision of a lunatic, ploughed through the mud, waded through swamps, beat his way through bushes and the entangled marshy growths, shooting all the time. There was something truly tragic about it. Once I saw him after a night spent that way. His eyes were bloodshot, he was coated with mud from head to foot, and his hair was plastered with it, but he was happy. He waved his pistol and jumped with joy. That night he had finally succeeded in killing one of the masonic souls. On examining it, he had found only a lump of pitch.

"From that time on his rifle became sacred to him. Once he was arrested for keeping his son out of school. The boy was left all alone to tend the goat, the man's one piece of property, while it grazed on the rubbish in the ditch, and also to mind a neighbour's child. One day the boy thought of playing a trick to frighten the child. He took his father's gun, aimed it at his own face, raised the cock, lighted a match, and put it to the vent.

"'I'm going to shoot myself, I'm going to shoot myself.' He brought the match nearer and nearer. The child was frightened and screamed. That moment the pistol went off. The cartridge struck the boy in his mouth.

"I happened to be passing by from school and shall never forget the scene.

"The boy bounded up in the air, turned round and round

in a circle, the blood flowing from his mouth and nose.   At each scream fresh rivulets of blood poured forth.

"The child did not understand.   It laughed at its guardian's funny leaps and screams.   But the goat seemed to realise the awfulness of the situation.   It broke loose from its stake and dashed off, jumping over the boy, across the wide ditches — it was terrible."

Marit was greatly affected.

"Yes, it must have been.   Did the boy die?"

"Yes, he died."

They walked side by side in silence again, so near, so terribly near.

"How beautiful you were to-day.   You had such an expression — an expression I've seen on you only once before — a year ago.   We were ever so happy.   Oh, those were wonderful, beautiful moments.   We were standing on the verandah in the evening.   From afar came floating the sound of the vesper bells.   On your face was the concentrated rapture that only happiness can give."

Falk quivered.

"I kept looking at you the whole evening.   I looked at you with profound delight because I felt you so near."

He pressed her to him, and seemed not to speak but faintly breathe the words, "Marit, I love you, I love you. . . ."

She felt the hot wave of blood flooding her body.

"For you, for you alone I came here.   In Paris I suffered the torments of hell longing for you.   And now I am overcome with a desire amounting to sickness to take you in my arms, press you to my heart, ah, press you so close as to feel your heart beating against mine.

"Marit, my happiness, my joy, I'll do everything, everything for you.   You mustn't resist any more.   You'll give me infinite happiness, you'll give me everything.   I suffered so all this time . . . my sun, my darling, give me this happiness. I have never yet loved so madly, so blindly — as you, you . . ."

She felt two bottomless eyes like two black stars upon herself. Her head swam. The fiery words fell upon her soul like drops of molten lead.

She felt him embracing her, felt how he groped for her mouth, drinking her in with his hot lips panting with desire.

She no longer resisted. Without will she yielded to his wild ardent kisses. And in her heart there was mad joy because she was walking on the brink of an abyss.

Of her own accord she flung her arms about his neck and kissed him, kissed him.

Falk had not expected such passion. He was deeply grateful to her.

" You'll be mine, Marit, mine. . . ."

Yes, it had to be, it was inevitable. Now something must happen — she herself did not know what — those eyes, those terrible eyes — and his voice, what transport, what rapture!

" Now let me go, let me go — I cannot breathe — I'll faint," she gasped.

Again they walked in tremulous silence.

" Will you be mine? "

" What — what — what did you say? "

Falk was silent.

" I don't understand —"

They said no more.

At the garden gate one mute short kiss.

CHAPTER IX

FALK slowly walked toward town. Suddenly he stopped.

"Shall I return, take her in my arms, carry her up to her room?"

"Yes — ask her permission to sit on the edge of her bed, or go down on my knees to her."

He pondered. Was it really a desire that could not be subdued? Perhaps it was only a wish to overwhelm Marit with the inspiration of novel sensations, to give her fresh proof of his wild passion.

He searched his heart, unable to decide what was genuine passion, what merely auto-suggestion. He had evolved so many plans of how to possess her, spoken so many words to enthrall her, both sincere and insincere that he had lost all perception of what was true in him and what false.

That very auto-suggestion now appeared sincere; his coolly calculated speeches assumed a passionate ardour. He had played with the feeling so long that it had actually become real.

In some spots in his brain, a new circulatory system seemed to have formed. Why was his heart so constricted? Why did it beat so tempestuously when he pronounced the word "love," whereas formerly he had uttered it a thousand times, coolly, without the faintest flutter?

He became absorbed in an endeavour to ascertain what form of love is called up by auto-suggestion.

An interesting subject. How was it to be treated?

He fell into meditation upon the interesting subject. His

brain, wrought up to the fever point, he insisted to himself, must be set at equilibrium.

"Let us say, for example, that some journal of psychology were to ask me to write an article on auto-suggestion."

Well, he would try. A frequently recurrent state in the brain marks out a path for itself along networks of new nerves, induces the growth of blood-vessels, and works upon them so long that they form a new network of circulation. Thus, a purely intellectual state becomes an emotional state.

"Ha, ha, ha! I was born to be a writer for a scientific *Bierzeitung.*"

A carriage passed quite close to him, so quietly that he almost fell under the horses. Evidently the tires were of rubber. He looked back and watched the two carriage lamps twinkle, dwindle, and disappear, then gleam up again at a bend in the road. His thoughts reverted to the masons' souls hounded by the peat-digger.

Marit was at home. Should he return to her? Maybe she was walking in the park to cool and calm herself. Or had she gone to the lake and was sitting on the large stone where they always sat together?

In the end he faced about and made along the road for town. Though his brain was fagged out, it turned persistently upon the minutest analysis of his feelings.

An extremely interesting subject. Not a thing to be done with it scientifically, but bully for a novel or short story.

And so a certain man is suffering from love induced by auto-suggestion.

Very well.

But at the same time he loves his wife unqualifiedly. And he loves her so much that there can be no doubt of the reality of his love.

In a word, he loves both the one and the other.

For he did love Marit, yes, he loved her — perhaps by auto-suggestion, self-deception; yet his soul was so full of longing and desire that the sensation could not be called by any other name than love.

Suddenly he felt a peculiar, rather unpleasant sense of satiety. A mere taste of bliss and cloyed already!

To-morrow, to be sure, he would go to Marit and his blood would again begin to boil; but the fact that at the present moment he, Eric Falk, felt satiated, remained a fact.

Apparently, therefore, he did not love Marit, because he never felt that way about his wife.

No, never!

He was keenly conscious that at the instant of releasing Marit from his embrace he had felt shame and hatred toward himself and her, as if he had been guilty of something low.

So it did not give him happiness?

No.

Was it anguish?

Yes, anguish, hate, shame.

Love, true love, not provoked artificially by auto-suggestion and self-excitation, love that does not analyse, that knows not the mind but only the heart, such love feels no shame.

If so, then what was it?

The matter was very simple. You, Mr. Falk, are both the accuser and the accused. You are both Mr. Falk and Mr. X.

And so you, Mr. X, accuse me of having lured a young girl and ruined her life?

Wait a bit, Mr. X. Not so fast. You know, *hors la méthode point de salut.*

When I first met Marit a strange, inexorable conviction was borne in upon me that I must possess her; and since I have never had a notion like that before, it deserves special attention.

How did it originate in my mind? I don't know. To be sure, I might ascertain it genealogically, assemble a thousand things that might have evoked it, but that would be mere intellectual sport. For one thing, I know, my brain is fooling me; I am, so to speak, a cicisbeo of my own brain. Therefore I say I do not know the cause that called up this thought. All I can do is characterise it, pronounce it to be exceedingly strong and of a passionate sexual nature.

When did I begin to recognise its sexual character?

One moment, one moment, let me think. I'll remember.

Last year, three days after I made her acquaintance. She was carrying a letter to the post office. I didn't see her or she me until we brushed against each other at the street-crossing. We were embarrassed. Why, why? Ha, ha! In our very embarrassment there was already an element of the sexual. I accompanied her home, then she walked half way back to town with me, and I returned to the garden gate with her. We couldn't separate. I talked a great deal, discussed religion.

Stop! That's interesting, most interesting. Explain to me, sage Mr. X, why did I from the very first try to upset her religious convictions?

You know me. You know I don't care a bit whether a person believes or does not believe, and I rarely speak of my convictions, for the simple reason that I have none.

So, you see, before I could explain what was happening, the sexual feeling was already at work with astonishing logic. So long as her religious faith, it said, is not plucked out by the roots, all my efforts and tricks will be futile.

It was not until a week later, I assure you, that the thought of seducing her first came to my mind. Near the churchyard it happened, on the path over which the weeping birches hang from the other side of the wall, but how, I really don't know. Presently I heard my voice becoming warm and tender, lowering almost to a whisper. It created an atmosphere of inexpressible mysterious agreement between us.

Only then I understood what is meant by "the call of the blood."

From that time on it grew in me, steadily, giving me no peace — and so it happened. But what difference does it make? There is a sort of inner excitation fermenting in me that bursts through every hindrance put upon it. Why? I do not know.

Ha, ha! I know you, Mr. X. The subject interests you. You would like to solve this brain-racking riddle.

Ah, you don't know how easy it is to solve riddles.

Explain, for example, what causes the menstrual flow in women.

You don't know? Why, woman herself, of course.

" Why ? " you ask.

Nothing easier. Didn't the first living substance inhabit the bottom of the sea? Now, as you know, the influence of the moon upon the sea is very great causing the tides. This influence upon the surrounding medium naturally extends to the living beings in it and is transmitted to the succeeding generations in the form of a very definite sign. Finally, by means of a colossal evolutionary series, it reaches down to man. *Quod erat demonstrandum.* Ha, ha! You don't like it?

But consider carefully. All logical and scientific proofs are in a greater or lesser degree just as valid as this very lucid explanation of mine.

Falk looked round. He seemed to see the editor saying

contemptuously: "Perhaps you believe in the fourth dimension?"

Listen, sir. You are an intelligent man of sane, positive views, a rationalist, a materialist; but until you prove that between me and you at this moment — at a given moment — there are not a thousand other beings — until then I shall not cease to admit the existence, not only of a fourth, but of a thousandth dimension.

The fact that you don't hear or see or smell or feel it is no proof. There are, perhaps, a thousand sensations in us of which we haven't the faintest inkling, but which will come out in the course of time.

Then why haven't they come out in the course of millions of years?

Ha, ha! Millions of years seem a tremendous length of time to us, but in relation to eternity are a mere mathematical line, which, as you know, has no real existence. However, let us set that aside. You shall not cease to be a man of great intellect in my eyes. You could very well serve the Lord God as a shovel for stoking men's brains.

Falk began to feel a peculiar tiredness. His thoughts twisted.

He looked up — the white monastery walls.

Marit, Marit!

Why did the monastery walls remind him of Marit?

Now, editor, explain why I suddenly thought of Marit. Explain, you the man who know, understand, and are able to explain everything scientifically.

You can't? I will.

I abhor monasteries, because it was the monastery that spoiled Marit's soul. And so every time I see a monastery I am set athinking of her. Were I to behold a million monasteries, Marit would always rise to my mind.

Anyhow, go to the devil! You're an ass!

But strive as he would to silence himself, to think and dream, to wear his brain out with all sorts of hair-splitting, nothing came of it. Athwart the mist of his thoughts and the chaos of his emotions there shone more and more brilliantly the one feeling — Marit, Marit!

Suddenly he trembled. Would a normal man think that way?

He walked on in a fever. Terror beat in his heart like a fiery hammer. He seemed to be falling down a bottomless pit. Then he stopped thinking. Nothing remained but a miserable sensation of fear before that terrible emptiness and darkness. Everything was so dark and hopeless. Again a thought leaped up in his mind — before him was life, with hellish longing and agitation, with the hot ferment of creation and destruction.

And why? Why all this? Why torture himself? Why all these efforts directed to one thing, the satisfaction of his passion?

He laughed contemptuously.

Wasn't it like a madman to torment himself so?

A diseased, hitherto unknown fear gripped him. In a whisper he put to himself the same question over again: "What for? For whose sake? Why? Why?"

Suddenly, in the hallucination that he was being pursued by a wild beast, he jumped across a ditch, but instantly recovered himself.

"I must think calmly, soberly. It will dissipate my excitement."

And so he was a tool of something, of some will that he did not know, but that was active in him, did with him whatever it wanted according to its own ideas and plans. And his brain had to co-operate, performing the function of an auxiliary — for example, deceive somebody, conceal the true culprit from somebody, lead somebody on a wrong path.

If, for example, he should seduce Marit, it would not be his fault, not at all. He would be acting under the compulsion of the unknown X in him.

Isn't it so, Mr. Falk? Somewhere in the unknown a mighty chain was forged, link joined to link, not to be sundered. Or somewhere a clock was wound up with wheels that must turn so and not otherwise.

And so I am still struggling with myself, still defending myself. But I shall have to yield, I shall have to yield.

A deep sense of misery moved him. Why this torture, why this misery? He could no longer struggle, had to let his hands drop at his side. Then happen what may — or, no! — what was fated would happen.

Fate, Fate!

Now he lost his last remnant of strength.

But like a rainbow after a storm he saw the little face of his Janko, and his soul filled to the brim with homesickness.

He was passing the landrat's house. The editor and the young physician were just leaving.

"Ah, Mr. Falk, where did you disappear to so suddenly?"

Falk was a little flustered.

"I had to take Miss Kauer home. The coachman was drunk. I couldn't leave her alone with the rascal."

"What do you say to our having another bottle at Pflaum's?"

Falk hesitated. Then felt again the clutch of that diseased, unreasoning fear always lurking in wait for him.— Only not to remain alone by himself. No, no!

"With the greatest pleasure, gentlemen."

CHAPTER X

THOUGH so late at night, the restaurant was still open.

The editor ordered wine.

"I am glad," he said, "to have made your acquaintance. But it seems to me you generalise too much and exaggerate."

"I know. I did it intentionally. Everything has a thousand sides. Every object is a stereometric figure with a multitude of facets. It cannot be envisaged as a whole. Seen in different lights it wears a different aspect. Moreover, the light falls on only one of its facets, so that in forming a judgment, a man can merely turn his attention to that one surface, or, at best, to two or three adjacent surfaces."

Falk gulped down a glass of wine.

"What does forming a judgment mean? How can we judge of anything beyond mere externals, like the struggle for a livelihood, for example? A purely intellectual judgment is a rope made out of sand. To express any opinion is impossible, I believe, but if I am asked to, well — then —. At any rate, to take whatever I say as absolute is futile. I merely give my personal experiences of one thing or another. I do not pronounce final opinions."

"That's metaphysics, Mr. Falk," said the editor. "I don't understand you."

The physician, who had been listening attentively, took it into his head to tease the editor. Falk had such a knack for chaffing.

"What is your opinion of the Socialist state of the future?" he asked in imitation of the editor.

The editor blinked suspiciously, scenting intent in the question.

"I said what I thought at the landrat's. However, I may add that Socialism interests me only in so far as it touches art. From that point of view I am in perfect accord with all the dreams, illusions, phantasmagoria that have been born, and may still be born, in the human brain. Once there is collective ownership, the artist will enjoy possible means of existence equally with the rest of the human kind, and will then be able to devote himself serenely to creative work. On the other hand, all those who take up art for the sake of gain, or out of laziness, or simply because they cannot find any other suitable occupation, will be happy when general equality and a six-hour day's work will enable 'iem to get positions in shops, offices, and so on. Then none will be artists except those who are called."

The editor, suspecting raillery in Falk's every word, gave an annoyed laugh.

"The further you go, the worse you get, Mr. Falk. You seem to have no great opinion of artists either."

"Of course not. They are almost non-existent. Those endowed with the divine spark quickly lose it in the compulsion of carrying their talent to the market." Falk grew serious. "To my mind no one is an artist except he who creates only under the irresistible urge of volcanic eruptions, who writes not a single word that is not a live, pulsing organism wrenched from his heart — and then —"

He smiled quietly at the editor's puzzled expression.

"Are there such people?" the physician asked in surprise.

"Yes, there are. But they are damned — *poètes maudits,* ridiculed, derided. And the crowd calls them fools. Ha, ha, ha!"

Falk went back in his mind a moment.

" Yes, yes," he continued, " I saw one of those tremendous geniuses going to rack and ruin in poverty — my schoolmate — the best man I ever knew, sometimes refined, sometimes coarse, sometimes gentle, sometimes rough, sometimes like bronze, sometimes like dark wood, but always beautiful. He was capable both of boundless love and Olympian disdain.—

" But, oh, hang it, let's drink, or the wine'll dry up.—

" Yes, he was a wonderful man. I remember when still a schoolboy he wrote the most improbable stuff on how to honour heroes after their death.

" Can you guess what he thought was the highest form of honouring dead heroes? "

" Well? "

" The greatest honour to a hero, he wrote, would be if peasants were to plough up his remains in the field and some shepherd were to make a pipe from, let us say, his shinbone and play songs on it composed in his honour.

" Wars, he once said, perform one of the highest cultural functions. The bodies of fallen warriors make far better manure than hypophosphates.

" I admit it's coarse. But then nature is coarse, too. Granted it is a cynical joke. But nature, too, plays cynical jokes on the human race."

The editor was offended.

" I am sorry Mr. Falk thinks we are not fit to be serious with. Aren't you carrying your quizzing too far? "

" Why, no, nothing farther from my thoughts."

" Then you are simply expressing your peculiar personal notions which from another person's viewpoint are at best only paradoxes."

Though irritated, Falk tried to control himself.

" My opinions, convictions, views are of significance to me

"My Darling Ysa:

"I am verily drunk with love of you. I long for you insanely. Nothing in the world interests me except you, you alone.

"Do you love me? Ah, tell me, tell me you love me.

"How will I find you when I get back home? Am I still your great, beautiful lord?

"Why was your last letter so sad?

"Ah, how everything is tugging me to you! What a thirst I have for you! Oh, if only you were near me now!

"And I, am I the same to you as you are to me? Light, air, life? Now I know for certain — my one law, my one dogma is, that without you I cannot live.

"So love me, love me more than you can; no, no, love me only as *you* can. For you, my only one, can love.

"I will write a whole library so that you may have what to read. I'll be your clown that you may laugh in moments of sadness. I will fling the whole world at your feet, will compel it to honour and extol you as my queen. Love me.

"In two days I shall be with you without fail.

Your husband."

After sleeping Falk read the letter over and changed the two days to five days, then carried it to the post office.

CHAPTER XI

FALK and Marit stopped, slightly embarrassed. From the road he had caught sight of her at the lake and went down to meet her.

" I have keen eyes, haven't I ? "

" Yes. I didn't think I could be seen here."

Silence.

The day was drawing to a close, the air was sultry, the sky overcast.

They seated themselves at the water's edge. Falk turned his gaze upon the smooth surface of the lake.

" What a wonderful hush on the lake. Only once before I've felt a hush like it — a super-hush."

" When ? "

" When I was in Norway — it was on the fjords. Oh, it was wonderful ! "

Silence again.

Marit was extremely uneasy.

" How did you get home last night ? "

" Oh, very well."

Conversation started and halted, and started and halted again.

" How sultry it is ! " Falk observed. " It's much cooler indoors."

They turned toward the house.

Falk made an effort at a more intimate tone.

" I spent the most delightful evening of my life yesterday."

Marit was silent, every now and then throwing him a scared glance.

Falk understood, but her tacit resistance annoyed him. To-day he must make a finish. It was inevitable, he felt, yet he was too faint to overcome her resistance.

He must muster up his strength. Oh, he knew himself well. The very second glass would do it. A strength of purpose knowing no obstacles would then leap up in his soul.

"Have you anything to drink in the house? I've swallowed such a lot of dust."

Marit brought a bottle of wine.

Falk drank it off quickly, then stretched himself in the arm-chair and fastened his stare upon her.

Marit did not dare to raise her eyes.

"What's the matter? Have you committed a crime, or what?"

There was profound sadness in the look Marit gave him.

"Be kind to-day. Don't repeat what happened yesterday. I suffered so the whole night. Oh, what a terrible man you are!"

"Really? Do you really think so?"

"You mustn't laugh at me. You have robbed me of everything. I cannot pray any more, because I keep thinking of what you told me. I think with your thoughts. You have removed all my shame."

"I can go away."

"Oh, no, no, no, Mr. Falk. Only be kind — do what you want — only not that. Don't ask that of me."

Her face was so tragic that Falk involuntarily felt compassion.

"Very well, Marit, I won't. Only don't say Mr. Falk. Call me Eric. We are so near each other already. Our relations are so intimate. Will you call me Eric? Yes?"

Falk stood before her.

" I will try," she whispered.

" Because you see, Marit, I love you to insanity. Whole days I roam from place to place thinking of nothing but you. At night I cannot sleep. What am I to do? I keep drinking, drinking, only to quiet myself. I stay hours at a time in cafés with those simpletons, listening to their vapid talk — it gives me almost physical pain — then when I leave I feel the same distress, am just as desolate. I know, I know, darling, it's not your fault. I'm not reproaching you. But you are ruining me . . .

" I know you would do everything for me — ha, ha! — except only one thing, the one thing indeed that is the sure proof of love.

" You may repeat that you love me a hundred times, yet I will not believe it; because love is either real love knowing no limits, no petty shame, is blind, unreasoning, neither high nor low, with neither sin nor merit in it, strong and great as nature itself; or — but there really is no " or." There is only one love. That love recognises not religion or shame. It stands above all the prejudices that fetter mankind. The rest is only whimsy, a palliative for boredom. Ha, ha, ha! "

He stopped before her and laughed his Satanic laugh.

" My dear child, I wanted an eagle to soar aloft with me to the heights of my solitude, and I found a tender, delicate, timid dove. I wanted a wild, proud lioness, and I found a rabbit always afraid of the gaping jaws of a rattlesnake.

" No, no, don't be afraid. I won't do anything to you."

Marit burst into sobs.

" Don't cry, Marit, don't cry. I'll go crazy if you cry. I didn't want to hurt you. But everything in me thrills and urges me toward you, my only, my beloved."

Marit continued to cry.

"Don't cry, don't cry, my darling." He dropped on his knees and covered her hands with kisses.

"Don't cry." He caught her in his arms, kissed her eyes, stroked her face, and more and more passionately caressed and clasped her radiant little head.

"My only, my darling, my, my —"

And she pressed herself to him, flung her arms about his neck, and their lips met in a long, wild kiss.

Finally she broke away.

Falk rose.

"Well, now, everything is all right. But just smile a little, smile."

She smiled.

Falk grew animated. He kept drinking, and told anecdotes, and joked more or less successfully, then fell abruptly into silence.

A dulness and heaviness hung in the room. They glanced at each other solemnly, breathing heavily.

It grew dark. The maid entered and called Marit out.

Falk looked after her a long time. He felt a cruel, rapacious desire, with a severity and relentlessness in it as in a rolling stone, which, though it knows it will drop into a bottomless pit, yet obstinately keeps on rolling.

The darkness in the room thickened. Dense clouds covered the sky. Each minute the sultriness became more intolerable.

Falk got up and paced the room, deep in reflection.

"Won't you come in to dinner?"

He took her arm and drew her close.

At table they held a stubborn silence. Conversation, notwithstanding Falk's attempts to keep it up, broke off and always had to be started afresh again.

They returned to the drawing-room.

After long pondering Falk said:

" Don't be angry with me, Marit, if I stay here later than usual to-night. A storm is coming up. Besides, I can't sleep. It frightens me to be alone — eh? — I'm not in your way, am I? "

Marit seemed to take fire.

For some time they sat in silence. Everybody had gone to bed. It was as if the whole household had died out. In the dull, stifling hush before the storm they could scarcely breathe. The tick-tick of the pendulum almost caused them physical pain.

" Aren't you afraid to be alone in this huge, empty house? "

" Sometimes I'm dreadfully afraid. I feel so lonely, as if I were the only human being in the whole world. I'm ready to sink through the earth with fright."

" But to-day you don't feel lonely? "

" No."

There was a long oppressive silence.

" Marit, have you still got the poems I wrote for you last spring? I'd like to read them."

" They are in my room upstairs. I'll get them."

" No, Marit. I'll go up with you. It is much cosier in your room. I myself am afraid of something here. You know in what a state my nerves are."

" But somebody might hear us going upstairs."

" Don't be afraid. I'll walk so quietly that no one will hear me. Everybody is asleep anyhow."

She still refused her consent.

" Don't be afraid, my sweet, my darling. I won't do anything to you. Absolutely nothing. I'll sit quite still and read my poems."

There was a clap of thunder.

"Very still. And when the storm is over I'll leave without making a sound."

At last they entered her room. He locked the door. They stopped on the threshold as though caught fast. The very air seemed to be panting and coiling itself round their bodies in live rings.

Suddenly Marit felt herself swept up in a mad, thirsty embrace. Her eyes flashed with all the colours of the rainbow. And in her soul she felt the mad joy of an insane dance over a precipice.

She flung her arms about his neck, hurled herself blindly into the abyss of sinful delight.

Suddenly she started away in fright.

"No, Eric, for God's sake — only not that!"

Her bosom rose and fell. She gasped for breath.

Falk released her from his embrace and came to himself. A long silence.

"Listen, Marit," he said coldly and sternly. "Now we'll separate. You see how cowardly you are? It's a shame to withdraw now. You are a rabbit, my dear, and I am a kind man. I'm a kind, soft-hearted man. You haven't the courage to tell me, 'Go, Eric, go and leave me my clean conscience. Leave me my useless, stupid virginity.' No, you haven't the courage to say that. I'm stronger than you. I'm a man, and therefore I go. Good-bye.

"I'm going away. I leave you your religion, your chastity, that absurd Catholic chastity — ha, ha! — your clean, tranquil conscience. I'll deliver you from so-called sin — yes, sin is what your Catholic eunuchs call the most beautiful thing in the world . . . be happy, be very, very happy!"

The storm grew fiercer.

Every moment the window lighted up with greenish zigzag flashes.

Falk turned to the door.

" Eric, Eric, how can you be so cruel, so cruel? "

All the pent-up, long-suppressed torture in her soul suddenly burst in a great storm of weeping.

" Eric, Eric," she cried, choking and gulping her sobs.

In a blind panic Falk caught her in his arms.

" Marit, Marit, I won't go away. I'll stay with you. I haven't the strength to tear myself away from you. It was only a momentary flash of insanity. I thought I'd be able to leave you. But I can't, I can't. I'll never desert you. Marit, my sun, my only happiness."

A great clap of thunder tore the heavy curtain of the air and rolled in the sky in immense reverberations.

Falk's breast was full of an unwonted tenderness, profound, passionate. He took Marit in his arms, rocked her like a child, fondled and caressed her, whispered ardent words of love, all oblivious of everything else in his life.

" I'll give you such happiness — such happiness —"

The rain beat in torrents against the window.

Now they were alone, all alone in the whole world. The rain, the thunder, the tempest cut them off from the rest of humanity. Marit pressed herself close to him.

" How good you are, how good you are, Eric! And you'll never leave me, will you? We'll be happy."

" We'll stay together forever and be happy," Falk said mechanically.

That cruel, rapacious something suddenly sprang into his soul again, that rolling stone moving downward into the pit.

He pressed her with prodigious force and passion.

They heard not the thunder, they saw not the lightning. All round them began to dance and whirl and blend, finally, in a madly careering, gigantic fiery ball.

Falk took her . . .

One suppressed cry, then a gurgling and groaning of insane bliss.

The storm ceased. It was already four o'clock in the morning.

"Now you must go away, Eric."

"Yes, I must."

"Go by way of the lake, then climb over the monastery wall, and you'll be on the road. Else you may be seen."

Half way home he was caught in another rainstorm. He ought to take shelter somewhere, he thought, but felt too weak to look for a place. Besides, what matter if he did get a bit wet?

Huge black clouds lowered in the sky again, closing in nearer and nearer to the earth.

A long-drawn, awful peal shook the welkin, the lightning split the sky in two.

Another thunderclap, flashes of lightning one after the other, and a downpour as if the clouds were precipitating themselves on the earth.

In an instant Falk was drenched to the skin. He scarcely heeded it.

Of a sudden he saw a gigantic sheaf of fire tear loose from the sky and divide into seven flashes. That same moment the white willow by the roadside was enveloped in flames. The lightning had rent it from top to bottom.

Life and destruction.

Of course. Where life is, there also must be destruction, annihilation.

Marit, yes, Marit was ruined.

In Falk's mind suddenly flashed the blinding thought that it was he who had ruined Marit.

Why not? I am nature, therefore I create life and destroy it. I pass over a thousand corpses because I must, and I create life also because I must.

I am not only this one I. I am also you and he, God, the world, nature — and something more whereby I know what you are, eternal stupidity, eternal mockery.

I am not a man. I am a superman . . . ha, ha, superman! He burst out laughing at the fantastic word. Yes, a superman, a cruel man devoid of conscience, but great and good. I am nature. I have no conscience, because nature herself has no conscience.

Superman! Ha, ha! It was a sick laugh.

Superman! Ha, ha! He went on laughing his sick laugh.

Out of the black sky he saw a fiery column tear itself loose and divide into seven flashes and on its way kill a dove. And it will divide again into a thousand flashes and kill a thousand doves and rabbits, and so it will go on forever, giving birth and killing.

For such is the will of Fate.

For I must do it.

For my instincts demand it.

For I am I. I am a criminal, diabolic nature.

And on this account I am to torture myself?

Ridiculous!

Does the lightning know why it destroys? Can it choose its course through the air?

No. It can only know that it struck in this or that spot, that it destroyed this or that object.

I, too, know, and am entering the fact in the records, that I destroyed an innocent dove.

The atmosphere was so permeated with electricity that a sea of fire seemed to be hovering in the air.

Falk walked on, enveloped in the mighty storm — he

walked and thought. He walked like a mysterious, formidable power — like a demon sent down upon earth, a demon with a whole hell of torments for scattering fresh creative destruction.

He stopped at the ditch. It was running full of water. If he walked round it, he would come out on the road. A little more or less wetness, what was the difference now? Yes, nothing mattered now, nothing, absolutely nothing.

So he forded the ditch. The water reached to his shoulders.

At home, after undressing and going to bed, he fell into a delirium.

CHAPTER XII

FALK awoke at noon. He was too weak to lift his head. It seemed to be weighted down with lead. Rainbow-coloured sparks danced in his eyes.

At last he raised himself up and tried to think, but still could not come to himself.

Something terrible was stirring in his brain — something he had to say to Marit.

What?

He did not know.

But it was something, and he had to go and tell it to her.

At length, with a great effort, he succeeded in getting out of bed.

He must, he must tell her something!

"Probably," he thought, holding back a moment, "this is only from a diseased imagination." Nevertheless, he must, he must go to Marit, he must.

He rose and sat down again, letting his bare feet touch the floor. The coolness of it was somewhat refreshing.

Ah, how pleasant! A little air in the open and he would recover. But what time was it? He looked at his watch.

So late, so late! Out of doors the air seemed to be fresh. Had there really been such a storm the day before? Or was it only a dream?

His clothes lay on the floor in a muddy puddle.

That excited him, but he quickly quieted himself down.

"Mother hasn't been in here yet, else my clothes wouldn't be lying there still," he reflected.

On the table stood an uncorked bottle of brandy. After drinking a whole glass at one gulp, he gradually recovered his full strength and dashed into fresh garments. The flood of energy streaming back almost made him cheerful.

Then he stole like a thief to his mother's room and listened at the door. She was not there — apparently had gone to church.

Falk drew a deep breath and felt a sharp, stitching pain in his side.

But now to Marit — to tell her everything, yes, tell her — but what?

"I'll remember on the way," he thought. "Then I can go back to bed and be ill if I take a notion to."

When Marit saw him she started back in fright. Falk had to smile.

"Don't be frightened. It's nothing. I've been feeling badly the whole week, and last night I caught a wretched cold. I had fever last night, ha, ha! Not last night — this morning. I ought really to have stayed at home. I don't know what drove me to come here to you. I can't imagine why I came. Give me some brandy, please."

He gulped down one glass after another.

"It was the hardest thing for me to get up to-day. But even if I had lain on my deathbed, I should have come to you."

Then everything in his brain got mixed up, and he began to wander. After a while he came to himself again.

Marit looked at him in horror.

"Ha, ha, ha! Why do you look at me like that? What terrible thing is this animal which a certain professor took it into his head to call the superman — superman! Oh, save me, Marit, or I'll die laughing. At any rate, this *Uebermensch* is a remarkable maniac. Listen! When I awoke, I remembered nothing of what I had dreamed, of what had been raving in my soul for the past several hours. All I could recollect were the inferences that my metaphysical soul had deduced — ha, ha! — deduced from my dream. One of the inferences was that I must go to you whatever befall. I am ill, perhaps very ill, but I was obliged to come to you."

His strength gave out.

He saw the sheaf of fire again, red fire, which divided into seven forks of lightning and killed the pure, white dove.

Marit was in despair.

"Eric, for God's sake, Eric! You are ill. Go back home! God, God, how terribly you look at me!"

"Wait, Marit, wait a moment. On the road there's a willow lying, split from top to bottom, the one-half of it bridging the ditch, the other half obstructing the road. When I was coming to you — to you — isn't it so, I'm with you, am I not? — What was it I had to say to you? What was it made me come?"

"Eric, my dear Eric, I'll take you home, you're frightfully ill."

She ran out and ordered the carriage to be brought round.

What did he want to tell her? *Had* to tell her . . . dove . . . lightning . . . home . . . dream . . . life . . . destruction. Aha! Destruction!

Ah, to destroy — ha, ha! — to destroy — to destroy!

A savage, rapacious ecstasy filled his brain — a wild, cruel thirst for destruction.

Things began to jump and dance queerly in front of his eyes.

Marit stood before him in her hat and cloak, all ready to go. She was greatly excited.

"Come, Eric, my dear, my only one, come!" She kissed his eyes.

"Once more, once more! Kiss me, kiss me!" he begged like a child.

"And now come, come!" Marit implored, dropping on her knees and kissing his hands.

"My dear husband," she smiled at him. "Come, my husband."

He jumped up abruptly.

"Marit, so I haven't told you yet? Why, I can't be your husband. I'm married already. My wife is in Paris — Miss Perier. You don't believe me? Here, I'll show you our marriage certificate." He fumbled in his pockets.

He came to himself a little and smiled constrainedly.

"God, what black balls are on your face! You are looking at me like a vampire! Don't look at me like that, don't! . . . I'm going at once, I'm going, I'm going . . ."

And he ran out like a madman.

"Here, please, in here. I'm going to drive you home."

"In here? Aha, here?"

Falk seated himself in the carriage.

"But where's my hat? I haven't got my hat." He was holding it in his hand. "That's odd. How did I lose my hat?"

Marit sat in the room stunned, almost out of her mind.

"Now he's gone home — has he gone home? No, no! Ah, he has really gone."

Her brain was a complete blank. And so she had died? No, it was only a dream . . . But no, it wasn't a dream. What he said was not a dream. It was the truth. She saw Falk's face with the diabolic derisive expression. He drank her in with his eyes like a vampire. "Liar!" her soul cried. "Liar!"

At last he had told the truth.

She sat like that almost a whole hour.

And so he is married!

"Married . . ." She repeated it coldly and sternly.

Her soul was as though congealed into ice. Everything in her twisted and turned. Her whole brain seemed to be in the vice of a single thought — married!

Her head was still in confusion.

She jumped up. "Good Lord, how could I have sat so long with my hat and coat on?"

She stopped before the mirror. She couldn't go into the kitchen with her hat on. She should have gone long before — they were waiting for her. She forced a smile.

She entered the kitchen. They were preparing to bake bread. She did all that was necessary, was more active than her wont. Then she returned to her room.

Over the sofa in a frame hung the Lord's Prayer with bright red lettering in Byzantine style. She scanned it attentively.

What a hideous dragon in that M! She read: "And forgive us our sins —"

No, no, wait, Marit.

She sat down on a chair.

No, it was not a dream. There Falk had sat and — what had he said?

"I have a wife!" it shouted in her ears.

Ah, yes, married to Miss Perier.

She crossed to the window and looked out into the garden.

How long the day was, how it dragged. That was natural. The twenty-first of June — the longest day of the year.

She looked at the clock. Five o'clock.

Her brother would soon be coming back from school. She must get his supper ready for him.

A carriage drove up.

"Marit, Marit, Mr. Falk is very ill," her little brother related eagerly. "When Macie brought him home, he had to be lifted out of the carriage. His mother cried and then the doctor came."

So Falk was really ill.

Marit was on the point of telling her brother that Falk was married, but checked herself.

Now the wife would come to the husband — ha, ha! His wife would again nurse her husband who had been ill of nicotine poisoning. She would bear all his whims with the most angelic patience . . . yes, yes . . .

Marit asked not to be disturbed, as she was very tired and wanted to lie down.

Falk was fearfully ill — he had to be lifted out of the carriage — his mother cried . . .

Marit paced the room.

"I must go to him — at once — this minute. He will die."

Her head was splitting. She clutched it with both hands.

"Married, married!" roared in her ears.

"I'll give you such happiness, such happiness — I'll never leave you any more."

She fell into an agony of sobs.

God, God, how he had lied!

Shame and hatred seized her. Every vein in her head seemed to burst with shame and hatred.

What had happened? Had it actually happened? Ah, yes, yes —

She felt how he had rocked her in his arms. His passionate kisses burned her. A convulsive thrill from the fire of those mad kisses shivered through her body.

She threw herself on the bed, buried her head in the pillows.

Ah, to dig out a grave for herself with her own nails! What shame, what disgrace!

It grew dusk. The sun dropped below the woods on the opposite shore of the lake.

Marit listened. She heard a stork snapping its beak. The girls in the vegetable garden were laughing.

Some one was singing . . . Oh, yes, her brother.

Finally she fell asleep.

When she awoke it was deep night.

She sat down on the edge of the bed and reflected. But her thoughts scattered, and she looked mechanically into the darkness of the room.

She was damned. God had rejected her. Now nothing mattered.

She began to think.— Was there anything that did matter, anything she cared for, anything she was not indifferent to? No, everything was so dull and stupid and unimportant.

Falk was ill. But Falk had deceived her, had lied, had promised her happiness, great happiness, when all the time he was married. Now his wife would come and would nurse him and Marit was damned, damned. If she went to Falk, his wife would drive her away like a dog, and she would lie like a sick dog curled up at his threshold. And what right had she to obtrude herself upon him? Ah, no, no, no! There was nothing left for her, neither in this life nor in God's world.

Everything was lost. There was no father nor mother. There was no God either — at least so Falk had assured her. It must really be true. There was no God, because He could not so torture a human being entirely innocent and guiltless . . .

At length she jumped up, stood in front of the mirror and fixed her hair.

God, how thin I've become!

Yes, she had grown thin — but what difference did that make now?

The house was silent as a house of death. It was deep in the night.

That was happiness, infinite happiness . . . he gave me happiness, he gave me happiness . . .

She took her hat and cloak and went to the lake.

She seated herself on the stone. She had called it the Cape of Good Hope when she had awaited Falk there every day.

On the opposite shore was a fisherman's hut. A light twinkled there, a little fiery dot elongated on the dark surface of the lake.

She looked at the long streak of light and on the deep darkness of the lake.

A peasant and his horses had drowned in that hole there the year before.

What difference did that make to her?

She was all, all alone. No one, no one loved her. She was like a dog driven out of doors in the rain and storm.

Now his wife would come and take him away, and she would remain behind alone, all, all alone.

Oh, almighty, all-merciful God, all alone, all alone . . .

Oh, no, no, no! Enough of this torture . . . The end was near.

A terror came upon her. She began to unbutton her dress.

One horrible thought flashed in her brain.

The world is coming to an end, the world is coming to an end. A flood, a flood!

She threw herself forward.

There was that hole, that hole . . .

She ran . . .

A noise and ringing sounded in her head. She saw nothing more, she heard nothing . . .

It's here, it's here!

No, still another little turn — here, here.— She shouted in the water struggling against the current.

Life . . . hole . . . ah, it's happiness.

CHAPTER XIII

IN a week Falk's consciousness returned.

His wife was sitting at his bedside asleep.

He was not in the least surprised to see her there. He scrutinised her face.

Yes, it was she.

He dropped back on the pillow and closed his eyes.

Now everything was all right.

Suddenly he saw the sheaf of red fire that divided into seven forks of lightning.

Marit was evidently no longer among the living.

He fell asleep . . .

END OF PART TWO

PART THREE

IN THE MAELSTROM

CHAPTER I

JANINA looked at Falk long and wistfully. How he had changed of late! As if fearful of some great, impending misfortune. Sometimes he would drop into an apathy lasting hours at a time, all oblivious of his surroundings. What was happening to him?

Ah, he was no longer frank with her, perhaps never had been. To her questionings he either declined to make reply, or put her off with hollow phrases. The signs of sickly nervousness in him frightened her. Sometimes his face would twitch, or his hands jerk, or a peculiar smile would draw his lips.

That smile, sardonic or despairing, he had brought back from Paris. Falk seemed to be coming out of a profound meditation. He rose from the sofa and put several pieces of sugar into a glass.

" Have you hot water? "

" You oughtn't to drink so much. It'll make you more nervous still."

" On the contrary," Falk countered impatiently.

Janina hastened to bring the water.

Falk set leisurely to preparing the punch. He looked at Janina who hovered about solicitously, trying to atone now for having dared to oppose him even for a moment. He was touched and turned very tender.

" No, Jenny, you're wrong. The punch has a soothing effect. Here, with you, I spend my best, my quietest moments. It's so pleasant to sit on this sofa and drink one glass after the other. Yes, I feel good near you."

He fell silent, seemingly engrossed in something widely remote from the present.

" Eric! "

" What? "

" You have changed frightfully since you're back from Paris."

" You think so? "

" You've never been like this before.   You are so nervous, so restless always."

Falk looked at her long but made no answer. He took a drink, looked at her again, then flung himself wearily against the back of the sofa.

" You are wonderfully kind," he smiled gently. " I feel so uncommonly cosy near you."

" Are you telling the truth? "

" Don't you see I keep coming back to you? "

" Yes, yes, but only when you are all worn out. What am I to you? A pillow for your weary head. Oh, Eric, Eric, I don't want to reproach you, but it wasn't right of you to leave me here for three whole years suffering so. And you never wrote me a word."

" Ha! I wanted you to forget me."

" Forget you? Never. No one could ever forget you."

He looked at her long without speaking.

" Tell me, Jenny," he said with sudden animation, " tell me perfectly frankly — was there really anything between you and Czerski? Now be quite candid. You know how I look on such things."

" No, there was nothing between us. We were engaged. That's all. I've told you so over and over again."

" All right. But it's so important to me, and you know how quickly I forget. The engagement must have delighted your brother."

" You know how much he likes Czerski."

" And you? "

"I? My God! I no longer dared to think of you. You had deserted me entirely, and Czerski was so kind to me. What was I to wait for? Besides, I have great respect for him."

"If he hadn't been sent to prison, you would have been a perfectly respectable housewife now. H'm, h'm. It would be interesting to see how the part becomes you."

Janina made no answer. A long silence.

"Did you go to visit him in prison?"

"Yes, twice at the beginning."

"And your brother escaped safely across the border?"

"You know."

"H'm, h'm." Falk rose and took a few restless turns around the room.

"Did they ever speak of me?"

"Who? Who should speak of you?"

"Well, your brother and Czerski."

"Of course. Very often. Why, you sent Czerski money. Have you forgotten?"

"Did they know of our relations?"

"No, I pretended to be cool and indifferent, as if I had never known you. I was afraid of them. They are terrible fanatics, you know."

"So they knew nothing at all?"

"I think not. You didn't speak of me to my brother in Paris, did you? You used to meet him there so often."

"We used to meet sometimes, but almost always talked about propaganda. Oh, yes, once he told me his sister would soon get married. Shortly after he left Paris."

"Now let's drop the subject."

Falk paced the room restlessly again.

"Listen, Eric. You never longed for me, did you?"

He smiled.

" Sometimes I did."

" Only sometimes? "

Again he smiled.

" Haven't I come back to you? "

" Yes, you have come back. But you don't love me."
Her voice shook.

" I love nobody. But I longed for you sometimes."

He glanced at her. Her face expressed suffering, and he
thought: " Next she's going to cry."

He sat down beside her.

" Listen, Jenny, I mustn't love. I hate those whom I
must love."

" Have you ever loved? "

" Only once, and then I hated at the same time, and my
hate was greater than my love."

" Don't let's talk about it."

He suddenly grew serious, distressed by the thought of
his wife.

" No, no, when a man begins to love he loses his freedom.
A woman penetrates everywhere. You have to remember a
thousand details. You must be her sweetheart, share a
room with her — the last, however, is not so essential — in
a word — you understand — I must be free. Any sensation
that ties me down even the least little bit stirs my hatred
and makes me vicious and ill-tempered."

He took her hand and stroked it gently.

" It's astonishing, Jenny, that you should love me so."

" Why astonishing? "

" My heart is so cold, so cold . . ."

Janina swallowed her tears.

" I love you just as you are. I don't ask anything of
you."

"That's good. That's why I feel so comfortable with you."

He lapsed into a long silence, then, as though catching himself, said:

"What do you think? Do you think I'm capable of loving at all?"

"Maybe you once were."

"But what if now — you understand, now — I were to fall in love with a woman so that she would mean my Fate, awful, momentous Fate . . ."

Janina gave him a frightened look.

"You understand me? If I loved a woman so that I could not live a single minute without her?"

Her eyes opened wide in a blank stare.

"Don't look at me that way. Don't behave like a child."

"Eric, tell me, tell me everything. What's wrong with you? You think I don't see that you are suffering, concealing something?" Tears returned to her eyes.

Falk replied with sudden animation:

"I don't understand why it bothers you so. I am not hiding anything from you. I am perfectly frank. It's a long time since I've been so peaceful and cheerful. I can't even bring back to my mind the suffering I've gone through. No, no, sometimes a wild desire comes over me to make mock of people, to torture them, and I do it with downright gusto. I feel an unquenchable thirst for love, but I feel love strongest when I torture the people who love me. Ah, my dear child, if I only wanted to, if I didn't have a little pity, you would see to what rack I would put you — just to feel your infinite devotion in my torture of you. I could tell you improbable things; for example, that I am married and have a legitimate child, whereas yours is illegitimate. Can't you appreciate an instinct of that sort? But don't take it all too much to heart. My mind is not always in order."

But he could not reassure Janina.

"Oh, no, no, Eric, dear. I understand it all very well. That is not what is really going on in your soul. I know the difference very well."

She mused.

"Tell me straight out — maybe it's Czerski that's troubling you."

Falk started.

"Czerski? H'm. I shall probably have to go through a good deal of unpleasantness with him."

"Why?"

"Well, I suppose I exaggerated. But still . . ." He broke off abruptly.

They fell silent.

"Czerski spent a year and a half in prison?"

"Almost."

"Odd that he should have been set free just now."

Janina looked surprised.

"Why odd?"

"Did I say odd? I must have been thinking of something else. But what was it I meant to say? . . . H'm. . . . Evidently Czerski is taking things hard. Of course, I feel for him. He's a strong man, bold to the point of rashness. I suppose now he has become an anarchist altogether? Well, well. Listen, Janina, did he cry when he found out?"

"No, he was perfectly calm. He said he was prepared for it, only blamed me for not having been open with him. Then he took Eric in his arms and asked after his father."

"You told him who the father is? — Well, of course you did. Why shouldn't you? Ha, ha! I have no reason to be ashamed of having helped to bring such a splendid citizen into the world out of non-existence. Ha, ha! Don't look at me so scared. Sometimes this nervous laugh catches me unawares. That's because I am fagged out. Ah, life is not so easy as it may seem to you in your childish, or, rather, girlish levity . . . Laugh, laugh. I said something funny."

Janina did not laugh. She looked straight in front of her, thinking sorrowful thoughts. That angered Falk.

"Why are you so dismal? It's as though an evil fate were pursuing me. Wherever I go, people put on funereal faces. They seem not to be able to behave differently in my presence."

Janina was frightened. It was a long time since she had seen him in such a temper. However, he controlled himself.

"Is little Eric well? Of course he is. What right has he to be ill? But you are still weak evidently. H'm, it's not so easy to give birth to a child."

He looked at a sketch hanging over the bed.

"You drew that with me, do you remember? It was fearfully hot. You were wearing a red cotton blouse, and when you bent over . . . ha, ha, ha! . . . that was the beginning of the end. . . ."

Janina gave him a long, sorrowful look.

"How happy I should be if I had never known you."

"Yes? Why?"

"I don't know.—And then, O God—there was a time when I was so happy with you, infinitely happy."

"Then what's the matter?"

"I'm afraid of you. I don't know who you are, I don't know you at all. I can't tell what you are doing or think-ing. Our relation has lasted ten years already. A long, long time! I wasn't fourteen years old yet. And you and I lived together, too, for a good while. Still I know nothing, absolutely nothing about you. You are terribly unfrank with me. Sometimes you seem to be speaking mechanically, without knowing what you are saying. But there's one thing you can't hide from me — you are dreadfully, dreadfully unhappy. That's the one thing I'm sure of. How I should like to pierce through and through you, penetrate your whole being and find out what is happening in your soul. The thought that I shall never be able to drives me crazy. You don't love me. You yourself say so openly. Yet I cannot resist you. I crave for you, feel I am your slave, a weak, pitiful creature, without a will, without a mind. What is your power? What is the secret of your strength?"

Falk smiled mysteriously.

"I possess a will that's stronger than yours."

"Maybe you would love me if I were stronger, if I did not yield so readily to your diabolic influence."

"On the contrary. Then I should *not* love you."

"Why?"

"Because I cannot tolerate another will against mine."

He stepped over to the window and stood there atremble, struck by the mysterious stillness of the night.

"Is it always so quiet here?"

"Yes, at night."

He looked down at the spacious asphalted yard. On all four sides large six-story houses, a regular prison-yard; opposite a light in one of the windows.

He sat down and sank into thought.

Then he said:

"Strange that your brother — what's his name?"

"Stephen."

"Oh, yes, Stephen. Strange that Stephen succeeded in getting across the border and poor Czerski had to take enforced rest. I suppose the police searched your apartment, too?"

"Yes, but they didn't find anything."

"H'm, h'm. I'm sorry that Czerski — he must have loved you very much."

She made no answer.

Falk looked at her a moment, then suddenly jumped up.

"I'm going now."

She looked at him imploringly.

"Don't go, don't go. Stay with me to-day, just to-day. Do."

Falk was upset.

"No, Jenny, no. Don't ask me to, don't ask me for anything. I want to be free. It's best for me to come and go as I please. Don't tie me down."

Janina heaved a deep sigh.

"Why are you sighing?"

She burst into tears.

That irritated Falk, but he sat down again.

She controlled herself with a great effort.

"You are right, Eric, go, go. It was only a momentary weakness. I was so worried about you. I shall not annoy you again." Her voice shook.

Then followed a long, gloomy silence.

"Is little Eric asleep, eh? I'll see him to-morrow. I'm coming here to-morrow or day after to-morrow." He rose.

"Do you receive letters from Stephen?"

"Rarely."

"Queer that he didn't know anything about our relation."

"How could he have? When we lived together, he was in America."

"Ah, true, true. Funny how I forget. Good-bye, Jenny. I shall probably call again to-morrow."

CHAPTER II

FALK had gone but a few steps on the street when he encountered Czerski.

They stopped and stared at each other in hard silence.

"You don't seem to recognise me," muttered Czerski through his teeth.

"I have the pleasure of speaking to Mr. Czerski, I believe. Delighted. But what do you want of me?"

"You'll find out directly."

"Yes? Very well. It's such a fine night we might take a stroll together, though I confess I should have preferred to be by myself."

They walked a stretch without speaking, while Falk made a prodigious effort to control his inward commotion.

"Tell me what you want of me."

"Ha, what I want? Nothing. But you knew I was a friend of Janina's."

"Indeed? I did not and still don't. That is, it was not until to-day that I heard of it, with half an ear, so to speak; and not as anything positive either, just as a surmise that you and she were almost engaged."

"Very well, let us say 'almost' engaged. But that doesn't concern you. Janina had the right to choose between you and me."

"Of course."

"Yes, she had a perfect right to," Czerski repeated and broke off.

A long silence fell.

"Now listen," Czerski suddenly cut into the quiet, "you have a wife and child."

A tremor went through Falk, and he stopped.

" What business is that of yours, hang it! "

" What business is it of mine? Very much so. I'm not referring to your having spoiled my whole life. My feelings have nothing to do with this matter. But you disgraced a woman I love profoundly. Yes, you disgraced her. Society is so organised that when a married man seduces a woman, the entire shame falls on her. And I ask why you, a married man, disgraced Janina."

Falk broke into a cynical laugh.

" Why, why? One of the questions, my dear fellow, to which there is no answer. An old question, as old as the world, and never yet unriddled. Why did I seduce and disgrace Janina? — That's the way you put it, I believe? — The very question I've asked myself a thousand times."

' Czerski looked at him fiercely.

" You dirty scoundrel! "

Falk laughed good-naturedly.

" We are all scoundrels. Or maybe *you* are not a scoundrel? However that may be, you are insufferable. If I weren't so tired, I should be pleased to slap your face. Go to all the devils! "

" Don't play off that chivalrous nonsense on me, please. You'd have to pay dearly for striking me. But listen. I am under certain moral obligations to Janina. So I want to know what you propose to do. Or, no, I'm not interested in what you propose to do, because you are to do what I propose."

Falk stopped and looked at Czerski in supreme astonishment, then burst out laughing.

" Tell me, Czerski, did you lose your mind in prison, or what? It wouldn't be surprising. On the contrary. Ha, ha! The most natural thing in the world for a man's mind to give way in that frightful solitary confinement. You were kept in solitary confinement, weren't you? What! I am to do what you propose? I? I? Ha, ha, ha!"

"Yes, you. You will have to do what I propose, what I order you to do."

"Ha, ha, ha! You are delicious. I like you. Well, what is it you order me to do?"

"Marry Janina."

"But you know I'm already married. Ordering me to be a polygamist! You surely must have lost your mind in prison."

"You are to divorce your wife and marry Janina."

Falk, dumbfounded, let a whole minute pass before answering.

"You certainly are crazy," was all he found to say.

"No, I am not crazy. I have thought it over a long time. I can't see another way out. You must do it or I'll make you. Your wife will put no obstacles in the way. After finding out that you have a mistress, I doubt whether she will want to live with you."

A delirium of terror overwhelmed Falk. Making a supreme effort he succeeded in taking a few steps more, then stopped from the weakness in his knees, stared at Czerski speechlessly an instant or two, and moved on again, wearily.

"Who is going to tell her?"

"I am."

"You? Why do you want to tell her?"

Falk cleared his throat and struggled to master the fearful tumult of his feelings.

"That's the only way out."

"It isn't. I won't do it. I swear to you by whatever is dearest to me, I won't do it. You cannot compel me to."

He spoke seriously and calmly.

"The only thing you'll achieve is my wife's misery and mine. You have thought out everything very well. You are right. My wife *will* drop me the moment she learns of Janina. I don't doubt it for a moment. But as to the result, you are mightily mistaken. I shall never in my life marry Janina."

"Why?"

"Because you cannot force me, I want you to know. Go ahead, tell my wife, spoil her life and mine. But, I repeat, I give you my word of honour, Janina shall never be my wife. You will accomplish nothing except to bring my vengeance down on yourself. I shan't be choice either in my methods of revenge. I like the words of the ancient Jehovah, 'An eye for an eye, a tooth for a tooth.' Listen. You belong to the Social Democratic Party. But the Party no longer trusts you. You are considered an anarchist — to a Socialist, you know, no better than a police spy. You have been in prison. Ha, ha, ha! What does that count for? A trifle, of no significance to a single Socialist."

Czerski looked at him in surprise. Falk laughed maliciously, though boiling inwardly with rage and excitement.

"You know, Mr. Czerski, I am the president of the Central Committee and enjoy the unlimited confidence of the Party. Since the Party knows very little about you, an enemy of yours would have no difficulty in creating general distrust of you. As it is, you are already under suspicion. Yes, yes. It is Kunicki's work. You remember you were so simple as to move his expulsion from the Party on account of his silly duel. So listen." Falk stopped and glanced sidewise at Czerski. "Ha, ha! You are greatly interested. Ha, ha! Quite natural that you should be. Now, then, listen. If they ask me about you — and in all likelihood they will turn to me for information — I need say only a single word — not even that — I need merely lift my brows, shrug my shoulders, nod. . . . In Party life that is more significant than a thousand words — you understand?"

"That would be vile!" shouted Czerski in a rage.

"Why?" Falk gave him a cold, contemptuous look. "Why? I don't know you. I am under no obligations to you. True, I sent you money for a propaganda tour. Even there the facts are against you. You didn't succeed. You made several attempts to smuggle literature across the border. The literature was always seized and so you only made further attempts impossible. What is more, during the last period of unemployment in Silesia you were so careless as to urge the workers to violence, that is, you played the rôle of the typical *agent provocateur.*"

Czerski looked ready to pounce on Falk. Falk smiled disdainfully.

"Don't be so furious. I feel infinite confidence in you. There's no man I'd rather trust. Only I wish to make it clear to you that in a given case I can wreak vengeance."

"You're a low-down rascal."

"So you've said more than once. I reply by returning the honourable epithet. My advice to you is, don't get so angry. By losing your self-control you only lose your advantage over me. There were moments when I thought I should drop down right here on the street, I was so struck by your threat. Now I am perfectly calm, and the balance is in my favour. Besides, you are careless in your utterances. For example, you *order* me, *compel* me — a manifest absurdity. You know you can't compel me to do anything.— Part company now? — No, we can have a perfectly quiet conversation. If you admit that the matter is as important to you as to me, then I can walk a little further with you."

" I don't want to have anything to do with you," Czerski hissed.

They were standing under a light. Falk became serious.

" There you are. You demanded an explanation, and now I have a perfect right to demand that you hear me out quietly."

" I have already told you everything."

" Can't you see your idea is an insane one? You are not looking well. You must be ill. I saw you two years ago at the Congress. I can observe the difference in your appearance.—Can't you understand it is madness to try to carry out your plan? What will you gain by it? Nothing, absolutely nothing. You'll only force me to do something low. Ha, ha, ha! You are a poor psychologist, Czerski. You feel embarrassed with me. Eh, am I right? Don't think I mean to ask a favour of you. Go on with your plan. I shall be pleased to see that you can carry out a scheme you have undertaken to the finish. Up to now I have not observed that ability in you. Besides, hang it all! I must add, you are a perfect fool."

Falk burst into a long, sardonic laugh, stationing himself in front of Czerski, who looked at him with an almost crazed expression.

" Did you really think that I, Eric Falk, would traduce you to the Party? You've got yourself excited about nothing."

Falk drew his brows together and seemed suddenly to relax completely.

" I'm not even a member of the Central Committee. I got sick of your Party, as sick as you've made me with your plans, your resolves and stupid notions of truth."

Czerski felt as if he had come out of a nightmare.

" So you don't love Janina ? "

Falk looked at him in surprise.

" No."

" Then you behaved like a vile skunk. I never expected it of you. I had profound respect for you. There's no one for whom I felt sincerer respect than you and Janina's brother Stephen."

Czerski sank into deep thought.

" I'm sorry, genuinely sorry," said Falk, " that I've obtruded in your life in this way."

Czerski interrupted.

" You mean to keep on living a lie? Fooling your wife? "

Falk took him in with a look of cold astonishment.

" My dear fellow, must you assume the rôle of judge and pass sentence upon my crime? Absurd! I don't justify myself to any one, least of all to you. But enough of this, more than enough. Do what you like. You are a very strong man, one of the few, perhaps, who cannot be called scoundrels. It's a great pleasure to know a decent man. But now, the devil take it, good night." Falk was intensely wrought up. " Go to bed, Mr. Czerski, or to all the devils, even to hell . . . Once more, I repeat — go to bed."

Czerski threw him a contemptuous look. A policeman passed and scrutinised the two men sharply.

" Go to bed! " shouted Falk.

He turned away and disappeared slowly round the corner, his strength almost completely gone from him. In the past he had always succeeded in mastering himself. Now he was in a frightful state. A cold sweat beaded his forehead. Speeding his pace up to a run, he kept going until completely exhausted.

" Misfortune is coming, advancing upon me surely . . . Nothing will save me now. Somewhere on high the wheel has been set in motion and nothing will keep it from turning. Yes, yes — clearly — nothing will keep that silly fanatic from carrying out his crazy design."

Falk wanted to grasp the immensity of the danger impending, but his brain was too fatigued. Only one painful thought thrust its sharp point into him, that soon he would be crushed, all undone.

A woman passing by jostled him. Two students were following her.

Dogs, knaves! God, how dirty and repulsive it all was! The devil take it! How dirty! What idiocy to stake your whole life upon five minutes of animal pleasure! A whole life? He laughed scornfully. What sort of a life? To stake a few minutes upon a few other minutes . . . ha, ha, ha! . . . One woman replaces another woman. *La reine est morte, vive la reine!*

He stopped and peered ahead as though blinded. Gradually, however, he began to distinguish the gigantic proportions of the Central Railroad Station. Round about he heard the whistling of the locomotives and the trains creeping slowly like serpents. Clouds of pungent black smoke filled his eyes and nostrils. He crossed the bridge to the other side. As far as the eye could reach spread the even roadway dissected by a network of shining rails lighted up by red, green and white lamps.

He saw countless fires, saw the signal lanterns, and continued to look at them until all these vari-coloured lights flowed together into one huge, rocking, flaming rainbow, or, rather, a gigantic sun in all the colours of the rainbow.

CHAPTER III

RETURNING home Falk found Ysa lying half dressed on the bed reading.

"At last you've come!" She rose and went to meet him. "I was homesick for you."

Falk kissed her on the forehead and sat down.

"Lord, how tired I am!"

"Where have you been?"

"In the restaurant with Iltis, so aptly named."

"Well?"

"Nothing."

"How pale you are, Eric!"

"It's nothing. Just a miserable headache."

Ysa sat down beside him, took his head in both her hands, and pressed lingering kisses on his forehead, hair and lips.

"Why do you stay away whole nights now? It's horrid to be left here all alone."

Falk looked at her and smiled.

"I must emancipate myself from you."

"Why?"

"Well, in case you should bowl me over."

"Ah, you!"

She embraced him still harder.

Falk rose, made a few turns about the room, then stopped, and looked at her with a smile of unwonted sadness.

"What are you thinking about, Eric?"

"You are so beautiful, so beautiful, Ysa."

"The first time you've observed it?"

"Ah, *I've* observed it before. Only after four years of

274

living together it strikes me as remarkable that you should seem just as beautiful as the first day."

She beamed at him.

"You know, Ysa, our life together has been very happy."

"I can't tell you how happy I've been the whole time and how happy I am now. It is a sense of happiness so full and deep that I fear it might not last. I know it's nonsense, just a woman's silly doubts and dreads. You love me, I am sure of it, so I needn't worry. Even if I felt like it, I couldn't be unhappy, not even when you are so nervous and away from home whole days. Do you know, Eric, I'll confess to you, sometimes it's pleasant for me to stay at home alone. Then I can sit still and think of our love, our happiness."

She fell silent. Falk walked to and fro in the room looking at her with a quiet, searching look.

Ysa spoke again.

"Your love is so big, so beautiful. I often think that I am the first and only woman you have ever loved. I know no other woman exists for you, and it makes me so proud. Maybe you don't understand that feeling."

"Oh, it must be a very pleasant feeling."

She looked at him with a quizzical smile.

"Tell me, Eric, tell me. You've never looked at any other woman like, like . . ."

"Like what?"

They laughed.

"You know yourself like what. I believe in the New Testament there's something about a look that bares a woman naked more than the grossest contact. Ha, ha, ha! . . . But I'm not doubting you. I'm so confident of your love."

"Confident? H'm, are you really so confident?"

Falk smiled enigmatically.

"There's nothing I'm surer of."

"H'm, h'm. Then you must have unbounded trust in me."

"I have, else I shouldn't be so happy."

Falk looked at her long and intensely.

"What if some day I were to betray you?"

She laughed.

"You wouldn't even if you felt like it."

"But if I should."

"I know you won't."

"But suppose some extraordinary circumstances made me take a false step, you understand? Circumstances under which a man is not responsible for his misdeeds."

Ysa looked at him in alarm.

"Queer that you can even assume such a hypothesis."

Falk laughed hoarsely.

"I *haven't* betrayed you, that's clear. Yet we can look at things from a purely hypothetical point of view. As a writer it interests me, you know."

"Well?"

"Listen, Ysa, sometimes I simply hate you. I've often told you so. I'm capable of hating you to the loss of my reason. I hate you because I love you so, because my thoughts are only of you, because there isn't a minute that you don't stand before my eyes."

"That's the very reason I love you so." Ysa kissed his eyes.

"No, no — wait, wait — Both my love and hate of you are troublesome. I should so like to be free of you. You know, to love is a great misfortune . . ."

He rose and began to pace the room restlessly.

"Do you grasp it? Can you understand it? Sometimes an impulse, an overwhelming desire comes over me to forget this torture — and a desire to have a pillow on which to lay my troubled head. Ha, ha, ha! — A pillow! Merciful heavens! A pillow may be a terrible tragedy."

His laugh distorted his face.

"What was I going to tell you?" He searched his mind. "Oh, yes, for example, suppose I know a woman, met her, let us say, ten years ago, a woman who gave herself up entirely to love, lives for love alone, I go to see her thinking of nothing, quite mechanically, simply because I happen to recall her existence in the world. Well, I find her at home. You cannot imagine how happy that makes her. She is simply not herself from superabundance of happiness." He laughed nervously. "Listen.— You look like a curious high school girl now.— But listen. Ha, ha, ha! Iltis, a specialist in these matters, you know, once told me there are moments when every woman is beautiful. That's true. Just think! I see a woman lighted up with the wondrous splendour of happiness. I quiver with desire. For me she is transformed into some other being. She ceases to be her own self. In her eyes is the radiance of that design of nature, terrible in its eternalness, to create a new being — ha, ha, ha! — that the existence of Mr. Falk may never end."

Falk broke off, his lips twisted with pain.

"Well?"

"Well? For God's sake! how can a man be held responsible? He doesn't know what he does. His very consciousness is untouched."

Falk rose and continued gravely:

"Man differs so little from an animal, just by a mite of reason, merely enough to be able to realise an accomplished fact. In the soul there may be a tiny sore spot the existence of which he has never suspected; then the sore becomes inflamed, the tiny spot grows to gigantic proportions, the trifling disturbance turns into an insane *idée fixe* and masters the whole soul. Here, for example, I see a drop of blood. Suddenly from an extraordinary combination of circumstances, I see whole streams of blood, no, a great sea of blood, a muddied clod of crushed human limbs running with blood. That's the way Garshin died — ha, ha, ha!"

He looked at Ysa in strange alarm, and burst again into a laugh that had a ring of great fear in it.

"Ysa, Ysa! There's terror in your eyes."

"No, no. Only you were so frightfully in earnest. Your eyes opened so wide — there was terror in your eyes, too."

"Terror, terror? Do you know I'm actually afraid of this strange man in me. Yes, there's something strange in me, something I don't know, and it fills me with mortal terror. Ha, ha, ha! Queer, how I always feel like laughing this way now — but wait, Ysa, I haven't finished yet. So I keep looking at the woman. She seems marvellously beautiful. Suddenly there springs up a curiosity in me, a passionate desire to possess the deepest mystery of her life."

"Well, then what?"

"Ha! I forget everything. I cease to be myself. That other, that strange man awakens in my soul. Ha, ha! And I possess her! Isn't it terrible?"

"Terrible, terrible."

"What would you say if it actually happened to me?"

"Eric, Eric, don't speak that way. I won't listen to it. Once something like it occurred to me and I thought my mind would go."

Falk looked at her in surprise.

"When? When?"

"I really didn't think of it. It simply flashed through my brain like lightning."

"But when, when?"

"Do you remember when you were at your mother's and fell sick there? A girl drowned — but what's the matter with you? You look so frightened. You turned so pale."

Falk stared at her with almost the last remnant of his self-control gone.

"Ha, ha, ha! Well and what did you think then?"

"You know, the thought of it now still frightens me."

"Simply because we're telling weird tales. But go on — what did you think then?"

"I was sitting beside your bed. I hadn't slept for three nights. I was awfully tired and dozed off."

"Well, go on, go on."

"Suddenly I awoke. You were sitting up in bed looking at me with the most fearful eyes, a host of phantoms peering out of them."

"I don't know anything about it."

"How could you? I myself am not sure it wasn't a dream. But I had a peculiar sudden conviction that that girl had drowned herself on account of you."

"Ysa, Ysa, have you gone out of your mind? You know she drowned while bathing. How could the idea have occurred to you?"

"I don't know. I can't account for it. I was frightfully fagged out. Your mother told me you and she had been together most of the time."

There was tumult in Falk's soul.

"It's strange that you could have thought such things of me."

"I couldn't rid myself of the notion. Never have I suffered so. A terrible certainty sprang up in me that if it

were true, then I must leave you at once.   I should not have
remained with you a single instant."

Falk looked at her terror-stricken.

"So you would really have left me?   You would?   That
very moment — that very moment?"

"Yes."

"Of course.   That's understood.   I've always known it.
While you were telling me this, my Fate seemed to be speaking in your voice, my Fate, awful, cruel."

"Your Fate?"

"Don't be frightened.   It's just that there's something
of Destiny in your voice, something prophetic.   When you
and I met, I didn't know you loved me, but your voice
sounded your love.   You speak differently from every one
else.   Just now your voice again revealed the terrible future,
the fate that awaits me.   How can I explain it?"

He paced the room with hasty steps.

"I am peculiarly convinced that you would not have hesitated a moment.   You would have left me without pity or
compunction."

He laughed.

"But why are we talking all this nonsense?   It is nonsense, isn't it, Ysa?   Ha, ha, ha!   And how is my precious
son?"

"He was very restless.   He carried on furiously and
screamed, and when I asked him what he was screaming
about, he said, 'I must scream, I must.'"

"Peculiar."

Falk continued pacing the room agitatedly, up and down,
up and down.

"An extremely nervous child, a future genius, evidently.
All geniuses have hot heads and cold feet, Lombroso says.
Ha, ha, ha!   Janko could afford to have a superfluous part

cut out of his brain. You know, Ysa, I believe there's a superfluous bit in every human being, and if it could be removed, then we should be *sicut deus,* as the most glorious of the gods, Satan, promised."

He laughed again.

"Ysa, a genius is a remarkable beast. Look at me. Perhaps you don't think I am a genius. I assure you, I am the genuine genius."

"You're silly, Falk."

"Well, let us assume I am a tremendous genius. To every five million people there are four hundred and ninety-nine million cretins and idiots. Therefore upon me as a genius devolves the deep moral obligation of improving the human race."

"In what way?"

"The only way there is — by begetting the largest possible number of children by the largest possible number of women."

"But once you proved to me, circumstantially and conclusively, that the children of geniuses are idiots."

Falk laughed with a show of spontaneity.

"You have a phenomenal memory. Yet it would be extremely interesting for our Janko to learn the individual peculiarities of his excellent father from living specimens. You'll agree that of a hundred children of mine by a hundred different women each one would be likely to inherit at least some of the unusual qualities of which I am proud, and so all of my remarkable qualities would be preserved."

"You're maundering, yes, you're maundering, my dear Eric."

She smoothed his face, kissed his eyes, and began to undress.

"Good night, Ysa. I'm going to write to-night."

" Stay with me to-night.   I don't want to be alone."

" Don't be a baby.   Our conversation will make a whole chapter for my new novel."

" All right.   Kiss me."

" No.   No kissing.   I must write, and my lady knows that kissing drives away thinking . . . Good night."

CHAPTER IV

FALK went into his room. He seated himself, clasped his head in both hands and drew a deep breath.

Vanished completely was the air of calm which he had made such an effort to preserve in Ysa's presence. He was plunged again in a flood of anguish and terror. A sharp gimlet seemed to be boring into his brain. The end of the world had begun, he was going to dissolution.

He jumped up and sat down again. He could not think.

All round him was sinking, bursting, collapsing — a frenzied orgy of annihilation.

In the oppressive closeness of the summer night he felt for moments as though he were drawing breath from lungs that had no air.

Opening the window, he recoiled in terror.

That sky, that terrible sky. He saw the stars in their astronomical remoteness. They seemed to be racing, breaking away from their places in the heavens, hurling into infinity, and shining and burning with a light that never was, like great blotches of gangrene on the bluish firmament. And that sky, that terrible sky — it seemed to be alive, to breathe, to palpitate with woe and despair, the unending despair of hell.

Perspiration stood out on Falk's forehead, his eyes opened wide and started from their sockets. For a minute — an eternity — his mind was void of thought and memory.

Then his whole life passed before his eyes, one period after another swiftly filing by, so vivid, so terrible, so harrowing. One act of destruction after the other. Once before had he seen his life that way, when he blasted the pure dovelike soul of Marit. My God, Marit, Marit! That hideous bootless murder!

He came to himself and smiled sardonically.

The devil take it, have I gone out of my mind? Or am I the prey of senile impotence? What have I to do with Nature's crimes? What! Must I plague myself because Nature, the accursed criminal, has chosen me as her instrument? No, no. God knows I don't want to suffer any more. Enough.

He grew heated.

Honoured and highly respected public — it would give me inordinate satisfaction to spit in your face — but that was only parenthetical — ha, ha! — Well, highly esteemed public, do you hear? Yes? Listen then. For I bring a new gospel. I will teach you to trap Nature in her fatuous cunning. I'll teach you to watch her hands when she performs ridiculous but successful somersaults. Listen. I'll explain all her card tricks. Hear me, because I bring you deliverance from the claws of Satan-Nature, a new redemption.

Hearken, hearken unto my new gospel. In the beginning was Nature, wily, evil, diabolic. She is great, you have been told, awful, indifferent, cold, proud, neither good nor evil, neither gold nor dross. A lie, highly esteemed public, a foolish lie. Nature is wicked, fiendish, lying, crafty. Ha, ha, ha! My highly esteemed public opens wide its mouth, so wide that a hay wagon and four horses could drive through. A shrewd fox is Nature, a malicious devil. What am I? Do you know? Does he know? Of course, of course. Your individualists, wise people, slapping their chests and shouting "I am I"— oh, *they* know! Ha, ha, ha!

I don't know what I am. Who am I? Whence did I come? Whither am I going? Ah, how terrible it is!

Terrible! Isn't it, Ysa? You alone can see this thing in its dread unfathomable depths. My actions, I feel, are the result of certain processes in my sex organs. And so it happened. What happened — what was perpetrated? Disaster, disaster. Hee, hee, hee! Listen to Satan laughing. Who perpetrated it? I? I? Who am I? What am I?

In his wild despair Falk approached the brink of insanity.

I didn't perpetrate it. How could I check what had been preparing in me for years, only awaiting the occasion to break into freedom and eject its all-destroying lava? Did I know what was in me? Could I keep a certain glance from piercing into my soul and conjuring up forces of whose very existence I was ignorant? And because that strange unknown thing in me produces unhappiness, must I suffer, bear the reproaches of a dull, heavy conscience?

No, lovely Nature, try your tricks on other people. I know your cunning ways too well. No, no, you're not going to torture me to death.

He filled a large glass with brandy and drank it off.

Czerski had thought it out wonderfully well. He'd simply go to Ysa and say in the calmest, most natural tone: " Mrs. Falk, your husband is a scoundrel. He has enriched his genealogical tree by another branch, an illegitimate one. You will agree to a divorce, of course, so that your husband may marry the girl and both genealogical lines be equally legitimate." Ha, ha, ha!

But, my excellent, though tedious Mr. Czerski, I didn't even dream of providing myself with two equally legitimate genealogical lines.

Nevertheless, I'll inform your wife so as to free you of the eternal lie. Like Tolstoy and Björnstjerne Björnson, I am fighting for the truth. I live to rid the world of falsehood.

For heaven's sake, Mr. Czerski, what nonsense! Both those gentlemen were suffering from senile impotence. Truth becomes falsehood and crime when it spells somebody's ruin. Can't you realise how happy I myself should be could I go to Ysa and tell her everything? Can't you see how cruelly I'm suffering? In this case truth would be tantamount to crime, fiendish crime. Yes, Mr. Czerski, crime, because it would destroy both Ysa and myself. Can you possibly be so obtuse as not to comprehend that in this instance truth is madness, ruinous folly, and no one would be the gainer?

Our thick-skulled philosophers, of course, cannot see it that way. And misfortune is pressing on. I smell it round me already. Ysa? Yes, Ysa will leave me, I am as sure of it as of death. She'll simply slip away — no, she will shake hands good-bye. Perhaps she won't, because my connection with the other woman is an insult to her. So she'll leave me.

What then?

God, what then!

He racked his brain as though to find the philosopher's stone, and drew nothing from out of the chaos dancing in his head. Each line of thought snapped before he came to the end of it.

Utterly faint he dropped on the couch impotently.

There was no doubt of it — that strange thing in him which he knew not, but which perpetually cropped up to the surface, had cut his legs from under him, had ruined him.

Falk, with all his wisdom, or, perhaps, because of his exceeding wisdom, had been ruined by the strange course of circumstances. But the ruin of Falk was a very different thing from the ruin, for example, of that sweet little Marit who drowned herself because she did not appreciate the great good fortune of becoming the mother of a genealogical branch of Mr. Falk's.

My thoughts are coarse, like a peasant's. But this coarseness brings misery, and for me misery turns into happiness. Besides, if I fall into the pit, I, with my reason, can control that fall from point to point, can make scrupulous note of each degree of descent.

Ha, ha! Now, after having torn Nature's mask from off her face, I still have the task of settling with my conscience, though, as a matter of fact, I no longer have a conscience. I have succeeded in overcoming it.

Mr. Czerski, you dull fanatic of truth, would you know why? Would you know? Then open wide your eyes and ears that you may perceive the full unfathomable depth of your stupidity. Listen to a wise rational man who has torn Nature's mask from off her face.

Nature is destructive. Very well. Perfectly agreed. Isn't it so? And in pursuit of her object of destruction she utilises various means, among them the so-called forces of nature, lightning, tempest, waterspouts, landspouts, and so on.

With equal satisfaction she also uses bacilli, those remarkable inventions of the devil.

Thirdly — no, go to hell! — no thirdly. I'm not a dry classificist. I'm a philosopher, and I omit the dreary enumeration of Nature's countless instruments of murder compared with which the most refined man-inflicted torture is an innocent amusement; and I pass on to the main theme, Man.

Man! Ha, ha, Man! Allow me to moisten my throat with some brandy and a dose of nicotine. Then I'll get right down to our theme. Now, then, Man. *Homo sapiens,* according to Linnæus, is a self-existent automatic apparatus provided with a registering and controlling clock-mechanism in the form of a brain.

Excellent!

But listen carefully. This is a continuation of my new gospel, of my work of redemption.

Nature began to be ashamed of her inane, purposeless murders. Nature is shrewd and cunning. She wanted to shake off the blame for her revolting crimes. So she gave man his brain.

Do you know what the brain is?

An ugly apparatus that cannot be put to any practical use. At best, all it can do is register, or, rather, affirm, the occurrence of something in the soul. But what? That it never knows.

The brain is always duping, deceiving, and never discovers its own deception until too late. It is only after the event that the brain perceives and says to itself, " Aha, cunning Nature has played a trick on me again."

But that's not all.

Closely connected with this nasty apparatus called the brain is something else, aptly named the conscience. Ha, ha! Fancy, Mr. Czerski, a curious beast trained by accursed Nature in the course of ages to impose torture upon man for the crimes committed by Nature herself.

Ha, ha, ha! Keen reasoning that! But it isn't all yet.

The brain has been at great pains to hammer into man's head that the possession of knowledge and a conscience is an unusual advantage and gives immense superiority over the creatures that are lacking in knowledge and a conscience.

Very keen, isn't it? For what's the difference between man and beast?

Man knows he is aping, the beast doesn't. The whole difference, Mr. Czerski, the whole difference. Ha, ha, ha!

See how stupid you are. You set yourself up on a pedestal, read sermons on nobility, insist upon my marrying a woman by whom I, through God knows what chance, begot a son. Isn't it absurd? If that doesn't make you laugh, then tickle your heels.

Falk gave concentrated attention to what was passing within himself. He laughed nervously. Gradually he began to disentangle the knotted thread of his thoughts.— And so man was endowed with a brain that he might understand Nature, render her thanks, bow before her might. Infernal knavery!

Listen, Mr. Czerski, prick your ears so that you get what I tell you. Isn't it the height of the ridiculous that the one distinction between man and beast is the possession of a brain, a conscience, that rubbish heap for Nature to dump her dirt on? The most laughable thing of all is that I, pitiful man, must be thankful to Nature for her tricks. The devil take knowledge and conscience. I don't want to be a man. I prefer to change into a microbe. If a microbe destroys, at least it doesn't suffer, or feel pangs of conscience.

Ah, that wise professor what's-his-name, oh, yes, Nietzsche! Ha, ha, ha! Nietzsche! The poor professor wanted to create a superman. The unhappy creature would probably have perished from a plethora of conscience and intellect the very day after birth.

Falk saw himself on the stage. So far from being daunted, he was pleased to be there, desiring to attract attention. He assumed the pose of a great man — or, no, not a pose — the rôle of great man came natural to him. And the audience waxed ecstatic over the great man who could be so simple and *aimable*.

Ah, you dull-witted audience, if only you knew what a risky path I tread merely to laugh at you and point the finger of scorn at every step. The dear audience, saved by sheer chance from being a herd of unreasoning cattle! God, I'll die laughing.

Suddenly he shook from head to foot. A great dread, like an evil black bird, swooped down on him, put out steely claws, and choked and strangled him.

But what could happen, the devil take it! What? What? What? — Ha, ha! What? Czerski would wring his neck — that's what would happen.

Now be serious, Falk.

I must prevent it. I have no time to lose. My hour has not yet struck, not yet. I must keep Czerski from his mad design — I must explain the whole matter to him, convince him with strong, logical arguments that he is mistaken in throwing on me the responsibility for what a certain power altogether outside of me did. It's absurd, eminently absurd. If you want to punish lying, Mr. Czerski, don't punish it in my person, but in the person of Nature, which functioned through me. It is not until after I have destroyed that I recognise the event. I am no more to be held responsible for my action than the microbe that eats your lungs.

Yes, I must convince him, must explain everything to him. Maybe he'll give in. Falk cleared his throat. He saw Czerski's face and figure as in an hallucination. Queer it didn't upset him. An interesting phenomenon.

Now I am a hundred per cent. better than an hour ago, I assure you.

He drank down a glass of brandy.

You are losing patience, Mr. Czerski. Don't be surprised that my explanation is dragging on so. I shall have to touch upon things horribly distasteful to me. That's why I am in no hurry.

Why do you frown? Aren't you interested in this sort of psychological problems? To dig into my own soul and other people's souls is a genuine passion with me. A soul is like a rubbish heap where one may come upon something unexpected. So, you see, my dastardliness, as you were pleased to call my noble conduct, was the result of a sort of psychologic curiosity, a kind of curiosity that distinguished the liberal bourgeois savant, Hippolyte Taine. You know, of course, he was a professor who conducted a factory for the production of bourgeois virtues. An ingenious idea, isn't it, to manufacture virtues just as we manufacture copperas. Ha, ha! But such is our liberalism, and humanitarianism — human inanity . . . These gentlemen liberals, what is it they don't know? But sit down, please. I see your knees are shaky. Will you have a cigarette, a glass of brandy? Ha, ha! Of course not — you don't smoke or drink. Walking on ethical stilts, you can't. Take care you don't trip. You are a philanthropist, soaring to unattainable heights of human virtue; and to sustain the style you scorn cigarettes and whiskey. Ha, ha! Don't frown. To me, you see, a man able to do without cigarettes and whiskey is an unintelligible creature, a square circle. No, speaking seriously, by not using alcohol, you are sinning against the organic law of compensation.

I see your startled look of query. Why? Why? H'm. Why? It's as clear as the sun. Primitive man, or, in other words, man without brains, that is, simply *Homo,* not yet become *sapiens,* is subject to sudden inspiration, ecstasy, prophetic vision, and so on. This prophetic vision strangely approaches insanity, which to-day, in our liberal-philanthropic-democratic society, is cause for putting such prophets in lunatic asylums. However, that's aside from the question. The point is, that these elemental outbursts are a mighty force. It is this force that gave rise to our culture, it is this rectilinear fanatic blindness that urged the people on to Jerusalem, that brought about the religious wars, stormed the Bastille, achieved the constitution, erected barricades, and last, but not least, guaranteed immunity to the pirates of the press. Don't frown.

Can't you grasp the significance of that inspired ecstatic power which enabled Samson to destroy a whole army of Philistines with the jawbone of an ass and impelled Ravachol to throw bombs and despatch some dozen pious souls to the bosom of Abraham?

You smile, Mr. Czerski? The Socialists, it seems, have some ground for suspecting you of anarchistic sympathies.

To return to our subject — that power which springs from inspiration, that outburst of elemental spiritual force which creates and destroys worlds, is an element in human life essential to its very existence, and yet it is lost to us to-day. The sober mind of the proper well-fed bourgeois has blighted it. But we, Mr. Czerski, we dwelling on the loftiest summits of humanity must preserve the sacred flame of inspiration. But how? Simply by pouring alcohol down our gullets. There's Suvorov, for example, a wise man. He knew it. Before every battle he allowed his soldiers to drink all the whiskey they wanted to — yes, whiskey, of course. And then they performed wonders of bravery.

Stuff and nonsense, you say? Evidently you have that very brain of the liberal-democrat which dethroned the all-wise, mystery-revealing God of the ancients. Ha, ha, ha! Thought is a product, like phosphorus, or the secretion of the kidneys . . . but I see you are genuinely bored. So I'll pass to our main subject, really the sole subject.

Pardon me for being so long-winded, but my heart is so heavy.

I am a married man. Happy? No. Unhappy? No. Well, then?

Maybe you'll have a drink of brandy. Excellent for the nerves. It dispels that feeling of depression, heightens your vitality, in fact, strengthens your whole organism.

You won't? Oh, yes, I forgot, you strut on stilts.

Well, here's to your health!

Falk took a drink. H'm, h'm. Deucedly unpleasant for me to talk to you about this.

He strode up and down the room in great agitation.

Have you ever reflected on the brain-racking problem the name of which is Man? No, evidently not. You are an anarchist; which means you are heir to the liberal brain that evolved materialism and eudemonistic ethics. Yes, yes. You have inherited that view of the world which — but hold on — do you know this passage in St. Augustine?

" And the people go and marvel at the high mountains and wide stretches of sea and the falls of the mountain torrents and the oceans and the courses of the heavenly stars, but forget about themselves."

The proper liberal bourgeois mind, you see, forgot Man. Now, in order to rediscover Man, we must forget the discoveries of natural science, we must restore the child's mind to which everything in the world looms awful, mysterious, fathomless. We must learn all over again to shudder with awe.

Ha, ha, ha! What an idiot! You are right to look at me with that disdainful smile. How else could you look at me, you adherent of the materialistic conception of the world?

You have found the key to all the riddles. You have torn off the curtain from all the mysteries — well, well, don't be angry, Mr. Czerski.

You really don't want a drink? A pity, a pity — to tell the truth, I'm not fond of teetotallers.

You are interested, would like to learn some intimate details of that mysterious Falk who sent you money for propaganda and wrote proclamations stirring up one class of society against another. *Provocateur* — ha, ha! — the official name for it. But it's not of myself that I wish to speak; it's of quite extraneous, so-called objective matters. Ha, ha, ha!

Has it ever occurred to you how a trivial circumstance may effect a radical change in a man? Yesterday, for example, I was at Iltis's. I am fond of him and should like to know his soul. He married. His wife is a beautiful woman, a wonderful woman. Well? Disaster. She could not have told beforehand that within two or three years she would become his wife. How could she have foreseen that there was a man in the world like Iltis? Before ever meeting him, she fell in love. Why not? Why not give yourself to the man you love? It's so natural. You cannot find fault with her for not having secured official sanction.

Logically she did quite right. But inasmuch as every woman exists only for the last man and that last man resents past encroachments on his wife, I admit Iltis's wife did not do well to give herself to another man first.

And Iltis . . . but, by heaven, I myself don't know whether it was Iltis. Maybe it was somebody else. Let us call him a certain somebody. Not bad — excellent! — We'll call him " Mr. Certain."

Mr. Certain falls in love with a woman who has already tasted of the forbidden fruit of the tree of knowledge, that famous apple of paradise, and marries her. She tells him everything, of course, and he — a man standing upon the very pinnacle of present-day culture, the leader of the most desperate Bohemia — a trifle, of no significance to him!

But gradually, gradually, Mr. Certain starts thinking. A tiny, scarcely perceptible wound in his soul opens and he sits up surprised, no, he lies down on the sofa — and keeps thinking, thinking . . .

So a man has already possessed his wife? A man has caressed her with the same words of tenderness and desire? And those endearments whispered in his ear — she has murmured them to another, has pressed her body in voluptuous embrace to the body of another? . . .

By a thousand devils, what is this? It hurts so, it hurts so . . .

Falk jumped up in terror.

That insignificant little wound seemed to blaze up into a whole hearth fire of gangrene and spread the fearful ache all over his soul.

Nonsense!

Mr. Certain is furious that such a thing, serving, no doubt, some mysterious purpose of Nature, has the power to excite him so. He assures himself it is sheer madness and the next minute has forgotten it. Just a tardy demand of his sexual organism, no more; and he is even delighted to have wrenched it so energetically out of his heart.

Stretching out on a sofa Mr. Certain whistles a tune — but *mit den bösen Mächten* — ha, ha! — you know Schiller.

A peculiar uneasiness comes upon him again, a savage, nagging curiosity. So he goes to his wife, is uncommonly affectionate, kisses her hands, fondles her face, talks to her about this and that, and then, *en passant,* as if he were broaching the most ordinary matter, asks, " How about your first husband, was he dark or light? " unconsciously injecting a mixture of hatred, curiosity, spite — call it what you please —

into the tone with which he pronounces the word " husband."

" He was dark, but had blue eyes."

Mr. Certain trembles. He cannot speak. He cannot comprehend what is happening to him.

Ha, ha, ha! Poor Mr. Certain I admit he is silly, ever so silly. But is it his fault? He has strength enough left to try not to think about the thing any more and succeeds in putting it out of his mind, when suddenly the tide turns and sweeps back with even greater force.

Now it becomes almost a delight for him to plague himself by scratching the sore that has begun to heal. He renews the examination of his wife, questioning her most delicately and tactfully, of course, so that she should not guess what is ailing him. How he thirsts to learn each detail, yes, Mr. Czerski, each of those detestable details.

So in a cursory way, from purely psychological interest, he inquires into the intimate circumstances of their relation. Bit by bit he finds out whatever it is possible to extract. Why should she conceal anything from him — from him who spoke so beautifully of the freedom of love — ha, ha! Both of them, besides, are so cultured that they had done with sex prejudice long ago.

Did she love him? She pondered. Oh, yes, she loved him, a good deal, in fact. Mr. Certain is all atremble, yet succeeds in governing himself. And the trifling details? Well, they are always the same, she laughs. He laughs, too, of course, then asks her to go into the minutiæ — from purely psychologic interest, mind you. These things are always so extremely interesting. Besides, if he learns the most intimate secrets of her heart, she will become closer and dearer to him. She hesitates; in the end, however, she tells him everything. And so the dark man implored her

to give him a concrete — ha, ha! — a beautiful demonstra-
tion — of her love! — asked her for *It*. Observe, Mr.
Czerski, the delicate allegoric phraseology I shall use in
telling my story.

She understood what "It" meant. That mystical It,
you know, is the one concrete proof of love.

A bluster of sound issues from Mr. Certain's throat — a
wheeze, the devil knows what — which he quickly turns into
a coughing spell.

So the dark man asked her for It, though advising her
to consider well before taking such a step. Think how wise
and noble was this dark man.

"As for you — you, of course, didn't deliberate about your
first It?"

Mr. Certain, observe, is a true psychologist.

"No, I felt it was going to happen. There was no use
thinking. It was inevitable."

"For whom? For you or for him?"

Mr. Certain quivers inwardly with rage, with a mad desire to shriek — shriek out his lungs. Why? He himself
knows not.

Not quite grasping the full meaning of his cynical query,
she looks at him with — you know — with eyes like a question mark, incredulous, distrustful and slightly contemptuous.

But Mr. Certain has already mastered himself — her suspicion was almost aroused — now he'll be warier.

So affecting an air of carelessness he continues to inter-
rogate her, cautiously, and finally — he knows everything.
The dynamic mechanics of love are always the same — moments of perfect equality for lord and peasant alike. Ha,
ha, ha! . . .

The cup runs over. Mr. Certain has an overwhelming

impulse to fling himself upon this woman, hurl her to the ground, trample on her, beat her to death with his fists.

Well, did he?

How can you ask, Mr. Czerski? It remained an impulse. Mr. Certain was too rational to translate it into action. Ha, ha! . . .

Oh, excuse me, Mr. Czerski, I didn't get you. I see now. You as a philanthropist asked why Mr. Certain should have had that impulse.

Why? To speak truly, he himself did not know why.

It would all have been highly comic had it not been so tragic.

The tiny sore in Mr. Certain's soul spreads rapidly. It is like a monstrous growth sending a million thin long roots down deeper and deeper into every cell of his being. Ha, ha, ha!

Why does he laugh so unpleasantly? Confound it, don't you know a man can die laughing?

Mr. Certain's delightful sensation expands infinitely. His imagination is stirred to its depths, and puts forth growths as luxuriantly as a virgin forest, turns pliant and inventive as Edison's brain, as sharp and venomous as an Indian's poisoned arrow, as patient in mental labour as Socrates, who stood barefooted a whole night long under the open sky unaware of the snow falling. Don't you think Socrates was posing a bit?

Mr. Certain draws a mental picture of the final details. She and the dark man were sitting in the room. He locked the door and tested it to make sure it wouldn't come open. She was combing her hair — Ysa was in no hurry, you know — then began to unbutton her waist slowly, the while he waited, all aquiver, looking at her with thirsty burning eyes . . .

Not a bad picture, eh?

Or, *passons d'une autre côté.* Mr. Certain looks at his child, and quick as a flash comes the thought, " By what miracle did she escape having a child by the dark man? " This question, the possibility of her having been a mother before belonging to him, brings him to the verge of insanity.

Or he reads a foolish novel about a woman who loves for the first time and gives herself with all the heat of untried virginal passion — ha, ha! Why wasn't he that first one?

Or he inspects her former photographs. So that's the way she looked before ceasing to be a girl — or after? Evidently before. And for whole hours at a time he examines the portraits diligently, loving her in them, loving her with a great ache. He is enraptured, bows to her, prays over her in an agony of rage and despair. Why — why didn't he get her pure as she was in those pictures, not knowing sin?

From this rough sketch you will have convinced yourself, Mr. Czerski, that Mr. Certain's psychologic state was not an enviable one.

Mr. Certain completely loses his balance. Eager to tear out the poisonous growth, he merely succeeds in pulling up a few bloody roots. Too late. There is no escape now from those terrible images and apparitions. Rage seethes in his soul, hatred of the woman darkens his reason. Contact with her becomes insupportable, that dark man always rising to his eyes. His soul is as if covered with wrinkles and gone grey. At the same time he is drawn to his wife with all the more magnetic force, crawls to her feet like a sick dog. Can you comprehend this?

Falk shouted.

Can you comprehend this? It's madness, past the stage of mere anguish. It's, it's . . .

Falk was himself affrighted at the lengths to which he had gone.

He rushed to and fro in the room with clenched fists swept by a feeling of exasperated rage against Czerski, who had forced him to go through all this once again and open the healing wound.

Why am I shouting? Because I have cramps of the heart and colic of the soul. Oh, if you were here now, you damned fanatic of truth — ha, ha, ha! Marry Janina? Ha, ha, ha!

Of a sudden he sat down at the window, utterly faint, wiped the sweat from his forehead, and gradually regained composure, sinking into a drowsy revery.

Then he jumped up again.

Now Czerski would at last understand how it was that he always returned to Janina.

He gazed up at the sky so heavy and sorrow-laden, as though sick with perpetual contemplation, and felt the space spread out and pass into infinity.

He listened intently.

It seemed as though the fathomless depths of eternity were falling down, deeper, still deeper, as if the awful hush of night were flowing into a vast rimless crater in whose jaws everything disappeared along with the light of the stars beaded with the sweat of woe. And time and space, the whole world, vanished, leaving nothing behind but the sick sky drawing a dark veil over his own poor head.

It was he, Falk himself, who was spreading the sky over his head, stretching that azure vault across the earth with his eyes and hands.

He jumped up.

The door, he thought, had opened and some one had entered.

No.

Terrible, terrible. That such a thing should be capable of destroying a soul. Why, why? Wrath filled him to the brim. What care I for that silly Why? Do I live to guess conundrums? Haven't I prodded her soul enough? Haven't I, with pedantic precision, ransacked the most secret corners of her being? Does man's limited knowledge help me to understand what is passing within me? Can't you see, Mr. Czerski, that in certain circumstances one may betray a wife, that there may come a moment of poignant hatred of her, when one would insult, besmirch her by a connection with another woman?

Falk's steps became more and more restless. He felt as if his head would burst with the ferment in his soul.

And now, just when the wound had begun to heal, Czerski wanted to tear Ysa away from him.

Of course she would leave him.

But that was impossible. Why, she was everything to him, he was riveted to her, could not live a single day without her . . .

The one thought that flashed clear and definite in his mind was, he must get Czerski out of the way. But how, how?

He almost went into a faint. Now all was lost.

Suddenly he quivered.

Olga would straighten it out, Olga, Olga — the one way out — Olga!

Ah, the cheering thought! Queer it hadn't come to him sooner.

With feverish haste he wrote a long letter, put a check in, sealed the envelope, then flung himself in the arm-chair, and stared at the ceiling with his mind a void.

He jumped up, stung to the quick again by immense hatred of Ysa.

She — she alone was to blame for his racking torture, for his having lost all faith, all purpose in life. She — she alone was to blame that these sick thoughts drilled into his brain and tore apart all the uniting threads of his life.

Ysa, Ysa . . . Oh, if it had not been! If it had not been.— Ha, ha, ha! — Yes, of course, Mr. Czerski, of course . . . it's evident.— Did I say evident? Nonsense, nothing is evident. All's a riddle, endless torment.

Ah, far better that it were all done, ended forever.

His heart contracted with a fearful pang that buried its long sharp teeth deeper and deeper.

The night was sultry, so profound, profound . . .

A great lassitude crept upon him.

The world is overthrown, the world is coming to an end, everything is going down to annihilation — annihilation . . .

CHAPTER V

"ARE you ill, Czerski?" Olga was greatly disturbed. Czerski looked up, half unconscious, until that moment insensible of some one else's presence in the room.

"No, I'm not ill. What's brought you here?"

"Would you like to go on a propaganda tour?"

"I've been thinking of it for three days."

"I've got money for you. But there's a condition attached — that you leave at once."

That was distasteful to Czerski.

"I'll not accept any conditions. I'll leave when I please and go where I please."

"But I can't give you the money unless you leave at once."

"Why at once?" He eyed her suspiciously.

"The literature must be across the border within at least two or three days. They've been waiting for it nearly two months already."

"It's not my aim in life to do services for a party. I have nothing in common with any party. I am a party unto myself."

Olga studied him.

"So you're a full-fledged anarchist now?"

"Neither an anarchist nor a Socialist. No 'ist' at all. I'm a party unto myself."

"But you hold views shared by the anarchists."

"If some of our views happen to coincide, that makes no difference. I shall never permit any party whatsoever to consider me one of its members."

Czerski lost himself in reflection.

"So you don't want to go?"

" Are there any other conditions attached to the use of the money?"

" No."

He deliberated a few moments.

" Well, I can take the books across the frontier, but I repeat, I recognise no programmes, no party. I submit to no orders, I accept no conditions."

" Very interesting. But I was told to give you the money in any event."

Czerski again rested his eyes on her, mistrustful.

" Tell me, was it Falk gave you the money to get rid of me?"

" How do you know?"

" I had a talk with him last night."

" With whom? Falk?"

" Yes."

Czerski pondered.

" Tell me, doesn't Falk love his wife very much? He seems to to me."

" Yes, he does."

" Then explain to me, that is, if you understand it your-self — How can Falk have a mistress? I've been thinking about it the whole night."

Olga gazed at him affrighted. Had prison unsettled Czerski's mind?

" A mistress, you said. Impossible! Quite out of the question."

" Yes, a mistress, the woman to whom I was engaged."

" Miss Kruk?"

" Yes. She just had a baby — a boy."

Olga was stunned. She tried to conceal her feelings, but her hands trembled, and her face went white with the rush of blood to her heart. Czerski, walking to and fro in the room in complete absorption, seemed not to take notice.

"Yes, it made me suffer — horribly. But I got the better of myself. At first, after she stopped coming to see me in prison — oh, the agony of it was frightful, frightful. But I conquered myself. And that's good. Now nothing stands between me and the idea for which I mean to live."

He fell silent.

"The last time I gave in to my emotions was three days ago on coming out of prison. A fierce hatred of Falk obsessed me. I wanted to disgrace him, make him miserable. Then the dread of a wedge being thrust in between me and my idea held me back. Ah, it's good, very good, to overcome one's feelings. Evidently Falk wants to get rid of me. But he has no reason to be afraid of me now. Tell him so when you see him."

He looked at Olga intently.

"Do you believe Falk sent the money so as to get rid of me?"

"When did you have your talk with him?"

"Last night."

"In that case, I don't think so. He was just waiting for your release from prison. He has a very high opinion of you."

"But he's a scoundrel, a downright scoundrel."

"You're wrong. Falk's by no means a scoundrel."

Olga spoke in a cold, parrying tone.

Czerski looked at her fixedly, without making answer. For a while he paced the room deep in reflection, then stopped abruptly and asked:

"Was it he who wrote that pamphlet purporting to be a bull of Pope Pius for propaganda in the villages?"

"Yes."

"A remarkably fine piece of writing. Excellent. However, I don't think he's serious about the cause. He's in it merely for his own amusement. It's a diversion with him. He's experimenting. He would like to be known as a great writer."

Olga was silent.

"Am I not right? You know him well. You don't answer? Ha, ha! Falk is seeking danger. I think he'd gladly go to prison, not for the sake of the cause, but to expiate his sins."

Czerski grew more animated.

"I often used to receive letters from him. Oh, he's extraordinarily keen and brilliant, he has got a lot of hate in his make-up, and perhaps a lot of love, too. Now I see clearly it's nothing but desperation. He wants to save himself and clutches at whatever he can for salvation. But he doesn't believe in a thing. Oh, he's nimble. Yesterday, I tried to insult him, but he made sport of me. He was very venomous and quick."

Czerski broke off suddenly.

"Will you have some tea?"

"Yes, please."

Czerski slowly put the coals in the samovar.

"Have you seen Miss Kruk?"

"Yes, straight after coming out of prison. She doesn't know Falk's married."

"Doesn't know?"

"He fooled her. His whole life is one long chain of lies and deceit."

Olga was fearfully shaken. To sit there quietly and listen longer was more than she could bear, and she rose to leave.

"I must be going."

" Please stay. After a whole year and a half in awful loneliness, I'm so glad to have somebody to talk to." He besought her with his eyes.

Olga, governing herself, sat down again.

" What I said of Falk grieved you, didn't it? I sympathise. We all expected otherwise of him. H'm, I'm glad he sent the money. How much is it? "

" Five hundred marks."

" A lot. A great deal can be done with that amount."

They were silent; then Olga asked:

" Is what Kunicki said true, that you and Stephen Kruk robbed a town treasury near here? "

" Perfectly true."

" So you resort to anarchistic methods? "

" All methods are good if they help me carry out my idea. But it's not an anarchistic method. Besides, I didn't steal the money. It was legitimate to take it. There's a great difference between that and stealing. I did the thing in the profound conviction of its rightness."

" You say stealing is permissible if sanctioned by your idea? "

" No, not stealing. I didn't say that. What you have in mind is the legal conception of crime. If I do something in the full consciousness and belief that it is right, then theft ceases to be theft and crime."

" According to you, then, the only test, the subjective test of crime, is an unclean conscience? "

" Yes."

Olga listened to him distractedly.

" Do you believe in God? " she asked abruptly.

" I believe in Jesus Christ, the human Son.— Don't interrupt." Czerski had lost his far-awayness and was speaking with great vivacity now. "What is it that determines the pleasure of a sensation? Not the fact that in itself it is agreeable. Opium smoking doesn't get to be pleasant until it's tried a number of times. So, in the final analysis, the essence of a feeling is determined by its enduring qualities."

"Consequently you wouldn't stop at any crime?"

"Don't say crime," he interjected hastily. "I wouldn't stop at any act that might help to realise my idea."

"But if your idea is false?"

"It cannot be. It is based on the one and only real truth — on love."

"But if your means are wrong?"

"They can't be wrong, because it is love that has inspired them. Besides, I don't like to use violence, even when necessary. I haven't programmes like the anarchists, and if a party includes the propaganda of the deed in its programme, I don't want it to reckon me among its adherents."

"You are very proud."

"Not at all. I have the great right that every creature has to exist, but I exist only by my actions. So my existence is what I do. That is my whole pride — to exist in my actions. Once I fulfil other people's orders, I cease to exist."

"That's all been said before and better."

"Quite possible. I don't deny it. But it came to me by myself in prison. It was through toil and effort that I thought up to it. So it is original with me. While a member of the Party, I got disused to thinking. Now I have left the Party so as to be myself, to direct my own acts with my own ideas."

"What do you mean to do?"

"Teach self-sacrifice."

Olga looked at him questioningly.

"To be able to sacrifice one's self is the first condition of any cause. And I will teach the delight of self-sacrifice."

"But your pupils would have to believe in the object of the self-sacrifice that you teach."

"Not at all. Self-sacrifice proceeds, not from faith, but from inspiration. All parties have faith, but not inspiration. In fact, they haven't even faith. They have dogmas. The whole Social-Democracy has petrified. Dogmas have taken the vitality out of it. It has become what Catholicism ended up in — dead faith in dogmas without enthusiasm, without the possibility of self-sacrifice. Point out to me the man to-day who would go to torture for his God. You can't. Show me the Social-Democrat who would unhesitatingly allow his head to be cut off for his idea. You can't. The Social-Democrats have wrapped themselves up in the security of a convenient peaceful faith, they have erected a Chinese Wall of dogmas beyond which they never step, indeed, never care to step. *I* want to create a fiery faith, a faith ceasing to be faith, transmuted into inspiration, into ecstasy, into a consuming thirst for sacrifice."

His eyes burned with rapture.

"You bank, then, upon the fanatic hate of the crowd?"

"Fanatic love!" he exclaimed with heat. "Fanatic love of the eternal race of man, love for the everlastingness of life, for the great thought that I and every living thing are one inseparable whole."

Czerski went on to develop his idea as a musician composes variations on a theme.

"I don't say, 'Sacrifice yourselves that your children may be happy.' I don't say, 'Sacrifice yourselves that you may live better than you have heretofore.' I teach the happiness of purposeless sacrifice, regardless of the future. Mankind thirsts for self-sacrifice. But Socialism and the Church, both of them satiated, take away this thirst. Mankind has forgotten the joy of self-sacrifice. It was in the great Revolution, in the purposeless Commune that people, just to intoxicate themselves with the sweetness of self-sacrifice, experienced that delight for the last time. By my actions I shall remind them of this happiness again."

He broke off and gave Olga a look of doubt.

"Perhaps you think I'm a foolish visionary?"

"Oh, no, what you say is beautiful. I understand you very well." She pondered. There was a long silence.

"Yes, you're right," said Czerski. "These ideas of mine are not new and have been expressed better. Why, Falk himself developed them splendidly at the last Congress in Paris. I felt like kissing his hands." He frowned. "But they didn't spring from his heart; they were the excogitations of his brain. The sacred fire of love was not burning in his soul. Oh, no, no, no! How can one utter such thoughts with icy calm and not sink through the ground from shame? It's that his very being doesn't quiver with these ideas. That's what makes him so brazen. Yes, he has a brazen intellect. He's a bad man. He is not clean enough to be worthy to think as he does. To think that way one should be a Christ, a God, the sacred source of happiness in self-sacrifice."

"You have changed fearfully, though I never really knew you; and Kunicki spoke so unfavourably of you."

Olga rose, viewing him with a certain awe. A radiance seemed to emanate from that spare, at it were, disembodied figure. She had never seen anything like it.

"You should take a little care of yourself. You are ill."

"No, I'm not ill. I'm happy."

He lost himself in meditation, then spoke again.

"Only last night I was a nullity, a weak man. To-day the weakness is all gone — gone " . . .

CHAPTER VI

FALK listened nervously. Olga was telling him drily of her visit to Czerski.

"Czerski's a visionary," he said at length. "His mind has got all mixed up. Perhaps he'd like to form phalanxes after Fourier — ha, ha! Bakunin has lodged too deep in his brain."

"I don't think he's a Utopian," Olga answered coldly. "Perhaps his reasoning is not quite clear, not well enough defined, but his ideas are original and not without chances of realisation."

Falk looked at her askance.

"Ahem, is that so? Well, well. The mere fact that he takes a stand in opposition to the official code is in his favour. —But tell me, what passed between him and Kunicki?"

"Two years ago Kunicki killed a Russian student in a duel in Zürich."

"In a duel?"

"Yes. Queer for a Socialist, isn't it? Czerski hit him at a meeting."

"What for?"

"He said he was punishing, not Kunicki, but the violation of the first principle of the Party."

Falk laughed sardonically.

"Extraordinary. And what did Kunicki do?"

"What could he do? He couldn't kill Czerski."

"A singular fanatic. And now he doesn't want to have anything to do with the Party?"

"No."

Falk sank in reflection.

"My actions make my existence — that's what he said, isn't it?"

Olga searched his face.

"Tell me, Falk, are you serious in your attitude to our cause?"

"Why do you ask?"

"Because I should like to know for certain." Olga was wrought up.

"You'd like to know? Very well. This so-called cause of yours is of no significance whatever to me. What have I in common with it? Humanity? What is humanity? Who is humanity? I know who you are. I know who my wife is. Perhaps I know two or three other persons. But humanity — humanity — I don't know what it is."

"In that case, why do you write proclamations and pamphlets? Why do you give money for propaganda? Why —"

Falk broke in hastily.

"I don't do it for humanity. Ha, ha, ha! How simple you are! Can't you conceive what capital fun it is to wash the eyes of those unfortunates, the blind working cattle, watch their sight come back to them, watch them develop as they grow in the knowledge of the injustices they suffer? What royal pleasure to see them throw off their yoke and with the fury of Spanish bulls rush upon the gentlemen who exploited them, until now with impunity, and took their cattle-like obedience and submissiveness as a matter of course! Isn't it as good as a comedy to see the masters, so certain of their absolute control, go dumb with astonishment at first, then fly into impotent rage and call for troops and insist upon the chastisement of the refractory slaves — ha, ha, ha!

"Oh, indeed, it's great fun to be picador to the bulls —

ha, ha! Look, here is the expense account of the last Silesian miners' strike. All my money, or, rather, my wife's money went into it, but the satisfaction I got out of it was rich compensation. The Theodoria mine is bankrupt, the Great Etruria has nearly gone to pieces, the Hubert is flooded. Ha, ha, ha! I know the owners. One has gone grey, the other almost lost his mind, and the third is actually insane. Ha, ha, ha!

"I ruined them, not because I take stock in your cause, but simply for the personal satisfaction I get out of worrying them. I'd be ready to give my last penny just to see those rascals go to hell."

Olga gazed at him long.

"How you slander yourself!" she said, smiling sadly. "Because you can't mean to fool me?"

Falk, in surprise, stopped in front of her, then burst out laughing. The next instant he turned serious.

"So you're convinced I'm doing all this from nobler motives?"

Olga made no response.

"You are convinced of it?" he probed impatiently.

Olga still remained silent.

"You ought to answer me," he insisted.

"Such mean, low, spiteful revenge, I believe, couldn't really satisfy you," she said at length, calmly. "No use misrepresenting myself. I know why you called the strike and lost your money — because the syndicate was paying twenty-five per cent. dividends when hunger typhus was raging among the workers."

"It never even entered my mind."

"It's not true, it's not true. For some time you've been taking delight in painting yourself as black as the devil."

"Ha, ha, ha! There's the making of a good psychologist

in you!" His laugh sounded forced. "And do you know why I sent Czerski money?" he asked suddenly.

All the colour left Olga's face.

"You lie!" she whispered hotly.

"Do you know?"

She was wretchedly pained.

"Say you're lying!" She bent toward him wide-eyed. "You wanted to get rid of him? Did you?"

"No," he answered, smiling sombrely. "I'm afraid of no one."

She drew a deep breath and sat down.

Both kept silence a long while.

"What are you going to do now with Janina?"

Falk went white.

"Czerski told you?"

"Yes."

Falk's head drooped. He held his eyes fixed on the floor.

"I'll adopt the child," he said at length.

"Terrible what an evil demon is in you. Why must you bring misfortune on yourself and others? Why? You *are* an unhappy man, Eric, aren't you?"

"You think so?" he said distraught.

He stopped before her suddenly with a strange smile on his face.

"Tell me frankly, Olga, did you think for even a second that I wanted to be free of Czerski out of cowardice?"

"Not for a second. Why, Eric, you are good. Only you are an unhappy man."

He kissed her hand and said drily, "Thank you," then began to walk about restlessly again. An unpleasant silence fell.

"When is Czerski going?"

"To-night."

Another pause.

"Olga, I believe in your love. I bow before it. I love it. You are the only person whose presence makes me good."

Olga rose in confusion, scarcely able to restrain her tears.

"Don't speak of it. Why talk about it? . . . But there's a great deal of unpleasantness ahead of you now. And when it gets to be very bad for you, Eric, come to me. Maybe I can help you a little."

"I'll come, I'll come when my neck is wrung."

"Come when you've got nothing else left."

With these words she quit the room.

Falk ran out after her.

"What's Czerski's address?"

She gave it to him and asked:

"Are you going to see him?"

"Yes," he replied, setting his teeth.

CHAPTER VII

AT the close of day Falk took a cab and drove to
Czerski's home.

His temperature was mounting and he feared one of those recurrent spells of fever in which he was likely to commit some blunder. However, he thought, that didn't matter very much.

The big thing was that ahead of him was the disagreeable duty of visiting Czerski and confessing that he, Falk, had been cowardly, that he had sent the money pretending it was for propaganda purposes when really it was to get rid of Czerski, and so prevent revelations to his wife.

The ride was interminable. Falk's thoughts were weirdly confused. He kept repeating a few senseless phrases, and, queerly, the inaner the phrases the more persistently they returned.

He looked at his watch. Eight o'clock. Czerski would probably not leave before midnight. So there was still time.

At length — there was the house Czerski lived in.

Falk stood still a while helplessly wondering: " On what floor, on what floor? "

" The attic, of course."

It was so dark in the hall that he had to grope his way. He made a few steps and started back, having stumbled up against some one.

" Beg your pardon."

" It's all right." The man's voice was disagreeable.
" An outrage not to have a light burning in a dark hallway like this," he fumed. " I'll report it to the police."

Falk was about to inquire on what floor Czerski lived when it occurred to him that the man might be a political spy.

"Can you tell me where Mr. Geisler lives?" he asked.

"Who?"

"Geisler."

"No, I can't."

Falk mounted the stairs trying to make as much noise as possible, and rang at the second story, asking for Geisler. The door was slammed shut in his face. He smiled contentedly, and went up the remaining flights on tiptoe. The spy would now be convinced that he had found Geisler on the second floor. Falk was pleased with his ruse.

But where now — to the right or the left?

He knocked at a venture.

"Come in."

Falk opened the door and entered. Czerski was sitting at the window.

Queer, Czerski seemed not in the least surprised, nor even to notice Falk's presence. He glanced round indifferently for a moment, then resumed his former posture, gazing contemplatively into space.

Falk did not open a conversation. He sat down opposite Czerski and studied him. His appearance was appalling. His eyes were sunken and lustreless.

At length it struck Falk that not a word had been said.

"Good evening, Mr. Czerski."

Czerski glanced at him with a strange calm that terrified him.

"What do you want, Mr. Falk?"

"I? Nothing, really. I'll leave at once, at once — I — I don't know why I came —" he said incoherently. Then he recovered himself. "Oh, yes, that's right. I came to tell you straight out, quite frankly, that I sent you the money just to get rid of you. I'm sorry I did . . . I don't want to live in lies any more . . . and I don't need to, either. — But what was I going to say? Oh, yes, don't leave the city. You are quite right to try to punish lying and extirpate it from the world. I'll be truly grateful if you will go to my wife now and tell her everything. I can't do it myself. I couldn't bear to see the torture . . . You know I'm terribly susceptible to suffering. I've been that way since childhood . . . My father once killed a dog I loved. In its death agony the poor creature looked at me with awful eyes. Since then I've never been able to stand the sight of physical anguish. Besides, I am of the opinion that one must never try to hold back the wheel of Fate. So, I think, the best thing would be for you to tell my wife."

"You're a coward."

"You speak truly. I am a coward masking my cowardice behind belief in Fate, though, as a matter of fact, I don't believe in Fate, because I don't believe in anything. I'm sorry I dealt you such a blow. Even last night I noticed how badly you look."

Falk was terrified to mark that his fever was going up. It took a huge effort for him to hold himself in check.

Czerski examined him keenly.

"You're in a fever. You ought to go home."

Falk was in the flush of fearful excitement.

"Who'll guarantee I'm not playing a comedy? I'm a skilful actor, you know. How can you tell that the fantastic notion didn't occur to me to feign physical abnormality and convince you that at times I'm not responsible for what I do and say? Ha, ha, ha!"

Czerski made no answer. That roused Falk still more.

"You're pretending not to hear me. Ha, ha! You want

to insult me. You wanted to insult me last night, too. You thought of a nonsensical plan so as to provoke me and put me in a rage . . . I understand you. You still feel respect for that Falk who did so much for the Party. You had to struggle with yourself before making up your mind to speak as you did. . . . Am I not right? To get up the courage to call me a scoundrel you had to overcome something in yourself, didn't you? "

Czerski fixed his eyes on him in a strange prolonged stare, and remarked almost solemnly: "Yes, that's so."

Falk was all unstrung.

" That's so? That's what you said, isn't it? But do you get what I am saying? I sent you money on condition that you leave at once. And even anticipating that you might have come this morning to tell my wife, I gave instructions to the servants not to admit any one."

Czerski laughed.

" I hadn't the remotest notion of going to tell your wife."

" No, really? " Falk thought a while. " I was positive you would. I heard you were rectilinear and vengeful, and I felt certain you intended my ruin. And the only way I can be ruined is by separating me from my wife."

He looked at Czerski almost in terror, then remarked abruptly:

" There, you see, my brain has lied again. It looks, God knows where, to find cause for the fact that I am already ruined. My wife is still with me, nevertheless I am ruined. And the cause of it is rooted in something entirely different. You know what a maelstrom is? Of course you do. It is a seething whirlpool. The water jets up in a raging geyser and sucks inward in a bottomless funnel. Sometimes a man falls in. The funnel drags him down, then the geyser tosses him up like a ball, and he is sucked in and thrown up over and over. Extraordinary. I saw a maelstrom on my honeymoon. I myself have fallen in. I may be dragged down and tossed up a thousand times still, but from out of its jaws I can never escape. I am irretrievably lost. Ha, ha! . . . Queer, isn't it?"

He wiped the perspiration from his face.

"Yes, I am lost. I speak of my undoing as one speaks of a tumbling wall or a piece of decaying meat in the summertime. Our souls, too, may decompose from excessive heat, and I, my dear sir, often have fever . . . Ha, ha! I once had pneumonia. Since then I'm bothered by fever. Ha, ha, ha! Inasmuch as I am already lost, you will help me by ridding me of people who love me. Every one who loves me is a source of unspeakable suffering, and so my enemy. I must lie, lie perpetually, because I cannot bear the sight of the torture caused by the disillusionment I bring. They love me because I appear great, whereas, in reality, I am nothing but a pitiful insignificant worm, a most common louse, Mr. Czerski. Can I tell them that? If I do they don't believe me. That's my misfortune. I have to lie because they take joy in believing my lies. Yes, God. preserve them from the moment when they believe my truth. Why, I have never interfered with any one's being good. But they always try to keep me from being bad, from being a scoundrel . . . Why are you laughing? Confound you!"

Czerski had not the least inclination to laugh.

"I'm not laughing. But I don't know what you want of me. You are uncommonly sincere and frank, yet I can't get what you are driving at."

"What I'm driving at? Ha, ha, ha! My sincerity and frankness are to lead you astray, move you, touch your emotions. I am an adept. I confess to sins I've never committed so as to hide the crime on my conscience. Ha, ha, ha! How naïve you are!"

Czerski smiled, though in his smile there was so much of suffering that Falk instantly turned serious.

"Listen, Falk, you are pounding water in a mortar. You are trying to throw dust in my eyes. I am very sensible of your misery. Calm yourself. I forgot Janina and you and your wife. What care I for all that? When I called you a scoundrel, I really didn't mean it. You suffer too greatly to be a scoundrel. You are not a bad man. I'm sorry I was so rude last night."

Falk looked at him with growing astonishment.

"You seem to be greatly surprised, Mr. Falk? You had a wrong idea of me.— But why speak of it? I have forgotten everything. I look at you, I see your despair, and I am sorry you suffer so, though, in truth, I feel like laughing at your trivial sufferings, just as I laugh at my own. You are in despair, you are dying of dread — and why? Because of an unpleasant sexual conflict. But, my dear Mr. Falk, there are greater sufferings, which a man experiences when he becomes one with the whole of mankind and his heart pulsates with the terrible trials of humanity."

He lapsed into silence and after a long pause resumed:

"I know that for you the concept 'mankind' does not exist. Your soul is too small to embrace the whole world. Your heart beats only for your wife, your mistress, and your children. You specialised in love. Men like you each take up some specialty in the province of love — one the family, another the brothel. What's the difference? What? Simply this, that one dares to break the laws regulating your paltry love and your petty desires, the other doesn't dare to. It's all so low and mean. And what constitutes your whole code of laws? 'Thou shalt not covet thy neigh-

bour's wife. Thou shalt not steal. Thou shalt not kill.'
What is your religion? What service does it do you?

"That after your labours of gluttony and drunkenness
here on earth, there shall be guaranteed to you a quiet corner for digestion in heaven. What is your philosophy?
I've read your Stirner and your Nietzsche. A pack of lies.
Mean, sneaking lies. You had to eliminate everything great
— love, pity, self-sacrifice, humanity, God — all because it
stands in the way of your digestion. You forever trot out
your Ego. A mere antidote to a guilty conscience. Your
Ego gives you the courage to break the small laws governing your small desires. For all your pompous individualism,
you are a small, insignificant man, Mr. Falk. What makes
up your life? Drinking and sexual dissipation. But no, no.
I have gone too far. You are a great artist, too. So you
have done a lot for despised humanity. But tell me, didn't
you do it so as to drown the reproaches of your conscience?"

He stood before Falk as though to defy him, then sat
down again.

"Bah," he said, "what business is it of mine? I have
nothing in common with you any more. Sitting here at
home to-day I've been thinking and thinking that there's no
binding tie between you and me. Everything personal has
dropped away from me. You don't know the concept ' humanity.' I don't either. But I love and comprehend
humanity as if it were an actual part of my own soul. I
have a feeling strong and substantial as an elemental instinct
that to sacrifice one's self for millions is far better than to
crawl to the feet of the first female who chances one's way.
And now, go, please go. I want to be by myself before I
leave . . . But just reflect — you are a small, insignificant
man, when you might have been one of the greatest. Yes,
yes. . . ."

Falk was deeply moved, yet, at the same time, ashamed that he allowed himself to be moved. His brain laughed satanically at his own helplessness.

"Are you addicted to opium?" he asked with an ironic smile.

Czerski looked at him coldly.

"Your mind is shameless," he observed solemnly. "Shameless."

Falk shrank before his inspired look and prophetic words. He felt in himself the struggle of two souls each striving to subdue the other.

"You're right. My soul, my mind are void of shame."

At that moment the soul of scepticism, the mocking, cynical soul, got the upper hand. He burst into a wicked laugh.

"What you said is excellent, though it's all been said before by Nietzsche, that very same Nietzsche for whom you express such contempt."

He was interested to see the effect of this on Czerski. But Czerski seemed no longer to hear anything, sitting at the window with his back turned to Falk. Falk became serious, and sad. He kept on talking, though only through dread of the silence.

"Yes, yes, my mind is shameless because it is unintelligible to me how your love can be based on anything else than your own personal griefs. And such is my brain that it doesn't take your feelings on faith. It analyses them microscopically. You were in prison. The woman you love gave herself to another. Solitude, grief, treachery, despair produce a desire to forget about yourself, about your own personal woe, and give yourself up to self-sacrifice. So, you see, your humanity is nothing but one long deceit. You are the dupe of your own self. To conquer your grief you save yourself from despair. Your humanity is simply the self-preservative instinct of the organism craving for respite and calm. The difference between me and you is this: You are happy in your great lie. I am not. Because my lie is small and insignificant. But what means great, and what means small? Good Lord, all my conceptions have become upset.

"However, that's not germane. What is logical reasoning to you? Simply an aid to digestion, also balm for the pangs of conscience."

Czerski wheeled round suddenly.

"Will you have some tea?"

"I should be most grateful.— But listen. You despise me. You called me a scoundrel. Why? For the reason that sexual love played a part in my great work of destruction . . . I say 'great work of destruction' because a whole series of people beside Janina are on my conscience . . ."

Falk drank off one glass of tea after the other. His fever was mounting.

"Sex, lust, voluptuousness played a rôle — very well —"

The thread of his thoughts snapped. He sat ruminating a long while, then jumped up with a solemn look on his face.

"Aha! Listen. Napoleon! The classic example!"

His face was radiant.

"You smile. Don't think I'm comparing myself to Napoleon. I'm simply trying to find a reciprocal connection between widely differing motives and actions. What motives governed Napoleon's soul? Ha, ha! Some say his was the part of the storm purifying the atmosphere. A foolish comparison. The storm's cleansing of the atmosphere is simply accidental — you're not one of those, I trust, who insist that Nature is purposeful? Ha, ha, ha! Will you let me have another glass of tea, please?

"Something must necessarily have guided Napoleon in his crimes. Ambition, for example. But what is ambition? We don't know. Its nature has not yet been decided. But isn't this palaver of mine boring you?"

"Go on, go on. I think it's soothing to you."

"Yes, it is. You're a good psychologist. Well, then, ambition, that extraordinarily complex sensation, is not like an elemental feeling, like love or hunger. It is the resultant of a whole series of simple sensations."

Falk broke into a nervous laugh.

"Excuse me, my head is a bit addled. I'm not quite well. I merely wanted to say, the motive for every action is more or less equally dependent on the feelings. Now, the root of each feeling is to be found in the most elemental sensations. Ha, ha! Therefore the results are the same.

"However, all these questions are extremely special in their nature. All I wanted to prove was that the motives for my noble actions are identical with the motives governing the actions of a Napoleon. In most cases, however, the motives of human actions are unknown. We don't know why we do this or that. Yes, yes."

Falk made a mighty effort to concentrate. His thoughts seemed to scatter in all directions.

Czerski, smiling, interrupted.

"But you are fighting windmills. Do you think Napoleon was great? In your eyes he may have been, supplying you, as he does, with an example of the pitch of coarseness and ruthlessness to which a man must go to satisfy his lusts."

Falk looked at Czerski with feverish concentration. All of a sudden he was beholding him as he had never seen him before.

"Astounding, astounding!" he repeated several times, then, abruptly, stepped over to him and said with great quiet:

"You are committing a terrible crime. Don't be angry at me. But you are perpetrating what people call a crime. I know it. I suddenly read it in your face. Before I thought you were simply ill, or that you used opium. But no. It's not that. I don't know how this prophetic thought came to me. All political criminals have the same expression on their faces. I saw Padlevsky in Paris an hour or so after he killed the Russian ambassador. And I had seen him a few days before, too."

Falk sat down again. Darkness gathered before his eyes, but in a moment dispersed.

"So you are going to destroy and kill, blow up mines and factories? And what is the incentive? Your love of humanity and pity for its sufferings? Very well. But where are the roots of your love and pity? Nowhere but in an indomitable striving to achieve your purpose. What difference is there between your desire to make humanity happy and mine to forget the ache in my heart, the ache that causes me to make a Marit or a Janina unhappy? Ha, ha! Just now you are thousands of miles away from here, with intentional scorn refusing to listen to me.— But yet, tell me, tell me wherein my crimes differ from yours? Only in this — that mine have not been provided for in the penal code, while yours will cost you your life. And I shall suffer the reproaches of conscience, while you will find happiness in self-sacrifice . . . self-sacrifice!" he cried out suddenly. "Self-sacrifice!"

Czerski quivered.

"Did you say something, eh?"

"Happiness in your self-sacrifice; in my heart torment."

Falk's condition bordered on pathologic ecstasy.

"You said you spit on everything. That's approximately what you said. Would you believe it, that brings us near each other? I, too, spit upon everything, upon myself, upon Napoleon, upon the superman, upon the whole world. It's all bosh and nonsense, Mr. Czerski, bosh and nonsense!"

Then, with tremendous seriousness, he said quickly, brokenly, incoherently, as though eager to pour out his whole soul:

"To no one have I ever said what I say to you now. I am in ecstasy over you. I love you. Do you know why? Why?" he asked with a look of mystery. "Because you have ceased to be yourself. Yes, you and Olga. I love you because you are the only ones who are able to love. And love's the one feeling I respect and love.

"Can't you hear my heart thumping? Can't you see my temples beating? — But to love as you love one must have faith . . . faith . . . faith, in which alone there is love — ha, ha, ha! Faith transmuted into love. Marvellous, you who would level the world down, you are the only true superbeings. Such is the power and might that this hellish love and pity give you. I? What am I? A man doomed to extinction. I am the last man. In the Polynesian Archipelago there's a peculiar race that'll die out of physical tuberculosis in about thirty years. My race is dying out of psychic tuberculosis. The lungs of the brain have been destroyed. Faith decayed, rotted away, killed."

Falk broke into a prolonged, nervous laugh.

"Ha, ha, ha! I just thought of one of my friends who was a superman like myself. Unfortunately he did not have my strength and died of drunkenness and debauchery. When he died, I went to a restaurant to realise that Boles was dead. I couldn't take it in. In the restaurant I saw a stout greasy doctor, one of the most depraved men I've ever met. He was deep in his cups. I sat down beside him and said, 'Boles died.' He thought a minute, then said, 'Well, what's surprising in that?' 'Why isn't it surprising?' I asked back. 'One must have convictions,' the drunken beast answered. 'The man of convictions never dies.'"

Falk rose, wiped his forehead and for a minute lost the thread of his thought.

"My dear friend, it is despair speaking from my mouth. You are wonderfully right, Czerski, my life is the life of a pitiful worm wriggling in woes, a life of petty love.

"How did you express it? Love for a family and attachment to a brothel? Don't be offended at the gross way I put it. But you know I spit on it all, on life, on myself, on you . . . No, not you. You are too great, too holy for me to spit on."

Falk suddenly bent over and kissed Czerski's hand. There was a strange solemn sadness in this thing that he did.

Czerski wrenched his hand away.

Falk looked at him a long time, then sat down and stared vacantly, not fully conscious of what he had said or done. He thought his fever had passed away.

Czerski was very white.

"Why did you come here?" His voice shook and broke.

Falk still looked at him without speaking. This continued for several minutes.

"I swear to you it wasn't a mere whim that brought me here."

"Are you telling the truth?"

"I've never been more truthful."

Czerski paced the room excitedly, then stopped.

"I take it all back, everything I said to you yesterday and to-day." He spoke quietly, making an evident effort to suppress his agitation. "You are not a scoundrel or a blackguard, Falk. Forgive me for having insulted you."

Many minutes passed in silence again.

Suddenly Czerski turned toward Falk.

"I didn't know you. I thought you had no conscience . . . And I'm sorry, fearfully sorry, I wrote about it to Stephen."

"So you told Stephen?"

"Yes."

Falk looked at him indifferently.

"H'm, perhaps you did well. But now I'm terribly tired. Good-bye, Czerski. I'm glad we part friends."

Without shaking hands Falk left and descended the stairs mechanically.

CHAPTER VIII

DOWNSTAIRS he remembered having encountered a spy there. He lighted a match and looked around. He saw no one.

Perhaps he had been mistaken or was suffering from persecutional mania. Cold shivers ran up and down his back. Evidently fever again.

And he walked and walked, taking no heed of the direction.

At length he set himself to thinking.

Home? Why home? To meet people who harried him with their love? Why? He hated it all. It was because he was beloved of some one there that the disasters had all come. No one could love Falk. Falk was a beast. No, not a beast, but only a pitiful wretch of a man.

"It's ugly that I kissed Czerski's hand — ha, ha, ha!"

Whose hands had Falk not kissed? But now he wasn't going to bother to be ashamed of it. Why should he be ashamed? Ha, ha!

A sense of great sorrow flooded his soul.

He stopped and stared straight ahead for many minutes.

Begin a new life? No, he hadn't the strength for that. And even if he had, the result would be no better. Ah, it would be best for the whole world to come crashing down on him.

Ysa, Ysa? My God, between us comes her past — her former lover is killing me.

But what else, what more do I want of life?

Art? Ha, ha! Yes, I was an artist, one of the greatest,

it seems to me, and I created because I felt the need to create. But suddenly in a moment of creativeness a tormenting idea got me into its grip — why all this? I look at the characters I create. New worlds open up under my hands. But it's all so ridiculous. Then how, amid all this, can one create, Mr. Czerski? How, how? To create one must have faith. And where is one to get faith from if one does not possess it?"

He laughed aloud, though there was a stab at his heart.

Ah, Mr. Czerski, I'll give you all my art, I'll throw all my fame at your feet, joyously will I yield up my entire past and future, all monuments raised in my honour, for only a little minute of happiness . . . Ha . . . Ha . . . And you, Mr. Czerski, disciple of truth, desiring to bring happiness to millions, try your power, give Eric Falk one single minute of happiness.

Suddenly he trembled.

What had Czerski said? What? He had written everything to Stephen?

Falk's knees almost gave way. Written to Stephen! He had heard the words without taking in their meaning. Now he felt a mad impulse to rush back to Czerski, beat him black and blue, trample on him, wring his neck.

But this gave way the next minute to a sensation of dread that sent a rush of blood to his heart. He breathed heavily. He was faint and walked slowly. A weight as if the whole world had fallen on him was squeezing his breast.

Things couldn't keep on that way, he would be undone. And yet he must live, he must still have at least a little more happiness with Ysa.

His brain began to work with surprising energy. He walked, taking long strides, and walking thought of how beautiful Ysa was. Were he to live a million years they would all flow together in that one second when first he caught her eyes. And were he to spread over the whole world, the essence of him would be concentrated in that one look, brimful of love. Ha, ha! A beautiful thought. Very beautiful.

Suddenly he saw Ysa in the embrace of another. He shuddered, recoiling with fright before that mental vision. Only not that — not that . . .

He must calm himself, must calm himself at length.

Funny, all this time he had forgotten to smoke a cigarette. He stopped. What time was it? Not yet half past eleven. Well —. He lighted a cigarette. How about going to Olga, talking a little about humanity, ideals? Ha, ha! She's a good woman, and I'm so much in need of goodness.

Suddenly a strange thought struck him. It seemed to him that he was entirely surrounded by spies and likely to be arrested any moment. The notion clung obdurately in his mind, mounting to veritable terror.

He looked around. The lights had already been put out and the street was perfectly dark. Suddenly he noticed some one directly in front of him. He trembled, but with a great effort subdued his alarm, and began to think. Evidently a spy. How to get rid of him? He faced about and deliberately went past the man, scrutinising him intently. The man seemed to pay no attention and walked on.

Falk laughed sardonically.

A stupid dodge! Pretends not to see, but sees very well. What was he to do? Take a cab? That wouldn't help.

He entered a restaurant, ordered beer, and picked up a newspaper.

He had scarcely glanced at it when a stranger came in, sat down opposite and began to stare at him with brazen effrontery. At least so it seemed to Falk.

Now and then Falk glanced up from his paper. Each time their eyes met.

It was insupportable. A sort of savage despair broke over him. He flung the paper away, paid the reckoning, and looked at the stranger derisively.

His heart stood still. The stranger had risen and was crossing over to him.

" Doesn't look like a spy, though," flashed through Falk's mind.

" Haven't I the honour of addressing Mr. Falk? "

" Do you want to arrest me? All right, but not here, please."

Falk rested his hand on the table, quivering all over.

" I don't understand you," the stranger said in surprise.

Falk recollected himself.

" Are you tracking me? "

" No, I met you accidentally. I've been looking for you some time, but not tracking you. I have an important matter I'd like to talk to you about, that's all."

Was he telling the truth, or did he mean to trap him?

" So you don't want to arrest me? Well, if you want to talk to me, come to see me at my home," Falk laughed sardonically. " I don't feel the least bit in the mood to enter into any sort of discussion just now, God knows. Maybe you want information about my activity in. the miners' strike? Ha, ha! Call at my house, and we'll talk it over."

Falk sat down. His heart pounded, and the blood rushed to his head. The stranger stared at him in growing amazement. Finally Falk rose and quit the restaurant.

On the street he drew a deep breath. All that had just

passed seemed to him remote, a million years ago. The only thing certain was that he had escaped a great danger.

Ha, ha! Strange! But what isn't strange in this terrible world? he asked himself with a sick smile. What is not strange? Ha, ha, ha! For an unknown man to fill me with such fear!

Evidently he's not a detective after all. Much more likely I made his acquaintance while drunk and promised him friendship. Maybe I told him he's the best man I've ever met. And maybe I even called him my one and only friend . . .

Falk laughed a long, convulsive, bitter laugh. Whom have I not said these things to? Is there a man alive to whom I haven't?

Ha, ha, ha! Now this fellow will be running about the city spreading the report that he saw Falk drunk, behaving like a lunatic and talking absolute nonsense, not knowing himself what he was saying. Ha, ha, ha!

Falk passed on.

"Only not to go home," he repeated mechanically.

And he roamed the streets for hours, a prey to mental torment and dark despair.

Suddenly he stopped at a corner in front of a large glass sign illuminated from the inside: "The Green Nightingale."

His spirits rose with a sense of elation. It was here he had been with Ysa on the day he first met her . . . He must go in, sit down a while, and live through it all once more.

The clock in a nearby tower struck two. Plenty of time still before going home. And he entered.

CHAPTER IX

THERE was only one guest in the little room at the Green Nightingale. He was sitting at a table with his head bent heavily on his hands, sunk in deep thought.

Falk started in fright.

For the Lord's sake! Grodzki! How had he come there? He was supposed to be in Switzerland.— And alone!

Roused to an uncommon pitch of excitement he seated himself at the same table and looked at him sharply.

Grodzki gave no sign of being aware that he was the subject of this intense observation.

"Have you fallen asleep?" Falk, in unaccountable irritation, impatiently touched his sleeve.

Grodzki lifted his eyes and stared at him, then shifted his gaze and looked into his glass.

"Can't you say a word?" Falk growled angrily.

Grodzki glanced at him again with a bitter smile.

Falk was about to say something, but getting a full view of Grodzki's face, stopped short. It was appalling, deathly pale. His eyes were deep-sunken and fixed with the immobile rigidity of death.

"Are you ill?"

Grodzki shook his head.

"Then what's the matter with you?"

"H'm, you'd like to know? Maybe you'd like to try your experiments on me again? Ha, ha! That time's past. You can't practise on me any more. I won't submit to your influence; I won't act as a medium for you any longer."

Falk seemed not to hear him.

"Strange," he said at last. "I just happened to mention you to-day. I was telling of your attack of insanity in the African Bodega, the time you made such an uproar. You behaved scandalously, absurdly."

Falk was violently excited.

"Tell me, why did you shout that way, eh? — My, how unpleasant this meeting with you is!"

Grodzki looked at him intently and smiled.

"It's unpleasant to me, too, perhaps more so than to you. What business have you to be knocking about nights like this anyway? How is it one can always find you in cafés at such unearthly hours?" He burst into a wicked laugh. "So you haven't given up dissipating yet?"

Falk shrugged his shoulders contemptuously. He was shaking with fever, his throat was parched, and darkness gathered before his eyes. "I'm really ill," he thought, wiping the perspiration from his forehead.

"You seem to have fever again?" Grodzki asked with a faint smile.

Falk felt his strength ebbing.

"Yes, yes, I think I'm ill. But it will pass away. I'm only very much excited."

He suddenly had a desire to converse and ask Grodzki about many things. But what *were* the things he wanted to ask about? He had forgotten.

"It'll pass away. It's not worth paying attention to.— Oh, yes, I haven't seen you for quite a while, ever since the scandal.— I get these attacks of fever very often now."

He reflected a long time.

"Yes, it was a terrible scandal. You ran away with that married woman — what was her name? How do you come to be here again? And where is she?"

"I suppose she died," said Grodzki abstractedly.

"Died? Died? Wait a moment. Do I understand you? You *suppose* she died, you said?"

"I don't know for sure." Grodzki spoke very slowly. "I don't know. why I came back here. I don't know anything. I told her in a café once that she was a burden to me. She left me at once. Then I lost consciousness, got brain fever, couldn't tell the difference between reality and my ravings. No one said anything, and I never asked any one what had happened. That's all I can tell you, because that's all I know. Besides, I don't care. I'm through, through with everything . . ."

Falk looked at him in dread.

"Is that true?"

"I don't know, and I don't care to know."

For about ten minutes they sat in deep silence.

"Listen, Falk, do you believe in the immortality of the soul?"

"I do."

"How do you imagine it?"

"Faith doesn't imagine. You either believe or don't believe. Besides, I don't believe in anything. I don't believe the soul is immortal. I believe in nothing.— Tell me, now, don't you really know anything about her?"

"About whom?"

"Her."

"No. Don't let's talk of it.— H'm, faith, faith.— I don't believe in anything either. But I'm in the grip of a terror."

"Terror?"

"Yes, horror. One never thinks of it. Life is so long. But when a man begins to want to, or, rather, has to die, then he constantly thinks about what is going to be afterwards. I've already settled my account with life.— Now

I'm going to die," he added, with a madman's smile, after a pause.

"You mean to die! You're wise. I couldn't advise anything better."

Falk eyed Grodzki curiously. Grodzki was buried in deep thought.

"It's really not terror," he said presently. "It's something quite different. When the desire to kill myself comes to me, I lose consciousness, I can neither think, nor control my conduct, I am in a fever. But what I want is to die in full possession of my consciousness, coldly, calculatingly. That's what's hard. It's true, there's a way. The moment you say to yourself you are not going to do it, you are not going to do it,— pull the trigger! But I shouldn't like to fool myself.— I believe the majority of suicides kill themselves that way. I don't want to fool myself. I want to die fully conscious that I am dying."

Falk listened, gazing intently at the speaker and wondering that his words produced not the slightest impression upon him. The only surprise to him was Grodzki's face. What a dead mask! His smile struck him especially. The lips moved mechanically, the muscles seeming to take no part in the action. He thought of what was passing in Grodzki's soul.

"Why do you intend to kill yourself?" he asked, his heart beating anxiously.

"Why? Why?" Grodzki countered, "I may as well ask why you still keep clinging to life? That's much queerer. I've at last come to understand you. I've thought about you a great deal. You played a great rôle in my life. Why, then, with your desperate, your guilty conscience, do you want to live any longer? Tell me." He broke into a laugh. "Whatever you do comes from

the unutterable pangs you suffer through your conscience.
If you ruin anybody, you do it only to have associates in
misery, to see others suffer as you suffer. You carry in
you a world of grief and misery, don't you?"

For a long while the two gazed at each other. Then a
sort of fury broke forth in Falk against this man, a fury
that seemed to communicate itself to Grodzki. Grodzki's
eyes suddenly opened wide and lit up with an expression of
mortal hate. Falk felt his face twitching. He rose and
sat down again. For a moment it seemed as though they
would rush madly at each other's throats. Their eyes glow-
ered in a stare that seemed as if congealed forever.

Suddenly the spell broke.

Grodzki burst into a contemptuous laugh.

"Ha, ha! You have ceased to be dangerous to me.
You are quite innocuous now. You are but the ruins of
the former Falk . . . I used to love you, love you more
than your extinct soul can grasp."

He turned serious and profoundly gloomy now.

"That dead mask," thought Falk, scarcely conscious of
what Grodzki was saying and unable to avert his eyes from
his face. He would have pierced that dead mask through
and through in order to fathom its strange mystery.

"I loved you very, very much. You were a god to me.
Now I have come to see you are but a man, an insignificant
man. I have the feeling of having at last awakened from a
hypnotic sleep. Yes, you are only a man, a variety of ape, a
mean man. I don't love you any more, no; and I don't
even know why I don't. I don't love anybody, I didn't love
her either. Some day you may have that experience, too.
Our kind cannot love. We may think we do, but it's only
self-deception. I always hated you, too, more than I loved
you . . . I was always on the lookout watching carefully

so as not to fall into Nature's snare. Nature wanted to entangle me in love, me, a man . . ."

They were silent a long while.

" Do you know, Eric, you are an insignificant man. However, that doesn't matter to me."

He regarded Falk for several minutes, playing mechanically with his wine glass.

" I have nothing more to say to you. A foolish chance has brought us together. This meeting is fearfully unpleasant to me."

Falk laughed maliciously, while Grodzki grew more and more serious.

" Maybe — maybe I'd feel some respect for you if you condescended to put an end to yourself. You know, Eric, I don't mean to trifle, to play the part of a keen, penetrating psychologist. But there are moments when one reads in another's soul with absolute clearness. I see your deep despair, your terrible aversion to life.— But it really doesn't matter to me."

" Don't say that so often, else I'll begin to believe you mean the very opposite," Falk answered with a sardonic laugh.

Grodzki suddenly grew excited, apparently forgetting what he had said the moment before.

" You think, or, rather, I think that it's impossible to want to take one's own life. You, my dearest Falk, will do it because you will persuade yourself that you have to do it. I will do it because I want to do it. Want to . . . must . . . *qu'est-ce que ça veut dire?* I take my life because I want to. You send a bullet through your head because you say to yourself you must . . . At least once in life to experience the satisfying sensation of having wanted something. It's so hard to want something. I wanted to do something yesterday, but got frightened and in despair unconsciously bit my finger. There is something in a man which revolts against death . . . Let him suffer pangs that words cannot describe, let him suffer so that his hair stands on end — it matters not. Once in my life, once only, my mind wanted something. And behold the miracle! — It was to die!"

He lapsed into silence. Falk looked at him with mounting dread.

"So you really want to put an end to yourself?"

Grodzki did not hear the question.

"Only you mustn't do it in despair," he resumed. "Every peasant maltreated in military service ends that way. It must be done calmly — yes, absolutely calmly —" He looked at Falk with his dead eyes. "Listen, Eric, I saw a picture once which produced a profound impression on me. A certain gentleman makes his entry into the region of death in patent-leather shoes, trousers turned up at the bottom, saunters in *sans peur, sans reproche,* a regular sport. On either side grow two lilies. And somewhere below stands Death yawning from boredom. You understand? Bored! Death bored. The foolish people think Death is great. Indifferent Death bored to death. You understand?"

He fell silent again.

"I can't say I'm afraid. I shouldn't be a bit afraid if I could send a bullet through my head. But I want to die decently, aye, beautifully. I don't want my brain to splash all over . . . Well, you see, I feel terror of the few moments when my brain will still be alive while my heart has long been dead. All my life will pass before me in those few moments. Suddenly an unquenchable thirst for life will come upon me. Everything will seem so beautiful. I shall be swept with a great craving to return to life; then terror that soon, very soon, all this will pass and that in one little tiny flash I shall cease to exist — cease to think. And I shall count every blade of grass, look at every leaf above me, think of all the tiniest objects, just to hold on to my thoughts. Gradually, gradually, my thoughts will grow confused, covered over with mist. And the very last thousandth fraction of a second I shall think of her — and a terrible tremor will run through my body. Then everything will begin to turn before my eyes in a mad dance, a fiery circle. I shall behold it wriggling, disappearing, going out . . . One more tremor of fear, a faint glimmer of light, not more than a minute dot in the black eye of non-existence "— Grodzki smiled insanely —" and all will be over."

A cold thrill of horror ran through Falk; but it was only a momentary sensation that left him quite calm. The one feeling he had was a tormenting curiosity to pierce through Grodzki's being, pierce it through with his whole soul, tear out of him the mystery that might enable him, perhaps, to solve the final riddle of existence. But his brain was as though enveloped in a haze. Darkness was before his eyes. He drank greedily one glass after another.

He saw with marvellous clearness the dead mask that Grodzki's face had worn and was now engraved on his memory. So that was the way a man looked who was about to die! Leaning across the table, he asked mysteriously:

" Are you really going to kill yourself? "

" Yes. To-day."

" To-day? "

" Yes."

For a moment they gazed at each other. But Grodzki seemed no longer to see anything or be conscious of anything. He looked into terrible infinite emptiness. Suddenly he moved toward Falk and asked with a mysterious air:

"Do you believe the Apostle John was mistaken when he said, ' In the beginning was the Word'?"

Falk gazed at him terrified. Had Grodzki gone out of his mind? His eyes had widened unnaturally and looked like two black shining balls.

"It's a lie," he cried, "'Word'— that's only an emanation. The Word was created by sex — sex is the emanation of the substance existence. Look. In me broke the last waves of evolution . . . I am the last. You are only a transition, a tiny link in the great chain of evolution. But I am the last. I stand higher than you by a whole heaven. You are manure for evolution. I am God."

"God?" queried Falk, in mounting terror.

"I will soon become a God. God is the perfect expression of non-existence, the foam that non-existence has spewed out of itself. I am more than God. In me is the perfect expression of existence . . ."

He rose, his face transfigured by a look of solemn exaltation.

"God is mercy, despair, and gloom — non-existence. And I am the will of the most beautiful product of creation, the will of my brain," he cried; but subsided abruptly, as though falling into collapse.

"If this keeps on much longer," thought Falk in a panic, "I'll go to pieces. Fever'll burn up my brain. Why doesn't Grodzki go? He should go! An end to it all!"

Every second seemed an eternity. It was only by a mighty effort that Falk forced himself to remain sitting in his place awaiting the moment when Grodzki would at last condescend to kill himself.

At length Grodzki rose, slowly, and with an air of not being aware of his actions. As if in sleep, he moved to the door and stopped there. Then he seemed to come to himself.

" Falk, do you believe there are worshippers of Satan? "

" I don't believe in anything. I don't know anything.— Maybe in New York, in the Crimea, or somewhere." He was going insane with impatience.

Grodzki still pondered, then passed slowly out of the room.

Falk drew a deep breath. It was as though a heavy stone had rolled off his heart. Suddenly a great fear possessed him. Only now he seemed to understand fully what Grodzki meant to do. He wanted to think it over, reflect on it — he could not. His sensation of fear grew. His heart seemed to stop beating.

He snatched up his hat and flung it away again, then began to look for his money, went through all his pockets, finally found it in his waistcoat pocket, called the waiter, tossed down all the coin that had come to his hand, and ran out to the street.

From afar he saw Grodzki stop at a clock, and inspect it closely.

Falk pressed up against the wall to avoid possible notice by Grodzki. That mad fear possessed him again. When would it end?

After long absorption, Grodzki moved on. With striking clarity Falk saw every movement of his, watched intently the strange hesitating gait. He thought he could calculate with mathematical accuracy the very moment of the rise and fall of his feet.

Then his attention began gradually to dissipate. He tried to walk, very softly, but it was so hard, so hard it made his toes ache. However, the ache acted as a counter-irritant to his racking sensations. What that immense curiosity meant, that excitement, that tormenting impatience, he could not comprehend.

A long time he walked behind Grodzki until he saw him turn into the park.

He was compelled to lean against the wall to keep from falling, so faint had he become. His nerves were strained to the utmost, the least sound gave him pain. From afar he heard the rattle of wheels, somebody's laugh. Shivers, growing ever more violent, shook his body. His teeth knocked.

Now it must happen at last — it must! He closed his eyes . . . Now, now! His heart contracted. His breath gave out. Suddenly a thought flashed through his mind.

"Perhaps I shan't hear the shot." His blood boiled and roared in his ears. "Maybe I shan't hear!"

He listened, every nerve strained to the breaking point.

"And perhaps he doesn't mean to kill himself at all," he thought, clenching his fists in a rage. "Maybe he was only fooling me. Of course he won't kill himself," he repeated furiously.

At that moment he heard a shot. He wanted to yell. His whole soul made for that saving cry of relief, but his throat was as though tied with a rope and all that escaped from it was a hoarse croak.

Suddenly he relaxed with a sense of joy that everything was over at last. And again there was kindled in him a savage hate of the man who had made him suffer so.

He listened. It was quiet. With every nerve he drank in that stillness; and yet he listened, yet his thirst was not slaked, though vast torrents of that hushed quiet seemed to sweep down on his soul.

Then he was overcome by a desire to see Grodzki, look

into his eyes, behold the fiery circles about which he had just spoken. Carefully he stepped forward, stopped, took a deep breath. But that instant a mad fear struck him, a feeling as though he himself had committed the murder. His knees knocked together, the blood rushed to his heart.

And he moved on, trembling, staggering, not quite conscious of his surroundings.

Suddenly he caught the sound of steps behind him. He remembered having heard them before, and summoning all his strength walked faster, faster, finally starting to run, not heeding the direction. His legs caught. Something dragged him, pushed him back, and he ran, and a furious din uprose in his head. It seemed to him that soon, soon all the blood-vessels in his brain would burst.

Bathed in perspiration he ran into the hall of his house and fell on the stairs unconscious.

How long he lay there he did not know. Coming to himself he slowly ascended the stairs, quietly opened the door of his room, and flung himself on the bed.

But suddenly he was on the street again. Queer! How had he come out of the house? The door was locked and he did not remember having opened it.

He stopped to ponder.

Strange, very strange . . . There at the corner was a new house. How was it he hadn't noticed it before? He read the large letters on the sign posted up over the front: "Mourning Apparel." He started back with a shudder. Why was he looking so hard at the crazy house? As yet he had no need for mourning clothes. Why did that sign upset him so? he wondered. Some one passed by. He had on a long frock coat with one button missing. Falk noted it distinctly.

Now he was passing through a large open square, on both

sides of which stretched long lines of vehicles. But there were no people in sight, not the slightest sound reached him. Dead silence all round.

He was struck with astonishment. An unreasonable dread set every muscle of his body aquiver. Why this fear? He tried to think, but unsuccessfully. A blur of cloudy, monstrous images circled in his head. And the whole world, torn into purple clumps, seemed to be dancing before his eyes.

He succeeded in calming himself again, and walked on — but where was he going to, where?

Aha! Here the street came to an end. And there was the park.

He trembled. Terror and fever shook him alternately. He could walk no further. The whole world fell apart into myriads of dancing fiery blotches, like blazing flakes of snow.

He did not understand what was happening to him. He closed his eyes, but something compelled him to look at one dark blotch — there — there lay Grodzki with his face upturned.

His fear was gone now and he only felt a mad, inexplicable curiosity. He did not see Grodzki clearly, only his face. His eyes were closed, his mouth wide open. Falk gazed a long time at this dead mask, and a wild fury of passion kindled within him. In the paroxysm of his suffering, unable to budge from the spot, he tried to lift his hand, but could not. Then he strained every nerve to drop on his knees and crawl on all fours. But he couldn't do that either. He could not tear his eyes away from the corpse.

Despair clutched him. The dead body seemed to lift its eyelids and reveal a malignant, mocking smile in the eyes. That was terrible.

The eyes — he saw it clearly — called him, and the parted lips suddenly widened in a revolting grin.

He felt an icy hand touch him, and a sepulchral cold went through his body.

As though struck by a thunderbolt, he jumped to his feet, and looked round. Where was he? So it had only been a dream! . . . This cursed fever!

If only it did not recur! The terror was splitting his head apart. Mechanically he took off his collar. The collar button dropped. He searched for it diligently, and the longer he hunted, the more impatient he became. Trembling with rage, he ransacked the room, felt over the floor with his bare hands, went under the bed, pulled all the papers from under the desk, frantically tossed them up, got into a state of desperation. Weeping and gnashing his teeth, he finally, with a tremendous effort, raised the carpet covering the whole floor.

There lay the button.

It made him infinitely happy. Never before, he thought, had he been so happy over anything. He laid it carefully on the desk, looked hard once again to make sure it was lying there, and with a sense of complete satisfaction sat down at the window. It was growing light.

He came to himself completely. So he had had a violent attack of fever. Perhaps he ought to call Ysa. Oh, no, no, no! She would faint away with fright. One should always have morphine at hand. Not to keep soothing drugs in the house was inexcusable negligence.

He must strain all his energies, must keep an eye on himself, must not lose consciousness again. That fearful delirium! He shook himself to get rid of the revolting images it called forth, opened the window, but got faint again.

Only one minute of calm, one little minute! . . . He lay down in bed.

A sort of strange sick hush fell. A thousand little fires were blazing on the distant peat heaps, careering in a mad race, then went out. The willows on the roadside groaned and crackled as though falling apart into sepulchral decay . . . A dog began to bark in the neighbouring village, another answered in a prolonged pitiful howl.

Suddenly he heard a plaintive howl, just as long-drawn-out, right at his back.

His heart went shut.

Once more that howl — louder. A terrible wail, then suddenly a fearful scream.

He turned round in wild terror and saw — nothing. There was no one there. Still he felt that something there behind his back, heard its groaning and howling and crying.

"What do you want?" he shouted. "It's not I, it's not I. I'm not guilty. I didn't do it. Let me go, Marit, let me go!"

Suddenly he had the sensation that some one was driving him with a fiery scourge in a hellish chase. His whole back was covered with long stripes and bloody scars. And he ran like mad. He must escape, must escape.

But the constant rains had softened the ground, and his feet stuck in the mud. At times he sank up to his waist. He scrambled out. Now, now he would struggle on to a dry place. But that moment some unseen hand grasped him from behind and threw him back into the mud. He choked, lost his breath, the dirt oozed into his mouth. Finally in his death agony he made a superhuman effort, tore himself away, crept out of the swamp, and started to run, this time on hard, smooth, even road. Again he heard groans in back of him, weeping and desperate cries. He lost consciousness, his strength gave out — he could go no more. Now, now the end would come . . .

Suddenly he stopped as though transfixed. On the marketplace of the little town stood a grey old man who nailed him to the ground with his eyes. He could not stand that gaze, turned around, but wherever he looked, he encountered hundreds of those terrible cruel eyes preying on him, burning him, drilling him through and through, tearing the soul from his body, glowing with thirst for vengeance, surrounding him with a fiery ring. He pressed close to the ground, sought in some way to escape unnoticed, but that ring of eyes shut in on him more and more tightly. In despair he determined to look once more, and beheld the grey old man — Marit's father.

"Murderer!" the old man shouted. "Murderer!"

Instantly a hundred fists rose ready to strike at him in a hail of fiendish blows, to mash him into pulp. With a terrible leap like a beast's he broke away from the crowd, ran home without taking breath, mounted to the first floor, and banged the door to.

He stood waiting, pressing against the wall. A long minute passed. It seemed to last a whole eternity. His blood pounded in his temples like a hammer. Thunder roared in his ears. The noise of it, he was afraid, would betray him. His strength gave out. His teeth chattered. He dropped to his knees, pressed against the wall, closer, still closer — the wall would support him, the wall would not give way.

There was a knock at the door.

He jumped up.

Marit, surely Marit!

Another knock.

A whole eternity seemed to pass.

Suddenly he saw the door beginning to open. An insane terror froze his limbs. With all the weight of his body he threw himself against the door, planted his shoulders against it, putting his full strength raised to the tenth power into the effort. But the door opened, wide, wider. A strange force pushed him farther and farther away. The crack, at first narrow, widened — now a head was thrust in, and he saw terrible eyes out of which inhuman suffering stared congealed.

Falk uttered a desperate shriek.

Before him stood a stranger.

"What is this, a new apparition?" he wondered. "Perhaps, though, it's reality. Maybe I've gone crazy?" he asked himself affrighted. Suddenly his eyes fell on the collar button on the desk. So it was not delirium, this sense of the presence of another.

He rose from bed, seated himself at the desk, and gave a scared look around at the stranger, who in his turn regarded him with uncanny calm.

A few moments went by.

"Did you come through there?" Falk asked uneasily, pointing to the door.

The stranger nodded his head yes.

Falk searched his mind, then, with a sudden recollection, said:

"I believe you wished to speak to me about something in a restaurant yesterday."

"Yes. You don't know me, but I know you. I used to meet you frequently. Pardon me for following you. I must speak to you. You seem to have had a nightmare. I know what it's like. God! How well I know it. I've been through it, just lately. You screamed. Naturally you would, being aroused suddenly from a troublesome sleep.

You are very nervous. I thought that by looking fixedly
into your eyes you'd awaken immediately. And so you did.
You seem to be highly nervous. I noticed it yesterday when
you asked me if I meant to arrest you. You didn't let me
say a word. I've been looking for you a long time, it's
true, but our meeting yesterday was purely accidental."

" How did you get into my room? "

" The hall door was unlocked. I entered and knocked at
a venture. And no one answering I opened the door.— I've
often met you. I met you a few times in his company, too."

" But what do you want? What can I do for you? "
cried Falk vexed.

The stranger seemed not to pay the least attention to
Falk's annoyance.

" Tell me, tell me! " Falk cried, losing patience completely.

Again the stranger looked at him with the same unnatural
calm.

" Don't interrupt me. So you see, the man in whose
company I met you carried off my wife.— I beg your pardon,
my wife carried him off by force . . . Ha, ha! I have a
theory on that subject, my own theory . . . Man is a louse,
woman's slave. And a slave doesn't carry his mistress off
by force."

" I think there are plenty of coachmen in the world
breeding plenty of children by their highborn mistresses,"
Falk laughed cynically.

The stranger seemed not to hear him.

" Woman created man. Woman is the first. Woman
forced man to develop his powers beyond all possible limits."
He broke off growing suddenly confused, and looked at
Falk with a queer, half-insane smile.

" Listen," he said at last with his mysterious smile, " what

was it that made primitive man take up a club the first time?
Why, woman. To fight for the female, to kill his rival,
that was what put the club in his hands. Isn't it true?"

"True," Falk answered curtly.

"You are an educated man, Mr. Falk, so of course you'll
say it was the so-called struggle for existence. You're mistaken. The struggle for existence is merely an effect. It
came after the satisfaction of carnal desire. Lust was the
means by which Nature gave man to understand the worth-
whileness of the struggle for existence."

He grew agitated and pale.

"But that's not what I've come for, to bore you with my
theories. The business I have in mind is very different."

He looked round solemnly.

"I'll tell you something, tell it to you and nobody else
. . . You have produced an extraordinary impression upon
me . . . The man who lured my wife away, that is to say,
who was lured away by my wife, has told me striking things
about you."

Falk could scarcely contain himself any longer. He did
not understand half the stranger was saying.

"Hurry. You see I'm ill. I've had a bad spell of fever."

The stranger smiled queerly.

"I've been through that, too. It's gone very bad with me
lately."

With a face so pale that it seemed to turn green, he moved
still nearer to Falk and whispered:

"Something urged me to come here to you, to make you
happy. To-day when you ran away from me —"

A quiver ran through Falk's body.

Was it delirium after all? He was fearfully alarmed.
The stranger's eyes kept boring themselves into him.

"What, what are you saying?"

" I wanted to give you happiness."

The stranger fell silent, lost in thought.

Falk looked at him distraught. A cold perspiration beaded his forehead. He shook like an aspen leaf. One button was missing on the stranger's coat. Where had he seen that man? Yesterday, yes, yesterday — but that was a dream — Oh, no, in that cursed restaurant.

The stranger seemed to be searching hard for the proper form in which to express what he was going to say.

" Do you know that strange sensation of peace? Of course you don't know it, you can't know it — that feeling of wonderful harmony . . . you don't feel pain, you don't feel your own body. All the physical fetters drop away from your body, and you are free. You sink into a sort of limitless, boundless infinity. Space widens, miles stretch into millions of miles, dirty hovels become palaces. You don't know where you are. You know no roads, no direction."

His eyes burned with the ecstatic fire of inspiration.

And again a cold tremor ran through Falk's body.

" In one second you live through a century. On the tiniest point of space you see a thousand large cities — What luxury! What beatitude! "

The light in his eyes suddenly went out. His face twisted with pain.

" At first fear comes over you. When the earth quaked under my feet and began to rock, when I found myself suddenly in a strange city, an unknown country, I simply had to fall down on my knees before the passersby and implore them to permit me only to touch the hem of their garments . . . Oh, those were trying moments, terrible moments, an ordeal."

" Aren't you apoplectic? " asked Falk, nervous.

" Oh, no, no," the stranger smiled an insane smile. " I'm

not ill. I'm happy. And I have come here to give you happiness also."

He pushed still nearer to Falk and whispered in his ear:
"These moments are terribly hard. But you can pull through them. Cast all thoughts away, absolutely all. They are but the support, the trusty support upon which rests the spirit of doubt and contradiction. Cast them from your mind. Free yourself of doubt, then sit down and concentrate, so that the full strength of your organism may flow into one point, so that you may feel yourself an atom, a vibrating, minute atom in the universe.— And then wait, long, patiently . . . Suddenly you will be plunged into a terrible chaos. An abyss will yawn before your feet, repulsive monsters will creep out of all the corners."

His eyes ignited with an unnatural fire.

"You will hear a hellish howl and din. The walls will become alive. They will begin to move on you, choke you, crush you . . . You will live through an agony that makes ordinary aches and pains seem like bliss. Then suddenly, all will vanish — something will lead you forth into the world, the whole of life will pass before your eyes with infinite lucidity. No more secrets, no more riddles . . . You will read in another's soul as in an open book. No more pain, no more sorrow, no more wrath, no more hate — I love the man who took my wife away. I followed him when he went off to-day to end his life by suicide — followed him with you. I wanted to save him. But at the moment of death one should not interfere."

Falk was beside himself.

"But what do you want of me?"

"You are responsible for his death. In your hands he was like wax. You were his god. You were his destruction. You filled his soul with poison. You brought him to the point where he became a criminal toward himself and toward others. Listen to me, Mr. Falk, come with me . . ."

The stranger fixed a stern look upon him.

"Oh, how hardened your heart is! Then why are you so pale, why so tremulous? He's on your conscience, yes, he's on your conscience!"

"Who, who?"

"Grodzki," whispered the stranger.

Falk groaned. His head dropped to his breast. Suddenly he leaped to his feet and cried: "I'm not sorry for it. I should like to destroy, annihilate the whole world. I laugh at your mystical ravings. I don't need them. I don't want happiness. I spit upon happiness. One thing only I regret —that I destroyed too little.— Do you understand me?"

"Spirit of evil, spirit of evil!" whispered the stranger, in terror.

But suddenly his face softened, his voice became almost tender.

"You are ill. I don't want to fatigue you any more . . . I followed you. I was afraid for you when you awaited Grodzki's shot."

He grew excited again. His voice quivered perceptibly.

"You had had such a long talk with him just before. Did he tell you anything about my wife? Did he abandon her? . . . Now she'll go to ruin."

"He didn't tell me anything . . . Go, for heaven's sake, go. You are killing me . . . Go, go."

Falk felt he could bear no more.

"You are so ill, so ill. Don't be angry at me, Mr. Falk. I'm going. I'm going."

And he passed out slowly.

Falk heard nothing, saw nothing. His head whirled. The room danced before his eyes — he fell unconscious . . .

CHAPTER X

FALK woke up. What was it? He heard a melody, a mysterious melody sung in a bass voice, and, like a distant echo, the mournful strains of a soprano. His whole being quivered and aspired to that divine air. How beautiful it was! All the heaviness, gloom, horror seemed to be melting away from his soul, changing to something divine. The delicate meaningless sadness of the sounds gave him a beatific sense of lassitude such as he had never before experienced.

It must still be night. But he could not decide to open his eyes. It was so delicious, this feeling of sadness. Yes, it was night. He felt the sweet desire for the coming day, the glad, warm, brief, brilliant autumn day. Now, apparently, it was raining, but in the morning the sun would come out, dry the earth, and burnish the leaves again with the same gay purplish yellow.

Had he really awakened?

He heard the melody still, softer and sadder. And he lay enveloped in a sick mournfulness that had ceased to be pain. It was like an ebbing away, like a recollection fading into dimness, a vague longing for remote tropical countries where the plants grow into giant trees, where every mountain top hides behind clouds, every river rushes impetuously, foam-covered. His heart beat with trepidation. He pressed both hands to it, and felt the pulsations between his ribs. At first he let it beat on his whole hand, then on two fingers only, and lastly just on his index finger. How it pumped! Was that the way Grodzki had found his heart? He sat up on the edge of the bed, holding his head in both hands.

358

Grodzki had shot himself! That he knew for certain. Shot himself because he wanted to die. He had died voluntarily from a sense of aversion, no longer caring to see the brilliant day and the purple yellow of the leaves.

But why think about it? Why break the blissful harmony reigning in his soul? What had that stranger said? " Falk, Falk, you don't know that harmony. It is higher than any peace, higher than all holiness and bliss . . ." But he's insane.

Falk trembled. He saw the insane man's eyes, and his fingers clutched at the blanket convulsively. A wave of terror swept over him again, but he calmed himself at once.

Evidently he had recovered full consciousness.

On the stranger's disappearing from the room he had fainted away in the arm-chair. But now he was lying in bed. So he must have been carried over and put to bed. And the collar button? There it was shining on the desk . . . So surely he had awaked in full possession of his wits.

That gave him purely animal joy. He flung himself back on the pillows and lay for a long time as though in a swoon.

Coming to himself again, he jumped out of bed and began to dress. But he was still feeling faint.

Half-dressed he lay down once more and stared vacantly at the ceiling.

What a silly pattern! The gas fixture should be in the middle. Well, all right. The ceiling has the shape of a parallelogram across which I will draw a diagonal.

Suddenly he fell into a rage. Ridiculous! The point of intersection is not there at all. The room disgusted him. Into that narrow space he was shut with all his torments and there beyond those walls the world was so wide.

He felt an immense craving to go away somewhere, far, far off, in the Pacific Ocean. Yes, the Pacific. That was emancipation. That was eternal quiet, eternal harmony without trouble or passion.

How his young heart had palpitated then! His knees had knocked with terror. He saw a multitude of people kneeling outside the church right on the grass imploring God for mercy. As he looked at them, his heart beat ever more violently, his anxiety grew, his sin burned on his heart like a stigma. Soon he would have to confess. He would have to tell a perfect stranger of a vile deed that he had committed. In awful anguish he opened a prayer-book and read a prayer to the Holy Ghost. And peace descended upon him. His heart was filled with bliss, and his soul became pure and big, like the hot noon shining down on him. Soon he would have to go inside the church; but did nobody see that black horseman on a black steed riding into church at midday? He crept cautiously up to the door of the sacristy, listened, then softly opened the heavy door, and shrank back in horror. There stood the stranger.

"You have ruined his soul," he said solemnly.

"I'm raving, I'm raving!" Falk cried, awaking and jumping out of bed.

Ysa was standing beside him.

"It's I, Eric, I. Don't you recognise me?"

For a full minute Falk looked at her in silence, then drew breath and said: "Thank God, it's you."

"Eric, what's the matter? Are you still ill? Aren't you better? I almost went mad I was so frightened."

With a tremendous effort Falk controlled himself.

"Hang it all! Why can't I shake off this foolish fever? Why can't I once and for all forget my pitiful trivial sufferings?" flashed through his mind.

"I'm all right now," he said almost boldly. "It was just

a slight attack of fever. Ever since — ha, ha! — I caught that cold at mother's I've been bothered this way. That's all."

His mind suddenly cleared.

"No, Eric, you're ill. You have high temperature. Lie down. Please lie down. This morning they found you on the floor and the doctor said you must stay in bed a few days."

Falk lost patience.

"Oh, let me alone. I haven't felt so well and bright for a long time. The doctors are idiots. What do they know ᷉ut me? Ha, ha, ha! About me?"

⌐Ie drew her down to himself, his heart filling with great tenderness for her.

"We'll make a night of it together. You'll bring wine and we'll sit here and talk and drink the whole night through — just as we did in San Remo on our honeymoon."

She glanced at him.

"I've never seen such a strong man! It's simply marvellous how strong you are."

"So I was lying on the floor?"

"You can't imagine what a turmoil you created in the whole house."

"But go now. You'll tell me everything later."

"Was there a visitor here?" asked Ysa.

"A visitor? No."

"Then I must have dreamt it."

"Evidently."

Ysa quit the room, and Falk began to dress.

"Yes, Ysa, you must have dreamt it. You dream strange dreams anyway."

He smiled a contented smile.

Should he put on a frock coat and a white neck-tie, he thought. To-day was the great holiday of peace, serenity, and eternal harmony.

He was in an exalted mood.

At last I have found myself — God!

But isn't it a disease? My thoughts are so feverish. Excitement pent up inside of me struggles to break its way to the surface. And perhaps this is only a physical reaction after all the torture and terror.

But what cared he? It had all been forgotten. His body straightened up with the joy of living and an energy long since unfamiliar.

" Ah, Ysa, back already? "

" Are-you doing gymnastics? "

" I'm expelling the disease. Give me something to eat."

" Come to the dining-room."

He ate, but with little relish.

" Ysa, I feel as though I had been born all over, quite new and young again. I am rejuvenated. I suffered a lot. But don't misunderstand me. I'm not referring to my personal suffering. It was as though the woe of all humanity had tumbled down on me and made me miserable."

Ysa beamed at him.

" Miraculous! The doctor said you would have to stay in bed at least three days and here you are looking stronger, more energetic, than I've seen you for a long time. You're not a bit like other people."

" Yes, yes, it's a new strength. Drink, drink with me. I am with you so seldom. Drink it all."

They finished their glasses.

Falk filled up the glasses again, then sat down beside her, took her hands, and began to kiss them.

" It's a long time since we've had a good talk," he said.

"Everything's all right now, isn't it?" she asked lovingly.

"Yes, everything's all right. We'll go away from here. What do you think of Iceland?"

"Are you serious? You always have so many schemes."

"This time I'm serious. It's more than a scheme. The idea occurred to me to-day or yesterday. I must leave this place, but I don't know yet when."

Ysa was radiant. She found Berlin, oh, so tedious, though she had considerately refrained from saying so to Falk.

"Picture a fisherman's hut on the seashore. Isn't it wonderful? And the autumn nights when the waves sing their awful song of eternity? But won't you get tired of it?"

"Do I ever get tired of anything when with you? Do I need another soul beside you?"

"But I shall often, often leave you alone. I shall go away with fishermen whole nights, and up into the mountains. And when we meet again, then we'll fling ourselves on the grass and look up at the heavens. But drink, drink . . . Oh, you can't drink as much as you used to."

"Look, I drank two glasses."

"And in that mutual confluence we shall be — you part of me — we shall be the revelation contained in us, the immanent substance."

He rose.

"Yes, we shall seek God, whom we lost."

Ysa was as if hypnotised.

"God whom we lost," he repeated half unconscious.

"You don't believe in God?" he asked abruptly.

"No," she answered thoughtfully.

"And you don't believe either that He should be found?"

"No, if He is not in you."

"That's what I think, too. To find God is to feel Him

in every nerve of one's being, to be convinced that He is here, to be possessed of a wild, supernatural force that comes from nothing but the feeling of God."

"You want to seek another god outside of God? What for? I don't require him. For I possess a direct sense of God. I feel Him as long as you are with me. Anything higher I have no need of . . . But you are not to feel the same way. Then I would not go with you."

He looked at her a long time.

"How beautiful you are! As though a light were shining in you."

He lost his self-possession and became extremely agitated.

"Yes, yes, I comprehend God, who is I and you. I understand the great holy Mine — You. Do you know what You are, my vague You? You are Jahve, Om, Tabu. My You is the soul never corrupted by the brain, my You is the holiday soul, which seldom descends upon me. Perhaps it did a single time, like the Holy Ghost, which came down to the Apostles only once. My You is my love, my faith, my guilty will. To find my god means to learn his ways, to understand his purposes in order no longer to do anything petty, paltry, ugly, mean."

Ysa was entranced. They squeezed hands.

"And you want to teach me to find that in myself?"

"Yes, yes."

He looked at her as though he had never seen her before.

"And you will be in me?"

"Yes, yes."

"I am yours — yours wholly, your You. . . . Is it so?"

"Yes, yes."

Falk suddenly became distracted.

"We are poor, Ysa," he said after a pause. "I lost all our money."

" Throw away what is left! " she exclaimed with a laugh and flung herself on his breast.

Terror came upon him.

" Listen. What if it shall pass away to-morrow? I so distrust myself."

" Then I will drag you after me."

" But perhaps it's only our extreme state of excitement now that makes us so ecstatic."

Falk jumped up.

" I'm lying! I'm lying! " he muttered hoarsely. " I've lied a whole lot, too much — now ". . .

He broke off. The idea of telling her everything down to the minutest details flashed up in his mind and instantly took on the vast proportion of a fixed idea.

" Ysa,"— and he looked at her as though to penetrate to the very depths of her soul —" Ysa, I must tell you something."

She quivered in alarm.

" Are you able to condone everything, everything bad that I did? "

A confession was struggling to his lips. He caught her hands, no longer capable of restraining himself.

" Everything, everything? "

" Yes, everything, everything."

" Even if I did that? "

" What? " she shrank back in terror.

She scrutinised him fixedly, then cried as though not with her own voice:

" Don't torture me! "

Falk at once controlled himself. He suddenly felt a cold sweat streaming down his body.

She ran to him trembling all over, and mumbled:

" What, what? "

He smiled strangely with forced composure.

Ysa saw nothing except that he had become deathly pale and his face was twitching.

" Are you ill? "

" Yes, I am.   I overestimated my strength."

He dropped down on the sofa, his head whirling round and round with the events of the last days.

He thought of Grodzki.

" I must have the strength of will to do it."

CHAPTER XI

"NOW you ought to go to Geisler and arrange everything, then we can leave the day after to-morrow."

Falk stood reflecting an instant.

"Yes, yes, we'll leave day after to-morrow."

He smiled absent-mindedly. "Do you love him very much?" he asked abruptly.

"Whom?"

"Geisler, of course. If something were to happen to me, you could marry him, couldn't you?"

"First die, then we'll see," she parried jestingly.

"Well, then, good-bye." He kissed her eyes.

"But don't come home so late again. I'm so uneasy about you now."

"I'll be back soon."

He went out. It was striking six. Streams of working-men were coming from the factories.

He turned timidly into a little narrow side street. Strange how everything alarmed him now. His heart beat with fear perpetually. At the least knock on the door he would start violently and remain many minutes with his nerves all a-flutter. Even little Janko's crying would give him a shock.

For a long time he had been unable to grasp how he came to have a son, and now, of a sudden, he had two, little Janko and little Eric, two dear charming children.

Ah, that wonderful eternal idyll! If only it weren't so ridiculous.

He walked along the streets in a brown study.

The events of the last two days span about in his head like a top and, whirling, fused into one feeling of vast woe. He felt as if he were choking. It caused him an effort to breathe.

What good would his running away do? It *was* a running away, an ignominious flight, not a pleasure trip. Well, he was running away so that his great lie should not be laid bare. But he couldn't live hidden with it longer. He could no longer look Ysa calmly in the face. Her trustfulness, her infinite faith were sheer torture. He was ready to spit on himself in disgust.

A strange woman, Ysa. Her faith hypnotised her. She walked about as in a somnambulistic sleep, unaware of his suffering, unconscious even of the possibility of such suffering. Ah, terrible when she should awaken from this sleep!

So I am doubly a criminal. I broke my marital faith and I committed a crime toward myself. I cut off the roots of my own existence. I cannot live without Ysa. I think and think in what manner of way I might live without her, and I find no way. And since I am I, hence God, because God is every one for whom everything exists, and everything exists only through me, therefore I committed a crime against God, and I am guilty of sacrilege.

However, I cannot be saying this seriously. Why, I don't even recognise the concept crime. Besides, I couldn't possibly have committed a crime, because crime presupposes a state of soul that — I swear it — has nothing in common with kind-heartedness — ha, ha! Kind-heartedness — which is called hard-heartedness. As for kind-heartedness, I have it to excess, the devil take it! My compassion for people and their sorrows is greater than anybody else's, including the sufferers themselves. So I am not a criminal.

He got himself extricated in these subtilizings.

But perhaps there's now arising a state of feelings that has not existed before. Perhaps that is accounted a crime now which has not seemed to be a crime since the evolution of civilisation, for example, since monogamy.

His brain was too worn out to develop these ideas further. Besides, it was all the same. That brain, with its lawyer's tricks and evasions, was absolutely powerless as against the feelings. So why keep on thinking?

And suddenly it came to him with terrible certainty that all this was to no purpose. Something awful, all-destroying was moving upon him with iron inevitability.

He trembled and looked about. No bench near. He dragged on painfully.

Though absolutely powerless to concentrate his scattering thoughts, he remarked various trivial details — a sign with a letter printed askew, a crooked rod in a garden railing, the peculiar gait of a passerby whose shoes seemed to pinch.

His mind finally wearied of these details, too.

Presently he uttered a subdued cry.

The thought that had been stirring in the most secret corners of his soul for several days, which he had exerted all his might to suppress, suddenly burst to the surface.

He must follow Grodzki's example. He had often before meditated suicide, but now it became an *idée fixe,* terrible, admitting of no escape.

He trembled, staggered, and leaned against a house.

Yes, there was nothing else left.

Now there was a profound hush in his soul. He tried to make himself think, but, unable to, walked on, his mind a blank, buried in that dull, dead stillness.

At one point he stumbled and almost fell. The unexpected shock of it pulled him up. After all it's not so hard

to take one's life. One must only train the will of the
brain to obey the will of the instinct, or *vice versa*.

And the compensation would be the end of agony at last.

For a long time he pondered what might not be agony,
but could form no picture; then what might not be lying —
but everything was lies. Perhaps a fact, a real fact might
prove to be the truth. But what is a fact? asked Pilate and
washed his hands of it. No — Pilate asked, What is truth?
and after that washed his hands.

Falk began to rave.

When he reached the building in which Geisler's office
was, his mind was a blur. That wasn't like the building.
Perhaps he had forgotten. He began to read the signs and
fixed his attention upon the one announcing, "Walter
Geisler, Attorney-at-law." Still he could not make it out.

He went inside and came out again and read the signs
all over. At last he recovered himself and shook with
fright.

Had he really gone out of his mind? Oh, God, God!
Only not that, not that!

He controlled himself with an effort. For fear that some
one might notice what was passing in him, he assumed a
light smile and tried to give his face the indifferent expression of a man who has idled in to have a chat with a friend.

He mounted the stairs and was admitted to Geisler's
office.

"Busy just now. Wait a minute," said Geisler.

After a while he turned from his desk and gave Falk's
hand a friendly squeeze.

"What's brought you here?"

"I'd like to get my affairs straightened out."

Geisler laughed.

"Ha, ha! There's nothing to straighten out. You

seem to have no notion of the state of your finances. No
more than 3,000 marks left."

"Very well. Then I'll drop in to-morrow. You can
have everything arranged by that time, can't you?"

"We'll see."

Falk suddenly bethought himself of something.

"You are to give me only 500, the rest you are to send"
— he mentioned certain amounts —"every month to this
address." He wrote down Janina's address.

"Who's this?"

"Oh, just the innocent victim of the ordinary villainy."

"Indeed? Well, and you? Going to the desert to
fast?"

"Perhaps." Falk smiled, then, recollecting his rôle,
laughed jovially.

"I nearly broke my neck looking for you."

"Where? When?"

"Yesterday. In a perfectly strange house. I wanted to
cover up my tracks, thinking a spy was following me. So
I stopped at the second floor and asked whether you lived
there. Stupid of me — seemed not to have been a spy at
all."

"Well, go on. Tell me the rest."

"No, it's a tedious story."

Falk lapsed into self-absorption. Geisler looked at him
in surprise.

"Aren't you ill?"

"To tell the truth, I am. Just had a bad spell of fever."

"Oh, yes." Geisler filliped his middle finger and thumb.
"What do you think of Grodzki's suicide?"

"Grodzki!" A cold shiver ran down Falk's spinal
column.

"The whole city is talking about it. He ran away with

an artist's wife, came back alone a few days ago, and shot himself."

"With an artist's wife?"

"Yes, the artist went insane, and Grodzki shot himself out of fright."

"Out of fright — fright of what?"

"They say he committed a capital offence and a warrant was out for his arrest. The woman seems to have disappeared. He was suspected of having made away with her."

Falk laughed.

"So that's why people commit suicide? Ha, ha, ha! And I thought it took a strong will to dispose of life and death."

"Probably it's mere gossip. I don't believe it. He was an able man. You knew him well. They're linking your name with his."

"My name?" Falk was strangely distraught.

"Yes, they're trying to trace a connection between you and him."

"They are? That's curious."

Geisler studied him.

"Your illness has soured you. You had better take care of yourself. How's Ysa?"

Falk trembled.

"You loved her very much, Walter?"

"To distraction."

"And no longer?"

"Ha, ha! A feeling of that sort doesn't pass away so quickly."

Falk seemed to be much pleased by this.

"It's odd that that should give you so much satisfaction."

"I'm settling my affairs." Falk laughed jokingly.

"What do you mean?"

"Well, an accident might take me off."

"Don't talk nonsense. You're ill; you ought to go to bed and stay there."

"You're right," said Falk, with a distracted air again. "But what was I going to say? You'll come to see us, won't you?"

"Gladly."

Going down the stairs Falk recalled that he should have advised with Geisler about the trip he and Ysa intended to take. But now he knew he should never go away.

On the street he thought of the farewell calls he had meant to pay, and the idea of the trip filled his mind again. But he did not want to consider it. It would involve too many complications — going back to Geisler, and the calls, and a lot of other preparations, and so on without end. No, no. His mind must be free.

"Should I visit Olga now, I wonder?"

He meditated upon this a long time and while meditating turned his steps mechanically in the direction of her home. That restaurant over there perpetually open exasperated him to the last degree, like the eternal lamp they kept burning in church, which had annoyed him even as a child. Absurd that it must never be allowed to go out! Then Olga appeared to him in the light of some sacred Vestal guarding the eternal light of that horrid tavern.— Well, well, Falk, you're getting stale and insipid.

He walked up the stairs and knocked.

Kunicki was sitting in Olga's room coatless. He was greatly excited.

"He shot a Russian in a duel," flashed through Falk's mind, and, with that, a terrible plan matured. Kunicki was a sure shot. He never missed aim.

"What are you discussing so hotly, as usual?"

Falk smiled affably, yet wickedly.

Kunicki gave him a sullen look.

" Well, Kunicki, what's wrong?   You look as if you were preparing to establish universal harmony to-morrow."   Falk laughed more and more gaily, and gave Olga's hand a warm pressure.

" How beautiful you look to-day! "

" Don't be foolish.— Kunicki is angry because you sent Czerski on a propaganda mission."

" Maybe Mr. Kunicki wanted to go himself? " Falk said over-amiably.   " This noble rivalry in a noble cause."

Kunicki threw Falk a look charged with hate.

" Keep your quips for a more fitting occasion.   This is a serious matter.   You know Czerski's an anarchist."

" No one knows it better than I do.   I had a long conversation with him about it."

" So much the worse.   Don't blame me if I open the eyes of the London Congress to what you really stand for."

" What care I about your committees?   I do just as I like."

" But we won't let you," Kunicki cried, fuming.   " You and this Czerski are undoing all our work of three years."

" Your work, your work? " Falk laughed scornfully. " What was accomplished by your work?   Ha, ha, ha!   A year and a half ago you unfolded your fantastic scheme to me.   You went into the matter very precisely, elaborating details of how you would remove each obstacle and organise a general strike of the miners.   I gave you the money for it, not because I believed in your nonsense, but because I wanted to find out whether you had the least ability to influence the masses.   You were to have shown me, so to say, in a microscopic preparation how the Crusades were set in motion, only with a changed slogan: *l'Estomac le veut.* Ha, ha! And what was the result? You returned in a week — plus a drubbing."

"You lie!" Kunicki shouted, in a towering rage, though still curbing himself. "You simply want to make a laughing-stock of me. If it affords you satisfaction, I gladly excuse your childish — ha, ha! — aristocratic-esthetic Nietzschean hunting after power and greatness, doubly comic in your case."

Kunicki laughed a forced acrid laugh.

"Continue," Falk returned wickedly. "I didn't mean to hurt you, and certainly wouldn't try to hurt you now that I see the extent to which your ridiculous rôle bothers you."

"If you think "— Kunicki's efforts to control himself delighted Falk —" if you think a man like you can insult me, you're mistaken."

Falk laughed a long laugh of sincere glee.

"I know I can't offend a man like you. Only, considering the efforts you are making not to take offence, you're protesting rather vehemently. But let's return to Czerski. You see, I don't believe in the Social-Democratic salvation. I don't believe that a party that dreams of a peaceful, rational solution of the social question can do anything. The dogmatic fabric it has erected rests on almighty reason. That's why it's so dull. Everything the workingmen have achieved so far is due either to stupidity, blind daring, or chance."

"Then you gave Czerski the money so as to stir up purposeless disorder through methods of unreason based upon the people's stupidity?"

"From the bottom of my heart I hope Czerski will perpetrate some impossible, some monumental act of folly. A few hung and beheaded revolutionists would leave a far profounder impression on the memories of the workers than your Party with its watery Marxian-Lassallean theories."

Kunicki laughed contemptuously, and muttered through his teeth:

"One might form a peculiar, though rather unflattering, opinion of you, Mr. Falk. A certain *provocateur* in Zürich expressed himself exactly the same way."

"The proper moment has come," thought Falk.

"So you take me to be a spy?"

Kunicki laughed offensively.

"I am merely calling your attention to the striking and suspicious similarity."

Falk bent across the table and struck Kunicki a sharp blow in the face.

Kunicki jumped up and threw himself on Falk, but Falk caught both his hands and twisted them so that Kunicki groaned with pain.

Falk was slightly excited.

"Let's not get into a fight here. If you want satisfaction I will gladly give it. I am stronger than you. I could easily thrash you."

He released Kunicki's hands with a violent shove that sent him staggering.

The pallor of Kunicki's face was deadly. He frothed at the lips. Putting on his hat and coat he quit the room.

Falk sat down. Olga stood at the window looking at him.

For a full half hour there was a painful silence.

Then he rose.

"He'll send seconds to me surely, won't he?" A veiled triumph sounded in his words.

"You provoked him, forced him to it. You want him

to kill you and so escape suicide." Olga laughed nervously and held out her hand. " So your strength is all gone? You said you love my love, and I thought you could live for the sake of my love. But you lied. You don't love anybody."

" I love you," Falk said in a perfunctory way.

" No, no, you don't love anybody. All you love is your own suffering, your cold, cruel curiosity, not me." She stood there wide-eyed, excited, her lips quivering.

" I love you," he whispered voicelessly.

" Don't lie, don't lie any more! You never loved me. What am I to you? You said, ' Be near me, I need your love.' But have you ever thought for even a moment that I live only for you? You are surrounded by a number of people who love you. But what have I beside you? Have you ever thought of me? "

" I always think of you," Falk rejoined in profound grief.

Olga wanted to say more, but her voice broke. She looked at Falk with eyes from which mournful tears streamed down quietly, then faced round abruptly toward the window, but immediately turned again and went to him, catching his hand with passionate despair.

" You mean to die? "

He looked at her as though not understanding. "You mean to die? " she repeated hotly.

" Yes."

" Yes! " she cried.

" Yes," he repeated almost in terror.

Her hands dropped.

" I don't love you any more. I don't love you as I loved you before. Why won't you give me even a penny of the millions you are taking away from me? Or have you grown so poor? Are you really so poor? "

She drew back and looked at him with a look full of woe and despair.

And Falk fell on his knees, seized the hem of her dress, and began to kiss her with a sort of reverence.

She dropped down beside him and taking his head began to kiss his eyes, his hair, his lips, and could not possibly tear herself away from that head which she loved with so much sorrow, such hopeless despair.

She jumped up.

" You don't love me."

There was a great weariness in her broken voice.

Falk made no answer.   He sat with his head leaning on both hands and suffered in silence.

Spiritual torment had broken him on the wheel.   A way out there was none.   His soul died away.   Only from time to time there flashed up in his mind an indistinguishable thought.

Olga sat on the edge of her bed, her eyes fastened upon him unwaveringly.

He looked at her.   Their eyes met.   He smiled unconsciously and gazed ahead of him vacantly again.

Suddenly he said as though to himself:

" I struck his face because he's just a mean worm."

" You're ill, Falk.   I see now your brain is sick."

She looked at him in growing amazement.

" And you've always been sick.   You are an abnormal man."

" I am abnormal.   Perhaps you're right.   Sometimes I ask myself whether I'm not insane.   But my insanity is unusual, different from other people's . . . Yes, yes, I have a great intellect.   Disgust is killing me."

For a long while he sat with drooping head and spoke quietly.

" Disgust of myself, of people, is eating me away like gangrene. Perhaps I could have done something in life, but dissipation gnawed down to the bottom of my soul. I walked, destroyed, and suffered. Oh, what terrible misery I have suffered! For all that, a diabolic force drove me on to do the very same all over again. People yielded to my influence — but why talk of it? Perhaps it is only my vanity speaking. As a matter of fact, I am pleased that I wielded such power."

He rose.

" Now I'm going. You were not just to me. I have always loved you very much."

He bent over her hand, which shook, and kissed it long. He stopped at the door.

" If the affair ends badly — you know what a good shot Kunicki is — then drop in on Janina occasionally. She was good to me. How ugly that I spoiled her life!"

He looked at her, smiling a strange smile.

" Will you?"

" Yes."

" Good-bye, Olga. Well — and — and — who knows whether we'll ever see each other again."

CHAPTER XII

FALK was awakened early in the morning. A gentleman was in the drawing-room on important business.

"Aha!" said Falk, and began hurriedly to dress.

In the drawing-room he found a young man, who greeted him with extreme ceremony.

"You come from Kunicki, don't you?"

He listened to the reply impatiently.

"*À outrance?* Certainly. Just leave me your address. But, for God's sake, no formalities. Of course, it's shoot to kill. But no fuss and ceremony."

The young man looked at Falk somewhat surprised, bowed and stepped out.

"Great!" said Falk, pacing up and down the room. Suddenly he felt a great craving for Ysa. He would go to her, take her in his arms, tell her everything, fondle her, caress her, implore her.

But the next instant his attention was attracted to a picture hanging over the piano.

A sky — a row of wide coarse stripes, screaming patches that did not blend, one long-drawn-out fearful cry of despair. A seashore — a long flooring. On the flooring two figures, the woman in a white dress, a single white blotch in all that desperate orgy of the sky, so awful, so mysterious that to look on it strained the nerves to insanity. The whole soul, it seemed, flowed into that white blotch. Yes, this was Fate, a white lightning, the world dancing in chaos.

Then he turned and examined a withering orchid.

"Now I must find seconds.— Geisler, of course — he will arrange everything."

He made a lengthy search for his hat, listened at the door of Ysa's bedroom, then resumed his pacing in the room. Many minutes passed that way.

"Now I must go, else I shan't find Geisler in."

He had no sooner left than Ysa walked into his room. She was feverish. Terrifying nightmares had haunted her sleep the whole night.

"Strange that Falk should have left the house already," she thought, disappointed. Talking to him would have soothed her.

Looking round the room she suddenly had the feeling of its being utterly strange, of it's not belonging to home. The very air in it seemed unwholesome, saturated with fever. Falk's papers were scattered about in disorder. She looked at a sheet lying on the desk. It was covered from top to bottom with a single word written countless times — *Ananke*.

A weird presentiment constricted her heart. She felt stifled. Sadness settled on her soul. It seemed as if all her happiness had gone up like a puff of smoke.

Whence that gloom came, she herself could not comprehend. She wanted to drive it away, replace it with cheerier thoughts, but her anxiety clung to her.

She returned to her room and began to dress slowly. The maid entered.

"A gentleman wants to speak to you. He says he must."

She handed Ysa a card. "Stephen Kruk."

Ysa read the name in astonishment. Impossible. Kruk had been obliged to flee Germany. There was a sentence of several years' imprisonment hanging over him. A wave of alarm swept through her. Her breast was weighed down with an evil foreboding. She had hardly the strength to finish dressing.

In the drawing-room was Kruk, pale-faced, with red, wildly roaming eyes.

Ysa stopped short, affrighted.

" What has happened? What has happened? "

" Where's your husband? "

His hoarse voice shook.

" He's just gone out. But what's the matter? How could you come back to this country? "

Kruk looked round as though unable to account to himself for the place he was in.

Ysa drew back in fright.

" Your husband is a scoundrel! " he suddenly cried. " He's dishonoured my sister."

Ysa heard a few more words: " mistress," " illegitimate child," " seducer," then understood nothing more. Kruk recovered himself. He saw that all the blood had left her face and her lips had turned blue. She reeled, but he had time to catch her before she fell.

" Your sister gave birth to a child? Recently? By my husband? A few weeks ago? Your sister? "

She looked at Kruk vacantly, and kept repeating, " A child, a child."

Suddenly she jumped up.

" I must see her. I must.— Impossible! No, no! "

She ran to and fro in the room.

" Why don't you say something? Say it isn't true, it's impossible. . . . Oh, God, God! Help me find my hat! Quick! Oh, God!— Impossible!— Ha, ha, ha! He asked me what I should say if . . . *Grand Dieu, c'est impossible* . . . How pale and solemn you are! Come, quick! "

She did not know what she was doing or saying. Not until she was seated in the cab did she recollect herself. They rode without speaking.

It seemed to her as though a black cold shadow were creeping up on her face. She laughed spasmodically, grew silent, and began to laugh again.

"I recognised you at once," she said, looking at Kruk with a sly smile. "I saw you in Paris twice. How you have changed! How pale you've grown! *Mais, c'est terrible, c'est terrible!* . . ." She glanced at the window with a wandering gaze.

Suddenly she became aware of the rattle of another cab behind. It was deafening. She saw nothing more, heard nothing more, only repeated mechanically: "*C'est terrible. c'est terrible!*"

At length the cab drew up, the one behind dashing forward and stopping abreast of it at the same moment.

Kruk's face changed. As Ysa stepped out of the cab, two policemen threw themselves on him.

"In the name of the law!"

With a movement quick as a flash Kruk pulled out a revolver, but that instant was thrown to the ground.

Ysa ran into the hall. She leaned against the wall to keep from falling. Her head whirled.

She looked around unconscious.

What had she come here for? To visit Eric's mistress? Ha, ha! Great God! She controlled herself and walked out of the doorway. Taking a few steps on the sidewalk, she stopped as though rooted to the earth. In one of the windows of the lower floors she saw a wan face — a girl holding a baby on her arm. The two women looked at each other a long time.— "*C'est elle,*" Ysa murmured, and saw Janina draw back from the window as if frightened.

Ysa entered and knocked. The door opened timidly, half way.

"Well, let me in." She pushed Janina back with force.

" I'm not going to hurt you.   I only want to see your baby.
— My husband is its father."

She entered the room.

" Why are you trembling so?   I really won't hurt you."

She burst into a nervous laugh.

" Well, Eric hasn't bad taste.   You are very pretty.   But
a mere child!   And Eric's mistress!   Ha, ha, ha! — But sit
down.   You have turned pale.— My God, how emaciated
you are, you poor little thing!   He's sucked the blood out of
you.   And that little mite is your child and Eric Falk his
father? " . . .

She laughed hysterically, looking at Janina with mad hate.
It lasted but a minute.

" Of course you didn't know Eric Falk was married.
How he lied, how he lied! "

Her strength gave way.

Janina threw herself on the bed sobbing.

Ysa rose.

" Have I offended you? " she asked coldly, and without
waiting for an answer stepped over to the bed in which the
baby was lying.   She looked at it long and intently.

" Don't cry.   I didn't mean to hurt you.— A lovely child.
— Why, you're not at fault.   You're but a poor weak child
yourself." . . .

She broke into laughter again.

" How strange that you should have a child!   How old
are you?   Eighteen, nineteen?   Well, good-bye.   Don't
cry.   I'll send him here.   He'll come back."

" Don't torture me so," Janina groaned.

" I torture you?   But I'll send him here — *tout de suite
— tout de suite.*"

Out on the street she stopped and remained standing on
the same spot for a long while.   Several loafers passed by

and threw indecent remarks at her. She looked about and walked off, faster, faster.

" Only not to return to that liar! " she whispered.

" God, what people live here! Why do they make fun of me? What have I done to them? " She gnashed her teeth in impotent rage.

Suddenly she felt an aching. Some workingmen had pushed her so hard that she almost fell. The pain brought her to herself.

Now she walked slowly past stone houses. She was timid, afraid, like a little child, a convulsive laugh tightened her throat. It took an effort for her to keep from bursting into sobs, but big tears not to be restrained rolled down her cheeks.

At last she reached a deserted square, sat down on a bench and quieted herself a little. Only now that she had completely recovered her senses, did she mentally realise the whole situation and feel the awful anguish of it. Her misery seemed to be making her insane. She jumped up. Geisler would give her money. Only to go away, run away from him — far — far away. Geisler would give her money — Geisler — Geisler —

She stepped into a cab and gave Geisler's address.

Her anguish grew intenser still, as though a whole Inferno were crumbling about her. Ha, ha, ha! *Mais non pas du tout; je suis au contraire très enchantée, tres enchantée.*— What were those gigantic letters: " Isaac Isaacson? "— funny! — Falk's a genius. He told me he wants to improve the human race by begetting children by as large a number of women as possible.— Here's where I can buy goods for a dress — Friedrichstrasse, 183. What *is* his name? Isaac Isaacson — 183 —

Suddenly she felt profound disgust.

Falk had taken her just as he had taken that girl, kissed her with the same lips . . . Her whole body quivered. She felt stifled, something so compressed her breast that she was ready to tear her dress.

"I only wonder why he didn't bring the girl into my bed. He might have performed that highly cultured act before my eyes."

She could no longer control herself. She contracted with pain and shrank together, drew herself up again, felt a painful stab in her bosom, in her head, everywhere — ah, everywhere —

Oh, que j'ai mal, que j'ai mal . . . Grand Dieu, que j'ai mal! . . .

She entered Geisler's office, tremendously jolly.

"Oh, how sweetly and kindly you look at me! You look like a bashful little boy. Ha, ha, ha! What a soft flannel coat you have on! Why do you look at me so, as if the sky of St. Anthony of Padua were opening up above your head? — Why, I am the legal wife of Mr. Eric Falk — you understand? We got married in the 15th arrondissement in Paris." She laughed heartily.

Geisler looked at her in amazement. But her laugh was so whole-hearted, it seemed, that he joined in.

"Listen, Walter, we haven't said how-d'ye-do to each other yet."

She held his hand in hers.

"Your hand is so large, good, warm."

"Didn't you meet your husband downstairs?" Geisler asked uneasily.

"Eric Falk, my husband?" she said, unable to catch her breath with laughter. "My husband! Ha, ha, ha! — *Mon mari! quelle drôle idée plus philosophique qu'originale, n'est-ce pas?*"

She glanced around and took a seat.

" Why do you look at me so dismally? — And — He was here? — Told you everything? " . . .

Geisler turned away and handled his cigarettes.

" Did he tell you about his little baby boy? And about his poor little mistress? Ha, ha — Maybe he wanted to unburden his heart to you."

" Listen, Ysa. Don't take it so to heart. — You are a woman — A man is so differently constituted."

She suddenly felt a terrible weakness, as if she were going to faint.

" Give me some water."

She drank off the whole large glass.

" Ha, ha! — No, I didn't see my husband. *Je ne l'ai pas vu depuis cinq jours.* It's delightful, so delightful to speak in one's own tongue — I've almost forgotten it. I studied in a vile German pension. I had to get up at five o'clock in the morning.— Oh, brrr! brrrr!— How different you are — good — and your hand is so strong and also so good."

She looked at him.

" Why do you look at me so mournfully? I don't need your pity. Just give me 500 marks.— You must give me the money —" she said firmly.

He looked at her frightened.

" What do you want money for? "

" H'm, a gentleman — ha, ha, ha! — and asks a lady what she wants money for! Give me money because I need it badly."

" Ysa, be rational for one moment. You're not going to do anything rash, are you? "

" What do you mean by that? "

" Listen. You know what you are to me . . . Something

has gone very wrong in your home. You understand me?
— How much do you need? "

"Three hundred — four hundred —"

"I'll give you six hundred."

She did not understand him. She only continued to look at him with growing ecstasy. Her head turned.

"Ah, how fine you are, how good! — Give me your dear large warm hand . . . Press me harder, still harder. *Oh, que j'ai mal, que j'ai mal!*"

And she burst into convulsive hysterical sobbing.

CHAPTER XIII

THE whole day Falk roamed about the city, restless.

Finally he went to a café and sat there several hours. He felt so broken he couldn't summon the strength to rise and ask the waiter for a newspaper. Oh, no, no! It was so painful to bring out even a word.

In a certain measure he was glad that everything was coming out so well — and Kunicki shoots true — to-morrow all will be over — Good!

He wondered that everything had become of so little import to him, yet it was his life that was involved.— His life . . . He smiled strangely. His life . . . He jumped up from his chair.

At home he felt so shattered that he threw himself on the bed at once and tried, but in vain, to fall asleep.

He must speak to Ysa, must speak to her about very important matters; but cautiously, very cautiously, so as not to arouse the slightest suspicion.

True, he might do it by letter. He pondered a long time. Otherwise evil thoughts might occur to her, or, indeed, good thoughts. He had better write her a letter.

He recovered himself entirely. His brain cleared and began to work.

Finally he said to himself definitely that to-morrow death would most probably close his eyes.— A shiver ran through his whole body.— Yes, a shiver and terror, though usually the knights of the revolver experience neither the one nor the other.

A strikingly vivid picture of the whole process of death in a duel rose to his mind. He would stand quietly, would see the muzzle of the pistol, a black point, then he'd distinctly hear the click of the trigger, then a loud report . . .

A cold sweat broke out on his forehead. It took a great effort for him to drive these thoughts away.

He yawned, yet that instant perceived that the yawn was but a substitute for terror.

Kunicki killed the Russian with his first shot — he won't miss me either.— And to leave all this — Ysa, the whole future —

However, he cooled down immediately. The future, the future! Whence this lie about the future again? A stupid lie! Ha, ha, ha! Strange that he should have to lie so to himself.— Evidently my mendacious soul was going to argue thus: " It's not so bad as it seems — It'll all come out right in the end."

Suddenly he sprang up in the air like a madman.

Why, Kruk cannot return to Germany! He's got a five years' term of imprisonment to serve.— So he can't get in my way.

He began to pace the room frantically.

Consequently Ysa will never know what has happened. She never opens my letters.

Until that time he had never had a moment of such direct pure animal happiness.

Such an abundance of good fortune! It seemed to deprive him of his reason. A passionate thirst for life filled his bosom. He could think of nothing else. One overwhelming stubborn thought possessed his mind — to go away as quick as possible.

Kunicki? Kunicki? What cared he for Kunicki now? What cared he for honour, what for dishonour? Only to run away, run away in all haste. His brain seized upon this thought with a desperate clutch.

And suddenly he roared with laughter, laughed long and hard.

Ha, ha, ha! My affairs are in a bad mess. I'm beginning to play comedy with myself. That's bad. What good will it do me if I run away? Will I rid myself of the lie and the disgust? Ha, ha, ha! What folly to think it can all still come out right!

He remembered a little lame Jew from whom he had tried to borrow money as a student. The Jew evidently had no money, or, more likely, had not wanted to make him a loan and invariably responded to Falk's plaintive pleadings with: " It'll all come out right in the end."

Suddenly his heart warmed. It seemed to him he had never felt so cheerful.

Now, in this cheerful mood, he could go to Ysa.

Entering the drawing-room, his eyes fell again on the crazy picture, with its mad orgy of despair.

In the dining-room he listened. From Ysa's room came the sound of sobs, groans and weeping.

It was as though a thunderbolt had struck him. He started back. His heart stood still. He ran to the door and knocked. No answer.

Suddenly a desperate shriek.

He knocked harder. Then he began to beat his fist on the door with all his might.

" Ysa! Ysa! " he shouted desperately.

Stillness. His mind almost went.

" Open the door! " he cried. " Open the door! "

No answer.

He fell into a fury, lost his reason. He threw himself on the door with the full weight of his body and broke it open.

Ysa jumped up to confront him, wild, distraught.

"What do you want? Go away, go away! Go to your mistress!" she screamed.

Falk stood trembling so violently he had to lean on the table.

"Go away, go away!" Ysa shouted, running about the room as if afraid he would catch her.

"Ysa!" he ejaculated at last.

"Leave me alone! Leave me!" she stopped her ears with her fingers. "I don't want anything. I don't want to hear anything, don't want to know anything. I can't bear to look at you! How abhorrent you are to me!"

Falk stood gazing at her with unsteady eyes. He heard only the hoarse shrieking voice, now a hysterical laugh, now convulsive sobs. He was surprised. That was the first time he had heard Ysa scream so.

Ysa's excitement reached the climax. She stamped her feet, uttered incoherent sounds, rushed around the table, and made for the door.

Falk recovered himself. He caught her hand. She struggled with him. He only squeezed her hand the tighter, so that his fingers buried themselves in her flesh.

"Let me go! Let me go!" she shouted.

"I'll go presently. But first you must listen to me!" he cried frantically.

"I don't want to hear anything. I hate you, despise you, you are detestable! Go to your mistress!"

She flung herself on the sofa with convulsive sobs.

Falk ran over to her in wild excitement.

Ysa's graceful delicate body serpentined and quivered in his arms. From her throat tore groans and cries of inhuman suffering.

Falk carried her out on the balcony, picked up a flask of

water, and moistened her forehead and temples. But she suddenly jumped up, and with all her strength propped her fists against his chest and pushed him off. Then she collapsed and fell on the sofa, panting. Gradually her strength left her, and she glided off to the floor. Soon, however, she rose and stood before Falk cold and proud.

"Well, what do you still want of me?"

"Nothing now any more — nothing," he murmured, looking at her with glassy eyes. "Nothing any more —" he repeated in the same muffled tone.

"You understand, of course, that all's over between us. I will not remain a single minute under your roof.— I'm going — I'm going —"

She flung herself at him and wanted to push him away from the door.

It grew dark before his eyes. He ceased to control himself and with all his strength flung her on the bed.

She jumped up, wanted to run, her hair became undone. He caught her hair furiously, and pulled and dragged her to the sofa.

"I'll kill you, I'll kill you!" He gnashed his teeth and laughed a mad laugh.

She no longer defended herself. She was all broken. There followed a minute of dreadful silence.

Falk, in supreme terror, dropped on his knees before her; then, suddenly, heard her weeping quietly like a tired child.

"Eric, Eric, how could you? How could you?"

Falk kissed her feet, then took her hands, and kissed them again and again. They were wet with his tears.

"Eric, what have you done?"

He made no answer, only pressed her hands harder to his lips.

"Get up now, get up. Don't torture me." She shed floods of tears.

He rose. Though trembling from head to foot he seemed to be calm.

"But don't go away from me," he gasped. "I — I loved you so."

He fell silent. No, he mustn't say it.

"I lost my reason. That other man always stood before my eyes."

She looked at him in fright, seemed not to understand.

"Who? What?"

"Who?" Falk repeated and recovered himself.

"No — no — no one —" He drew back a few steps — "But don't go away from me — do what you please with me — only don't leave me."

Her voice sounded weary as she said:

"Now nothing will help. You are a stranger to me. That which I loved in you has died never to come to life again. You are as ridiculous as all the others. You are a beast like the rest of the men with their stupid, brutish lust. — I thought you were different.— But now don't plague me any more. I despise you! You are abhorrent to me — let me go! Eric, let me go! I cannot remain with you a minute longer."

She stepped to the door.

A mad rage seized Falk.

"I won't let you. You must stay with me, you must. I command you. I'll kill you if you go."

He wanted to seize her. She fell back in terror.

"You have gone out of your mind," she shouted.

He caught her and pressed her in a wild passionate embrace. She resisted with all her might, but he held her too hard. She could not tear herself away. A passion, a sickly passion, clouded his brain — a beastly desire to possess this woman, possess her for the last time.

"Let me go, let me go," she screamed in terror.

Powerless to control himself, he carried her over to the bed.

Suddenly she managed to free one hand, bent all up in his embrace, clenched her fist, and struck him full force in the face. He let her go on the instant. His soul, it seemed, had died away.

Ysa he did not see. He was looking into an abyss suddenly gaping at his feet. Then he rested his eyes on her fixedly and came to himself.

Her face was as though turned into stone. The only sign of life in it was the expression of aversion and hatred in her eyes.

At length he realised that she no longer loved him.

"Don't you love me?" he asked with an icy smile. There was really no reason for putting the question.

"No, I don't," she answered, cold and firm.

Falk smiled, himself not knowing that he smiled, pushed pieces of the door with his foot, and was about to quit the room.

Ysa jumped up with savage hate.

Falk stopped and smiled.

"And that girl —" she laughed as though gone insane. "That girl who drowned herself — ha, ha, ha! — accidentally, while bathing.— You did it — you, you, you,— a year after our marriage! Ha, ha, ha! Well, tell me of all your other exploits, you fine monogamous husband. I suppose you have several other girls on your conscience. Maybe one of them hung herself on your account?" She walked up and down the room and talked, no longer conscious of what she was saying.

" Ah, that lie, that perpetual lie — ha! — but let us leave that! Now all's over. Go! Go! You would do well to look out for that girl a little. She looks very pitiful. *Adieu, mon mari — je n'ai plus rien à te dire —*"

" *Adieu, adieu.*"

Falk no longer heard anything, no longer felt anything. He wanted to sit down somewhere and remain there long, long, in profound silence.

Ysa flung herself on the bed. Falk quit the room quietly. The bell rang.

Falk opened the door.

He looked blankly at the messenger and waited.

" Is Mr. Falk in? "

" I am Mr. Falk."

" I have a letter for you."

Falk took the letter, went to his room, and put it on the table. Then he seated himself in his arm-chair and gazed long at this strange missive, until finally he compelled himself to read it.

From Geisler, saying everything had been arranged, the duel would take place the next day at five o'clock in the morning.

Falk smiled, threw himself back in the arm-chair, and stayed like that the whole night. He lost all sense of time. He did not want to sleep, and sat there smoking one cigarette after the other, wondering why there wasn't a single thought in his head.

" I'm chemically purified of all thoughts," he repeated, smiling.

When Geisler came for him at the appointed hour, Falk lifted surprised, smiling eyes.

" Time already? "

" Yes. Haven't you slept? "

"No," Falk answered apathetically.

He took his old slouch hat.

"Good Lord! You can't go that way. Put your silk hat on."

Geisler looked at him uneasily.

Falk grew indignant.

"Why are you looking at me so distrustfully? Do you think I'm afraid?" He spoke, then lapsed instantly again into his deep apathy.

When they reached the appointed place, Kunicki was there already with his seconds.

The formalities were soon over.

With a calm surprising to himself Falk saw Kunicki aiming straight at his breast.

The advantage is on Kunicki's side.

Kunicki never misses aim.

Strange sport — to lay me dead —

But how reconcile the two things — Kunicki a Social-Democrat, yet fights a duel? Ha, ha! *Un citoyen cosmopolite du monde entier.*

All these thoughts flashed through his mind. He wanted to laugh aloud.

That instant a bullet whizzed close past his ear.

One idea possessed him wholly: *Un citoyen cosmopolite* with lame principles and will have to be lame himself . . . It took an effort to keep from laughing. He aimed with marvellous calm. A suppressed laugh convulsed his breast. The bullet struck Kunicki in the leg. Kunicki sprang into the air and fell.

"The devil take it! Give me a cigarette!" he shouted.

"Will he be lame?" Falk asked on the way back to the city.

That was the only idea that lodged in his mind.

" I don't know."

" *Citoyen cosmopolite — un citoyen* with lame principles
— Ha, ha, ha! — The finger of God! Now he's going to
be lame himself."

Geisler was unpleasantly affected by these words, but Falk
took no notice.

" Whatever you say, this is a devilish mean sort of a satisfaction!" Geisler said, just to break the distressing silence.

Falk looked at him.

" Kunicki and I were great friends. He has a good intellect. He completely demolished Rodbertus."

Again they were silent.

" Has Ysa left already?" asked Geisler.

" Why, was she preparing to go away?"

" I thought so."

Geisler seemed to be highly wrought up.

" Do you want to go home?" Falk asked in alarm.

" I'm extremely tired."

Falk looked at him with an odd smile.

" You seem to be troubled about something. Ha, ha, ha!
All right. Leave me. I'll go lie down, too."

CHAPTER XIV

FALK pressed up still closer to the wall. There was complete darkness in the room. He trembled, having caught the sound of a voice in the hall. He listened.

"Mrs. Falk and the little boy left to-day. Mr. Falk has stayed in his room all day. He seems to be ill. He doesn't want to eat anything, and won't speak."

There was a knock at the door.

Falk did not stir. Presently the door opened, a stream of light poured into the room, and darkness again.

"Falk," Olga called softly.

"Hush, hush."

"Where are you?"

"Here."

"What are you doing?" she asked frightened.

"Somebody has died."

"Died? Who?"

"She, she — Sit down near me — here, here —"

"What have you in your hand?" asked Olga.

"A letter from her. She's gone away and will never return, that is to say, she has died."

They sat a long time holding hands. In that mysterious stillness and darkness her head began to turn.

"You haven't gone out of your mind?" she asked softly, with dread in her voice.

"That's over."

For a long time they were silent.

"How good it is that you've come," he said, breathing heavily.

"But what now?"

He made no answer.   She did not dare to ask again.

After the lapse of some time, she was about to question him once more — he was asleep.   She did not stir for fear of waking him.   Even in his sleep, he held her hand.   A long time passed that way.

Suddenly he jumped up.

"I may go to Czerski.   Will you go with me?"

"I will."

"*Vive l'humanité!*   Ha, ha, ha!" he laughed a bitter, sardonic laugh.

THE END